A DIFFERENT WORLD

A Different World

Zulfikar Ghose

THE OVERLOOK PRESS
WOODSTOCK, NEW YORK

First published in 1984 by

The Overlook Press
Lewis Hollow Road
Woodstock, New York 12498

Copyright © 1978 by Zulfikar Ghose

Library of Congress Cataloging in Publication Data

Ghose, Zulfikar, 1935-
   A different world.

   I. Title.
PS3557.H63D5   1984   813'.54   84-42674
ISBN 0-87951-982-7

. . . your immodest demands for a different world,
and a better life, and complete comprehension
of both at last . . .

Elizabeth Bishop – 'Arrival at Santos'

Book Three

A DIFFERENT WORLD

CONTENTS

Chapter 1

PROEM: TO AMÁLIA

A woman drove me back to Rio. Yes, I admit – it was madness! Any ordinary fugitive, one, say, with no greater reputation than a student revolutionary from '68, would have thought a million times before taking such a risk.

But I, Gregório Peixoto da Silva Xavier, am known the world over! Brazilians whisper my name from Manaus to Pôrto Alegre; and there are men and women in New York and London, Frankfurt and New Delhi who talk of my exploits – as, indeed, people do everywhere else where freedom is cherished or tyranny silently and stoically endured. But I am a Brazilian; what more is there to say in this matter of women?

Tell a Brazilian that the only way he can get to his woman is by swimming through a river full of alligators, piranha and electric eels and he'll not think twice before plunging right in. The eyes of Brazilian women are flames and their voices are the ocean calling. I swear it! How else do we burn and drown in their arms?

And ah! my dear Amália, for the five years of my solitary existence in the remote wilderness of Goiás, on the border of Mato Grosso, my body had smouldered with your touch while I kept my distance from my pursuers. But one's mind and one's passions conspire against the security of the body and, hearing that Amália was in Rio and that for five years she had kept herself faithful to my memory, duplicating my exile by herself withdrawing from society, I was suddenly overwhelmed by an emotion that would admit no restraint of common sense or prudence.

Even the thought that Amália might well have fallen into the hands of my enemies and through the usual techniques of

11

persuasion been compelled to make precisely that gesture which would draw me out of my hiding, even such an obvious doubt which in any other situation would have made me doubly careful, did not restrain me. Amália would never be a traitor, my heart insisted, not she whose body conjoined to mine a thousand times had dissolved both our identities, making of our two souls an insubstantial fragrance in the air; and on urgently taking a plane for Rio I simply refused to listen to my mind, which babbled many an argument against my going like a tribunal of elders shaking their grey heads and indicating the inevitable pitfalls of my wilfulness. I railed at my mind, in fact, for having such an idea: not she, O not my Amália, whose body had been my shelter when I was in need of a refuge, whose lips and whose breasts had nourished me with hope when I had been ready to surrender to despair, not my Amália who had once whispered into my ear that the greatest gift she could expect from this life would be a child from me and whose noblest sacrifice had been to secure my survival by herself going away: no, she would never for any consideration in this world, whether of money or a new love, draw me to Rio only to betray me.

And my heart feels vindicated now, even though my life can never be the same. I could not tell then, deciding that I simply had to abandon my solitary life if only for a brief visit, that my going to Rio was to be more than a furtive tryst with a lover. I saw only Amália's dark eyes and the fire that burned there; and how can the inspired mystic who sees only the pure flame of God's presence know that there might be men waiting for him to mortify his miserably weak flesh? I was in that frame of mind in which one thought becomes so dominant that it's easy to forget that there are barbarians in this world who, discovering those feelings in us which are the intensest because they comprise our inner truth, proceed to practise the full extent of their own corruption on the very part of our soul which is the purest.

Friends, do not believe that age brings wisdom; alas, it only rejuvenates folly! My forty-two years, the last five of them spent in a self-imposed exile from society, seemed hardly to have

12

advanced me beyond infancy. It is my good heart, I suppose, my charitable disposition: I whose heart ought to have been a stone by now.

I had understood the temperament of barbarians when I was not yet thirty and had learned to will my flesh into thinking of itself as made of steel; and I had become – for one assumes the habits of one's adversaries in order to survive in their world – a barbarian myself. What happened when I returned to Rio was a shock, but not for the reasons I had ever anticipated in all the elaborate calculation of possibilities which awaited me; and if it was a sort of extinction of my self, the manner of it was the least expected, leaving me to wonder whether my continuing existence was not some cruel joke. No, Amália did not do this to me; I realise now that I myself am responsible, that my life which has seemed to be concerned with the political destiny of a country has, at another level, hidden from me, been something else altogether – that my subtlest enemy has been my own blood.

During the contemplative years of my exile, I have understood a great deal about destiny and about the cold determination that shapes our most hot-headed actions; I have, I hope, in spite of foolish compulsions, been made wiser by reflecting on my own peculiar past, where somehow my soul has always been present in a living body whenever Brazil has been at the crossroads; and yet one's immediate existence is so constricted by banality and incomprehension that one needs to look back again, re-live a life that is not over and yet seems to be finished, in order to satisfy the fierce questioning that goes on in one's brain, demanding again and again: why this horror, why this situation from which there is no escape?

I have to narrate so many stories here. Alas, I know not where to begin.

Amália, Amália, O the loveliest woman in all of Brazil, why do you torment me, why have you turned my brain into a quivering mass of jelly that I can no longer think of any thing but images of your body and the whisperings from your sweet lips which always assert, even in this late vanquishing of my day, their imperial dominance so that what rationality my poor mind is capable of is utterly confounded? And I to whom so many thousands have turned with admiration and with hope, the common, credulous people who have heard in my voice and in my words a more melodious future for their constrained lives, who have experienced ecstasy merely on seeing the brightness in my brown eyes; I through whose reincarnated body, again and again, for four centuries, Brazil has revealed the elaborate pattern of its history and of its destiny; I who have undoubtedly been chosen by the gods to reveal truths to my nation – yet what am I now? A mere lover, one who is unsure if his mistress is faithful or so subtly and so cruelly deceiving him that his mind has no more substance in it than a gutter has water during a prolonged drought. There's a rage within me which I must learn to discipline in order to tell the most curious story of all my lives. I have some sanity left even though I am continually being driven to distraction by memories of Amália's body. God, her breasts!

But I say to my soul: stretch out your wings, let your flight be towards that brightness which is the purest truth, still this sordid heart of mine and, O soul, let my brain not mirror the chaos it has witnessed but cull an order out of that chaos.

Amália, I shall come to you, as I have come a thousand times, to hold your body, to love you and to be loved by you, but give me rest now so that I can tell this, the most complicated and difficult of my stories, from the beginning: O my tragic heroine, O my love, I have asked so little of you all these years.

Chapter 2

THE EDUCATION OF A POLITICAL ANIMAL

The dry season showed no signs of ending that year and at the time, late in 1954, I was more concerned about the cattle on my father's farm than with the fact that the recent suicide of President Getúlio Vargas had plunged the country into a period of political turmoil which was not to end until ten years later, when the military overthrew a precarious and wholly meaningless democracy and established a dictatorship. Well, I was concerned about another matter besides the cattle. I was twenty and had my own problems, not the least of which was the disease that just about every Brazilian male contracts soon after he realises that the passing of water is only the lesser and boringly mundane function of the organ which has so fascinated him since childhood; and, Brazilians being precocious scientists of the body, eager to experiment in matters of partners and positions, the results can be devastating, so that one can be fairly sure that there's always an epidemic raging behind the bikinis and swimming-trunks of those glorious young bodies you see on Copacabana and Ipanema, those beaches of paradise on which everybody appears to be god-like. I'd discovered this disease on my body at the age of eighteen but it was not until two years later that I was secretly seeing a doctor and undergoing treatment, having, out of the usual feelings of guilt and shame, neglected to do so earlier, thus making my condition much worse than it need have been. And here was Getúlio, much beloved by the working man and despised by the political parties and the military, this powerful dictator of Brazil whose wily stubbornness had significantly touched every Brazilian's life – President Getúlio Vargas of our great nation had just shot himself, and even when

15

I heard the news on the radio at our farm I still could not take my thoughts away from the misery attending my cock, such is the irrelevant human absorption with some distracting detail concerning its own self that keeps us unimpressed by great contemporary events.

The revelation of my condition had come to me as a cruel joke during a most hilarious moment. It was something that one often teased other boys about. I was forever telling my younger brother Anibal (Lord knows what possessed my parents to give him that name) who, in the manner of younger brothers was quick to grasp the essentials of life, 'Anibal,' I'd tell him, guessing what he'd been up to in the stables with a servant-girl, 'better get some of mother's cold cream and put it on your cock and sheathe it in a banana skin when you go to bed.' And my elder brother Vicente would add, 'Yeah, Anibal, the pox gets every third Brazilian male and it's just too bad you're the third. But Gregório doesn't know what he's talking about. A banana skin won't help you. Let me give you the benefit of experience. The best thing to do is to get that saucer Iolanda uses to give the cat milk, pour some kerosene into it and when you go to bed make sure you sleep in such a way that your cock's immersed in the saucer. You want to keep it soaked all night. And don't smoke in bed while you're at it!' Anibal would usually reply, 'Why don't you bastards piss off?' and run away.

Well, one night the three of us were by the swimming-pool at the back of the house. Our parents and sister Iolanda were in Rio and the three of us had been playing the fool. Drinking a full bottle of *cachaça* between us, we'd decided to sober up in the pool and, stripping completely, had run out to jump into the water. At one point we decided to see who could piss the farthest, a really stupid sort of contest but then, three brothers together make for stupid company, probably the worst group of idiots you're likely to see. We stood on the deck at the deep end, Anibal in the middle. Vicente and I exchanged meaningful looks, and Anibal said in his shrill voice, 'Right, here goes!' and immediately shot out a thick, silvery arc that splashed into the pool, and Vicente did so too, a second after him, so that if you didn't know what was going on you'd think there was a fountain dancing lyrically on the pool.

But I was stuck, couldn't get a drop out for a whole minute; instead, I felt a horrible pain at my abdomen and thought I was going to fall right into the splashing created by my brothers. They were shaking out their last drops and Anibal was saying, 'What's the matter, Gregório, got the pox?' when I finally came up with a few drops, after which I suffered another pang of pain, and then out it came in a powerful arc that went right beyond where my brothers' efforts had landed. It was no release, however, for the discharge was attended by an excruciating pain and, what was worse, my bladder seemed to have the capacity of a petrol tanker, so that Anibal said, 'Watch it, Gregório, the pool's going to overflow.'

I finished just then, nearly exhausted by the attempt, but, in order to accomplish what Vicente and I had agreed to with that earlier look he and I had exchanged, said, 'Watch it yourself, Anibal, your're going to be in it!' Simultaneously, Vicente and I seized Anibal by each arm and, since he was a short, light fellow, swung him up and down twice while he yelled and howled, kicking his legs, and at the third swing threw him in the air so that he landed right in the middle of all that piss.

He swam to the nearest edge faster than a lizard darts across a path, and pulled himself out of the pool. He came running towards us, yelling obscenities, but stopped at the corner seeing that we stood waiting for him and looked set to fling him once again into the pool. 'You mother-fuckers,' he screamed. 'I'll make you eat shit for this!'

Anibal went off crying and even half an hour later he was still in the bathroom, under the shower. I could hear him there, probably soaping himself for the tenth time, while I lay in bed with my newly discovered pain. First thing I resolved to do was to give up all liquids, take only a little water out of necessity, put my bladder on a fast so that I didn't have to suffer the agony of emptying it more than twice a day. On coming into the house I had hastily put on a pair of pyjamas, and avoided looking at the offending member, for I was certain that it had been transformed into a tiny cactus, the kind people put into a pot, green with

17

yellow spots and covered with thorns,. The thought that my future was wrecked and that I might as well say goodbye to this world and enter a monastery kept me awake far into the night.

Our farm was in a wide valley among the mountains north-west of Rio, just off the road to Vitória, and consisted of a little over ten thousand acres, most of it lush pastures where the cattle fattened. There were banana plantations on the slopes of the mountains, some of the fields were given over to pineapple or corn, and there were large wooded areas where, beneath the thick vegetation, orchids and flowering vines hanging from the trees, we spent our childhood, playing the fearful games of boys, dividing a territory and raiding a neighbour's possession. Here, too, ran a cataracting river which at one point seemed to lift a white, foamy head over a huge boulder and fall some thirty feet down into a deep hollow. A tree arched its limbs over the waterfall, and when I was only five years old my brother Vicente, who then was twice my age and therefore nearly an adult in my imagination, barefooted and wearing only a pair of shorts, climbed up the tree, crawled along the branch that hung some twenty or thirty feet above it, directly over the hollow where the water fell, the branch moving in a spring-like action while Vicente crawled over it. I was terrified, expecting the branch to break at any moment and send my brother crashing against the boulder, and yet I watched fascinated, for Vicente's concentrated look and his taut muscles had that beauty which comes from a total commitment to a voluntarily chosen action, and it seemed that he and the tree were one, each expressing a mutual trust by not harming the other. He reached the point above the hollow, the water crashing down below him. The branch which supported him was quite thin now and had bowed a few feet under his weight; it seemed the most perilous position to be in. Then, suddenly, Vicente sprang up, kicked the branch away as if it were a diving-board, curved through the air, straightened when he was some ten feet from the water and plunged into it in a perfect dive. It was the most beautiful thing I had seen a body do: perfection was a risk one took, but without the aim of perfection there could be no beauty; the island of one's body needed to be located in the paths of hurricanes so that its survival – the palm-trees still against the calm, glittering blue – possessed a thrilling heroism.

Naturally enough, Vicente was the hero of my childhood, always astonishing me with surprising physical feats. He taught me to swim and to ride a horse; how to catch a snake by its head and to let it loose far from the house (for Vicente didn't believe in killing snakes since they ate mice and were themselves the food of some predators), and how to survive in a jungle, armed only with a machete. By the time Anibal was born, which was three years after me, there was already a bond between Vicente and me, and even when he was a baby lying in his cradle in the front veranda, being fussed over by a maid, Anibal must have seen Vicente and me running around the front of the house playing those mock-aggressive games that are really an inverted expression of affection.

Anibal was the most precocious child I ever saw: he was crawling at six months and had acquired a wobbly sort of walk in his tenth month, and one could see that he was serious about it, for his face was set in a determined, wrinkled knot and he resented anyone trying to hold him when his knees appeared to give way. When he was shown a picture-book in his second year his instinct seemed to inform him that the big black words beneath the pictures were more important, for when mother pointed to the picture and said, 'Look, Anibal, *elephant*' he pointed instead to the letters ELEPHANT and yelled out '*Phunt!*' and sneered, a look that passed for a smile in his childhood but which stayed with him throughout his life, growing progressively uglier. He understood language before he could be taught the alphabet, so that father, at first flattered by the cleverness of his youngest son, began to worry that Anibal might be a genius and hired a tutor for him. But Anibal showed no inclination to learn, for he perversely behaved like a born idiot before the tutor, driving the poor man to despair when he tried to show Anibal the rivers of the world on a map or gave him the dates of Brazilian history to learn.

Father concluded that perhaps Anibal's genius lay elsewhere and, after long discussions with mother, bought a grand piano (which took up so much room the entire drawing-room in the appartment in Rio had to be refurnished), obtained the services of an Italian piano-teacher, a sharp-looking old man with long, grey hair and a wispy goatee through which he ran his fingers continually, and waited for the prodigy to emerge. Anibal, however, refused to have anything to do with the piano except to pound the keys with his fists, enraging the Italian for whom the instrument was an object which had to be approached with adoration and touched delicately with the piety of a lover's hands. One day when he heard the Italian enter the apartment Anibal jumped up on the piano, positioned himself in such a way that he could, the moment the teacher entered the room, kick at the keys with his heels, and presented an image of such destructive recalcitrance that the poor Italian, seeing the perverse little demon mock what was sacred to him, flung up his arms and ran out of the apartment. Father finally abandoned any attempt to develop Anibal's genius and treated him as he did Vicente and me, leaving us to grow up as normal kids, learning what we could at the school in Rio and spending the weekends and holidays at the farm, discovering worlds of our own. That's what Anibal liked best, to be on his own. He had created within his mind an atmosphere of distrust and suspicion, and whenever one caught him unawares there was always an expression of loathing on his face, whether he looked at one of us or at a complete stranger, his mouth open in a sneer, his eyes lowered and looking sideways at one in a gesture of contempt.

When I was fifteen Vicente took me camping among the mountains on the western boundary of our farm during the summer holidays. Of course, he asked Anibal too, but Anibal was in an especially surly mood in which he seemed to be convinced that any gesture to treat him as a normal human being was a calculated strategy to put him in a position so vulnerable that he could only expect death by strangulation, so that he refused, saying, '*I* don't want a boa constrictor wrapped around me, no thank you. You can have your camp and good luck to you!'

Vicente and I went off on mules, loaded with hammocks and blankets and carrying rifles. It was exciting because of the risk we were taking, for we carried no food with us and would depend on what we could hunt, and yet it was an acceptable risk since we could, within a few hours, come back home in case we found it impossible to survive in the jungle. We did take a bottle of *cachaça,* however, to keep us warm at night.

'Anibal's turning out to be a right pain in the balls,' Vicente said as we rode away. 'What the fuck does he want?'

'I don't know,' I said. 'He seems to have unnecessary suspicions.'

'You know, Gregório, there's three of us and our sister. But there's no competition among us as far as I'm concerned.'

'Me, too,' I said.

'What I mean is, the four of us will inherit equal parts, but we don't have to divide it. It can remain the same property, the *fazenda* Xavier. The way I see it, there'll never be a reason to split it up in four.'

'Sure, that's how I see it, too,' I said.

'But Anibal seems to have got it into his head that we're going to do him out of his share. It's just too sad. I mean, I've nothing against him for being the third son and, anyway, the law gives him an equal share.'

'He's only twelve, maybe he doesn't understand that.'

'Yeah, but he's not a child. He's damn smart, he's growing up to be a right old son of a bitch.'

'I guess he'll soon discover the world's not a conspiracy against him,' I said.

'I don't know,' Vicente said.

We had come to a stop since we were fording a shallow river and the mules had sunk their heads in the water and were drinking.

'Hey, *mula,* enough!' Vicente shouted. 'We don't want you bloated with water, there's a lot of climbing to do.'

He pulled at his reins and dug his heels into the sides of the mule, getting him to climb up the bank and take the narrow path through the thick vegetation. I followed, using the same language to my mule and imitating Vicente to urge the reluctant beast to forego the water. There were vines hanging across the path, stretched low between the trunks of trees, and Vicente hacked at them with his machete. We were hot, sweaty and thirsty, but since I was convinced that the more difficult the journey, the more it approximated to adult experience, I was thrilled by what I considered to be the hardship that I was going through.

'This is nothing,' Vicente said when the path was really thick and he had to dismount to cut away the creepers and the profuse underbrush before we could make any progress at all, so that I was excited to think that the trials I was enduring were only a prelude to greater hardship. And I must say I longed for hardship, some harsh experience that would give me an opportunity to prove that I was a man.

We reached the mountains late that afternoon, having stopped earlier by a river for our lunch, which consisted of raw *palmito,* the heart of the slender palm-tree which we found near the river. I agreed with Vicente that it was delicious and that it was great to live on what nature had to offer, but I must say that I didn't tell him that I wished we'd brought some salt and pepper with us. We climbed beyond a banana plantation at the foot of the mountains and found a clearing near a stream where the land was fairly level. The view, looking back on our *fazenda,* was a beautiful panorama of rich green fields with the cattle grazing there, plantations of banana and pineapple scattered across the land and large areas of tall grass and sugar-cane specially planted as feed for the cattle. Someone travelling the world in search of the most beautiful landscape and coming to the spot where we stood might have wondered, as his heart missed a beat, whether he had not at last found it.

'There's no reason why that view should ever change in our lifetime,' Vicente said.

I looked at him with admiration, and he went on 'You know what I believe in, I believe in doing nothing that will create changes. I'm a conservative in the real sense of the word. People talk a lot of politics but it's all shit if you want to know. Politicians are forever promising a new era, and do you know, Gregório, there are actually communists in this country who want everyone to be a communist? They want to redistribute the land, they have all kinds of ideas for change. You'll learn about all these things soon, but one thing you must always remember is that you are a landowner and that as a landowner you don't have power over people so much as responsibility to the land. Your duty is to see that the land is never harmed. Can you imagine what would happen to that land if every peasant on it owned an equal share of it? Each one would be master of a squalid plot unable to grow enough on it to feed himself. The fields on which the cattle graze would be fenced into tiny sections to grow beans. The forests would be cut down for housing of the cheapest kind. No, we have to be conservatives, we have to keep things as they are, or this world will vanish.' .

We hung our hammocks between trees on the edge of the clearing, tied the mules with long ropes so that they could graze and, taking our rifles, went off into the jungle in search of game. The animal kingdom seemed to have received advance warning that there were hunters in the jungle, for every little creature had vanished from it. There was not even an ant to be seen. Hungry and sweating in the heavy humidity of the jungle, we positioned ourselves near a stream and waited silently for over an hour. Towards sunset there was some rustling in the vegetation and soon what looked to me to be a jaguar or a leopard came to the stream. I instinctively raised my gun but Vicente put out a hand and, touching the barrel, lowered it, putting up the hand in a gesture of silence. We watched the animal drink, look around him, lick at his sides and walk away contentedly.

'What a beautiful cat!' Vicente said in a soft voice.

'What was it?' I asked.

'A panther. I'd been told they were extinct, but it's terrific to see they're not. Isn't it fantastic to have panther in the state of Rio?'

It was sunset before we found anything to kill. A flock of wild ducks descended on the water, dropping almost silently from the sky and then suddenly landing in a noisy flutter of wings and becoming instantly silent once they were on the water. There was none of the squawking one associates with ducks. Silently,

23

Vicente and I raised our guns and, taking great care, for we knew that if our first shots missed the ducks would fly away, shot three birds within half a minute while the others, beating their wings and letting out shrieking cries, flew away.

We returned to light a fire and had the ducks roasting just when it grew dark. Vicente hadn't shown any anxiety at all, but I had been worried all afternoon whether we were going to have any dinner or not.

We kept the fire burning long after we had gorged ourselves on a duck each, putting the third one away for the next day, and sat swigging from the bottle of *cachaça*. I must say I felt very grand and grown-up. Vicente told me he planned to go to Europe after taking his first college degree in Rio.

'But dad wants you in his business, doesn't he?' I asked.

'He's done without me for twenty years, he can wait five more. Besides, what's running a tourist shop in Copacabana? Even Anibal could do that.'

'It's important for dad, though,' I said. 'It's his business and you know he loves it.'

'It's only a hobby,' Vicente said. 'I don't even think he makes much money from it. The wealth comes from the *fazenda* and from the rented apartments in Rio, all of which he inherited. The good thing about father is he didn't spend it all the day he came into his inheritance.'

'What will you do in Europe?' I asked after a while.

'Oh, I just want to live there, spend a year each in London, Paris and Berlin. Wander about Italy and Greece, take a look at Portugal.'

I looked puzzled and he said, handing the bottle to me, 'Think of it this way. Brazil is a European *idea*. Oh, sure, when the Portuguese came here in the sixteenth century they were supposed to be on their way to India. But don't you believe a word about the great European race for spices and silks. It was just that Europe suddenly *knew too much*, had too much excess energy, the mind was bursting with visions, the body was restless, and there were a good many merchants with surplus fortunes looking for speculative ventures. And surely, while everyone went lusting after gold at first, wherever a man

24

pitched his tent or took a native woman for a wife he brought to that place the foreign words of his language and with that the entire memory of that language, its great bank of ideas. Or think of it this other way. Brazil is still a new world. Whatever happens here, even a hundred years from now, will not greatly diminish the country's potential, there'll be people in Brazil who'll still think of a *new* world then just as people in Portugal nearly five hundred years ago were enlivened by a dream to which they gave the name "Brazil". But Europe itself has already lived out all its dreams, it is a world that has come to an end though its peoples, possessed by the illusion of an infinite continuity, obviously do not think so. In a strange way I'm attracted to its decay. While I would not want anything changed here, I'd like to be there where I know no change is going to help them. Here, I'm bored by the endless possibilities; there I shall be fascinated by the elimination of a future.'

'Vicente,' I said, passing the bottle back to him, 'I think I must be drunk. I hear your words clearly, but don't understand a thing.'

'That's all right, Gregório,' he said. 'You'll understand them one day. All I was going to say was that I want to understand Europe so that I can understand Brazil. Our culture is our own but without European culture it would not exist. Maybe all I want to do', he added, smiling, 'is to go and screw European girls.'

'Now *that* I understand! Why, I'll even drink to that.'

'My secret wish', he said, taking a swig and passing the bottle to me, 'is to belong to the real old world, marry the daughter of a titled family with a long history and live in a castle.'

'But wouldn't you want to return to Brazil?'

'Ah, it's only a dream, Gregório. But if it came true, then, no, I wouldn't return. And if I don't, you can have my share of the land.'

The fire had burned low by the time we finished the bottle. I was congratulating myself, for it seemed a remarkable achievement for a boy of fifteen to have drunk half a bottle of *cachaça* and to remain cold sober, when, attempting to rise from the ground, my legs felt as though the bones in them had melted and I collapsed in a heap. Vicente laughed and pulled me up, supporting me and half dragging me while I worked my tottering legs and painfully made it to my hammock and climbed into it with his help. As soon as my eyes caught sight of the bright stars the entire sky began to spin and grow vivid as if it were bursting all over with fireworks. I turned my head and shifted my body to curl up in my hammock. I must have passed out soon after that.

The next morning I awoke before Vicente. It was just beginning to be light, a few birds were singing. What woke me was neither the light nor the birds but the consciousness of a splitting headache and a fierce pressure at what I was convinced was my heart. I tried to climb out of my hammock but fell out of it, hitting the ground with my knees and forehead. During that same moment there was a great surging pain within me and, my hands and knees on the ground, out came the chewed up duck in a vile-looking liquid. I had come out in a profuse sweat while I vomited. I rose finally, surprised that I had not died, feeling miserable with nausea, and walked desperately to the stream where, removing all my clothes, I plunged into the cool water.

I remained in the water for some twenty minutes, swimming up and down as vigorously as I could and then floating on my back or simply standing up and allowing myself to sink beneath the surface until the cool water in my hair massaged away the headache. Vicente was still in his hammock when I returned but I noticed something that I had not observed earlier. The mules had gone. Our rifles, which we had placed beside the trees from where our hammocks were hung, were no longer there. Our machetes had been taken, too.

'Vicente, wake up!' I called, shaking his hammock. 'We've been robbed. The mules are gone.'

Vicente raised himself, holding his head, and said, 'Jesus!'

He obviously had a hangover too, for he didn't seem to grasp the crisis in which we now found ourselves. He got out of the hammock and I repeated that we had been robbed.

'Shit, let me go and clear my head first,' he said, walking away to the stream. 'One problem at a time.'

I sat down on a rock and stared at the ashes of last night's fire. I was overwhelmed by a sense of misery. We were twelve or fifteen miles from home. It would be a long day's walk, mostly through the thick vegetation. Adventures into the interior were all right provided one had the means with which to cope with physical danger; but to be in the position of a mountain-climber who, half way up a sheer face, sees all his equipment fall ten thousand feet into an abyss wasn't my idea of adventure.

'Well, let's eat, and then we can think about our problem,' Vicente said cheerfully, returning from the stream.

'What are we going to eat?' I asked.

'Why, the duck, what else? I hung it there from a tree next to my hammock.'

Walking in that direction he stopped, looked down upon the ground and said, 'Shit!'

I went to see. There were some bones lying on the ground and large red ants were going up and down them.

'I couldn't have tied it too well,' Vicente said, 'it must have fallen.'

'Or some creature must have got at it,' I said.

'Well, let's go and find something else,' Vicente said.

'Vicente,' I said, not believing that he could be so unconcerned by the gravity of our situation, 'we don't even have our machetes, what are we going to kill with? And don't you think we should start walking back home? We'll be lucky to reach it by sunset.'

'I don't believe this,' he said. 'Why should anyone come here to steal our mules and things? I bet you it's a trick of that fucker Anibal. He must have followed us and watched us get drunk.'

'I don't know what he'd have to gain by it,' I said. 'But we can't hang around here and speculate about it. We've got to get moving.'

We folded and rolled up our hammocks and blankets and, carrying them under our arms, began to walk away. We hadn't walked ten paces when Vicente stopped, saying, 'Shit, this is stupid! We shouldn't give up so easily. Why don't we look for the tracks of the mules?'

'O hell, Vicente, what tracks are you talking about? It's thick underbrush all around here.'

'But there's bound to be droppings or something.'

Just then I saw some dung and said, 'Look, there's your evidence. It's obvious they were taken toward the farm, or at least that's the direction they aimed for from here.'

Vicente agreed to make for the farm but as we proceeded he kept looking for any evidence that suggested the mules might have changed direction. To be frank, I was scared of getting lost in the jungle and wanted to be transported to the farm at once, if some magic power could do so; I scorned now the feeling I'd had while eating the duck the previous evening, that life in the jungle was terrific: it was all right, I realised, while one had mules and rifles. Then one could even admire a panther's sleek body, but I didn't want to run into that same cat now.

There was no visible track and I said, 'How can we be sure we're heading for the farm?'

'As long as we keep going downhill we won't go too wrong.'

That made sense when I gave it a moment's thought, and I felt even more encouraged when Vicente added, 'We're bound to come across some banana pickers soon. We could borrow a mule.'

I felt considerably cheered, for I imagined ourselves coming out of the thick woods in a few minutes, encountering some banana pickers and riding home in the greatest comfort. But half an hour later we were still in the dense jungle. The underbrush had become thicker, it was dark. We could not tell how high the trees rose above us, for we were little more than ants in the massiveness of vegetation that had become our world.

'How can you tell we're going downhill?' I asked, suffering one more cut on my arm as I stooped below a vine and tried to avoid its thorns.

'Gregório, you're not scared, are you? Listen, you don't have to worry about a thing. You're on your father's land.'

That didn't answer my question but encouraged me nevertheless, until I remembered that there were snakes and wild beasts on my father's land. We came to a small clearing and for a moment felt a sweet relief as if we had come to a vast plain. We sat down on the ground, sweating and hungry, and already our clothes were torn and dirty. I could see that Vicente had lost some of his confidence and when he showed no eagerness to move from the illusory security of the small clearing it occurred to me that he was afraid of committing himself to an uncertain direction. I sighed to myself, throwing my head back in anguish. At that moment I saw a patch of blue sky high above in a circle made by the tops of the trees. I had an idea. I rose and began to climb up the most accessible of the trees.

As I climbed I almost expected to see the bay of Rio from the top. There's nothing like an ocean view to strengthen one's notion of freedom, for all other perspectives, whether they be of wide plains or of valleys among lush mountains, finally inform the imagination that there has to be something else beyond them; but come to a beach and you need not fear what might come from beyond the horizon and so you stick your chest out and breathe in all the sea air your lungs can contain. I had that expectation of coming to a view of the ocean, but I managed to climb only half way up the tree. From there I had a view of other trees and I would have needed to be the most inquisitive of botanists to appreciate how advantageously I was placed. As it was, it occurred to me in a passing moment that the best solution to my predicament could well be for me to relinquish the branch I clung to and let the darkness beneath me decide my fate.

'Can you see anything?' Vicente called from below and his voice sounded like someone who had fallen into a well.

Just then I looked down at a direction that I seemed to have missed earlier, for I saw a mud hut not a hundred yards away from our clearing.

'Yes,' I called to Vicente, 'there's a house there.'

Fifteen minutes later we found our way to the hut and discovered a huge pot of beans cooking over a fire outside, and not too far away a pig tied to a tree. A man emerged from the hut, our own faithful administrator, José Formigueiro, who had been born on the land, worked as a peasant on it from his boyhood and had risen, during my lifetime, to the position of general administrator, for father valued his experience and trusted his shrewd handling of the peasants.

'O Zé!' we cried simultaneously in our delight at seeing a friendly face in the middle of the jungle.

'Vicente, Gregóriozinho!' he exclaimed. 'Welcome, a thousand times welcome to my humble abode.'

His wrinkled face looked old and had that toughness of skin common to peasants who spend a lifetime working under the sun, but he was not yet fifty. He stood erect and, pushing back a soiled felt hat on his thick black hair, he smiled at us, his gold teeth glinting. Vicente explained the misfortune that had befallen us when Formigueiro had brought out a couple of folding chairs for us, and he sat on the wooden steps below the door of his hut. While Vicente talked I watched Formigueiro, his hands clasped firmly in front of him, for a warm affection for him surged within me in the relief I felt at having found him. I had always known him as the man who solved father's problems on the land; he would come to the house in the evenings whenever father was on the land, stand outside the veranda – in deference to the master's presence in the house – leaning against the railing near where father sat in a wicker chair, and discuss all that had been done during the day and plan the schedule for the next day. Father transmitted all his orders through Formigueiro and never dealt directly with the peasants, so that Formigueiro enjoyed something of the power of a prime minister in a constitutional monarchy. He knew every detail of the land and was one of those wonderful people who, without any education, has an engineer's sense of where a canal should be dug, an agronomist's judgment of how the pineapple yield could be improved and a doctor's understanding of an illness, all his knowledge coming from having spent his entire life in this complete world of the farm where his only tutors had been observation and experience. He had learned to read and write and was the only peasant on our land at that time who owned a radio, but his actions were inspired only by that lore of the land, that collective knowledge which belonged to the people who for several generations had no life outside the farm. It was understood that, being the ad-

30

ministrator, he made some money for himself in his dealings with the merchants who came to buy bananas and pineapples to take to the markets of Rio; but that was the price one had to pay to have so reliable a man.

When Vicente had told his story, Formigueiro rose and fetched some bread and butter and two bottles of beer.

'You could eat some beans if you waited an hour,' he said, laughing, 'and if you stayed till the evening you could have some of that pig there.'

'Looks like you're preparing a feast,' I said.

'Oh, a *festinha*,' he said. 'Some of the men get together here, once every six or seven weeks. We roast a pig, drink a lot of beer. It's a way of maintaining good relations among the men.'

'But why here?' Vicente asked, for Formigueiro had a substantial house not far from our own.

'Men have to do this sort of thing away from their own homes,' Formigueiro said, giving us a wink.

We laughed knowingly and he too laughed, saying, 'You see what I mean?'

'And you do all the cooking yourself?' Vicente asked.

'I prepare the ground, if you understand what I mean,' he said, giving another wink and making a gesture with his hand, pointing a thumb over his shoulder to indicate that someone else was in the house. And naturally, although he had said nothing at all, we understood that he had a woman there.

We finished our odd breakfast of bread and butter and beer and asked him which was the quickest way back to the farm.

'By horse!' he said.

'But we just told you we don't even have mules,' Vicente said.

'No matter, but you will have two horses,' he said. 'They're tied at the back of the hut.'

'You have *two* horses?' Vicente asked incredulously, which I thought was rather silly of him since Formigueiro had already hinted that a woman had come with him.

'Vicente', Formigueiro said, smiling, 'and Gregóriozinho, I am your friend. You lost your way in the jungle and like magic you found me in the middle of nowhere. And now you need horses and like magic two horses appear from nowhere. Think

31

nothing of it. But do me one favour, please. Give me the benefit of your discretion when you get back to the house, you know by now that there are some things that must remain as secrets among men. Just take the horses to the stables and tell Joãozinho there to tell a couple of the men to take two mules and lead the horses back here tomorrow morning.'

Of course, we were so grateful to be able to borrow his horses that it would be a point of honour not to reveal his secret. What we had no way of realising then was that we were not protecting Formigueiro's marital honour and that, if we were protecting him *from* anyone, if was from ourselves. It is one of the absurd truths of life that whenever we come across a male friend in some unexpected place and he, giving us a wink, hints to us that he's there for an assignation with his mistress, we immediately connive with him to keep his secret. Formigueiro knew this elementary piece of human psychology and used it to his own advantage, and Vicente and I, enjoying the speedy return to our house, joked knowingly and rather affectionately, with many a praise for Formigueiro's discretion, about what amounted to a brothel which he had set up in the middle of the jungle for half a dozen peasants. The secret sexual activity of one's friends is always something to congratulate them upon, whether the affair involves high drama or, as with Formigueiro, is hilariously comical. When, two hours later, we passed the six or seven men, all neatly shaven and spotlessly dressed, on mules, we greeted them jovially and cracked jokes about the succulent pig that awaited them, but neither Vicente nor I noticed at the time the solemn, conspiratorial air among the men. Nor did it occur to either of us that, while we had seen the men, we saw no women heading for the festivities which we had already imagined and laughingly described to each other. We were too caught up in our own freedom to return home to question any missing evidence as suggesting an implausibility of explanation. The other absurdity of this episode was that we hurried home as fast as we could when, had we not lost our mules, we would still not have moved from our camp and might well have spent another night in the jungle.

The question of the mules puzzled us for a while after we had left Formigueiro's horses in the stables with his instructions to Joãozinho. Our principal suspect, brother Anibal of the sneering face, had left for Rio with our parents early in the morning. Unless he had superhuman powers, it seemed impossible that he could have spent ten hours, and those too in utter darkness, riding to our camp and back through the jungle. Since then I've witnessed more remarkable feats from Anibal, but that, I am certain, was not one of them, even though he was precocious in his villainy. It is conceivable, however, that he had paid some peasant to do the job for him.

Having the freedom of the house to ourselves, Vicente and I soon forgot about the mules and talked of the wild orgy we could have in the house if only we found some women. Formigueiro had put not a few ideas into our heads but, of course, ours was only a clowning with fantasies, for we would never take a peasant girl into the house during our parents' absence. It was a taboo that our blood had understood long before our minds had ideas. In the house the family maintained an impeccable purity, even if one came to it having just lain in a field, one's knees in manure while possessing a girl.

Naturally, I generalise, not myself having done any such thing on the farm by the age of fifteen. I believe Vicente too was innocent in this matter, for, without having been instructed, we knew that it would be compromising for a son of the family to attach himself, however briefly, to a peasant girl. Gone were the days when owners and sons of the big farms considered it almost a virtue to impregnate any slave girl – in those days it was an economic virtue to breed more hands to cut the cane or to pick the cotton. Now, after nearly a century of emancipation, the peasant not only enjoyed an independence of sorts but also began to be conscious, however dimly and feebly, of being a political animal. One came across a quiet, sullen face in the fields sometimes and had an uneasy feeling that, were some seditious radical to give him a few ideas, the quiet face would soon learn the vocabulary of revolution. Of course, I did not understand any of this when I was fifteen but I must have had an instinctive knowledge of it; and let me give a simple piece

33

of advice to any landowner: whip a peasant if you have to but never make love to his sister or daughter. Vicente and I suspected that in this matter too our younger brother was a traitor: his nature was contrary to all the principles which ought to inform the behaviour of someone of our class.

'Hey, Gregório,' Vicente said when we had tired of clowning about the house, 'we're not going to find any women on the farm, old Formigueiro has cornered the market.'

'Why don't we go to Rio?' I suggested. 'I bet Anibal's not sitting at home studying algebra.'

We drove off to Rio with the unstated intention of going to the kind of festive place that Formigueiro had instituted in the jungle for his friends.

I might as well say it now that I was no stranger to these houses, having been initiated into them a year earlier when I was fourteen. Vicente and I had been sitting in the sidewalk restaurant of a hotel on Avenida Atlântica, drinking beer for which I had only recently acquired a taste. It was a hot afternoon, the beach across the road was dazzling white, the ocean calm. There were few people in the restaurant, one rather large man sitting in a corner eating fried chicken with ravenous gestures and a young couple whispering to each other, heads close together, Coca Cola bottles in their hands, straws at their lips. A young mulatta sat alone three tables away from us, beside the sidewalk, smoking a cigarette and turning her brown head from time to time towards the strollers on the sidewalk in a bored manner and yet with an open stare, as if she were waiting for a friend. She had on a light-blue cotton blouse with a low neckline and her breasts swelled out each time she inhaled from the cigarette. A bottle of Fanta stood on her table but she had hardly taken two sips of it. Vicente and I – both of us sitting facing the ocean and therefore in a position to see the woman – were talking some nonsense but suddenly there was a merry glint in Vicente's eyes and he said, 'Gregório, I think the time's come to make a man out of you!' Before I could ask what he meant he rose and went and sat at the mulatta's table, giving the impression that he was an old friend of hers. She leaned forward and the two whispered together like the lovers at the other table. She threw her head back a moment, looked at me in a curious fashion – the eyes narrowed, the lips pouted – and then smiled at Vicente, nodding her head. It struck me as very strange. Then I saw Vicente lean to his side and put a hand in his trouser pocket. Well, it was hot enough for a young man to want to scratch, and maybe that's what Vicente was doing, for he turned his trunk sideways in an absurd contortion and I didn't see the rest of his gesture. A moment later he came back to me with a big smile on his face; in the background the mulatta lit another cigarette, inhaled deeply and, looking at me again with narrowed eyes, sighed tragically.

'Hey, Gregório,' Vicente said, 'life is full of surprises. That's Maria Theresa from Minas. I met her some time ago at a party and didn't recognise her until a moment ago. Come, let me introduce you, she has some fabulous records in her room.'

'Gregório,' she sighed, making my name a line of a poem when she took my hand. 'Ah, you're such a smart young man.'

She looked sad and I thought that perhaps I'd reminded her of a brother who had died young. The three of us walked into the hotel and across the lobby to the elevator where Vicente suddenly said, 'Damn, I left my cigarettes on the the table! You two go ahead, I'll come up in a minute.'

Maria Theresa and I took the elevator and she pressed the button for the fourth floor. It was a small, slow elevator and I stared at the numerals which lit up for each floor, only they went dead for a long time between floors before one of them feebly lit up. Maria Theresa was two or three inches taller than I and her accentuated female form – the blouse drawn tightly down into her skirt where a brown leather belt made her waist seem narrower than it was, the white skirt flaring out from the hips – suggested softnesses beneath the rigidity of her attire, and if the thrust of her bosom seemed aggressive it also possessed a deliquescent quality, as if the glorious sun that one watched at its setting was perfectly beautiful not because it was full, round and heavy but because what the imagination held of it was its quality to dissolve and cease to exist. Her form contained all the women that I had stared at during this stage of awakening sexuality; but right there, in the elevator, her strong perfume (which had never existed in any of my fantasies of women) combined with the cigarette that she still smoked were suffocating me; I had a strong impulse to get out of the elevator when it stopped at the second floor and run to a window. A huge, dark-skinned man with a cigar in his mouth stood at the second-floor door, however, and came into the elevator and pressed the button to go down to the ground floor. The elevator resumed its upward progress. The man, who now occupied three-fourths of the elevator, wore a white linen suit which had become crumpled, a black tie and a grey felt hat. He had a bulging face, two enormous cheeks with eyes like a couple of coffee-beans stuck far back, and a massive double chin. Those beady eyes were looking down at me while his lips worked at the cigar, blowing out little puffs of blue smoke. I was certain that I was about to faint when Maria Theresa said to me 'Is your mother well?'

'Yes, she's fine,' I said, wondering why she had asked me such a question. Perhaps when Vicente had met her at the party he had mentioned he'd said something about mother, perhaps she had had a fever at the time.

'And your good father?' Maria Theresa asked.

Good? I wondered, thinking Vicente must have told her everything about our family, and I answered, 'Better than ever.' And to put her fully in the picture I added, 'Iolanda had the 'flu but she's fine now and Anibal's his usual self, strong as an ox and stubborn as a mule.'

'That's good,' she said.

The fat man was looking at me as though he suspected me of lying. Then I saw his eyes light on Maria Theresa's bosom, fall out of their deep recesses for a second and then withdraw and become tiny slits while two weary eyelids covered them. When he opened his eyes again he looked at me with what I interpreted as disgust. The elevator stopped at the third floor and two old ladies, one in a pink dress, the other in blue, and both thin and fragile with sunken chests and hunched backs, walked in. Maria Theresa squeezed me into a corner, the fat man pressed himself against her and, as if to show that the occasion afforded him no pleasure, he looked up at the ceiling, the cigar still stuck in his

36

mouth. The elevator began to ascend and the lady in blue said, 'Julia, why do we always have to go *up* in order to go down?'

'That is modern life, my dear,' answered the lady in pink.

'It is a desperate *bore,'* said the other.

When we came to the fourth floor a family of six stood waiting for the elevator. The father had a crew-cut, wore Bermuda shorts and a camera hung from his neck and rested on his protruding stomach; the mother carried a white, patent-leather handbag that matched her white cotton dress and high heels; the two boys of seven or eight were the exact image of the father and two daughters, about twelve and thirteen, that of the mother. They stared at us and we stared right back for a moment after the elevator door had opened. 'Oh Christ!' exclaimed the father. 'I guest we better wait,' the mother said, and the younger son said in a shrill voice, 'Why don't we all walk down?' Maria Theresa thrust up an arm, saying, 'Hold that door!' and the lady in blue said, 'Julia, *what* is going on?'

Maria Theresa explained to the ladies that they would need to step out of the elevator to allow us to exit. It took them a couple of minutes to comprehend the statement, which had to be reiterated by the fat man and the man with the camera on his belly before the ladies, shaking their heads as if suspicious of being tricked into some fraud, stepped out but, determined not to be cheated, they immediately turned around and began staring at us, stopping our effort to follow them out. The fat man decided to make it easier for us by attempting to evacuate his elephantine bulk from the elevator, causing another little crisis for the old ladies. He finally managed to persuade everyone outside to retreat so that he could get out, and in order to allow him to do so Maria Theresa, who had been holding the door, let go of it for a second. As soon as he went out, the door promptly closed and the elevator began to descend in its laborious fashion. We heard mixed cries from above, one of the boys was cheering, the father was swearing and the ladies were making squeaking sounds. The elevator did not stop until we were on the ground floor.

'Why don't we walk up?' Maria Theresa said. 'We don't want to see them all standing at the door.'

We began to climb up the poorly lit stairway. As we were coming round the flight to the first floor the two boys came running down. They were followed by the two girls and then their parents and the father, seeing us, said 'Oh, for heavens sake!' and went on while his wife, following him said, 'I told you, Henry.'

When we were coming to the third floor the fat man was making a cumbersome descent, holding on to the banister, staring down at the steps with a craned neck, still puffing at his cigar. He looked up when he heard us coming and even in that poor light his eyes seemed to pop out of their deep sockets to stare at me with disgust. We hurried past him and, just before coming to the fourth floor, heard one of the old ladies say, 'But Julia, are you *sure* you can *see* where you're going?'

'Oh my god,' cried Maria Theresa seeing the lady in pink holding on to the banister like someone clinging to a cliffside and staring down the stairs as though it were some abyss. A few steps above her the lady in blue was kneeling on the top of the stairs and peering down at her companion.

Maria Theresa persuaded them to return to the elevator – apparently, seeing the others walk down, the ladies were convinced the elevator was faulty – but I shan't go into the extended discussion that took place before the ladies finally departed for the lower world.

The room we entered had a cleanly made bed in the middle, a wash-basin in a corner and, in the opposite corner, an easy chair with a small table next to it. I made straight for the window and thrust my head through it to breathe some fresh air and looked out on a wall full of window airconditioners on the next building. On withdrawing from the window I collapsed into the easy chair and Maria Theresa, walking across the room, drew the curtain across the window, saying, 'It'll be cooler this way.'

It was darker, too, and it took me a few minutes to get used to the dim light. She walked back and sat on the edge of the bed, bent down to her raised feet, one at a time, and pulled off her shoes; a most graceful gesture, I thought, reminding me of an 'artistic' photograph I'd seen on some calendar.

'Whatever happened to Vicente?' I suddenly asked.

'To whom?'

I thought that perhaps she had not heard me clearly, and said, 'My brother, he went back for his cigarettes, remember?'

'Oh, don't worry about him! Just relax.'

I thought this a remarkably incongruous statement. It was then that I looked round the room for a record-player and saw that the room did not even contain any luggage, which surely someone living in a hotel ought to have had lying about. As my eyes, travelling around the room, fell on Maria Theresa again, I suddenly realised what was going on even before my eyes transmitted their perception to my brain – that, during the couple of moments that I'd taken to glance around the room looking first for a record-player and then for luggage, she had slipped a few buttons out of their holes and taken off her blouse. It did not take me another moment to interpret what my eyes had just communicated, though for a while I stubbornly refused to believe myself and played with the possibility that the heat was too much for my new friend. She next slipped off her skirt and sat there, on the edge of the bed, in her bra and underpants while I looked shyly away from her and, thinking that I should say something, came up with, 'A good, clean wash-basin is a mark of civilisation.'

She made a vague sound deep within her throat, a pure female sound charged with sexuality which would have made any man throw off his clothes and leap at her, but I innocently looked at the ceiling and wondered how long it was since it had last received a coat of paint. Having begun to stare at the ceiling, it occured to me that it would look ridiculous if I suddenly took my eyes away from it without saying something about it and, not having anything interesting to say, except for the paint job that it badly needed, I kept staring stupidly at it. After a while Maria Theresa said, 'What's your favourite subject at school?'

'History!' I exclaimed immediately.

'That's wonderful,' she said.

'Ask me anything in history. Go on. Anything.'

'When was Brazil discovered and by whom?'

'By Alvares Cabral in fifteen hundred. Go on, ask me another!'

'Who was the last Emperor of Brazil?'

'Dom Pedro Segundo,' I answered, having by now stood up, my chest held out, my arms at my sides and my head high. 'That's too easy, ask me something difficult. Ask me the date of the French Revolution.'

'What was the date of the French Revolution?'

'Seventeen eighty-nine!' I yelled.

'Why, Gregóriozinho, that's fantastic!'

'Go on, ask me some more dates.'

'Well... you're so clever, I don't know what to ask.'

'Ask me the date of the Norman Conquest of Britain. Ask me about the Hundred Years War. Lincoln's assassination. The emancipation of the slaves. The Empire. The Republic.'

'Oh, Gregório, you're such a genius!'

I sat down, since it was apparent that she had no more questions to ask. I was about to look at the ceiling again when she said, 'You're the most brilliant *man* I've ever met.'

I have to confess that the flattery implied by her emphasis had me confused. To tell the truth, I knew by now that she was a whore and that Vicente had tricked me into coming with her. I remembered his words about my becoming a man and I also remembered how he had turned in his chair to hide from me the fact that he was taking money out of his pocket to give to her. I suspect I knew this all along but had somehow decided not to think about it even when the lady sat on the edge of the bed in her underclothes. You have to remember that I was fourteen at the time – which, I have to agree, is nothing remarkable for a Brazilian youth. I mean, to be with a whore at that age, for one's elder brother, if one has one, or one's father usually so contrives circumstances that a Brazilian boy finds himself happily initiated into sexual matters no sooner than he has discovered the possibilities of his manhood, the elder brother's impulse being to play a joke while the father sees himself as doing the sensible thing, for consequently many a young girl of respectable family remains a virgin for a little while longer – perhaps, with luck, as long as her wedding-night. At least, this was the common custom some twenty-five years ago. Well, there I was with Maria Theresa, having finally begun to face my reality; and if I had evaded it so far, the truth was that I did not know what on earth I should do, so I was almost relieved when she said a moment later, 'You *are* a man, aren't you?'

For with those words she rose, stood a few paces in front of me, pushed back the straps of her bra so that it hung most provocatively from her breasts, showing almost all of them and yet by concealing the vital parts seeming to show nothing, and at the same time pulled down a little on her underpants so that a section of black hairs showed without the truth about her sex being actually visible. She made a clicking sound with her tongue, pouted her lips and, putting out a hand to me, said, 'Come, my little genius.'

I don't believe women understand the nature of male sexuality, especially when the male in question is a fourteen-year-old whose best flights in this particular realm have hitherto been propelled manually. There had been times when not the presence of female flesh and not even a memory of it, not looking at a photograph of one or remembering a close-up of a heroine in a film, but merely a sudden rememberance of a poorly printed photograph in an old newspaper, a blurred grey image on yellowing paper made even more distant by being only a thing that is remembered – this form seen at so many removes had been sufficient to set the manual machine in motion. So, imagine a youth of such sensitivity, whose dreams have rarely dared to go beyond the desire to procure a colour photograph of a film star, having before him a beautiful mulatta in a state of provocative undress saying to him, 'Come, my little genius.'

Well, I came, right there in my pants in that chair. While women have no understanding of such a happening, for they see it only as a tribute to their own particular selves, which is to say their vanity, they do have a wonderful sense of sympathy. The fact that man is forever condemned to ejaculate makes him a pitiable creature while making the woman believe herself to be invulnerable, which is why the man is always the beast and the woman a goddess, for she, like all superior creatures, can look

41

down with a contemptuous silence, for she alone is gifted by nature to dispel no evidence of her own sexual state. With this natural advantage the woman, suddenly seeing a revelation of her strength, discovers that she is not the weaker sex after all, and so becomes imbued with a magnanimity; and while she might not always forgive a man a premature ejaculation, she will sometimes pretend that nothing has happened.

So that when I found myself in this situation with Maria Theresa my condition was such that I was convinced that even a virgin with no knowledge of male procedures would have realised that I had been rendered temporarily useless. And this is where I had my first experience of female magnanimity. For what Maria Theresa did was to pull up her underwear, put on all her clothes and to go and lie in bed, asking me to lie beside her and teach her some history. I took off my shoes and lay beside her with my clothes on and proceeded to astonish her with my knowledge of Portuguese conquests in Africa and Asia. After about fifteen minutes, while I talked about the slave trade from Angola, she began to stroke parts of me, first my hands and arms, then my chest then slowly going towards my stomach and points beyond. She snuggled up beside my shoulder and begged me to tell her about the Paraguayan war, and while I did so she quietly took my hand and slid it into her bosom. I was just then in the middle of a passionate denunciation of the Paraguayan dictator Lópes, and with a great willpower continued my speech, speaking the more rapidly the closer I came to the end of what I'd learned by heart for a school exam, so that by the end I was babbling as fast and as loudly as one of those football commentators on radio. My speech was stunningly brought to a close by Maria Theresa putting her lips on mine and her hand down where I seemed to have recovered from my earlier false start.

O glorious woman, my first whore!

I was inspired to kiss her everywhere, her mouth, her cheeks, her chin – do I have to write a catalogue? And as I did so I was grateful for my earlier spillage, for there seemed to be a more durable quality to my new potency. And then, when I was ready, I turned her over so that her knees were on the bed and her beautiful buttocks stuck up in the air. I stroked them, kissed them, rubbed my cheeks against them, hugging her from behind, and then, kneeling behind her, tried to remember what I'd seen dogs do in the street and bulls on the farm. I seemed to be getting nowhere with my attempts at insertion, and after a while Maria Theresa said, 'Gregório, are you sure *that's* where you want to put it in?'

I was dumbfounded. What could she mean? Before I could think of what to say she made an accommodating suggestion: 'You can do what you like.'

I was more confused but had a brainwave and said, 'No, *you* can do what you like.'

She hesitated for a moment and I took that to mean that I was to continue, and so began parting her buttocks to see if I could not enter this time, when she dropped herself flat on the bed, turned round and, holding my index finger, said, 'Think of it as the battle of Waterloo.'

With those words she pushed my finger into a warm, moist area, pulled it partly out and pushed it in again, several times.

Thanks to Maria Theresa's instruction, I've never made a mistake again in my life; and because of the memory of that first time my subsequent forays in this battleground have always been attended by a sense of Napoleonic confidence of victory and an ultimate feeling of wretchedness and loss.

I suppose from that day can be dated the misery that I was to suffer in my late youth, but already in my middle years I'm beginning to be sentimental and think of Maria Theresa with great fondness as a pure, angelic creature, one of those naturally generous women to whom the society and the times and the double standards of sexual morality have conspired to leave no recourse but to become either nurses or whores, giving everything they have to keep intact the vanity of men. The simple-minded Maria Theresa, brown-skinned and black-eyed, remains in my mind as an elegant lady, but I've forgotten all the others who exist in my imagination as a riotous crowd in some debauched drawing-room, a confused assembly of naked women, white and black and mulatta, for I was the normal

43

young Brazilian male in those days, strutting about the beaches believing that my handsome body was the object of everyone's desire, driving up and down the avenues along Copacabana and Ipanema and, once a week, going whoring. Of course we had girl-friends, but they were only companions to take to a party or to the movies; and, of course, one formed attachments, believed that one was in love, and sometimes even went so far as to abstain from visiting a whore for two or three months by way of proving the seriousness of one's love. With these girls from respectable families one was engaged in established social rituals: to them one expressed the poetry of love, both verbally and through gestures of tenderness, while one continued to practise the prosaic commerce of sex with the whores.

It was, I can say without perverting the true meaning of the word, an innocent life. But adolescent fantasies during expeditions into the jungle and the purchase of sexual confectionery were not all that preoccupied my youth. Look at the early history of your greatest hero and you will discover that much of his time was spent not fighting dragons or courting women but staring at words in a book. Actually, much of my staring was not at words but at the ocean; I'd spend hours, either sitting on the terrace of our apartment or down on the beach, just staring at the blue waves as if I expected one of them to bring me some special message from some distant world. The books I read were by Brazilian authors; these were tattered and poorly printed volumes that somehow came my way.

But father, who professed a great respect for the written word (although I never saw him read anything but the newspaper) and used his business connections to order entire catalogues of books at greatly reduced prices, had built up an impressive library both at the apartment in Rio and the house on the farm; so that Thucydides and Herodotus, and Shakespeare, Dante, Molière and Goethe were as much at home on the walls that surrounded us as were the beetles and roaches, especially on the farm. It was a comprehensive library of the world's classics, all beautifully printed and bound in leather, which none of us read, except our sister Iolanda who read just about everything. Although she was a year older than me, she behaved as if I ought to know more and would suddenly ask me such questions as, 'Gregório, do you think that Hamlet was mad because he could not love Ophelia as much as he did his mother?' Not having any knowledge of what she was talking I would come up with such answers as, 'It is, as you know, a matter of speculation.' For I'd realised that a vague evasiveness always satisfied her that she had engaged in an intellectual dialogue, whereas if I said, which I did before I perfected my technique of evasion, 'Oh, Iolanda, how the hell should I know?' she would be put into a foul humour. I had, out of self-defence, hit upon a technique known among certain intellectuals as 'critical acumen'.

To keep his library up-to-date father also subscribed to the *Illustrated London News* and the *National Geographic,* so that when we had guests even Anibal, at the age of eleven, could astonish them by answering correctly which of the Queen's horses had won at Ascot, and Iolanda by describing accurately the life of veiled women in Afghanistan.

Mother would sigh ambiguously on these occasions to suggest either the sacrifice of parents who had so much to teach their children or to indicate, especially when the guests applauded the children's knowledge, that, alas, there was so much more that the poor creatures would have to learn before they attained true adulthood. She herself, being French by birth and confining her literary allusions to classical writers of her native land, had a way of saying, 'Ah, Molière. . .' and, with a look of profound inner beauty in her eyes, would leave it at that, so that one was supposed to appreciate the depths of her own understanding. Father would look affectionately at her at that moment and nod his head as if he understood her feeling precisely, and occasionally, when a guest did not proceed with the conversation, father would put in, 'Such is the quality of genius.' And mother would look at him with a smile as if to convey her gratitude for his perception of her own idea. I was always impressed by this solemn dialogue because I never understood it, and it was only some years later that I realised that the words she used were 'Ah, Molière' and referred to a French playwright, whereas all through my childhood I'd though she was saying 'A mulher.'

45

The only guest who did not care to hear what the prodigious memories of the four Xavier children had to recite was a middle-aged banker named Ernesto Moreira. It was rare for fewer than four guests to come to dinner, usually there were ten or fifteen, but this time, because there was only one, we all paid him a lot more attention.

'Children', said Senhor Moreira, 'should be seen and not heard.'

Even at that time I was certain that someone else had spoken the same words and spoken them ironically, but from the solemn Senhor Moreira's lips they fell like a heavy weight upon the dining-table and Iolanda, who had just taken the first spoonful of soup to her lips, held it there, thought to herself for a moment and put the spoon down. I don't think anyone noticed that she was making a protest and, had I not been so hungry and the soup not made of potatoes, I believe I would have joined my sister. I was glad, however, that after a while mother noticed and said, 'Why aren't you eating your soup, Iolanda?'

Iolanda did not reply but looked blankly at mother, so that father had to look at her and say, 'Iolanda, your mother asked you a question.'

Iolanda looked at father, then stared for rather a long moment at Senhor Moreira and looked again at father and whispered, 'It's too salty.'

'Oh, nonsense!' father said.

'It's just perfect,' Senhor Moreira said, his mouth full of bread.

'In that case. . . ,' said Iolanda brightly, smiling at everyone, and commenced vigorously to eat her soup.

I don't believe anyone understood that she had scored a point but she had satisfied herself and didn't utter another word during the rest of dinner.

Senhor Moreira sucked greedily at his soup spoon, tore at his bread and, his mouth full of both bread and soup, said, 'Politics, that's what life is all about.'

I put down the words as if he spoke them clearly, but every time he talked his mouth was full and a word like 'politics' sound as 'poashicks' when it was emitted through thick lips by two bulging cheeks. He looked up at father, who was nodding his head, and at mother, who had her spoon poised before her mouth, and, satisfied that his audience was attentive, he stuffed some bread into his mouth, worked his jaw two or three times smacking his lips, sucked a spoonful of soup and, rolling the resulting paste about his mouth, said 'Yes, politics, that's what life is all about, but business is the master of politics. There's no government without politics and no politics without business. Now! Take the common factor away and you are left with government and business. Therefore, government is business and business is government.'

Even I, who was only a boy then, could tell that the man was an idiot as I watched him conclude his statement with a triumphant flourish, pick up what was left of his bread, rub it around his empty soup-plate until he had polished it and stuff the bread into his mouth.

'But Senhor Moreira,' mother said, sitting elegantly upright in her chair and looking as if she were about to ask a difficult question of a very learned man, 'how can business be the master of government?'

The plump banker was lost for a moment, not having any food before him, then seized his glass of wine, put it to his thick lips and sucked as if he were drinking hot coffee, and said, 'Politicians cannot live without money.' He paused, looked with an aggressive brightness of eye at mother as if he had made a telling point, and went on; 'Look at any successful politician, you will see that he is backed by some business or other. Politicians are the tools of businessmen.'

He turned his bright stare at father, apparently convinced that he was uttering a profound truth with each platitude. And yet this man was a respected banker and I received the impression that both my parents took him seriously and believed that their children were learning the important facts of life by listening to him.

He remains in my mind as a singular example of an overfed, inept buffoon who looked up at one with a bullying manner, when his face was not attending to food, and bore himself with

47

such ponderous gravity that he gave the impression of being preoccupied with profound thoughts; who used pretentious words in long-winded, meaningless combinations, who exhibited a fundamental vulgarity, and who passed in the world as a shrewd businessman. I have seen many versions of Moreira in my life and it was seeing that original example at the table that taught me that the simplest way to succeed in life is to give such fools the notion that one takes them seriously and to feed their vanity from time to time by calling their ideas progressive and their methods dynamic and by bestowing upon them some fashionable label, such as 'the new technocrats.'

It was some years later that I discovered that father used Moreira to finance his business. I was in the office of the shop in Copacabana where tourists from the hotels on the ocean-front came to buy semi-precious stones, framed butterflies, rosewood bowls and a thousand other objects. Father had a notion that he could instil sound business principles into his sons' minds by having each of them occasionally spend a day with him at the office.

'Gregório, why don't you open the mail,' he said when we arrived in the room which served as an office at the back of the shop, 'and sort out the letters, putting the invoices in one group, bank statements in another and so on? A businessman must do everything in a businesslike way.'

I sat down at his desk which, apart from an extra chair, was all the furniture in the office. On an earlier occasion father had pointed out that the most important thing in an office was not that it had a teak desk, an oriental rug and potted palms but that it had an efficient filing system. I opened the letters one by one, most of which were invoices from various wholesalers. There was only one letter as such, from a merchant in Minas who, referrring to the great demand for icons, saints, candlesticks and 'other objects of antique value', as he put it, including refectory tables, chairs, cabinets, carved doors of solid wood, ceramic tiles and bits of broken plaster which some tourist valued as worth putting into a glass case in his drawing-room, offered his services of procuring the said rare objects for our esteemed clients, for he had access to many hundreds of churches which his ancestors had been good enough to construct in the state of Minas some two hundred years ago when the rivers and the mountains had been blessed with gold. The letter, signed in a florid hand with several flourishes by a man named João Joaquim Balbi – where he compensated for the brevity of his surname by making the most of the two J's and giving the q an extravagant flourish so that it seemed the centre of some flower – ended by stating that objects in special demand and of great rarity could be manufactured by skilled craftsmen 'to specifications of genuine antiquity'.

Two financial statements in the mail intrigued me. First there was the one from Moreira's bank giving the monthly status of a recent loan; the second was from a broker on Wall Street in New York and it gave, for three pages, a list of securities held by father, stating the value of each and giving as a grand total the staggering sum of $223,747.

Father came back from the shop, sat down in the other chair across from me at the desk and said, 'Well, give me a résumé of the mail.'

I pointed to the pile of invoices and gave a general idea of what they were for.

'That's quite a lot of money to pay out!' father exclaimed.

'Yes, sir,' I said.

'Now, Gregório, what does that teach you?'

I thought for a moment and said, 'I'm not sure if I understand.'

'Oh, come, young man,' father said, looking at me seriously. 'The question is very elementary. If you get bills for a thousand contos then what can it mean but that you have to pay out a thousand contos?'

'Well, yes,' I said.

'Well, yes, what?' he said, frowning a little.

'I mean I can see that.'

'Then why didn't you say so?'

'Well, I thought it was too obvious an idea to be the answer to your question.'

'No, simple things first,' father said, pushing his chair back to

49

give himself room to cross his legs. 'Remember your geometry? The shortest distance between two points is a straight line. All great systems are built on simple foundations. All right. The next question is, if you have to pay out a thousand contos in bills, where does the money come from?'

'Why, the bank.'

'The *bank?* Do you think a bank is a tap you can turn on and money comes pouring out like water?'

'No, I meant the money you put in the bank.'

'Ha! And what money do I put in the bank, do I pluck it off a fig tree?'

'The money which is earned by the shop.'

'Very good,' he said, nodding his head. 'Now, have you ever spent a day working the shop?'

'Yes, you know I have.'

'Never mind what I know!' he exclaimed, and I irrelevantly thought that he'd seen some crime movie and had been impressed by a court scene.

'Yes, I have,' I said.

'Have what?' he cried, pointing an accusing finger at me. 'Eaten a banana? Gone fishing?'

'Spent a day at the shop.'

'Once or twice or many times?'

'Many times,' I answered.

'Good, we're getting somewhere. Now, answer this. When you have spent a day at the shop, you have seen people come in and buy things we sell, have you not?'

'Yes, sir, I have,' I said in a firm voice.

'And you yourself have taken their money in payment for their purchases, sometimes in cruzeiro notes, sometimes in dollars and sometimes in travellers' cheques, is that not correct?'

'Yes, sir, it is.'

'At the end of the day you have counted the day's cash receipts, have you not?'

'Yes, I have.'

'Good,' he said, smacking his lips. 'Now tell me, what has been the largest sum that you have counted as a day's receipts?'

50

I thought for a while and said, 'I can't truly remember.'

'Has it been a thousand contos?' he asked, pointing his finger again and his eyes bulging out as if he were on the point of proving to the court that I had been at the scene of the crime.

'No,' I said.

'Five hundred?'

'No.'

'Less than five hundred?'

'Yes, sir.'

'How much less?'

'I don't think it was ever as much as two hundred contos.'

'Do you want to stick by that fact? That the shop never took in more than two hundred contos in one day?'

'Yes, I swear to it,' I said, hoping that my use of court-room terminology would impress him.

'All right, then, Gregório, tell me now why I have been at such pains to put these questions so specifically to you?'

I had long understood the point of his questions but, not wishing to suggest that it was all child's play, tried to give the impression that it was difficult to answer and so said, 'You're trying to teach me business, sir.'

'Yes, of course,' he said, looking a trifle vexed as if he had a miserable idiot on his hands, 'but that doesn't answer my question. Think about it.'

I looked up at the ceiling, rolled my eyes in a gesture of one struggling with a complex thought and then said, 'I believe we are talking about income and expenditure.'

'Income and expenditure!' he shouted, nodding his head approvingly.

'Also about profit and loss,' I said.

'Profit and loss!' he shouted again, as though wanting to declare to the world that his son was a genius at understanding business.

'Overheads and taxes,' I said, finding a new combination that went neatly together.

He looked at me in amazement and then shouted, 'Overheads and taxes! Quite right, my boy, overheads and taxes! So, you've learned the very important fact about this business, that the

51

money you take in daily is not all profit but only a percentage of it is. And there is a moral to this. You have to accumulate cash reserves in order to meet your obligations. All right, what else was there in the mail?'

'There's a statement of a loan from the bank.'

'Ah, yes,' he said, frowning.

'Can I ask a question, sir?'

'Yes, what is it?'

'If we accumulate cash reserves to meet our obligations, then why do we need such a large loan?'

'Good question, Gregório, very good question. What else was there in the mail?'

'Pardon me, sir, but you haven't answered my question.'

'I know, Gregório, and I will answer it in a moment, for it requires an understanding of complicated issues. Let's finish the mail first.'

'There's only one other thing,' I said, picking up the communication from New York, 'a statement of stock exchange transactions on Wall Street, giving the current total value of your securities as $223,747.'

'Ah, the market is on the upswing again,' he said with satisfaction.

'What I don't understand', I said, 'is that, when you have that amount of money in New York, a business here with a good turnover, why then should you ask a bank for a loan?'

'For the simple reason that I can get it!' he exclaimed. 'Never pass up an opportunity to get a short-term loan.'

And he began a long monologue that touched upon accountancy, tax laws, working capital, cash flow, and ended with: 'If you want to get rich, never spend your own money. Borrow it, double it, pay back the loan, add the profit to your real capital, and with that solid wealth to back you up, borrow again.'

I was deemed to have done a hard morning's work and was rewarded by being taken to lunch at a *churrascaria* where we ate heaps of roast beef and rice and beans.

'That man Balbi is a scoundrel,' father said as if he were speaking not to his teenage son but confidentially to some

52

business colleague.

'Do you know him?' I asked, trying hard not to be distracted by a beautifully tanned blonde who sat across the room.

'Yes, the man's a nuisance, he sends long letters every month and once a year even comes to Rio.'

I chewed thoughtfully on the meat, trying hard to concentrate on the conversation and to dispel the fantasy in which I saw myself with the blonde on a satin-covered mattress floating across the blue sky among soft, billowy clouds.

'People like Balbi are destructive,' father said. 'You can have no idea, young man, so please pay attention and stop dreaming about the young woman behind my left shoulder, she's beautiful, I know, but there are thousands like her, so don't think you're missing anything.'

I looked at father with an innocent stare, and he went on, 'You have to realise that the beauty of women is a very banal thing, especially here in Rio where there's no reason why any woman under twenty-five should not have a perfectly tanned skin, a fine figure and, with a little make-up if necessary, stunning features. So, you're not going to lose by not having that lady's affections all to yourself and, as you can see, she has eyes only for the young man with the curly, poetical hair, so you'll be better employed listening to me.'

'That's all I'm doing,' I protested, 'listening to you, but tell me, how do you see all these things?'

'Oh, don't be such a child, Gregório! You know very well there are mirrors on the walls and that for the last twenty minutes I've done nothing but study the young couple while talking to you!'

I looked behind me. There was, indeed, a large mirror there in which I saw the face of the blonde, looking with smiling eyes at her companion, and in spite of all that father had said, I thought to myself, O my God, why can't she look at me like that?

'So, if I may return to the boring business of Senhor Balbi, let me say that by listening to me you'll learn more about not only being a successful businessman but, being one, you'll also realise that that's the surest way to win the type of woman you can't take your eyes off.'

'Father, I'm looking only at you!'

'You hardly flatter me by saying so. What kind of a son do I have who, given the presence of a beautiful young woman, looks only at his old father? Would you like to change places with me? No? Well, that's more like it! As I was saying Balbi's type of businessman has to be avoided, and let me tell you why. What he has to sell are objects which he's stolen from churches. He goes to villages which were thriving towns once, back in the days of the gold boom, but which are nearly deserted now except for the old, the infirm and the cats and the dogs. He gives a miserable gift to the priest there and proceeds to ransack the church of all its furnishings, including whole altars, and sells these to people in Rio and São Paulo who call themselves antique dealers and who, in turn, sell them to anthropology professors from America or museum curators from all over Europe or to that type of acquisitive bourgeois from Europe and America whose great destiny is first to reduce the world to his own execrable level of vulgarity and then to destroy it altogether by his avarice. Now, if I didn't have any scruples, I'd be hand in glove with such a barbarian as Balbi, for there's a great deal of money to be made in that criminal trade which passes itself off as a business. And this is what I want you to listen most carefully to, Gregório, if you will only take your eyes away from those two deep green wells in that gorgeous blonde head behind my left shoulder. The making of money in itself is no great thing; one has to observe principles in this life. Anyone who robs churches is a thief, there can be no two words about it. What is worse, he's robbing not only the house of God – that would be no great crime considering there are thousands of God's houses for which even God appears to have no longer any use, oh yes, I've seen them, in Tiradentes or in Ouro Preto, overgrown with creepers and even the cobblestones in their yards uprooted by weeds – but also, and this to me is the crime, robbing the heritage of our country, taking away the objects which belong to your grandchildren and selling them to people whose only satisfaction in owning them is one of vulgar ostentation.'

54

I had never thought of grandchildren of my own but must confess that, just when father mentioned that word, my eyes were again on the green-eyed blonde and I was having the fantasy of being the father of all her green-eyed children.

'Well, I can see there's no point in talking to a young man who will think only of pretty girls.' father said.

'But I heard everything you said!'

'I should hope not!' father exclaimed. 'If a son of mine is not interested in women, he can be good for nothing and there can be no future for Brazil! I hope by now your elder brother has had the sense to introduce you to the facts of life.'

'Yes, he has, father,' I said, thinking of Maria Theresa who was my one indisputable fact.

'Why, that's excellent! Why didn't you say so before? You can stop drinking that miserable Coca Cola! Waiter! Bring us whisky, will you?'

When the waiter had brought a bottle and two glasses and father had poured me a good measure, I picked up my glass, held it to my lips and threw it back in one go, and said, 'This is nothing, father. Vicente and I have drunk an entire bottle of *cachaça* between us in a couple of hours.'

That pleased him and he re-filled my glass. When I had drunk that with another exhibitionistic, manly gesture, he said, 'Well, that's enough, there's work to do, let's go.'

When we rose from the table he took my arm and drew me to the table where the green-eyed blonde still sat smiling at her companion. I was dumbfounded when, reaching her table, father said, 'Ah, Mônica, you continue to be indescribably beautiful, I believe you've stolen my son's heart. Please do me the honour of shaking my son Gregório's hand and forgive me if it's trembling.'

In fact, my legs were trembling, but no one could see that and I was too overcome by the sudden realisation that father knew the girl I'd inwardly been sighing over for the last hour to become nervous, and I put out my hand, saying, 'My father's taste in beauty is an education to me.'

The young man who was with her looked petulantly at her while she said, holding out the softest hand I'd ever touched,

55

'Why, Gregório, hel*lo*! You have your father's deep-brown eyes and he knows how irrestistable *his* are!'

I assumed that to be just playful nonsense, and father and I walked away, nodding our heads to her young man who didn't look happy at all, and father said, 'Yes, she knows these eyes, ah, yes!'

I decided not to believe father's implication that Mônica had been his mistress but realised that an older man, even one's own father, once given the opportunity to muse upon his sexual conquests, especially where the partner had been less than half his age, could not resist describing all the details of the affair. I wished, however, that father had been less effusive about a girl I'd spent all lunch looking at and thinking about in the most intimate images. One of my fondest fantasies at that time was being with a most beautiful woman in a bedroom bathed in a rosy light, the white, satin sheets aglow with a soft pink, bouquets of red camellias on either side of the bed, pink rose-petals strewn upon the pillows, and there, on gently undressing this beautiful woman, caressing her flawless skin and her golden hair, hearing her whisper in a voice indescribably beautiful that she has never known a man before, that she has kept her treasure only for me. And every time I saw a beautiful woman, as with Mônica that afternoon, my mind obliterated the presence of other men and took her away to the secret world of my fantasies where her breasts, kept concealed from all humanity since she was five years old, offer their nectar to my lips. Such being the nature of my imagination, it was distressing, to say the least, that the woman who in my fantasy gave her innocence to me had given it to another in reality, and that the scene in which I had acted with her in my mind she had already performed with my father.

Later that afternoon, Mônica and her young man turned up at the shop, some three hours after we had met them at the restaurant. She had changed into a flowery cotton dress and wore a wide-brimmed straw hat, the blonde hair coming down to her shoulders in straight, neatly brushed silken strands, and her bearing had the queenly poise which comes naturally to beautiful women, especially after they have bestowed a little of their bounty on a fawning and lustful male companion and have no doubt that, whether they are walking up a boulevard or entering a shop, men are going to turn their heads and look at them with a sudden flaring of desire. The two of them had come to the shop because Rudy, her young man, wished to buy her a present, and I had been called out of the office because Mônica insisted that I should serve her. Rudy, rather thick-set with deep-blue eyes, obviously of northern European descent, seemed to be in a state of belligerent elation. I suspected that he wished to give the impression that Mônica was his mistress and that they had gone and made love after lunch, whereas I believe the truth was that his male ego had been piqued by the flirtatious little dialogue between father and Mônica at the restaurant, that she had allowed him the preliminaries of love, intensifying his lust without appeasing it, so that he had become reckless, the sort of mood in which a man will mortgage his life just to prove his own delusion that he is deeply in love. He seemed also obviously anxious to show off his possession of Mônica as if a mistress were like a new car one had bought which one drove up and down Avenida Atlântica until one was convinced that the entire neighbourhood knew of one's good fortune. Had Mônica taken him to a jeweller he would probably have bought her the largest diamond in Rio; instead they had come to our shop, and that, I thought, was not without a subtle meaning.

'Rudy wanted to buy me a souvenir of Rio,' Mônica said, smiling at me with her full lips while I stared at her large, green eyes like a dog.

It struck me as absurd that someone who lived in Rio should be considered as wanting a souvenir of the city. But I was overwhelmed by Mônica's beauty and nervously went about pulling things down from the shelves to show her, talking rapidly when no one said anything and finding nothing to say when I was asked a question.

'No, no, something of more taste,' Rudy said, dismissing several of the things that I showed them, 'something more expensive.'

57

I was fascinated by the fact that Mônica actually picked up with a fondling gesture the things which I had put down on the counter. Her hands caressed the objects with a soft, delicate touch, and I imagined myself on future occasions, whenever I came to the shop, looking sadly at these objects and experiencing a profound unhappiness at being beside things which *she* had touched.

'No, no, something more precious,' Rudy said. 'Something which is a souvenir also of love.'

I knew, when he said that, that he was watching me with cynicism and complacency and probably hoping that his casual remark about love, calculated to show his complete possession of the woman I so desired, would provoke my envy, but with a supreme effort I restrained myself from looking at him with anger and hatred and affected an emotional indifference. It occurred to me that the object of this game was not that he should please Mônica but that I should suffer torment, and I decided that if that were the case I would make him pay for it, so that, instead of frantically going about the shop bringing down more things, I talked as if I had been twenty years a salesman and persuaded him that the best souvenir would be a collection of all the souvenirs of Rio that we had in the shop, to be placed in a special glass cabinet in Mônica's bedroom. She was delighted by the idea and, smiling generously at me, informed Rudy that that was precisely what she would like. The thought surely ought to have crossed his mind that he was being taken for a fool but, instead of reflecting that he could buy a gold watch with the amount of money he was about to spend on worthless trifles, Rudy eagerly accepted the suggestion, for he was more interested in showing his money and flaunting the idea of his wealth than in expressing his taste. I was convinced when they left that Mônica thought to herself that she had demonstrated what a power she had over men and that he was intoxicated by his own certainty of possessing Mônica, for had he not shown a potential rival or a former lover – for my father would surely know how much money he'd spent – that he alone was worthy of her love? Frankly, I found such behaviour trivial and, had it not been for the pleasure of receiving Mônica's wonderful smiles, I would have been bored by the entire affair; but at least I'd grown a little wiser, for here were adults engaged in foolish guiles for no better reason than to pacify their slightly enraged vanity, and all because of a few words spoken in jest.

Coincidentally, however, it was the largest single sale we'd ever had in the shop, for no fool, even from Germany or the United States, and of these there were plenty, had ever bought silver replicas of the Sugarloaf and of the figure of Christ on Corcovado, trays made of rosewood with an inlay of iridescent butterfly wings, silver tea-spoons with semi-precious stones in their handles and a lot else, all at once. I was congratulated on my success and would have been in danger of being appointed a permanent salesman had father not observed the transaction from behind the fake mirror between the shop and the office and realised that it was due more to his own words spoken at the restaurant than to any gift of persuasion on my part. While to me he was full of jocular hints that Mônica had never cost him such extravagance, father nevertheless had the generosity to praise me to mother and to his friends for the sale I'd made, making of the episode an elaborate and amusing story.

But what will men not do for beautiful women with whom they are not even in love! I believe that we go about attempting to fulfil ideas of ourselves which we have projected during an idle fantasy, for we realise in our imaginations certain notions of perfection, and there's no more easily grasped imagery for it than to see ourselves, immaculately dressed, driving up in a Rolls-Royce with the most beautiful woman in the world and parking precisely outside an expensive shop and buying her all the frivolous objects that she desires. Ah Gregório, you who understood this at the age of fifteen are in your present predicament precisely because you, in your own self-conceit, thought it was true only of the vanity of other men! And how easily do you forget that the woman who professes to love you is obliged out of the necessity of her own vanity, to spend hours in which she does not have a single thought of you! But we shall come to all this in due course, my friend; besides, Mônica has not yet left your world.

59

My day's work at the office and the shop gave father great pleasure, especially as it proved his belief that one learned business from practical experience, and while mother heard every detail of my day with interest, she was restrained in her expression of approval, being convinced that too much praise, even when merited, went to a child's head. She was given to worrying over our future and was afraid that we would grow up as barbarians. She had been born in northern France, had been brought to Brazil at the age of five, had only once visited Paris, when she was not twenty and that only for a month, but considered herself a Parisian and thought it her duty to temper the natural boisterousness of her Brazilian children with the civilising experience of European manners. Etiquette was one of her obsessions and she trained us meticulously at table, sitting upright herself and sharply correcting the slightest infringement, as if she expected one of us to be appointed ambassador to France one day.

She would take the four of us to gatherings of French society where people sat solemnly listening to chamber music in absolute silence and coughing in between movements. Iolanda always sat with her eyes wide open, staring at the musicians in their black suits and ties, but Vicente and I gave meaningful looks to each other to indicate our complete boredom while Anibal would fall asleep until mother saw him and tapped him sharply on the knee. Sometimes we would be taken to the Alliance Française where a visiting Frenchman would give a lecture on life in Algeria or on French furniture of some period, but the lectures were always in French of which we had no more knowledge than of Chinese, but mother believed that our merely imbibing the atmosphere of French culture was an educational experience in itself.

None of it meant anything to us boys, however, but Iolanda began to think of herself as a French lady, went through a tiresome phase when she criticised everything by saying, 'That's not the French way,' but from the age of sixteen, after she had been snubbed by some of her school-friends for her French airs, began to study the language with a great passion and to express a genuine intellectual curiosity instead of a boring snobbery. It pleased mother, of course, who regretted that she had not spoken French to us when we were children. The time came when mother invited a group of her friends, dressed Iolanda in a specially designed robe which made her look like a Greek statue, put chalky-white make-up on her face, loosened her hair to let it hang dishevelled about her shoulders, and had her enter the room where the guests sat in expectation of a surprise: Iolanda stood in the middle of the room, held her hands in front of her as if carrying a plate of food across the room, turned her eyes to the ceiling and declaimed in a shrill voice speeches from *Andromache.* Vicente and I, who had been forced to stay in the room, squirmed with embarrassment in our corner on hearing Iolanda's rapid and toneless declamation, but her performance, to our astonished surprise, was a resounding success, for the guests, alluding to certain phrases, remarked how Iolanda's rendering of the words gave a new meaning to the speech and reminded them of some great actress.

The success of this event led to the formation of a dramatic group which, fortunately for us, was so successful that mother, becoming totally absorbed in rehearsals and the reading of scores of French plays to discover those in which Iolanda could appear as the heroine, had no time for us. Their greatest success was *Cyrano,* which had a paragraph written about it in a newspaper, was revived for three more performances, and even seen by some Brazilians who knew no French. For a long time afterwards mother would talk of the success as though it belonged to some distant past and had happened not at a salon in Rio but at the Comédie Française in Paris, and Iolanda went sadly about the house, making tragic speeches aloud, especially in the afternoons when everyone else was trying to have a siesta.

I might as well abandon a strict chronology here and jump some years to describe where Iolanda's success in the amateur French theatre in Rio led her. I have no idea why the *Cyrano* success was not followed by even more ambitious productions; perhaps some happy instinct informed mother that it was better to be remembered for a modest success than to be despised for having over-reached and produced a colossal failure, so that for nearly a year she prefaced many of her statements with, 'When I was planning the production of *Cyrano*. . .' and in subsequent years she would interrupt a conversation among her friends with, 'If you remember that year when we did *Cyrano*. . .' and inevitably a legend grew about the famous production and its beautiful, tragic heroine, Iolanda, who, of course, continued to live the part by always looking pale, sad and like one who expected her days to end very shortly.

A young Frenchman by the name of Jean-Baptiste St Clair arrived from Lyons where his father was an importer of coffee, paid a very cursory visit to a coffee plantation in the state of São Paulo, spent most of his time in society in Rio, and fell in love with Iolanda. My sister, who by now was convinced that hers was to be the fate of the heroines of classical tragedy, dutifully fell in love with him with every expectation of nothing but an acute misery ensuing from the affair. When Jean-Baptiste went away to São Paulo for five days, for Iolanda it was a cruel parting decreed by malignant fate. At lunch and dinner she sat staring sadly at her plate, not touching the food and protesting that she had lost her appetite; mother, sharing Iolanda's mood and perhaps regretting that she herself had no reason to expect suffering, made the occasion out to be one which men could not be expected to understand (for mothers and daughters in alliance regard fathers and sons as imbeciles); to match the awesome sadness projected by Iolanda, mother affected a noble silence and, if any one of us uttered a word or two to begin to say that nothing actually had gone wrong, she gave, with an imperial tilting of her head, a look of scorn and disdain which was enough to make one feel a complete fool. Father simply scratched his head and drank a little more than usual, while Vicente and I wondered at the mysterious world of women which, without actually saying or doing anything, made us feel as though we had done it grave injury, reducing us to talking in whispers and to walking about the house on tip-toe. When not at the dining-table Iolanda sat by a window, looking out at the ocean and listening to the radio, becoming nervously apprehensive each time the news came on, for she was convinced that the next newscast would announce the death of Jean-Baptiste either in some accident or at the hands of some brutal murderers.

Nothing of the sort happened, of course, and Jean-Baptiste came back to Rio earlier than he had been expected, wrote, sitting in our drawing-room, a long report on the coffee plantation to send to his father and read it aloud to us. Since it was in French only mother and Iolanda understood anything of it and both of them seemed to be greatly moved by it, as if it were the last act of some tragic play, while to the rest of us it sounded farcical since all we heard was a passionately declaiming voice which enunciated exaggeratedly poetical effects to say nothing more profound than that the coffee plantation had recovered from the previous year's frost.

During the third and last month of his stay in Rio, Jean-Baptiste and Iolanda were married, and that, too, for mother and Iolanda was an occasion of high tragedy. At first there was the suspense of whether or not Jean-Baptiste's parents could come to the wedding; there would be a cable from Lyons announcing their imminent arrival and the following morning another cable regretting their inability to come: it went on for two weeks, culminating in a phone call to Lyons, made in our drawing-room, with Jean-Baptiste shouting in French into the phone while mother and Iolanda stood on either side of him, not knowing whether to cry for joy or for sorrow and remaining poised on the verge of tears, while father shifted his weight from one leg to the other, nervously looking at his watch and wondering how much all this drama was going to cost him. It led to nothing, for the parents did not come. When that had been resolved there was a new cause for Iolanda's suffering. She was to live with her husband in France – something that was both self-evident and inevitable and yet she and mother spent many hours with Jean-Baptiste debating the matter, discussing the advantages and disadvantages of living in France and comparing them to those in Brazil and finally convincing themselves that it was through some rational procedure that they had chosen to live in France when it was quite obvious that they had no choice in the matter; once having decided, however, Iolanda felt that fate was about to part her cruelly from her

63

beloved parents and her devoted brothers (on which last point, had she questioned us, we would have relieved her of all anxiety). For mother, Iolanda's going to France was a cause of sorrow because it meant not so much that she was losing a daughter but that Iolanda could live the life that she herself might have lived if she had never left France. The two cried regularly each evening between the engagement and the wedding and then wept copiously on the great day itself.

For the rest of us, it was a great relief when it was all over and the married couple had taken the ship to France, all that dramatic suspense and tension had been too much for us, for we too had begun to think that some tragedy was bound to occur and give Iolanda the inverted sort of happiness of her life having lived up to her dramatic expectations. In fact, the only tragedy that occurred in her life was that she had as happy an existence as any bourgeois housewife can expect, giving birth to a boy and a girl and remaining (as she still is) married to a prosperous husband devoted and presumably faithful to her.

It was many years later, when I had opportunity to read widely, that I realised that *Cyrano*, which had been mother's greatest success and had changed Iolanda's life, and which was the only play which they performed in full, producing only selected scenes from the others, was in fact one of the worst plays in the whole body of literature – which fact, though it has no bearing on my story, nevertheless amuses me enormously, being a perfect example of how mankind never learns to discriminate and, more often than not, prefers the mediocre, for it always looks for that mirror which is most engaging to its vanity; so that it must follow as an undeniable law that the shallower a writer or a politician the greater his following.

Bourgeois happiness is not to be despised in spite of the superior stances affected by people incapable of achieving it and I've often idly wished that, instead of having this feverish mind of mine which insists on speaking to all mankind, I'd had a mind complacent enough to live quietly with a homely wife who desired nothing more than that I take her to the theatre on her birthday or on our wedding anniversary and who, bored

64

and left entirely cold by *Phèdre* or *King Lear,* would on seeing *Cyrano* cling to my arm and, putting her head on my shoulder, weep bitterly. How easy life would be if one could really enjoy, like millions of people do, the soap-operas on TV everyday!

But everything that happened in my early life conspired to fill my soul with agitation; born in the lush tropics, the journey of my life has been towards a desert.

Some pages back I left you with some tantalising remark about Mônica. Since I've no desire to create an artificial suspense, my aim being to give you a cold narration of the facts, and since I've already abandoned chronology in any case, let me narrate the Mônica episode here, for it's not without consequence to the significant events in my life, some of which, I know, you have read misleading and inaccurate accounts of in the newspapers.

We found each other by chance at a fancy-dress ball nearly a year after she had come to the shop with Rudy. I was seeing the world through one eye since I'd gone dressed as a pirate and had a patch across my right eye, which, believe me, is not a clever thing to do, especially if one is young and is looking out for pretty girls. But Mônica had done something even less clever, she had come as a mermaid! The party was at the house of a politician who must remain nameless for the sake of discretion; let's simply say that he was involved in the succession to the presidency at the death of Getúlio Vargas and leave it at that. The house was on the top of one of the hills overlooking Rio and commanded a glorious view of the bay, and I remember unwittingly uttering the prophecy that someone who was already an emperor of his world could scarcely expect to rise higher. The garden had a large pond full of water-lilies and splashing fountains, and prior knowledge of that had inspired Mônica's costume. She was a great hit early in the evening, but there's a limit to how long you can dangle an artificial fin in a pond; besides, the fin was made of foam rubber and consequently Mônica's legs grew cold and numb inside it. Also, a carnival party is an occasion for dancing, and mermaids, while they may sit on rocks in the middle of the Atlantic and brush

65

their hair and sing sensuous melodies to drive sailors mad, have never been known to dance. So Mônica was stuck in her mermaid-suit which, in the early enthusiasm when she received so much admiration for her originality, she had kept dangling too long in the water with the result that the lower part of her body was cold and the upper part sticky with sweat. Only I, who had become increasingly frustrated seeing the world with one eye, recognised her plight and sympathised with her. Everyone had congratulated her on her brilliant idea and then left her, but by the time I came to her she was alone and, hearing me say I was sorry she'd put herself in a strait-jacket, she burst into tears and then, taking possession of herself, pleaded to be driven to her apartment so that she could change.

I drove her down the hill to her apartment in Copacabana. I don't know why it didn't occur to me to remove my eye-patch while I drove but, since I sat on her left and had the patch on my right eye, I didn't see her while peering at the traffic with my left eye as if I were driving through fog. Actually, Mônica had a zip at the bottom of the fin and by putting her feet through the opening she could walk; even dance, when I think of it; but by unzipping the fin the entire effect was ruined and she looked ridiculous, and someone who creates an astonishing impact in the first five minutes of a party doesn't want to go about receiving ridicule the rest of the evening. Anyway, we arrived at her apartment and she went directly to her bedroom to change. I sat in the elegantly furnished drawing-room glancing at a fashion magazine, and after about ten minutes I heard her call. She was in bed, lying under a sheet, and said her legs had gone very numb. I was about to offer to massage them when I thought that that would give an impression of taking advantage of her situation, and said she ought to have a hot bath.

'Will you run it for me, please?' she asked, having agreed that it was a good idea.

I ran the bath and looked at my own ridiculous face with the eye-patch and crude make-up of rouged cheeks and a painted moustache. I took the patch off and washed my face clean. The bath was ready.

'But I can't move my legs!' Mônica cried.

There was nothing to do but to carry her to the bathroom, to see her undress herself and then to pick her up and place her in the bath.

'Gregório, what are you staring at me like that for?' she asked when she was comfortably relaxed in the bath. In fact, I was just about to leave the bathroom. But she added, 'Haven't you seen a naked woman before?'

'Mônica,' I said, being suddenly inspired, 'I've seen naked female bodies before but, if you want to know the truth, you're the first woman that's come into my life.'

If the real truth has to be told, I might as well confess that when she had undressed I'd been concerned more for the relief that she would experience from the earlier oppression of her insane costume than for the passion that her nudity might arouse in me. It seems remarkable to think about it now, but observing one of the most beautiful women I'd ever seen in my life drop her underwear on the floor did not make me look at her with any physical desire; instead, my mind was entirely upon whether or not she was going to recover from the numbness in her legs, and even when I lifted her naked body to place her in the bath it was as if I were carrying a sick child and not a woman whose soft buttocks were resting on my arm.

'You look as though you could use a bath yourself,' she said. 'Why did you have to put that brown paint on your chest when you were only dressing up as a pirate?'

'Pirates are all sunburned,' I said but, taking her hint, added, 'Maybe I'll have a shower when you're finished.'

'Gregório,' she said, 'this bath is almost as big as a double-bed.'

Well, a moment later there I was with her in that watery double-bed. It wasn't that double believe me, and after trying several positions we decided that the most comfortable one was to sit opposite each other with the legs intertwined. I have to state here that I found my situation unbelievable, for here I was looking into those deep-green eyes which had so bewitched me a year earlier and staring at the silken blonde hair which was partly under water; what's more, I could hardly avoid looking at her round breasts which seemed to have discovered a

67

buoyancy in the water and, while they appeared to float half-submerged with the nipples just above the surface of the water, they suggested a weight and firmness which intoxicated my mind. In the meanwhile, Mônica could hardly fail to notice that what floated between my legs was no tiny sardine but, if one must pursue this miserable sea metaphor, a veritable trout. The truth is, I'd never in my post-adolescent life submerged myself into a hot bath without being astonished by my own virility; I suppose it went back to the days of self-experimentation which were necessarily carried out in a bath.

Anyway, at first we pretended that there was nothing extraordinary about our situation and talked about trivialities as if we were walking down Copacabana and looking at the shops. Then, suddenly, Mônica shifted her foot and tickled what, after the previous imagery, I can reasonably call my gills. I responded by squashing her left nipple with my right big toe. The next thing, we'd moved positions so that I lay where she had been and she now sat on me, her back against my chest, her shoulder at my mouth, my hands, coming from under her arms, clutching her breasts, and her buttocks on my thighs facilitating the trout to enter her deep waters.

It was perfect while one remained still but rather painful to me if the desired rhythm had to be executed: it was a strange impasse, for remaining still was fine, but boring, while any attempt to proceed towards a climax was painful to my hips and to the small of my back, so that I alternated between the two frustrating situations of inaction and action and was relieved to get it over with, after which my only thought was to be allowed to remain alone in the bath for a few minutes to enjoy the more real pleasure of my own body relaxing in the warm water.

To anyone who has no underwater experience let me say that it's a waste of time, there's no pleasure in it if it's not a pervertedly psychological one. The water has an abrasive effect which negates the natural oily moistures of the body, so that one emerges sore from the performance. It's not worth it unless the lady is a mistress of long standing and you crave novelty for its own sake. My only pleasure with Mônica on that occasion was that she had begun the evening by presenting herself in the guise of a mermaid and I as a pirate, so that our underwater union seemed intellectually appropriate; only, at the climactic moment, even this purely mental pleasure was a little diminished by my remembering some ambiguous words which my father had spoken the first time I saw Mônica, which now reminded me that she had very probably once been his mistress.

We returned to the drawing-room, she in a dressing-gown and I in my underpants, put on records of carnival music, drank Scotch and danced. My pleasure in being with her was not only that she was a very beautiful woman but also that she was nearly ten years older than me. What thrilled me was that to men twice my age (forgetting, for the moment, about my father) she was a young girl greatly to be desired and that, being older, she could choose from a hundred men and yet had accepted me. I did not realise then that to her the love of a boy in his middle teens was a triumphant confirmation that she herself was also young and had not aged at all.

'I made a horrible mistake going as a mermaid,' she said when we were sitting down, drinking and exchanging kisses on the sofa. 'But then, it's thanks to my stupidity that I met you, so everything has a reason.'

'Who took you there?' I asked.

'Oh, you don't know him,' she said, evading the question. 'Some insurance man. The mermaid was his idea, I think he wanted to find a way of having me anchored to the pond while he went and had a good time.'

'If anyone believes he can have a good time by ditching you he has to be out of his senses.'

'Gregório, you're such a sweet-natured young man,' she said, touching my cheek with her soft lips. 'Oh, I'm so glad it was you, who're so innocent and young, who saved me and not some politician.'

I didn't want to tell her that I wasn't that innocent or that I didn't consider myself young, and said, 'Yes, most of the men there were politicians. I've come to know some of them through father and all I can say is that their main interest seems to be to have a new mistress every month.'

'Gregório, you're so wise! You see the truth about everybody.'

Receiving such flattery, I did not see the truth – that she might well have been, or aspired to become, the mistress of a politician, for there must have been many advantages to such a rôle. She looked at me in an oddly searching manner for a moment, as if trying to evaluate my loyalty, and then said, 'Gregório, let me tell you something. My father has a *fazenda* in Goiás the size of Cuba, my mother lives in an apartment on three floors in Ipanema with a swimming-pool on the fourth floor. She has seven servants and there are probably three or four hundred peasants at the *fazenda*,'

'Well,' I said, not understanding her meaning, 'and you have a fine apartment on Avenida Atlântica. What are you complaining about?'

'That's it, Gregório. I'm complaining about my own class of people, our greed is monstrous. Our politicians, you see, serve us, and not the people.'

'So what do you want, to go and live in a *favela* in Recife?'

'I want a revolution.'

'What do you mean, a revolution?'

'Don't you see? We uphold an unjust society.'

'Mônica, who's been putting these ideas into your head?'

'No one has! Can't I think for myself?'

'Tell me something. What happened to your friend Rudy?'

'He's in São Paulo, constructing hotels. But I know what you mean, you don't have to try scoring ironical points off me, you know. Well, he was just a fool inflated with his own vanity. My only revenge was to make him spend money on things I could throw away.'

Naturally, I was more attentive to the endearing way in which she punctuated her talk with kisses – soft little nibbles at my ear, a slight, swift licking of my cheek or a small smack on my mouth – and did not listen to her too seriously. I assumed that she liked to talk and to give the impression of being an intelligent, sophisticated person and not merely one who dumbly acceded to the lustful passion of a young man. I gave every appearance of listening to her and even responded with statements which must have been appropriate, for I don't remember her disputing anything I said, which could well mean that I played the politician and bided my time, or that, like all people possessed with their own ideas, she heard my words only as an affirmation that I was listening to her. The point, however, is that neither of us could have listened to the other seriously; otherwise she would have soon realised that I was only going through the motions of a conversation in order to keep her interested in me, and I would have understood that she was not merely playing at being intellectually sophisticated.

What astonishes me in retrospect is that a young woman like Mônica existed over twenty years ago when Vargas was still the dictator of Brazil, or, at least, a good nine or ten years before the military dictatorship came to power. No, let me be more precise. I am not astonished by the fact that Mônica had ideas advanced for the time; I am astonished by the fact that *I did not see the truth.* What I should have realised was that the ideological talk emanating from Mônica's sweet lips, which I took to be a novel sort of sexual foreplay, could not have been born spontaneously, or independently, in Mônica's mind. There already existed an atmosphere for such talk and when I heard it from Mônica I failed to see the signal; I failed, too, to realise that the threat to the established order in a society comes not from the illiterate peasants and workers but from those very people who have most to lose by seeking a change. Mônica's revolution would have hurt her landowning father more than it would have benefited any peasant. I am convinced now that humanity is trapped by a neat paradox: one's own intellect, once it is free of crude ignorance, resolves that first it eat one's own body and then extinguish one's own soul in a self-denying, cannibalistic orgy, all in order to give resolution to some idea which had suggested itself to the intellect as a theoretical speculation.

Mônica had a further surpise for me. After the bath we had danced, we had sipped Scotch and we had sat in a casual embrace, talking. All this time I had assumed that the final sequel would have to be that she and I would spontaneously rise, walk to her bedroom, she would slip out of her dressing-gown, etc. So that when she said, yawning slightly, 'Ah, I'm tired!' I thought that that was the hint I'd been waiting for. I rose, offered her a hand and she lifted herself up heavily. We walked together towards the bedroom, but just by the door she said, 'Uh-huh, this is where you stop. You go through *that* door.'

She pointed to the door out to the hallway and the elevator. I smiled indulgently, pretending that she was merely joking, rubbed my nose on her forehead and lifted a hand to her breast. She stiffened up, retreated a step, looked reproachful and sternly pointed to the exit.

In deference to my vanity I will not describe the rest of this scene which ended by my being dismissed from the apartment in a state of frustration and anger of such violence that within half an hour I had bought the only perversity that could appease my enraged mind, choking a woman's throat to seek my relief. A sordid sort of peace came to my heart, but even then I could not understand why Mônica, who had behaved like a woman of easy virtue in the bathroom, should have been so adamant in her refusal later and have considered my proposition to have been an affront to her honour. It seemed contradictory. But again, I was too confined by the narrow point of view of my own vanity to arrive at any responsible explanation. I thought of it only as a tiresome example of the universal sexual war, when it was no such thing, and what confused me even more was accidentally receiving the information some days later that, instead of going to sleep when I left her, Mônica had returned to the party from which I had earlier rescued her. On hearing that, the entire episode seemed even more meaningless, and yet, once again, I was restricted in my search for an explanation by continuing to seek it in terms of what my own behaviour had been. The question I should have asked was not 'Why has she done this to me?' which naturally I asked again and again, but one which should have excluded my person: 'Why is she mixing among politicians?' Had I done that I'd have discovered a truth which only dawned on me ten years later: Mônica was only one, and a rather ineffectual and transient symbol at that, of groups of young people devoted to a radical

72

ideology who were attempting to infiltrate the establishment. But, instead, all my thoughts led me to conclude that there was no purpose to my pursuing Mônica. She had used me for her own ends, no doubt finding a sexual gratification in the attentions she provoked in me, while thinking only of how she could advance in the political circles that she had already penetrated; she did not, I realised, possess the generosity of spirit to understand that there was a world which existed outside herself – and I say this because I observed in due course that all her actions were mimicry, she had no notion of what her rhetorical political posture meant, for otherwise she would not have ended up by marrying one of the more corrupt politicians; what poor Mônica possessed was the narrow vision of the majority of mankind; she never doubted that everything existed only in so far as it impinged upon her own expectations of life.

A lot else happened in my early youth which would be relevant to this narrative only if I were concerned with demonstrating that even the lives of heroes are composed of long periods of mundane occurrences. Let me instead attend to the few remaining events that shaped my destiny and then proceed to the real substance of this chronicle.

After the affair with Mônica, which left me so depressed and disgusted with myself – depressed because a beautiful woman had behaved in a manner which insulted my male view of life and disgusted because of my brutal treatment of the whore whom I'd been driven to after being thrown out by Mônica – I kept away from women for a considerable period. I just went about in a resentful mood, perhaps unconsciously expecting Mônica to come and apologise to me. Nothing of the sort happened, of course, and, in fact, when I ran into her once she pretended not to know me. She was playing too subtle a game for me to comprehend and the only game I could play in response was to appear among my friends as one who is weary of this world. It was at this time that I met a political activist (though that's hardly a label he'd approve of) who was to have a profound effect on my life. I'm obliged to give him the pompous

73

name of João Capistrano de Magalhães which he jokingly chose for himself. He lives in Mexico now and will no doubt smile when he reads this and discovers that his old friend Gregório has kept his secret.

'Call me Capistrano if you ever have to talk about me,' he said once. 'Let's make that sound good,' he added, laughing and puffing at his cigarette. 'What about João Capistrano de Magalhães? Really aristocratic, eh? People will imagine me as a tall nobleman descended from some great family in Portugal, black hair and deep-set brown eyes solemnly contemplating the distant horizon, a gentleman given to profound thoughts. Ha, what a joke!'

It doesn't sound like a joke now but it did at the time, and I laughed heartily, looking at my short, thin friend contract his sunken cheeks as he took another puff at his cigarette, his grey eyes glinting merrily.

The occasion of our meeting was itself farcical or deadly serious, depending on one's attitude to the famous disease which I mentioned at the start. My condition had so degenerated that I had no recourse but to go to a doctor, and naturally I avoided our family doctor and sought out one who knew nothing about me. There, in the reception room, sitting in a chair opposite the mulatta receptionist, was Capistrano.

The receptionist was laughing when I entered, one of those restrained laughs with the hand held in front of the mouth and the head tilted towards the bosom. It was obvious that the man sitting opposite her, leaning back in his chair with his hands clasped at his knees, where he also held a straw hat, had provoked the laughter. The girl became serious on seeing me and, just when I began to answer her questions so that she could fill out a form for the doctor, the doctor himself appeared at the door and beckoned the man into his office. I briefly saw him walk towards the doctor and noted absently that he was short and thin in his white, cotton suit which was not too crumpled and that he looked about thirty years old. But I had no reason to register more facts on my mind since my attention was again on the questions being asked by the receptionist, and also I could think of nothing but the moment which was rapidly

74

approaching when I would stand in front of the doctor, take my pants down and reveal the absurd cactus developing there.

The moment came and went in due course, and one thing I can say about unpleasant experiences is that, if you dread them acutely enough in advance, they usually turn out not to be so unpleasant. And if some experience turns out to be exceptionally painful, I have a neat trick of making it bearable by convincing myself that it has already happened, that as a matter of fact I'm lying comfortably in a bath and eating strawberries and cream and it just happens that the memory of that painful experience involuntarily passes through my mind. In all the circumstances that might inflict us with pleasure or pain one can make the self withdraw from the body by insisting upon the intellectual truth that all reality is only a construct of the imagination: and surely, when it comes to survival we're all obliged to become poets.

To my surprise the small gentleman who had preceded me to the doctor was still with the receptionist when my examination was over. They were both laughing. I stood by her desk, waited a second for her attention and said that I needed an appointment for the following week. While she was making a note in her diary the man said to me, 'If you're going to Copacabana perhaps we can take a taxi together.'

'I have a car,' I said. 'Can I give you a lift?'

And so the two of us walked out together, exchanging pleasantries.

'You were certainly a great hit with the receptionist,' I said.

'Ah, it's an old weakness, I can't resist a mulatta!'

It was only many months later that I realised that he'd stayed behind after he'd seen the doctor in order to become acquainted with me and that, while flirting with the receptionist, he'd managed to look at my name and address on the form she had earlier filled in; for at that time Capistrano never missed an opportunity to draw young people into the circle of his influence.

As we walked out of the doctor's he went on to say, 'But look at me, I see a doctor for a cure and end up by spending more time talking to his receptionist, hoping to pick her up, and what do you think will happen? The doctor will cure me of the disease and she will give it right back to me!'

The car was parked three blocks away and we walked towards it. Capistrano talked in a jocular manner of how his love of mulattas had brought him to his present misery. It was all said in a lighthearted vein, and within twenty paces I was so taken by his charm that I felt I was walking with the closest of my friends.

Suddenly, he pulled me by the arm, dragged me a couple of steps towards the entrance of a building, and fell forward on the dirty sidewalk, pulling me down, all in a couple of seconds.

Even as I was falling clumsily, holding my hands out in front of me at the last moment to prevent my face from crashing against the mosaic stones of the sidewalk, I heard the burst of machine-gun fire and several pistol shots. Then there was the sound of a car being driven away at a great speed. We rose to our feet. Several people appeared from all directions and went hurrying towards two figures who had fallen, one of them in an army uniform. By the time we approached the figures a circle had gathered around them. Capistrano took a quick look, held my arm again, directing me away from the crowd, and said, 'Come, let's get out of here, there's going to be trouble.'

When we were driving away he said, 'That was Carlos Lacerda they tried to get.'

'Who!' I exclaimed in astonishment, knowing Lacerda's name as a political opponent of Vargas, although at the time I had no detailed knowledge of the confused politics of my country.

'He looked as though he was all right,' Capistrano said, 'but the army guy looked dead.'

'I must say you were pretty sharp the way you saw it coming,' I said.

'I have a sixth sense,' he said. 'I can always tell when bullets are going to fly.'

His casual, jocular manner was only an outward appearance; at his most relaxed he was more alert than anyone in the president's bodyguard.

Police cars and an ambulance went speeding towards the scene. People were running, there were shouts in the air, the word 'Lacerda' echoing from the buildings.

'There's going to be trouble,' Capistrano said. 'We're back to the politics of assassination. What could have come over Vargas?'

'Do you think he sanctioned it?'

'There are some events rulers don't sanction but approve of with a flicker of the eyelids.'

We arrived at his apartment and, since we both needed to wash ourselves after falling on the sidewalk, he invited me in for a drink.

'Fascinating, this subject of politics,' he said as we took the elevator. 'One can talk for hours and still feel there's more to say. I suppose it's because politicians have a monopoly over the most interesting subject: what's going to happen next in our lives? Will we have to pay more taxes if a new party comes to power? They've a monopoly over half-truths and ambiguity, too; the newspapers are forever trying to interpret what politicians say. Ah, here we are!'

The apartment was modest in size but was tastefully and luxuriously furnished, with Persian rugs on the parquet floor, leather chairs, rosewood tables and cabinets that were full of books. The walls were covered with pictures, among which I recognised Debret prints and was later to learn that several of the imposing paintings were by contemporary Brazilian artists, Capistrano's favourite being Portinari.

After we had washed ourselves we sat sipping Scotch for two hours, talking politics; to be more precise, he talked and I listened, for, while I was becoming more and more fascinated by political talk (for it seemed to guarantee that one had become an adult), I had little to contribute myself: at the time I knew the names of the former emperors, the dates of the abolitions of slavery and the founding of the Republic, the fact that Getúlio Vargas was our president and one or two other dates and names, but I knew very little of the present politics of Brazil. History had absorbed me at school but I'd always thought of it as a subject about the past, full of glorious figures like Napoleon who expressed an awesome authority; now I was learning that history was made of living events and that the people who were its architects did not have authority granted them as a natural right but that they had to win it for themselves by engaging in intrigues, by lying and by hypocritical actions; that power did not fall upon those who merited it but on those who schemed for it – with the added irony, of course, that, once the force of their monstrous vanity had made them succeed in acquiring power, which they exercised with a complete disregard for common humanity, they were then given a place among the nation's heroes and after their death were considered to have sacrificed their lives for their country. Capistrano had a neat way of putting it: 'Your Churchill or your Roosevelt doesn't sacrifice his life for anything. On the contrary, it's the people who sacrifice their lives so that a Churchill or a Roosevelt may enjoy his greatness, for ask yourself what would such a man *do* otherwise? Probably spend his time playing chess with the local idiot.' I could not deny Capistrano's conclusion, since he gave many examples to prove it – that the man who ended up in the history books as a great leader was invariably one who had been a scoundrel to his contemporaries.

Seeing how enthralled I was by these ideas, which struck me as revelations of the true nature of politics (and not, as actually was the case, as merely Capistrano's interpretation of the world), my host finally confided to me: 'What I'm interested in, Gregório, is to preserve the mental health of Brazil. Or, to put it in another way, I want to fight the barbarians who, impressed by some foreign examples of socialism, delude themselves into thinking that they have a better programme for Brazil's future. Now, understand this, Gregório. Anyone who is at all interested in politics is interested in power for himself. There are very few exceptions. Thomas Jefferson, perhaps, or Mahatma Gandhi. But just about everyone else convinces himself that his main interest is mankind when the truth always is that he's thinking of his own profile on a coin or on a postage stamp. Well, that's being a trifle cruel, but it's not far from the truth. So what these men will do is to find any old theme which can be popular, even if it means importing what was current twenty or thirty years ago in America or Russia.'

'Excuse me,' I said 'but your own statements imply that you, too, are interested in power.'

'No, my friend. I'm interested in politics but not in being a politician. My part in this game is to thwart those who will try to impose radical solutions. The truth is that there are no radical solutions for the simple reason that there never are, in any society, complex problems. Oh, everyone has problems, like France has with Algeria right now or, let us say, the Negroes and the coloureds have with their government in South Africa. But they are nothing that the passage of time, education and the normal changes that take place with each new generation will not resolve. My answer to everything is slow and natural evolution. Let us always debate the problems and their solutions and let us through the inevitable tensions of conflicting opinions inch our way forward along lines of compromise, so that the whole society benefits a little rather than one section of it gaining all and the others losing. But let us never allow a group of people, calling itself whatever party, Progressive or Socialist or Democratic or what have you, to hold a gun up to us and say: "*Our* solution is the *only* one." Do you not see what goes on in their minds? In the name of humanity and equality they are prepared to kill you when what it really means is that they will kill you because you dare to deny them the power they seek. There are among them some people who're so convinced that they're right that they will establish a tyranny, if given the chance, to prove their virtuous love of the people.'

'So you don't approve of Communists?' I asked rather naïvely.

'I've nothing against Communists, nor against Socialists or Conservatives or Ultras or any other label. I'm against extremists of any party, those who're too convinced of their own righteousness. I'm against illiterate peasants who think they ought to possess their master's land as I'm against the intellectuals who produce theories about wealth and its distribution. You see, it's only in the twentieth century that man can have *now* what he desires. If we want to go to Paris, we can catch a plane and be there on the same day; a couple of injections and some tablets will look after most of our illnesses; so that we have acquired the habit of having immediately available that which we think will improve our lives. In the past our wars lasted for thirty years or a hundred years, while in this century they have lasted four or six years and we all know that the next one will last only a few minutes. And now, having acquired this habit of an impatience with time and simultaneously having obtained the connivance of technology to make quite irrelevant the old concept of time, we therefore demand of our political institutions not that they gradually take us forward but that they bring about a most extraordinary utopia immediately. *Right now.* We no longer accept the mute rôle of humbly acceding to nature's designs for us, but instead we actively tamper with nature, for her designs no longer count, only ours do. We've become agitators for the most miserable and useless thing which exists in the world, the human *self*; the fulfilment of that self is the end of all our vociferous campaigning. And I'm against that for the simple reason that no *self* ever did anything which was not motivated by selfishness or greed or a thousand other demands of vanity. And what I am *for*, a slow and continual progress – I envy the selfless, immobile rocks, the vast stretches of sand, the oceans – unfortunately such an evolution is becoming an impossibility. Our tragedy is that we were born in geological time with the beautiful destiny of becoming fossils but we live instead in a time of our own invention which ticks to a nice harmony with the heartbeat, with our destiny having become burdened by the absurd notion of immortality. And, since we've become creatures of political contention, what you will have from now on will be either a repressive government which will keep wealth and power confined to a privileged class of people, or a radical revolutionary government which, in an inverted way, will also be repressive, for don't you believe that any revolutionary will ever distribute power to the people since he will say "I am the people" and keep it all to himself. This business of politics, Gregório, is a quagmire, and I understand nothing of it, to tell you the truth, except that I do recognise the forms that barbarians take from year to year. Now they're the trades unionists and now the Liberals and now the Conservatives. And it's the barbarians, whatever their shape or colour, that I work against.'

I must say that I was impressed by the forceful flow of

Capistrano's speech; perhaps it was because in my previous conversations with men the subject had mainly been women, and now, hearing a man talk so passionately about what I was certain was a serious subject, it seemed that I had suddenly entered the world of adults which had always appeared distant and mysterious. It was with the most adult mannerism that I rose, when he paused and I had nothing to say, walked ponderously to the cabinet where the drinks were and poured more Scotch into our glasses.

'My cause', he went on, 'is that of the vast bulk of humanity which has no cause but would like its government to produce the ideal conditions in which human beings feel no threat to their existence and can go about their mundane pursuits in an atmosphere of security, for the truth is, Gregório, if you want advance in this world, you have to create the conditions of bourgeois content. Never underestimate the bourgeoisie, that solid middle class of industrious merchants concerned only with business profits, mortgages and the education of their children. Without the taxes they so submissively pay there can be no good government.'

'But will not that lead to a vulgar society?' I asked.

'I can see that you're an elitist. God help you if you ever enter politics!'

'I don't intend to,' I said, though greatly flattered to be labelled an elitist, I was that naïve. 'I was only considering the implications of your argument.'

'Not just an ordinary elitist, but an *intellectual* elitist, ah, well!'

I have to admit that I felt an intense pleasure on hearing him say that, as if I'd been elected to some peerage.

'Brazil is not yet ready for that sort of elitism,' Capistrano went on. 'Remember, it's not yet a hundred years since the slaves were emancipated and the Empire overthrown. We're not obliged to be the victims of history.'

'But it's difficult,' I said, 'when one looks back on events, not to see a determinism boring away at the future as surely as woodworm in an attic.'

'Maybe the fact that we're determinedly opposed to the next inevitable set of events is also part of historical determinism!'

'Certainly.'

'Therefore, it's best not to think in terms of determinism,' he said, 'whether historical or spiritual. Let us assume that our destiny is in our own hands, that God has made us the wonderful concession of becoming gods ourselves so that we can go about creating alternative worlds to see which one suits us.'

We talked on, the dialogue becoming more and more theoretical and speculative, but that was what I found exciting: the more abstract the ideas, the greater the thrill I experienced within my mind. In another hour we would have solved all mankind's problems in the refined haze of pure thought and might never have come down to earth had there not been a knock on the door. Capistrano went to open it and that is when I first saw Amália.

She was sixteen years old then, timid and quiet, and had come to Capistrano's apartment with her elder sister Odila who, apparently, though only twenty, was a long-established friend of Capistrano. I felt no such thing as love at first sight for Amália, nor she for me, the truth being that on that occasion I had eyes only for Odila, who was more fully developed and seemed very self-possessed, with bright, confident laughter, whereas Amália, who was being taken out by her sister for the first time to such sophisticated company as Capistrano's, was nervous about being initiated into adulthood. If anything passed through my mind the rest of the evening it must have been an envy of Capistrano that he could attract so beautiful a woman as Odila; actually, I think, little passed through my mind. As with Amália, it was my first awakening into adulthood in so far as I thought, in an access of self-flattery, that I'd had a profound conversation with Capistrano, understood everything he had said and made some telling points myself. I cannot now say whether it was a delusion or whether the matter of knowing the precise moment when one becomes an adult is of any importance; but if it means anything, I felt important that evening, perhaps too important to conceive that the sixteen-year-old shy girl with the round, apprehensive eyes was going to play a part in my life.

I became a close friend of Capistrano, discovering in him the sort of wisdom which I believed would guide me through life. I saw him nearly every day, at his apartment or in some bar or café, often in the company of other young people he had attracted around him. Wherever we met, Odila was always present, sitting next to him, sometimes holding his hand in an ostentatiously possessive manner; Amália, too, would be there from time to time, and it is a measure of Capistrano's hold over the minds of the young men around him that we looked more at him than at the girls.

Leaving his apartment one day I found myself accompanied down in the elevator by a tall young man of my age, Rodolpho Rubirosa, who had suffered the misfortune in childhood of having his dark, nearly black face pitted by smallpox, so that when one talked to him one stared past his shoulder in order to avoid having to look at his ugly face. He too came to listen ardently to Capistrano and rarely said anything himself. Now, in the elevator, he surprised me by saying, 'Well, what do you think of our Socrates?'

'Capistrano?'

'Yeah, who else?'

'I'm learning a great deal from him,' I said guardedly, not liking Rubirosa's sneering manner.

He made a sound which suggested cynicism. We walked out of the building and he said, 'You know what I think? His main interest is to screw young girls.'

'Whose isn't?' I asked, covering an uncomfortable feeling with a forced laugh.

'Have you seen the girls stare at him? Not just with their eyes, but with their whole bodies, leaning forward and asking to be taken. That's what he likes, to show us younger men that girls younger than us want only him.'

I understood that Rubirosa was jealous – the poor man was so ugly that no girl looked at him – but it did not occur to me that Rubirosa, for reasons of his own, might be trying to test me or to sow the seeds of animosity against a friend. It was a conversation that I soon forgot, but many years later I was obliged to remember this encounter: the two of us confined in the small elevator, his sneering, ugly face which I tried not to look at but was overwhelmingly conscious of, and even when I looked at the little brass plaque stating the maximum number of persons who could safely be accommodated by the elevator I saw only the pitted skin of Rubirosa's nearly black face.

It was very probable that Capistrano slept with several of the girls but I neither begrudged him that privilege nor felt any envy. I myself had experienced an instant attraction for Odila the first time I saw her but, realising that she was Capistrano's mistress, I excluded her from my lustful fantasies as far as was humanly possible, which is to say for about a quarter of the time. But one day I saw Amália looking at Capistrano in the manner Rubirosa had described, *with her whole body*; I was astonished to discover a sudden choking sensation within me and realised that I was jealous. I went and drank some water. I do not know what passed through my mind or my heart, for apart from the usual lewd desires which tickle a man's fancy on seeing any pretty body I had given no particular thought to Amália; and what surprises me even now, after that current of jealousy had passed through my body, I returned to my previous state of having no clearly defined feeling for Amália, and if I had any longing at all it was to receive greater wisdom from Capistrano as if I too wished to be possessed by him, but in the only way (as far as I am concerned, for I leave others to their own predilections in such a matter) I could be possessed by a man: intellectually. It was certainly an odd situation, for here was a girl whom a moment's breathlessness within me indicated that I was already in love with and yet I sat listening with the greatest interest, affection and esteem to the very man she seemed to be eager to be seduced by and who, for all I knew, had already obliged her. What will seem even more inexplicable is that, soon after coming to the realisation that my feelings for Amália were complex and profound, I ceased to go to Capistrano's altogether and did not see Amália for the next two years. Explain it how you will, I have no suggestion to make in the matter; I can only say what happened.

I stopped going to Capistrano's not because I wanted to suppress my feelings for Amália; but then, perhaps I did, how can I know? Perhaps I was jealous that Amália and the other girls could possess Capistrano in ways that I could not, but I would be the last person to subscribe to such an idea, for I have no respect at all for the explanations of human behaviour offered by modern psychology which, with all its scientific approach of experiments, diagrams, statistics and an impressively obscure language, offers us no more truth than the mumbo-jumbo of astrologers and palmists. I was involved in self-contradiction; perhaps, who knows? It was not a conscious decision I made, not to go, it simply happened that school exams, going away to the farm in the summer, family affairs, my companionship with Vicente and the petty feuds with my younger brother, Anibal, and a thousand other things kept me away from Capistrano for several months. And then, when I had the opportunity to go, I did not, and finally, when I did call on him again, he had sold his apartment and moved to São Paulo.

It was soon after the dramatic collapse of the Vargas régime that Vicente left Brazil in pursuit of the dream which he had confided to me: to live in the ancient cities of Europe and to absorb their culture. Father was reluctant to let him go, for Vicente had received his *B.A.* in economics and, as far as father could see, all that remained for Vicente to do with the rest of his life was to put the classroom theories into practice and make a great deal of money. He could not understand that a subject which concerned everyday commerce should be studied outside the realm of the practical and assume for itself degrees of complexity and abstraction which meant nothing to the most successful businessman. He had no doubt that the higher study of economics was only a conspiracy by some intellectuals who could keep themselves lucratively employed as professors and government advisers by elevating a few basic principles to a body of elaborate laws which belonged to some secret religion; and just as a religion's main purpose always was to increase the numbers of its devotees, which to it was a higher goal than to use its professed moral principles to influence political leaders to work for the general good of mankind, so, father argued, the study of economics only produced economists, and the more learned your economist was, the less he had to do with the simple matter of carrying on a business. And just as no religion ever

85

stopped a Hitler, no economic theory had ever stopped a depression.

'Business is business,' father said, 'you buy and you sell.'

Vicente patiently pointed out to him that there were such things as banking, international trade, marketing and a dozen other matters which needed studying.

'But if the purpose of it all is to make money,' father argued, 'then what good is a knowledge of international trade when you can make your fortune raising pigs?'

Vicente said that there was more to economics than carrying on a trade, for the economy of the country did not depend on the success of the peanut-seller on the beach.

'The economy is healthy if every peanut-seller in the country makes a profit,' father said with some vehemence. 'Don't talk to me about your clever economists! Not one of their theories prevented the crash of the 'twenties, and look at our own dear economists, they've made a speciality of producing runaway inflation.'

They were going round in circles, repeating their arguments and examples, and father, probably knowing the stubbornness of sons and yet not wanting to accede to it, kept rejecting Vicente's ideas while he, knowing of the closed minds of fathers, believed that he, at least, by taking a clear and a rational approach, would make father see an objective truth. There seemed to be no resolution to their argument until mother intervened with the very simple statement that there was no harm in Vicente's going away for a year, he was still very young.

I believe father was reluctant to see Vicente go because he had in his own mind a dream of his sons entering his business and enlarging it to some magnificent enterprise. He probably imagined some rosewood-panelled board-room in which he sat at the head, an oil portrait of himself on the wall, Vicente opposite him and Anibal and me on either side, discussing some profound matter of corporation policy while a blonde secretary hovered around the room and from time to time came and placed significant memoranda before each one of us. It must have been an annoyance to have his dream postponed. If mother had found a simple compromise between the two, it was

86

not without a secret thought for herself: if Iolanda was already in France and Vicente was also to be somewhere in Europe, would that not be a good excuse for the rest of the family to visit Europe next year? In the past, whenever she had expressed the idea of the family going to Europe, father had always found a reason not to do so: the children's education must not be interrupted, the long summer holidays coincided not only with the long, cold winter in Europe but also the carnival, the tourist season in Rio when the shop made the most money, so that mother, whose long-frustrated dream of going to France had become an intense longing ever since Iolanda had gone, saw in Vicente an unlooked-for carrier who might yet transport her to her beloved native land: with two children in Europe, it might be easier to persuade father.

Vicente too had his secret dream. He had no intention of studying economics, which he despised, and did not expect to return after a year. When I questioned him, it appeared that he had no plans to do anything; only that he wanted to go and live in old cities, learn their languages and customs, and in the process acquire the wisdom of the Old World. I must say that I did not understand the purpose of all this but, thinking that what Vicente really wanted was complete independence for himself, I sympathised with him. Well, off he went in a D.C.6 of Panair do Brasil, promising to write to me of all his adventures, while I, in the loud bravado of one trying not to weep, said, 'I'll come and visit you in the summer!' And he, perhaps also suppressing a similar emotion, said with an extravagant laugh, 'I'll have a pretty English girl waiting for you!'

I began to go to college at about that time, with every intention of devoting all my waking hours to hard study, but anyone who has spent as much as five minutes in Rio will sympathise with me: there, indolence seems to be a prescription of nature, and the soul asks of the submissive student, 'What can you achieve with all your studies which is not already yours, these glorious beaches and the wonderful young women in their bikinis?' I don't believe anyone has an answer to that question unless he's a hypocrite. But to serious study I went with a willpower deserving of a wider reognition than one's family's approbation of the good results at the end of the first year. It was then that I met Amália again, newly enrolled at the college, a year behind me.

I was amused at first by the happy coincidence but soon began to believe that one's destiny was inescapable. She kept to a group from her class during the early months and I too maintained a deliberate distance. The unnecessary barriers one creates! It maddens me to think now of the precious months we wasted avoiding each other. One day we met in the library and, since neither of us had our respective groups to go to that afternoon, we ended up by going to a café together. At first we talked of the one person we had in common, Capistrano. I was a little uneasy, for when she talked of him I could only wonder within myself whether or not she had gone to bed with him. But soon we went beyond Capistrano and began to talk of the things we were studying, she in government and I in history. That is when we realised that we were a generation apart from Capistrano's and that, however much we'd been influenced by his ideas, there was still a world to discover for ourselves. It was a natural development from then on that we should see each other often, and soon every day. A month later we were neglecting our groups and seeing only each other, and the more we did so the more the conviction grew that the two of us, symbols of primeval man and woman coming together at a new dawn, were going to create a new Brazil between us.

I cannot say now what specifically engrossed us in our endless talks – and feel constrained to add that such phrases as 'symbols of primeval man and woman,' while they represent the truth of what Amália and I thought at that time, are not a little embarrassing when I put them down now, some twenty years later. We had plans for everything, from the re-creation of Rio as a futuristic city to the development of the vast interior of Brazil as the largest agricultural region in the world. Strange topics for a twenty-one-year-old Brazilian male, you might say, to be discussing while holding the hand of a beautiful girl! But Brazil was our passion and, while most young couples talked of their future in terms of a house and the number of children they planned to have, for us the future was the dazzling concept of realising the most perfect society mankind had ever witnessed. I suppose our talk must have been vaguely utopian; I'm almost embarrased in my attempt to recall it with specificity, for each sentence only makes it seem no more than the idle talk of hopeful youth. And yet, of course, there are few experiences in life so thrilling as such optimistic talk, however idle, about the future that keeps young lovers looking into each other's eyes long after all the world has gone to sleep; and love then is not at all a sexual desire but the far more prolonged pleasure of intellectual ecstasy: the beauty of words and the aesthetic structure of pure ideas which the words represent create a far more enduring love between two people than any sexual compatability ever could.

One weekend I took Amália to our farm where my younger brother, Anibal, now nearly eighteen years old, had installed himself as a general manager. Finishing school, he had decided not to go to the university, and when father had tried to persuade him of the advantages of an education Anibal had reminded father of what he himself had said to Vicente – when father tried to dissuade Vicente from pursuing further studies in Europe – that the true business was to be learned in the practical world.

The early signs of genius that the family had perceived in Anibal had long since vanished but, in his queer way, he continued to choose the unexpected. Now he lived in the style of a peasant, dressing in a pair of faded and worn trousers and a dirty cotton shirt, and when he came into the house after an afternoon in the fields he sat with his muddied boots on the table, leaning back, holding a bottle of beer in a dirty hand, swigging from it in a coarse manner, wiping his mouth with the back of his hand, letting the beer dribble down his chest, and belching. He had grown large and strong, with broad shoulders and thick, muscular arms, but one could not say about him that his was a handsome physique, for the word which came to one's mind was 'loutish.'

When Amália and I arrived in the late morning Anibal was

already in the fields and I was glad not to have his uncouth presence while I showed Amália the house and the grounds around it. After taking some coffee we went for a long walk across a pasture into a wooded area. I showed Amália many of my childhood scenes, the waterfall where Vicente used to dive from the swaying branch of a tree, the rivers where we had played.

We returned to the house just before two in the afternoon when lunch was on the table. Anibal arrived on a horse the same moment as we did, and I must say he cut a rather impressive figure when he rode up, though his body, shining with sweat, took on all its loutish characteristics when he dismounted, his soiled clothes darkened in patches where they had clung to the sweat pouring from his body. There was dirt about his eyes and mouth and, as he passed his sweating hands across his shirt at the stomach, I saw his nails were black. I introduced Amália to him and, after making a grunting sound and giving her a large, filthy hand, he said, 'Well, let's go and have lunch.'

Amália and I went to wash our hands and rinse our faces with cold water, and when we came to the dining-table Anibal had already begun to eat; apparently, he had gone straight to the table after greeting Amália. He had heaped his plate with rice, beans and thick slices of beef and was shovelling it all into his mouth as fast as he could, chewing with a disgusting smacking of his lips and pausing either to swig from a bottle of beer or to throw a scrap of meat to one of the three cats scrambling about his feet. The scene would have shocked Amália had I not prepared her for it by telling her while we drove from Rio that my younger brother had developed a savage nature; hardly a nature, for it was an act meant to imply that all the niceties of society were irrelevant to the actuality of existence: somehow, people who come up with such a philosophy always seem to argue through their actions that actuality can only be experienced by reverting to barbaric modes of behaviour, that one is closer to truth by becoming animalistic: propositions without any logic whatsoever. However, here was Anibal offering us the image of himself as natural man, leaning back to scratch his crotch when he was not revoltingly chewing away at large chunks of meat. He had nothing to say when we came and sat down, and while we ate he kept his head bowed to his plate, raising it to swig from his bottle or to scratch himself or to throw something to the cats. I tried hard to think of something to talk about to distract Amália from this wretched spectacle, but my mind went completely blank since it was filled with the sounds of Anibal's eating.

When he had finished he picked up one of the cats by the scruff of its neck and put it on the table to let it lick his plate, leaned back and lit a cigarette.

'You must have a healthy life, working on the farm,' Amália said to him with a smile.

He looked at her with his old sneer and grunted, 'Yeah.'

'Anibal,' I said, 'if you have work to do, let's not keep you.'

Fortunately, he took my hint, threw back his chair and stomped out to go to his room where he slept for the next hour. I asked a servant to take away the cats and Amália and I finished our lunch in a comparatively civilised ambience.

Afterwards we sat on the veranda, drinking coffee, and I explained to Amália in a soft voice that Anibal's manners were now tolerated by my parents because they hoped it was a phase he would outgrow; but, I added, here we were at the farm at the weekend and my parents, who in the past rarely missed an opportunity to spend the weekend at the farm, were in Rio. It was not the first time they'd found an excuse not to come. My mother absented herself for months, for she had been driven to despair by Anibal's manners and been made to feel wretched when, once, on her prompting, father had severly scolded Anibal but had received insulting replies, such as, 'If you like, I'll go and eat with the servants.' For mother the tragedy was compounded by the thought that she could not take a specimen such as Anibal to France, so that to see him was to be reminded of a double unhappiness: Anibal was not what a son of hers should have been and, being what he was, he impeded her plans to visit Europe, for father, who liked to consider such plans and went so far as to consult the schedules of the shipping lines, always, when it came to a final commitment, found a reason to postpone the journey, almost as if he feared he'd lose his life the moment he left Brazil, and now he would say, 'What would it look like if you turned up in Paris with a country yokel like Anibal?'

Father learned to live with the failures of his sons. Oh yes, Anibal wasn't the only thorn in his flesh! He grew to tolerate Anibal because it soon became evident that Anibal's management was producing good results, and he hoped that through the evil of Anibal's ostentatious uncouthness might be achieved the greater good of a more prosperous farm. As for me, I did not say anything because I found my brother's behaviour beneath contempt; also, father had found something in me to disappoint him: after I began college I refused to have anything to do with his business, a resolve that started as the arrogant posture of one who wishes to suggest that, living in the world of pure ideas, he has no time for such trivialities as shopkeeping, and ended by becoming a fixed principle. It seems that with the best of intentions sons cannot help being obnoxious to their fathers, and my father seemed to believe that he was triply cursed. Vicente, having spent his year in London, from where he'd written me very banal letters to do with visiting the Houses of Parliament and the Tower of London, had moved to Paris and showed no intention of ever returning; Anibal had turned into a monster; and I was recalcitrant, to say the least. The odd thing was, I said to Amália, I understood all these things, saw the sadness which had come over my father, was hurt to see him suffer, and yet I could do nothing to bring him any happiness. If, firm to my principle, I refused to spend a day in the shop so that father could be free to make a visit to São Paulo, he went into a rage and said I'd abandoned him and preferred to spend my time among hooligans and whores; and if, not being able to bear the suffering that I experienced from the knowledge of *his* intense suffering, I offered, out of pity and a desire to prove my love to him, to spend two days at the shop so that he could take a holiday, he would turn away in despair, believing that my gesture was intended to be cruelly ironical.

Amália and I had been talking for an hour when Anibal came stomping out of the house, walked across the veranda and down the steps, mounted his horse and rode away. Amália and I

92

changed into our bathing-suits and loitered to the swimming-pool set in a garden of azaleas and hibiscus at the back of the house. Later, we went down to the stables, chose horses and went riding. Everywhere on the land the effects of Anibal's management were apparent; the pastures were cleaner than ever before, the banks of rivers which used to be covered with thorny vines and bushes were now planted with a special variety of grass for the cattle, canals had been dug to make better use of the rivers which flowed through the land. The banana-pickers coming down from a plantation in the hills, their mules loaded high with bananas, seemed to be proceeding with a remarkable sense of urgency and not at all in the indolent manner I'd always associated with them. We cantered across a field and saw Anibal on his horse in the distance, on the edge of the pineapple plantation, the old administrator, José Formigueiro, with him, also on horseback. Anibal was making gestures with his hand, pointing this way and that, and Formigueiro was nodding his head. We trotted away in another direction and found ourselves going past a line of timber-and-mud houses where some of the peasants lived. I was surprised to see how clean they all were and remarked to Amália on the contradiction in Anibal's character that made him insist on bringing an unprecedented tidiness to the land while assuming a degeneracy of manner himself. I had seen some of the improvements on previous visits but had not made so extended a tour of the land as the one on which I conducted Amália and admitted to her that my brother had very nearly transformed the original wilderness – but then, of course, I also admitted, no two people ever had the same vision.

We returned to the house, had another swim to cool off and then sat by the pool drinking tea. We talked as usual of our favourite subject, the great future that we envisaged for Brazil.

In the evening we had to go through the trial of listening to Anibal eat his dinner and simultaneously feed the cats, but I was a little more inclined to accept him now that I had a fuller knowledge of what he had begun to accomplish on the land. Only it was impossible to talk with him: any remark to him met with a vaguely grunted response at best or a gesture of the eyes that one associates with a drunkard; yet he had a perfect command over speech, for he talked with the servants and especially with Formigueiro.

Formigueiro came up to the house when Anibal had finished eating. In the old days, when father attended to the affairs of the farm, Formigueiro would come and stand by the railing of the veranda, but now he walked right up and took a chair beside Anibal. He rose when, a moment later, Amália and I came out to the veranda and greeted me with his usual warmth and expressed poetical sentiments on being introduced to Amália.

'Zé, this is something new,' I said, 'working on Saturdays.'

'Senhor Gregório,' he said, smiling, 'a man needs money, a man has to work.'

'I remember a time when you spent Saturdays bringing a little happiness to your men,' I said with a wink.

'But what am I to do, Senhor? The men would rather make more money.'

'What good is money without pleasure?'

'We do our best,' he said, giving me a wink this time, and added solemnly, 'but we're servants of circumstances.'

Amália and I went out for a walk in the grounds in the cool of the night, leaving the two men to their conference. I told Amália of the time Vicente and I had come upon Formigueiro's hut where, we had been convinced, nothing but debauchery took place.

We saw Formigueiro ride off and shouted good-night to him from a distance. By the time we returned to the veranda Anibal had already gone to his room. Amália and I sat talking for an hour and then, although it was not yet ten o'clock, went to our separate rooms. I fell asleep almost immediately. Very early in the morning, when the light outside was a milky grey and the dawn had not yet broken, I awoke from my profound slumber but remained in bed, hoping to fall asleep again since there was no point in getting up so early. I needed to go to the bathroom but, measuring in my mind the relative discomfort of holding on and the bother of walking down the hall to the bathroom, decided to try and suppress my need. I dozed off for a while but

94

then the pressure on my bladder began to obsess me, and if I still held on it was partly because I thought that, had I gone to the bathroom when I first felt the need, the business would have been over by now and I would by lying in peace; instead, here I was wondering why I had not already gone and worrying that in another ten minutes, if I did not go *now*, I'd be blaming myself for not having done so. It was a circular dilemma, but finally I decided to do what I'd often done as a boy – climb up on the window-sill and water the lawn outside.

When I had positioned myself and was about to commence I heard a noise, and froze. I came off the window-sill, stood on the floor and looked out of the window, slowly and carefully putting my head out. Two windows along a figure was just at that moment jumping out. It made a slight thud as it landed on the grass. It stood up and began to walk along the wall in the direction of my window. It was a young woman, and the thought that I should raise some sort of an alarm crossed my mind only for a fraction of a second, for I immediately realised the game my savage brother was playing. I leaned back so as not to be observed and saw the girl go past dreamily, recognising her to be the daughter of one of the peasants.

The first thought that came to my mind was that, had she been a moment early in her departure and had I not heard or seen anything, she would have received much the same sort of baptism as her lover had some years earlier. And then I began to think of the serious matter of Anibal's impropriety in choosing his women from among the peasants; one of these days he'd either have to marry one of them or be ambushed and stabbed to death by someone's father.

The girl having gone, I proceeded to complete the business which had woken me up. At the sound of my splashing a bird gave a cry somewhere, a cock began to crow, several birds sang out in a frenzied melody and the first ray of light shot into the sky. I fell back into bed again and slept soundly until Amália knocked on the door and said it was eight o'clock. Breakfast was already on the table when I joined her there. Anibal had breakfasted some half an hour ago, Amália said, and gone away on his horse.

She laughed when I described to her what I had witnessed. 'It's not funny, believe me,' I said. 'There could be a terrible scandal.'

'Why, Gregório, you talk like a bourgeois!'

'No, it's not that,' I said. 'The age when masters' sons could seduce their peasants' daughters is gone. There could be trouble.'

'But what if they're seriously in love?'

'You know that's highly improbable.'

'I don't think so,' she said. 'Anibal seems devoted to the peasant life, perhaps he intends to marry a peasant girl.'

'You don't know Anibal, he was born a subversive. If I hadn't seen the progress he's made on the land, I'd give him a piece of my mind.'

Amália laughed again and said, 'How contradictory you are!'

'I don't know what you mean by that,' I said, a little hurt that she should not sympathise with me fully.

After breakfast we went riding. I kept ahead so that we wouldn't have to talk since I had been slightly annoyed by the morning's conversation. She had nearly treated as a joke what to me was a serious matter. The riding was exhilarating and rid my mind of the irritation it had felt. I led Amália up a path into the hills and, fording a shallow river, realised it was the path Vicente and I had taken once when we had gone camping. I had not thought of it because the path had looked different; there were no overhead creepers, the underbrush had been cleared. Amália was enjoying the climb, for the view broadened and became more spectacular each time she looked back. Before I knew it we had come to the hut which I remembered as Formigueiro's secret hideout – and if we appeared to take a comparatively shorter time reaching it, it was because time and distance seem longer to a young boy and also because one no longer needed to dismount frequently in order to clear the path of vines and underbrush.

Formigueiro's hideout didn't look very secret any more, for there, sitting on the ground in a circle, were some twenty men, Anibal among them. I was slightly embarrassed and at the same time vexed, for Formigueiro seemed to have won the complicity of my degenerate brother. The men looked silently at us. Formigueiro shouted an amiable greeting. My only thought was to go away from there as soon as possible, and so I said, 'Don't let's disturb you, friends but we'd appreciate a cold beer.'

We remained on our horses. The men continued to stare at us. Formigueiro went into the hut and came out with two bottles of beer.

'I only want a sip,' Amália said, took a drink from the bottle and passed it to me, while I returned the other bottle to Formigueiro.

'Senhor Gregório, once again you're too early to eat some rice and beans,' Formigueiro said to me with a smile.

'Maybe one day I'll come by invitation,' I said.

Formigueiro laughed. I handed the bottle back to Amália who took another drink and returned the bottle to Formigueiro.

'Well, thank you,' I said. 'Please accept my apologies for having disturbed your party.'

'Not at all, Senhor Gregório,' Formigueiro said. 'You could be one of us.'

'Next time, perhaps.'

We rode away. All the time we had stood there, just outside the circle of men, everyone had looked silently at us. The expression on the men's faces was one of apprehension and unease. Anibal, however, kept his face to the ground. I explained to Amália more fully than I had done the night before what I thought went on in that hut, telling her of my previous encounter with Formigueiro in the same place, and having a few more abusive words to say about my brother.

'They looked like conspirators,' she said.

'That's what men look like when they feel guilty,' I said.'And of course, in a sense they're conspirators against their own women-folk.'

Returning to the house, we had a swim, enjoyed lunch without Anibal's disturbing presence, had a siesta and drove away to Rio at four o'clock, by which time my brother had still not returned from what I assumed was a Sunday of debauchery in the hills. We spoke little on the drive back. Amália was exhausted from all that riding and I was driving too fast to have any thoughts.

I was obliged to slow down in the traffic of Rio, and I put a hand on Amália's thigh, caressing it. She held my hand and pressed it. I had to change gear and withdrew my hand. She shifted in her seat, drawing up her legs, clasping her knees in her arms. I left her at her parents' apartment in Botafogo and drove home.

I don't know why I felt relieved leaving her. I had grown uneasy in the silence of the drive back; it seemed so banal for two people to be sitting in a car and staring stupidly out of the windscreen. I wanted all our moments together to be brilliant, as so many of our hours together at the college had been when we had talked passionately of Brazil's destiny, and as I was certain our future life together would be. The roar of the wind as we drove into Rio seemed to have intruded into our intimacy; being boxed in the car seemed to have dulled our bright perception of the future. Driving down to Rio from the farm, seeing luxuriant landscapes on the way, the densely forested mountains and the wide and brilliantly sunlit valleys and perspectives which seemed to take the eye deep into the very mystery of the land, one always ended up in a traffic-jam on Avenida Brasil on entering Rio.

At home my parents were sitting down to dinner when I arrived. I had little appetite but I joined them since it seemed the appropriately dutiful thing to do. There was an uneasy silence nowadays between my father and mother. They had had several disputes concerning their children, especially after Anibal had taken up living and working on the farm. At first my father blamed mother for having spent her life in fantasies of France or of giving her maternal attentions almost exclusively to Iolanda while her sons grew up as louts. This was unfair on mother but when I attempted to defend her I received such abuse from father that I kept out of their future disputes and remained a passive spectator of their sad drama. It hurt me to witness what I did, especially when my own behaviour (which I beleved to be impeccable and precisely what I needed to do for my own future) was partly the cause of their quarrels. I secretly resolved that one day I'd do something truly wonderful for them to make them happy and to prove to them that all these years, when I'd appeared recalcitrant, I was in fact working towards their happiness.

In her turn, mother accused father of having been too indulgent to his sons, for she at least could not be blamed as regards Iolanda who, she was proud to say, had lived up to the highest expectations of any parent, thanks to her mother's watchful care and training.

As for Anibal, he ought to be put in a cage, she said. I would have agreed on this point if the family had asked for my vote, but father brought out his account books to show how the land was making a greater profit under Anibal's management, and the boy, he added with an amazed look, is scarcely eighteen. Mother disagreed; it was unhealthy for a teenage boy to be running a small empire, he ought to be in the streets chasing girls. Such are the contradictory minds of parents, for when, a few years earlier, it had been obvious that Vicente and I were chasing girls we were reprimanded for not being serious in life, and now that Anibal was, in his own perverted way, being more serious than even father had ever been so far as the administration of the land was concerned, he was supposed to be committing a crime against his own youth. Add to this the further contradiction of father approving among men his elder sons' venery but whenever mother suspected anything taking up a posture of stern censure, and you have a situation where one was always obliged to appear to be both doing and not doing what was both approved and disapproved so as not to appear offensive to either parent.

Mother refused to go to the land again, for she was no longer prepared to be insulted by Anibal's refusal to wear a clean set of clothes when he sat down to dinner. On his occasional visits to the land father was torn between hating Anibal for behaving in a manner which had introduced another divisive element into the family and admiring him for his business success; he could not bring himself to censure Anibal after the first few attempts to scold him had produced no effect, except for the reaction of a primitive grunt, and he soon realised that the only sanction against Anibal would be to banish him from the land, which, of course, would be the equivalent of killing the goose that lays the golden egg. It was obvious that in his coarse way Anibal had won a degree of trust and eagerness to co-operate from the peasants which made the administration far more efficient than it had ever been. In the end father accepted the offensive means through which the desired end of higher profits was achieved; for mother, her concept of civilisation was a principle which she would never abandon; it was no use making money if one could not quote from Racine and Molière in a conversation at dinner. Father's trouble was that he agreed with mother at least as far as observing an elegant style was concerned, though he could have done without the classical quotations of which mother had only a small repertoire, and he had heard them all several times; but he had no intention of losing money for no better reason than not to hear Anibal's animalistic sounds when he ate.

I rather suspect that their disapproval of their sons' behaviour and the quarrels which resulted over their separate interpretations of the disapproval were really an indirect expression of their own despair at getting old.

Sitting down to dinner that evening I wasn't sure whether I should talk of the good changes I'd seen on the farm and please father but at the same time aggravate the pain which Anibal's name caused to mother, or whether I should keep quiet out of respect for mother's feelings but in the process hurt father by appearing callous. I ended up by talking of the poor roads and the heavy traffic, thus giving gratification to neither of my parents but, in spite of my desire to be kind, making each considerably irritated by my irrelevant chatter.

The next day Amália said, 'Gregório, we know nothing of Brazil.'

'What do you mean by that?' I asked, but she remained silent as if to suggest that I didn't deserve an explanation. I was annoyed and, saying that I had studying to do, left her and went to the library. I sat there staring at some book and wondering about my relationship with Amália.

We loved each other but were not lovers in any sexual sense, having tacitly assumed that we had an entire lifetime ahead of us and that the present was a time more of sharing intellectual enthusiasms than sharing a bed. At least that is what I assumed, for I took it for granted that we would be married when we finished college. Apart from innocent embraces, I scrupulously maintained a puritanical distance from her, believing that any expression of sexual ardour would arouse her repugnance since I thought that her idealism had no room for such base longings. Little did I understand that, in her feminist pride, she was not prepared to disclose even through the vaguest hint that what she wanted most was a gratification of those very longings. Had I known, had she spoken or made some significant gesture, had we not assumed that the other's idealism was purer than one's own, we would not have fallen into an awful misunderstanding as a result of which she was moody and silent, believing she was not attractive enough for me, and I was similarly reticent, thinking that I had no new brilliant idea with which to impress her. Each of us interpreted the other's silence as a rebuke, mistaking a feeling of anguish directed at one's own self as an unspoken comment upon the other.

A few days after she had made the remark about our knowing nothing of Brazil Amália was absent from college. I assumed she was indisposed and thought nothing of it, and it was only when she had not come for an entire week that I decided I should call at her parents' apartment to see if she were not ill. But on that very day I received a brief letter from her. She had gone away to São Paulo, she said, for she was tired and needed a break. She gave no real explanation, and I took the words to mean that she was tired of me. I was sufficiently angry to make up for several months of abstinence from the haunts which Vicente had introduced me to, but even that did not relieve me from the oppression I'd begun to feel. At the back of my mind was the idea that Capistrano now lived in São Paulo but I kept that idea, and all its associations, suppressed: I loved Amália but was not as yet prepared to go mad on her account. She gave no address, saying something vague about being with her sister, and I was too proud to call on her parents to ask for it. I simply

101

maintained my silence and thus reinforced our misunderstanding: we loved each other, but her going and my refusal to seek her signified only indifference.

For the next year and a half I did nothing but study, avoiding friendships which were not ephemeral and superficial and, when it came to love, preferring to purchase it rather than enter into a new relationship. After taking my degree I spent the best part of a year in Rio, working for weeks on end at my father's shop and, just when he'd begun to conclude each time that I had at last become the son he'd hoped I'd become, doing what he wanted me to do, I'd fall into a mood of disenchantment, or merely of boredom, and go away to the farm where, in order to avoid my boorish brother, I'd go for long walks into the hills. One day, after another period of work at the shop, I was again in a mood of frustration and despair and was driving out of Rio to go to the farm when, without thinking of it, I took the road to São Paulo, and visited Capistrano.

He received me amiably and invited me to stay with him for as long as I liked. I stayed four days. He had not changed, the eyes still held one, the voice was more compelling than before. Groups of young people came each evening to sit at his feet. I did not see Amália, heard no one speak of her and was too proud to tell Capistrano that it was a misery in my heart which had brought me to him and to beg of him to tell me, if he knew, where I could find her. Looking at him, observing the superior air he had about him at certain moments as if he guessed what was on my mind, I felt convinced that he not only knew where she was but also had her as his mistress. I resolved that I should not even mention Odila's name in case Capistrano thought that I was doing so only in the hope of some chance information about Odila's younger sister.

On my last night at his apartment a young girl remained behind when the crowd of students who had spent several hours listening to political talk had finally gone. She was a very pretty brunette named Alícia and she looked at him as that pock-marked Rodolpho Rubirosa had described girls looking at Capistrano, with her whole body. But Capistrano said to her,

102

'Alícia, why don't you take a taxi home? It's too late and my friend Gregório is leaving tomorrow.'

She went obediently, and I said to Capistrano, 'You didn't have to forgo your pleasure for my sake, I'm sorry to have been in the way.'

'Think nothing of it, Gregório,' he said. 'I've had enough of Alícia, there are times when it's a greater pleasure to sit and talk with a man.'

'I'm flattered,' I said, 'but Alícia is extraordinarily beautiful, and who can have enough of her?'

'You should have seen her three years ago, when she was sixteen. Ah, she was something then! Now, having followed me from Rio and getting tons of money from her parents on the pretext of going to the university here, she hangs around as a matter of habit and I've to be rude to her to get any peace. One thing you have to understand: for a good many people revolutionary politics is only another way of finding a sexual partner. A good many young men who think they're getting some sort of a high talking about revolution don't realise that they're usually only getting an erection because the person listening to them with such interest is a pretty young girl who, on her part, thinks she's having profound ideas about the future of the working classes when what's actually on her mind is a bourgeois marriage – which fantasy includes having a servant to cook her meals and clean her floors and bathrooms and another servant to take her children out to the park while she sits and reads a work of anthropology. People like to think of themselves as the new wave of intellectuals but do not want any change in their own lives apart from continuing to live in an ever superior world where they can continue to speculate on the problems of the working classes; and with the majority of these people all you have is only a language game in which words are used as things in themselves, merely as signs which reveal the tribe's allegiance, there's no meaning, certainly no relevance whatsoever to the reality of existence. So it is with Alícia, she has no idea of what we talk about here, only that these are the words she ought to be hearing and using herself. So, you believe that I don't care for her, that she bores me? And, Gregório, how do you tell a nineteen-year-old girl that she's too old for you?'

'A woman of thirty can be young,' I said, 'it depends on what one wants from her.'

'Oh, don't be such a saint,' he said, laughing in feigned mockery. 'You know very well what any man wants from a woman! When girls of sixteen give it to you it becomes very boring when women of twenty expect it from you and impossible when matrons of twenty-five demand it of you. Especially if they're the same ones getting older.'

He talked at length on this subject, enjoying the pleasure of a double voyeurism by observing a vicarious voyeur listening to his graphic descriptions, so that he was seeing himself via the images he projected on my imagination. Finally he exhausted the subject, or tired of it, and talked of politics again, saying, 'Kubitschek, what a joke! We don't have a president, we have a pharaoh. That's what the idea of Brazil does for a man. It's not enough for Brazil to have been discovered where there was nothing before in order to fulfil the buried dreams of Europe but, once discovered, it has to exceed the expectations of the most poetic imagination. You've had your dazzling emperors in Europe and Asia but they rarely got past building churches or temples, if they got that far, for most of them were too busy butchering entire nations. Louis XIV is remembered for the chairs and tables designed in his reign but our Kubitschek has to build a glittering new capital in the middle of the god-forsaken interior to commemorate himself, and he's not even a king!'

When he had exhausted the theme of abusing Kubitschek, though the criticism was in language which implied an admiration for the president's daring, he said, 'You know what you should do, Gregório? You should go to the United States and study politics there.'

'Why should I do that?'

'Because the United States is big and developed and Brazil is big and undeveloped. Because one day the United States will exhaust itself and Brazil will step into its place. Greatness will be thrown upon Brazil, Brazil will be expected to lead the world simply because there won't be anyone else big enough and rich enough to do the job.'

'But I'm not a politician,' I said.

'Oh to hell with politicians, they're a bunch of dumb idiots! They see only petty details. We need dreamers who believe in grand destinies. You, Gregório, have been asleep all these years, you've never had anything interesting to say, but you're the biggest dreamer I've known, and I want you to wake up now before your dream turns into a nightmare.'

His words, I'm convinced now, were meaningless rhetoric, but they inspired me. I could hardly sleep that night, and all the way back, driving to Rio, I kept thinking of the idea of going to the United States. I believe I wanted an excuse to leave my parents in any case because of the depressed state of mind my relationship with them frequently put me into; but at that time, entering Rio again, I felt that the voice I'd heard was not Capistrano's but that of my destiny. Needless to say, it was not easy to convince father to finance a project which sounded to him similar to Vicente's, but he agreed in the end, especially when I threatened to disappear into the interior and never see him again. What did he want, a son who could be proud of his father for having given him a handsome education, or a son who loathed him?

'Will you promise to return?' he asked. 'Or will you vanish like Vicente?'

'Father, I can't promise anything, for how do I know what the future holds? All I can say is that I intend to return.'

It was 1960. Kubitschek's term of office ended with his great dream of a new capital in the interior being accomplished. Grudgingly, people who worked in government were leaving Rio for Brasília which, by all accounts, was a sea of mud from which rose incomplete buildings which looked like ruins. I was twenty-six years old and I, too, was saying farewell to the beaches of my beloved city.

I made a last visit to the farm. Anibal had grown into a huge man and drove about in a jeep on the greatly improved roads. He had acquired two trucks which were constantly delivering bananas and pineapples to Rio. He had bought a pick-up on which to bring down the bananas from the hills and a tractor with which to plough the land and to clear the wild underbrush. The peasants wore a uniform of blue cotton trousers and red shirts. Efficiency had become institutionalised. I missed not seeing the mules coming down the narrow paths, overladen with bananas; I missed the distractions afforded by wild underbrush, the ferns swaying in the breeze or some jungle flower suddenly catching one's attention. I missed the infinity that the earlier wilderness had suggested, for it had possessed mysterious depths. Instead there was order everywhere, the limits of everyone's actions were precisely defined, and the noise of the mechanised vehicles filled the air all day long. I was glad to return to the city and to spend my last two days lying on Copacabana beach when I was not attending to the details of my departure.

It was on the very last night that Amália called. She was at her parents' apartment, she said; she had heard that I was going to the States and wanted to meet me.

Twenty minutes later we were sitting at a table in a sidewalk café, leaning forward, holding hands, our elbows on the table and staring into each other's eyes.

'How can I explain?' she said.

'Three years and not a word, how could you have been so cruel!'

'No, Gregório, don't say that, please. I thought of you all the time, I loved you all the time.'

'Tell me the truth, then. Why did you go to São Paulo? Was it. . .?'

I could not bring myself to mention Capistrano's name.

'I was in São Paulo only a month,' she said. 'It was to see Odila, that's all. She's married some professor. I took a bus from there to Goiânia.'

'Whatever for?'

'Remember what I said once? We know nothing of Brazil, I said. I went to find out. I went everywhere. Cuiabá, Belém, Recife, Salvador, everywhere. I've stood among the prophets of Aleijadinho in Congonhas, I've knelt in the church at

106

Tiradentes. I've been a beggarwoman in Bahia and a whore in Recife.'

'Amália, what are you saying!'

'No, don't take me literally,' she said, smiling softly, 'what I say is true only in my own mind. But I have seen everything and I have been every Brazilian I've seen.'

'But what madness, Amália, for a beautiful young girl to be travelling alone.'

'I was at home, I was everywhere, and everywhere I was at home.'

'You've become mystical,' I said.

'Perhaps, why not?'

'If you'd told me what you were going to do, I would have come with you.'

'I was tempted, but I thought that you at least should finish your studies, that way together we would know everything. I would be the body, you the mind, together we would be one.'

'But why didn't you write?' I asked.

'And risk your abandoning your life for me? I loved you, I wanted you to discover your own world for yourself. I wanted a purer love than my body desired, I didn't want my body to be between us.'

This and other answers to my questions made no sense; if it was not some paradox it was a contradiction, and even what appeared to be a simple, direct answer possessed levels of ambiguity and, on consideration, was no answer at all.

'What can we do now?' I asked. 'I'm going to the States tomorrow and may not be back for two years.'

'I'll wait for you even if it's longer.'

We kissed and parted. It was a tender embrace, without passion. I had not known what to believe of her explanations. It was difficult to imagine a lonely girl going among villages and cities and surviving. None of her answers possessed a specificity, they were more like riddles, and for all I knew she might have been in Rio all this time, or in São Paulo, living as someone's mistress. Also, I tried not to think of the coincidence of her having arrived just when I was departing, for if it was not a coincidence there were implications which I preferred not to contemplate.

The next morning I suffered a silent breakfast with my parents, bid goodbye to their pained faces and took the Pan Am flight to New York.

Some day in the future, if I'm still alive, I shall tell the story of my experiences in the United Sates and describe how I realised very quickly that the supposedly greatest nation on earth was also the most insular. Apparently the United States had built a huge mirror around its frontiers, it could only see its own beautiful face each time it gave the impression of looking beyond itself. Brazil meant nothing to my contemporaries at Columbia University, it was just another South American country where, from time to time, some revolution took place. Those who thought they knew about Brazil turned out to be people who had seen some movie with Carmen Miranda, and whenever one mentioned the fact that one came from Brazil they'd immediately do a funny imitation of a samba, roll their eyes in an idiotic fashion and recite the well-worn line from the Carmen Miranda song, *Mamãe, eu quero*, as if that made them experts on Brazilian affairs. The United States was interested only in itself and its Press talked of little except the country's new president as if he were a dashing young monarch, going to such a silly extent as printing photographs of the president's little daughter wearing her mother's high-heels, proving I don't know what, if it wasn't that the greatest nation was given over to a banal sentimentality. At least in Brazil, I thought, a president didn't have to stoop to such a base level of having to make a hit with maudlin, provincial women.

I mixed with a bunch of Africans, Asians and South Americans, all of who shared my contempt for Kennedy whose incredible popularity seemed to us the result only of public relations tricks. A few Europeans and a number of radical Americans attached themselves to us but I was convinced that the latter's radicalism was shallow, for they were the kind of youths who'd have attached themselves to any cause that mimicked the rhetoric of revolution for no other reason than they thought it was an interesting – or *cute*, as they would have put it – thing to do; at least it was different from what their parents expected or wanted them to do, and therefore they equated in their minds a satisfying feeling of rebelliousness with the idea of revolution – unless, of course, their idiocy was a mask, for they could well have been C.I.A. agents keeping an eye on likely subversives who, after Castro, could be found among any group of South American students. As for me, I despised both the radicals of the American variety and the Castro-inspired revolutionaries among the Latin Americans. No one seemed to realise that truth is not obtainable through positions of extreme ideological commitment, that such commitment only enslaves one to a partial view and thus makes of one both a hypocrite and a liar. If I learned anything at Columbia, it was not in the classroom or from my friends but by observing what the new revolutionaries proposed: it was no less, so far as I could see, than the imposing of a radical tyranny on peoples who were supposed to be oppressed; I had ample proof of what Capistrano had repeatedly told me, that the most destructive threat before mankind was not the old-fashioned kind of dictatorship which we had in Brazil under Vargas but the kind of people's democracy proposed by intellectual liberals. They were so impressed by their own virtue that they were eager to legislate it among people to whom it meant nothing at all.

And this is another subject, of course, which is not entirely relevant here, for I have no intention of writing a treatise on the miserable beliefs to which a few people would like to convert all mankind. I make a few observations merely to indicate my impatience with beliefs, whether they be religious or political, for the truth is that there has been no belief in the history of mankind which has not, in arrogantly asserting itself, killed off a score or a thousand or a million people for the crime of not accepting it.

I did not take any degree from Columbia, for I was there for only a year and a half and did not complete all my courses. In the middle of my second year I received a letter from Amália giving me the news that my parents had been killed in an air crash.

Earlier in the year, in my correspondence with my father, I had suggested that he and mother might take a trip to Europe to see Vicente and Iolanda and visit me in New York on their way back, since the airlines allowed a stop-over in New York for very little more money on a return ticket to Europe. Older readers of this chronicle will remember that there used to be a Brazilian international airline called Panair do Brasil which went out of business in the early 'sixties (and which has been superseded by Varig, a private and not a national airline). It was on one of the last flights of Panair do Brasil that my parents were booked to fly. The jet accelerated down the runway but instead of taking off into the blue sky it crashed into the bay, taking my parents to their watery grave.

I felt guilty because it was at my suggestion that they had commenced the journey which never left the ground. How our good intentions mock us! In order to show I was different from Vicente, who had long abandoned writing to any one of us, I kept up a regular correspondence with father, describing my life in New York to him; and it was to show what a loving son I was that I had suggested they come and visit me, further demonstrating my love of the family and my selflessness by suggesting they visit Iolanda and Vicente first. Had I remained cruelly silent, like Vicente, they would not have died when they did and perhaps might still be alive – probably cursing me for my aloofness. Or had I insisted they come to New York first, they would have been on a different flight; in short, the one gesture which was calculated to be the most considerate and loving was the one which proved fatal to them.

I was surprised that the news reached me via Amália. What, I wondered, was my beastly brother Anibal up to? Surely he would have been the first to have been informed? I decided to return to Brazil. My studies at Columbia would equip me for nothing. They had provided me with valuable experience, I supposed, but I could not see a degree making any difference to my future. There was nothing to do but assume my adult responsibilities, whatever they were going to be.

Two weeks later I had flown back to Rio. A thousand things

seemed to happen simultaneously: seeing lawyers and bankers, attending to the management of the shop and the apartments which were rented out, sending long letters to Vicente and Iolanda describing the various properties in Rio and asking them for their intentions since father had left no will. The inheritance would go through a slow legal process and in the end we would all receive an equal share, but there were many questions, such as should the rented apartments, which produced a good income, be sold or continue to be rented. I was engrossed in these maddening details and sometimes wondered why I bothered when none of my three siblings seemed to lift a finger while I ran from the lawyer to the banker and from the banker to some petty government official. I was most annoyed to find that Anibal had not deigned to come down from the farm and I resolved to have it out with him once and for all as soon as I had the opportunity to go there. Vicente and Iolanda replied very briefly, telling me to do what was best, which was the same as saying that they did not wish to be embroiled in the harassments with the lawyers, though Iolanda did give the name and address of her bank in France to which her share of the income from the rented apartments was to be remitted. I hired the services of a young accountant named Virgílio to handle this and several other matters, but still had little time to myself for many months. Had I not had the consolation of being reunited with Amália, I doubt if I could long have preserved my sanity.

A new president, Jango Goulart, had come into power and he seemed bent on turning the country into a Communist state. Amália told me of what had been happening during my absence and said there was a lot of talk of confiscating property. I pressed my lawyer to try and have our inheritance settled quickly. Each time I saw him he presented me with an account of his expenses, and I began to think that, if the government did not take it all away, the lawyer would.

'As for the farm,' he said one day, 'it's not clear who owns it.'

'What do you mean?' I asked. 'My father owned it, and his father before him.'

'There's some confusion,' the lawyer. said. 'It'll take some

111

working out.'

I could see what was coming: we would need to bribe a hundred officials, it was Brazil's way of distributing the general wealth.

Finally I found the time to drive up to the farm. There was a new iron gate across the dirt road at the entrance, a barbed-wire fence marking the boundary of our land. A man sat inside the gate, smoking a cigarette and reading a comic. A pistol hung from his hip and, although he had obviously heard me drive up to the gate, he took no notice until I sounded the horn. He walked up heavily and, standing behind the gate, looked at me enquiringly.

'What's the idea of the gate?' I asked. 'And that damn fence?'

'I only work here,' he said and shrugged his shoulders, flicking his cigarette away into the dirt.

'Well, open the damn gate and let me through, will you?'

'Are you on official business?' he asked, throwing a glance to where the cigarette had fallen.

'Fuck you,' I shouted, not being able to restrain my anger. 'This happens to be my land!'

The anger had been building up within me while driving from Rio. The mere idea of having to meet Anibal filled me with revulsion. And now I exploded, thinking it was typical of the son of a bitch to put a fence across the land which had been the freest place in the world. The gatekeeper, totally cowed by my abuse, let me through, for he was of that order of men who are hostile and bad-mannered when one treats them as equals but become immediately meek and servile, in spite of a gun at the hips, when one abuses them.

I drove up to the house in a rage, hardly observing the bright, new huts which had been built everywhere in groups of five or six, each group beside a field on which there was some cultivation. There was a young man in the house who sat in one of the former bedrooms which was now furnished as an office.

'Where's Anibal?' I demanded.

'I'm Pedro Azevedo,' he said, not rising from his desk. 'I'm the accountant.'

112

'I'm Gregório, Anibal's elder brother. Will you please tell me where he is?'

'I do not know, Senhor Gregório. He left after giving the farm over to the peasants' co-operative.'

'The peasants' *what*?'

'Co-operative.'

'It wasn't his to give, what nonsense has been going on?'

'No nonsense, I assure you, Senhor Gregório. The land belongs to the people. Senhor Formigueiro is the general overseer, he lives in this house now, but only temporarily, until his own hut is completed. After that this house will be demolished.'

'Listen, Azevedo. I've seen a lot already and have no reason to doubt that what you're telling me is true. But how could this have happened? This is Brazil, you know. This was my father's land and I don't see how one of his sons could have given it away during my father's lifetime.'

'It was done before I was hired. I don't know the details. I only work here.'

'All right, but tell me, where can I find that fucker Formigueiro?'

Just as I said that I realised in a flash that the hut in the hills which Vicente and I had taken to be a place of debauchery was in fact a meeting-place of subversives, and in the same moment I was reminded of the time Amália and I found ourselves there by accident and she used the word 'conspirators' to describe them. Anibal had been among them the second time, and I realised too that all these years Anibal had only been a puppet trained to move to the remote wishes of Formigueiro.

'Senhor Formigueiro is in Brasília,' Azevedo said. 'President Goulart is interested in his experiment,' he added brightly, as if to impress me.

I left soon after that, for I did not care to hear Communist cant. I was more convinced than ever as I drove away and saw our old, wonderful land parcelled out into little, tidy lots that the most dangerous people in the world were those who believed they could change it. The lots of land with the neat huts beside them had a mean look. An ancient dignity had gone out of the land. It was not a price I wished to pay to increase mankind's happiness, that most fraudulent concept of all, or to bring about human equality, that absurd chimera attempting to attain which people achieve only a demoralising degeneration of values in their lives. I drove slowly back to the gate, greatly saddened and embittered. My younger brother, passing off his treachery as improvement and efficiency while my parents lived, had wasted no time in taking his own profit and disappearing as soon as they died; and my elder brother, who had been the first to teach me the value of the land, had expressed no desire to return to it when I'd written to him on returning from America to say that he might come back and become its new master. It now fell on me to begin litigation to get the land back or be compensated for what amounted to an expropriation. But what satisfaction would there be in re-possessing those mean lots, and how could money replace the dream of freedom? It was like waking up crippled.

The gatekeeper let me out. I drove slowly away and, coming round a bend, stopped the car and switched off the engine, finding an intense emptiness within me which took away all my energy. The land here, adjacent to our property, was as ours had looked. A disorder of underbrush, a proud independence of trees. I put my arms upon the steering-wheel in my weakness and, resting my head against them, began to weep uncontrollably. I wept for my father and my mother, I wept for the land which had been theirs, which they had touched but not wounded, I wept for myself who had seen the world begin to be taken over by barbarians.

Chapter 3

THE FLIGHT

On a Monday morning, during the rush-hour, a dark-blue Volkswagen collided with a bus on Avenida N.S. de Copacabana. Braking hard and swinging to the left at the last minute, the bus failed to avoid the Volkswagen, whose driver apparently had jumped the lights; the dark-blue car crashed into the right side of the bus just where the door was, and the evasive action taken by the bus-driver not only failed to prevent the accident but also caused another collision to the left of the bus, where a little red Renault taxi was in the process of overtaking the bus. The entire street was blocked.

A similar accident took place at the same time on Barrata Ribeiro, the main street parallel to Avenida N.S. de Copacabana and going in the opposite direction in Rio's one-way system of streets. In one of the narrow streets which joined Barrata Ribeiro and Avenida N.S. de Copacabana a truck broke down, so that the driver had to come out and look at the engine, shrugging his shoulders in a helpless gesture at the traffic behind him which had become blocked; in another street a delivery van stopped on the edge of the road and two men, trying to carry an old bed across the street, shouting instructions to each other, dropped the bed and stood abusing each other while the traffic in the street came to a standstill. Since these two events in the side-streets occurred at the same time as the two accidents on the main streets, an entire area was a solid mass of stationary cars and buses, many of the drivers of which shouted from the windows, asking what had happened. Many simply blew their horns by way of futile protest at not being able to move and not knowing the cause of their immobility. From outside the great block of stationary traffic could be heard the sirens of police cars and ambulances, but they might as well have been outside the walls of a fort.

Inside a bank on Avenida N.S. de Copacabana, just beyond the corner where the Volkswagen had hit the bus, so that the next block was completely free of traffic except for one car parked outside the bank, several people were lying on the floor and all the tellers were standing behind the counters with their hands above their heads. Two young men with machine-guns stood in the middle of the lobby; a third was walking away with two large brief-cases. A moment later the three ran out to the waiting car and drove into the next side-street; there they abandoned the car for another one and drove as fast as the traffic allowed to Avenida Atlântica and came up to my apartment, where Capistrano, Amália and I had been sitting on the terrace, looking out at the ocean and drinking coffee.

'Gregório,' Capistrano said, 'I think your plan worked.'

'I never doubted it would,' I said.

'The revolution has begun,' said Amália.

This was early in 1967, during the summer of heavy rains when *favelas* in Rio and even an apartment building in the district of Laranjeiras had come crashing down. It was some five years after I had sat outside my ruined land and wept. My life underwent a profound change during those years; from a passive observer of humanity's incompetent blundering I became an active leader, persuading Capistrano to return from São Paulo and join Amália and me. It had been Amália who had urged me not to withdraw from the world, which everywhere was being taken over by the barbarians, but to do something about it. 'Put all those ideas we had into practice,' she suggested, adding that I ought to persuade Capistrano to join me in Rio, for after all that theoretical talk we now had a practical responsibility. Capistrano had come and taken a small apartment in Ipanema but spent much of his time with us. Call us a group or a movement, we did not want a label like the revolutionaries of the time who'd picked up a second-hand ideology from a foreign folk-hero called Che Guevara and played out desperately suicidal rituals.

Amália herself had come to live with me after my father's properties in Rio had been legally settled on his children and I had acquired two apartments, using the sumptuous one overlooking Copacabana beach for myself and paying for our expensive life by collecting rent from the other, and I also had some money, which came from the sale of the shop, invested to produce a tidy income.

By now Amália and I shared a whole world of ideas and it seemed entirely absurd not also to share a bed. If either one hesitated, it was, ironically enough, me. For I proposed to marry her rather than that we should merely live together; but she scorned the idea of marriage for reasons which I understood at the time to be idealistic but discovered many years later to be something else. But I do not wish to look back to that time from the perspective of my present knowledge; at the time, after I'd agreed that we should live together, I thought ours was a perfect relationship, a marriage of ideas in which love, engendered and sustained by physical attraction, was the purest of the intellectual abstractions which we cherished. She had still not explained the years of her absence from Rio before I went to New York and, when I questioned her about it once or twice, she never went beyond saying that it was a time which had become a blank in her consciousness. I wished sometimes that that had not happened, or that she had a simple, plausible explanation to give rather than the vagueness of a metaphysical pretension which she affected; but I suppressed my own desire to know, telling myself that it was odd in human behaviour to prefer some such improbability as her having lived those years as a social worker in some slum or as the mistress of some criminal to her evasive suggestion that all she did was to travel around the country: we find it easier to accept an unpleasant truth, provided it conforms to our preconceptions, than an explanation which commits no offence to our person but which strikes us as meaningless. With time, however, I learned not to question her on those missing years and, although I suppressed them myself, they lived within me as a gap which one day had to be filled.

The men had left the two brief-cases in the drawing-room and quietly withdrawn from my apartment. Capistrano, Amália and I continued to sit on the terrace, watching the ocean and drinking coffee. A police car went screaming down Avenida Atlântica but did not prompt the slightest change of facial expression in any of us that might have indicated that we were aware of some crisis in the street. A little later Amália and I rose from the terrace, went and changed into our bathing-suits and walked across the road to spend the rest of the morning on the beach.

The traffic on the avenue and the crowd on the beach were the same as always, only thicker. The 1964 coup which had ousted the socialist president Goulart and established a military dictatorship had not touched outward existence and, outwardly, we too were only two bodies in the crowd with no other desire than to enjoy ourselves on the beach. The defeat of incipient socialism ought to have solved the problem of our land, but far from it; the farm was still under litigation even though Formigueiro had vanished into the interior after the coup. In spite of my letters, Vicente showed no interest in returning to Brazil and Iolanda did not understand the legal proceedings and only wrote when for some reason there was a delay in sending her the rent collected from the apartment which she had inherited. As for Anibal, he might have been in Siberia for all I knew; in fact, I wished that that was exactly where he had found himself.

Amália and I crossed the avenue and found ourselves a spot on which to spread out our towels on the sand.

'What happens next?' Amália asked as we lay there.

'We go to Minas tomorrow,' I said. 'Nothing very serious, but it has to be done in such a way that the others think it's really serious. There's a lot of pure pantomime in this game. In any case, it'll be a nice little break for us.'

She rose to go into the ocean. I saw her slim, tanned body pick its way through the crowded beach, her brown, wavy hair falling to below her shoulders. I lay back on the sand and dozed. Two women sitting near me under a red, white and blue striped parasol were discussing a movie they had seen and interrupting their chatter with shouted exhortations to their children who were playing near the water. The vendors were walking through the crowds of sunbathers calling out the names of the refreshments they carried – *mate gelado, coca, maracujá* –and there was the rhythmic thud of a wooden bat hitting a rubber ball as a couple played fresco-ball on the wet sand.

Amália came back and lay on her towel, beads of water on her shoulders. Capistrano joined us a little later, his thin body looking taut and strong in his maroon bathing-trunks. He stretched his towel on the sand and sat down, casting a casual look around at the women on the beach.

'Any phone calls?' I asked from where I lay across from Capistrano, Amália between us, my eyes at the sky and my words muttered very softly.

He was looking away from me at a young mother and said in an off-hand manner, 'Just one from São Paulo. Funny, there was nothing on the hourly news on the radio, but the guys in São Paulo had heard about it.'

'Well, that's all right,' I said, turning over and speaking into the sand.

Capistrano lay back, looked up at the sky and said, 'Will they understand it, though?'

'They'll get the message,' I said. 'At least it already proves how they operate.'

'The water was delicious,' Amália said, speaking into her towel, her arms above her shoulders around her head.

Capistrano and I rose and went into the ocean, swimming past the crowd of children in the shallow water and past the youths diving into the breakers.

We were quite far out in the ocean, alternately swimming and floating on our backs, when Capistrano asked, 'What's the rehearsal for Minas?'

'Amália and I drive out tomorrow morning,' I said. 'Nothing will happen till the day after. Nabuco goes to Havana.'

'That tit! He never had an eye for women. The best people to give power to are lechers. They screw women and not the country.'

'Nabuco is the eager type,' I said.

119

'A harmless idiot, yes. He'll do the trick.'

'I hope so,' I said.

'What about the men in Minas?'

'They're O.K. I'll talk to them. But they'll make their own action. We don't want to know what we should not know.'

We began to swim back to the shore, and Capistrano said, 'Amália was right, the water's delicious.'

We waded past the children screaming and laughing in the water. The beach was crowded the length of Copacabana, the calls of the vendors filled the air, rising above the noise of women and children with the muffled roar of the traffic on Avenida Atlântica in the background.

Amália lay with her back exposed to the sun, a film of perspiration making her skin sparkle in the sunlight. I collapsed beside her, falling on my knees and staying kneeling a moment, stroking her warm skin. Capistrano stretched out on his towel, putting a forearm across his eyes. I rose and went for a walk along the water's edge where girls in pairs, in brightly coloured bikinis, walked, talking and laughing, their teeth perfectly white and their dark eyes sparkling; or there were young couples taking very slow steps in the wet sand, their arms at each other's waist, their eyes to the sand; or there were groups of youths parading the perfection of their sixteen-year-old bodies or just playing the fool at the water's edge. I walked for some half a mile before returning.

Capistrano had propped his head on his hand, the elbow in the sand, and was talking to Amália who had sat up and was listening to him with profound interest. On seeing me Capistrano said, 'Come on, Gregório, let's go and eat lunch, I'm starving!'

We went back to the apartment. The radio was on while we ate and when the news came on there was a brief item towards the end about a huge traffic-jam in Copacabana, but there was no mention of a bank robbery. While we were having coffee on the terrace I received a phone call.

'Who is this?' I asked.

'You will recognise me when you see me. Be in the restaurant at the zoo at three o'clock. Come in a taxi, not in your car.'

'Who was it?' Amália asked.

'He didn't give a name,' I said.

'You'll know what to say if he's from the secret police,' Capistrano said.

'Make sure you contact the bank,' I said to Amália before going.

'Yes, of course,' she said. 'I know my part. Be careful.'

It was a hot time of the day at the zoo, even the monkeys had withdrawn into dark corners and were asleep. I walked past the cage full of blue and yellow and red and green *araras* dozing on their perches, stopped a moment to look at a peacock dancing incongruously for no one's benefit in a narrow cage, and turned towards the elephant-house. Not far from it was the restaurant, actually only a refreshments stall, with metal chairs and tables on a paved area around it. There was a family which was obviously from the provinces on a visit to Rio. The father looked merrily at his three children drinking from bottles of Fanta, his hand clutching a bottle of beer which he rested on a stomach which bulged out as if he carried a water-melon under his shirt; the mother, squat and vast at the hips, looked worn out. I bought a bottle of beer and went and sat as far as I could from this family. Two foreign tourists, a middle-aged couple, were walking among the cages in the distance and slowly making their way towards the refreshments stall, stopping frequently to take pictures of each other in front of some animal or other behind bars. There was no one else about. I took a sip of my beer and looked around again. A well-built, tall man, dark brown, nearly black, in colour, was buying a beer at the stall. He must have come from the other side of the stall, I thought. He walked towards my table. He was dressed in khaki-coloured cotton trousers and a white shirt of which the collar had curled up. He walked with his chest well out, an effect heightened by the fact that the two pockets on the shirt were full, one with a thick note-book with a black binding, so that there appeared to be a black band across the area of his heart. The other pocket had some folded papers in it and a row of ball-point pens clipped there. I recognised him as soon as I saw his

121

pock-marked face: Rodolpho Rubirosa, who used to come to Capistrano's apartment some ten years before. He carried more weight and walked with a sense of measured purpose, like one who had acquired some authority in his world. He put out his hand when he arrived at the table, saying, 'Remember me?'

I took his hand and said, 'Rodolpho Rubirosa, why, of course, how are you?'

'One of the advantages of a face like mine is that no one ever forgets it,' he said, sitting down.

'I've a good memory for names,' I said, not wanting to gratify his desire for self-pity, and wondered to myself why he should have called me to this rendezvous. His past connection with Capistrano put all sorts of doubts in my mind.

'If you're wondering why we're meeting here,' he said, 'the answer's simple. I happen to live within walking distance from here and had come home for lunch.'

'Why did I have to take a taxi?'

'Where would you have parked? But please forgive the slightly melodramatic approach. One acquires a taste for certain types of games. All clichés in the end, I'm afraid. Still, it's good to sit out in the open air, one feels free to talk.'

'What do you want to talk about?' I asked.

'About old times and new,' he said with a slight chuckle.

'To what purpose?'

'Because it's my job to acquire information.'

'Are you with the police?'

'Yes and no. You'll soon find out.'

'But your orders come from Brasília?'

'Yes, ultimately they come from Brasília.'

'From the dictatorship? Ultimately?'

'Let us say a ministry is involved.'

'Why these vague answers?'

'Rules of the game,' he said. 'Military games in which camouflage is always a principal factor. They make life interesting, give it a nice touch of the unexpected. Otherwise work, even this work, is too dull.'

He had said enough to convince me that he was working for the secret police. As a student he had frequented Capistrano's group and perhaps also other groups of one political conviction or another; and surely one way to acquire power was to become an agent of the government and use one's experience of radical and other groups to help the government stay one step ahead of any subversive activity.

'Well, what would you like to know?' I asked.

'How is old Socrates?'

'Capistrano? He's fine,' I said when he nodded his head. 'He's only forty-five or six.'

'Yeah, I know,' he said. 'Five-foot five, dark complexioned, grey eyes, I could draw you a verbal picture of him. But what's he talking about nowadays?'

'The same as ten years ago. The old theme of common sense, a hatred of government that serves the politicians and not the people.'

'And you, what do you think about that?'

'I'm still his disciple.'

'But you went to America for two years.'

'For a year and a half.'

'All right, one year and seven months if you want me to remind you of the actual duration. I might surprise you by giving you the precise dates.'

'I've no doubt you could.'

'There was no Capistrano in New York,' Rubirosa said. 'Your companions were Chileans, Puerto Ricans and American radicals.'

'They were also Cubans who'd been exiled by Castro,' I said. 'While there were some who hung the poster of Che Guevara on their walls there were others who covered the walls with nude pin-ups. So what are you trying to suggest?'

'Nothing that's not already on your mind,' he said. 'What do you know about Capistrano's disciples in São Paulo?'

'Ask him, I know nothing. I don't know of anyone in Rio either. I'm the wrong man for that sort of information. Do you know what happened to my father's land?'

'Yes. The government could work that out for you.'

'I see! So you want to make a deal, is that it?'

'No, I've no power to do that, I'm only a kind of middle-man.

123

We could help each other.'

'Why did you choose to speak to me and not to Capistrano?'

'You are more interesting. Besides, you and I are the same age, we speak the same language, while Capistrano is as old as Socrates in my mind.'

'And what's more,' I said, 'we both, you and I, love Brazil and want to do the right thing for our country, isn't that true?'

'Of course, no doubt about it.'

'But do we have to sit in this heat? Even patriotism doesn't demand that one be uncomfortable.'

'I'm sorry. We could walk under the shade of the trees over there, if you prefer.'

'Depends on what else you want to ask me,' I said.

'Oh, just a few simple questions. I'd like to take you to a curious place afterwards. Which reminds me of something interesting that happened this morning in Copacabana.'

'Yes, I know. There was a big traffic-jam. I heard it on the radio.'

'There was a big bank robbery, too,' he said, looking keenly into my eyes while I stared back blankly at him, trying not to look at his hideously ugly face.

'Is that something new?' I asked.

'No,' he said, 'there's always banditry in every country and it need not mean anything. Even in your so-called civilised countries, like England, bank robberies are not uncommon and they usually mean nothing except that a few people think it a quick way to acquire money.'

'Do they mean anything else in Brazil?'

'The trouble with you and me, Gregório, is that we're friends and you think nothing of asking me more questions than I ask you.'

'I'm sorry, I didn't know I'd been called for an interrogation.'

'There you are! Making a statement in such a way that it's calculated to make me feel apologetic.'

'Please think nothing of it. Ask what you like, and let's get it over with.'

'As I was saying, the bank robbery. I received a phone call from São Paulo and my colleagues there said that there was a subversive group there which took credit for it.'

'Responsibility, I should say,' I observed. 'Nobody can take credit for a criminal act.'

'You have the time to be precise in such matters,' Rubirosa said. 'All right then, responsibility. But my guess is that, if they were so eager to communicate a confession, then they must surely be innocent. It can be no more than bravado. But at the same time they must know that this was no ordinary bank robbery but one with a political motivation. O.K., let's walk in the shade.'

He rose hastily while making the last statement. I noticed that the foreign tourists had come up to the stall, the woman had sat down at a table directly between us and the stall and the man, standing there waiting to be served, was taking a picture of the woman: we would have been in his picture, in the background, probably completely out of focus but still there had Rubirosa not walked away and I followed him. It seemed an empty piece of melodrama to me, for even if the couple had been merely posing as tourists there was no reason why anyone should want to document Rubirosa's presence with me; the entire gesture, I thought, was calculated to keep me tense and a little confused.

We walked down the central avenue where there was some shade from the palm-trees and stopped to look at the leopards and the jaguars in their cages.

'What I wanted you to know,' Rubirosa said, 'is that it's all right for the radicals in São Paulo to suggest what they do. They're only digging their own graves. We couldn't have engineered things better ourselves.'

'I'm not sure I understand what you're talking about,' I said. 'I don't know why you imply that I should know anything about the robbery.'

'You don't have to,' he said. 'I just thought you'd like to know that there was a robbery, that the radical factions are eager to take responsibility for it, as if such a trivial thing will bring the government down, and that we have no reason any longer not to crack down on a number of people. You work that out, friend, and you'll know why I called you.'

125

We walked out of the zoo and stood by the road waiting for a taxi. There was little traffic at that time of the afternoon. Even the ice-cream seller outside the zoo had sat down under a tree and dozed off. We stood by the road for five minutes before a taxi came along. We said nothing while waiting for the taxi, expecting one to come at any moment and preferring to resume our talk when there was no possibility of interruption; also, I had no intention of saying more than was necessary, and I suspect that Rubirosa remained quiet in the hope that, pondering what he had already said and wondering what was to come next, I would be kept in a state of suspense and possibly even become nervous and say what I ought to keep to myself. He gave the taxi-driver an address in the business district, in Castelo. In the taxi we talked of the hot weather and of some girls we had known only by name and sight in the old days at Capistrano's.

The building in Castelo had an airline office on the ground floor. We took the elevator down to the basement where two armed, military policemen sat in the hall just outside the elevator door. Rubirosa waved a hand at them in a dismissive manner and they turned their eyes away from me to their own inner reveries. I noticed that our steps made no sound and saw that the walls and the ceiling were covered with acoustic tiles and that the floor was of cork. Another policeman sat by a steel door at the end of the hall. He rose and opened it on seeing Rubirosa, and we entered an office. It had a grey steel desk in the middle with three telephones and some scattered papers on it. A man in a military uniform sat at the desk, speaking into a phone. He waved almost absently at Rubirosa as we walked past to open another door and to enter another office which had a similar desk in it. Rubirosa walked to the chair behind it, sat down and spoke what I assumed were code words into a phone, rose and motioned me to follow.

A door led out to a narrow, dimly lit corridor, at the end of which was a staircase of stone and metal. There were other doors along the corridor and I assumed that each was shut on some other office like Rubirosa's. He led me up the stairs and out of a locked door, to which he had the key, and we came

126

out to a square courtyard bounded by the high walls of the building. It looked like a car park, for there were several jeeps and trucks parked there with the words *Policía Militar* stencilled on them in large, white letters. Five policemen with rifles stood in the shade by the door and Rubirosa, pointing to an armoured van which was parked nearby, asked, 'When did that arrive?'

'Five minutes ago,' said one of the policemen. 'The driver's still in there, waiting for orders.'

Rubirosa and I walked up to the driver's window where a thin, young soldier was sitting smoking a cigarette and staring out of the windscreen.

'All right,' Rubirosa said to him, 'bring them out.'

The soldier alighted from the van and went to unlock the rear door. Meanwhile, Rubirosa shouted an order to the policemen, three of whom came marching up, rifles at their shoulders. Four raggedly dressed men in handcuffs stumbled out of the van and were prodded by the policemen's rifles to walk towards the door of the building, where one of the other policemen, receiving a message from Rubirosa's eyes and a jerking of the head, unlocked the door. We followed the four prisoners and the three policemen down the stairs, our feet on the stone steps echoing loudly in the stairwell. Rubirosa overtook the men when we reached the corridor in the basement and opened one of the doors. It was a much larger room than his own office and had no furniture in it. The bare walls were painted a glaring white which made the holes of the several electrical sockets look like black, menacing eyes. Some cables and wires lay entangled in a corner and looked like a nest of snakes.

The prisoners were relieved of their handcuffs and then made to remove all their clothes.

It is not a pleasant sight to see four bedraggled, unshaven, dirty-haired men be forced to lose what little dignity they possess, and, were I not studiously excluding my own emotions from this particular narrative, I would graphically express the compassion I felt, especially when their loss of dignity was accompanied by humiliating words and gestures from the policemen and by the terror evoked in them by the empty room with only the wires lying in the corner. Their misery was mine, although I had no reason to identify with them, their wretchedness was a spot which I seemed to have discovered on my own soul. But I was obliged to appear dispassionate, disinterested, merely an objective observer. I looked at them coldly as if they were smears which had dirtied the wall against which they stood.

Rubirosa whispered some words to the policemen and then led me out of the room. We returned to his office where he asked me to take a seat while he himself sat behind his desk and spent a few minutes speaking into a phone, so that, briefly left alone with my own thoughts, I could not help imagining what the policemen must have begun to do to the prisoners; but, realising that this was precisely what Rubirosa wanted me to do, I took hold of myself and stared coldly at him. A young soldier brought us cups of coffee and when he had gone Rubirosa said, 'You see, it doesn't take us more than a few hours to catch bank robbers.'

'I compliment you,' I said, 'you must have a fine organisation.'

'Of course, those men haven't confessed as yet,' he said, drinking the coffee from the little cup in one jerking movement.

'But they surely will,' I said.

'Would you like to see them do so?' he asked with quite a sinister grin.

'Oh, I'm sure your methods are infallible.'

'Yes, you should see our methods, you might find them instructive.'

'I will, if you insist,' I said, 'but believe me, I've complete confidence in your organisation.'

He looked at me without speaking and I said, 'Well, what else would you like to show me?'

'Some little tricks we've learned from the American army, which invented such methods for Vietnam. We have some interesting electrical equipment which might come as a shock to you, but most people are quite impressed by it and always respond favourably. Do you ever find that when you try to think of your past, even something so simple as where you were yesterday and whom you met, your mind goes blank and you just can't remember? Well, we have a fascinating machine which brings the past back vividly and in complete detail, it's extraordinary how it never fails. Perhaps some other time, I can see you're anxious to return to your friends. Yes, when you come again, knowing what you're going to expect, I'll show you these machines, you could grow quite attached to them. Please convey my compliments to Capistrano,' he added, rising, 'and to your beautiful lady Amália, long may she preserve the rosy bloom of her youth.'

'At least the secret police know we exist and are something to be reckoned with,' Capistrano said on the terrace of the apartment when I had returned and described the meeting with Rubirosa.

'I doubt if that's the sort of impression we should be making on the secret police,' Amália said. 'For people like Rubirosa, to be seen acting mysteriously and brutally, or merely to have a reputation for doing so, becomes an end in itself.'

'What do you mean?' I asked.

'It doesn't matter to Rubirosa who gets it in the neck as long as someone does.'

'True,' Capistrano said, 'the world will never know who's innocent and who guilty, all it needs is the image of a victim.'

'And Rubirosa', Amália said, 'will end by making a victim of each one of us.'

'Oh, I don't think *we* have anything to fear from that pockmarked son of a bitch,' Capistrano said.

'Precisely because he's pock-marked and a son of a bitch', Amália said, 'he's bound to attempt to disfigure other people. Look at all the tyrants the world has had who were born ugly and impotent. Remember too that, when these people take to torture, what they go for are your genitals, those very vital parts in which they're deficient themselves. Nature provokes them to take revenge in circumstances in which they can pretend they're only piously doing their duty.'

'We can manage Rubirosa,' Capistrano said. 'We can play along with him. All he needs is attention, for someone to look at his ugly face.'

'Those four men,' I said, 'they had nothing to do with the robbery.'

The first reference to the bank robbery on the radio news had been in the afternoon, after I had returned from Rubirosa. Four men, it was said on the news, had been arrested in connection with the robbery.

'You're jumping to conclusions,' Capistrano said. 'You saw four men who had been arrested for some reason and then you hear that four men have been arrested for the robbery, and you assume that they're the same.'

'But the point is,' I said, 'although Rubirosa must bave been lying to make an impression on me, suggesting that they were arrested for the robbery, whoever those men are, they're the wrong ones. *We* know that.'

'It could also be', Capistrano said, 'that no one has been arrested in connection with the robbery, that it's only a lie to convince people of the efficiency of the police.'

'The real point surely is that the arrests have nothing to do with us,' Amália said. 'We know very well that, whatever happened, someone was bound to be arrested. That's how the police work, they have to play their vicious games. Besides, Rubirosa is probably dying to know what we're up to and is trying to put on a little psychological pressure.'

'You're not beginning to have a conscience, are you?' Capistrano asked.

'It's because I have a conscience that I'm involved in this,' I said. 'I never subscribed to the theory of ends justifying means.'

'Neither do I,' Capistrano said. 'I have the greatest contempt for your Lenins and Maos who have thought nothing of human life when it has been considered a price they have to pay to win their ideological victory. But in this case we're talking of the means used by the police and not by us, for our motives are neither vicious nor criminal: no one was hurt and the money has already been returned.'

'I know,' I said, 'it's just that I felt rotten looking at those men.'

'That's nothing, Gregório,' Amália said. 'Wait till you have to look at yourself in that situation. Or at me. You've already seen

130

on your own land what kind of soulless degradation the barbarians are capable of inflicting on the world. *That* is what we're fighting against, aren't we?'

'Yes,' I said softly, looking at the ocean.

'Now all those theoreticians in São Paulo and here in Rio will have to act,' Capistrano said, reminding us of our original aim. 'All those endless talkers will have to put down their cups of coffee and go out into the streets. Even the government will be forced to act with urgency. In a year we shall have either a free society or a tyranny of the right or of the left.'

'What if the military restores democracy?' I asked.

'Not while there's a threat from the left,' he said.

'And that's only just beginning,' Amália said.

'Expect no miracles,' Capistrano said. 'Life will never be what we desire it to be and that, believe me, is a great mercy. The kind of world we used to dream about ten years ago would be a great bore if that is where we had arrived at today, for our idea of the future is always changing, which is why any dogmatic ideological approach has to be foolish because that's a sure way of trapping yourself in a world which you cannot allow to change. One must always allow oneself the liberty of a counter-revolution; the most hideous place in the world must be where there is always summer or always winter. I'd be glad to be a Communist provided I was guaranteed my right to renounce Communism if I wanted to. You must have noticed that at any given moment there's something that you're discontented with, it can be the views expressed by the president or by some newspaper columnist, it can be the behaviour of a lover or of a mistress, it can merely be the state of your stomach, but always there's the conviction that things will or ought to change for the better, and it's this general discontent that gives you the energy to act. Discontent is an elementary force in our natures, it should never be suppressed, for therein lies a nation's will to change. Suppress this force and you're going to have a dying society with a dead culture. There are no reactionaries and no subversives in nature, only human beings who desire a different character of change.'

'But what about people who belong to a party?' Amália

asked. 'There are always some who're committed to a certain type of society.'

'Alas, poor suckers, what can one say about them! Remember, as I've said before, that the kind of man who becomes an easy tool of any system is not your illiterate peasant or worker but someone who has convinced himself that he's an intellectual and who, simply by having acquired the facility of repeating certain ideological formulae, is led to believe that he's capable of thought. You should see the journals which come out from England and France and the United States, each one radiant with the halo of its own beliefs, full of the cant of committed writers who never had a single idea of their own but are invariably eager to claim originality for themselves. Where would these smart-asses be without their Marx and their Heidegger, their Lévi-Strauss and their Merleau-Ponty? Originality of ideas comes only from writers who're committed to no cause but that of the freedom of their own mind to choose from a world of fertile speculation a phrase whose beauty is its own.'

'That is truer of artistic creation', I said, 'than of political thought.'

'All thought is a function of language,' he said. 'We have to look at language to discover new thought.'

'Who can deny your abstractions?' I remarked. 'But we were talking of action, more precisely about political actions.'

'Yes, but let us never forget what directs the course of those actions. A truly independent mind. Without that, we too shall be trapped by someone else's cant.'

A feeling of refined well-being came over us as we sat there staring at the ocean; as if the mere expression of the words 'independent mind' gave us admission to a select society. Six floors below us the traffic roared up and down Avenida Atlântica, mixed with the cries of children playing on the sidewalk.

Early the next morning Amália and I drove away for Minas in her old, beige-coloured Volkswagen. There was fog in the mountains near Petrópolis which slowed us down to a crawl

132

behind a line of traffic and deprived us of the spectacular views which always thrilled me with a fresh wonder each time I drove on that road. Then the traffic halted altogether. We got out of the car but could only see vague forms in the swirling fog. There were muffled shouts in the distance which would suddenly go dead to produce an eerie silence. The mountain-side beside us was dripping with streams and covered with red and orange flowers and I knew that across the road was a sheer drop of a thousand feet and down in the valley was a banana plantation. Word passed from car to car that we had been brought to a standstill by an accident ahead of us. We assumed that some fool had lost his patience and had decided to overtake in the fog, but soon heard that a huge rock had torn itself from the mountain-side, crashed down to the road where it had struck a car, sending it hurtling down the valley, and come to a stop in the middle of the road. There were murmurs in the air, quiet whisperings among people standing outside their cars, and then a few moments' deadly silence in which everyone probably had the chilling thought that the car knocked off the road by the rock could easily have been their own. One listened uneasily to the sound of water dripping from the mountain-side and wondered if more rocks were not about to be dislodged; looking at the solid wall of granite and being able to see only a few feet of it in the fog, with the flowers growing out of crevices, one felt the crushing pressure of its enormous weight.

A line of traffic began to pass us slowly in the opposite direction, ghostly forms of people sitting silently in cars and buses; the headlights, diffused and menacing in the fog, crept up and vanished, the loud wailing noise of the engines of buses and trucks in low gear creating the impression of an imminent explosion. Our line began to move and we passed the scene of the accident without seeing anything and only knew it was the place because two policemen were directing traffic there, allowing only one line to pass at a time.

Five minutes later the fog suddenly vanished, the sky appeared dazzlingly blue, and the traffic thinned out as the road began to descend. At nine o'clock we stopped in Areal for coffee and, seeing that some fresh bread-rolls were being delivered, ordered those too, and thus duplicated the breakfast we had had two hours earlier. It was a typical bar-café of the sort one comes across in the country, red, formica-topped tables, a 'Kibon' ice-cream chest just inside the front door, and dust-covered bottles of *cachaça*, whisky and gin on the shelves behind the counter. The middle-aged man who came from behind the cash-register to serve the coffee asked if we had heard of the rock falling down the *serra*, it was just now on the news, he said. We told him how we had been delayed by that accident and he somehow felt that his prestige was enhanced by meeting people of whose discomfort and inconvenience he had only just heard a description on the radio; we were to him like celebrities walking out of a television-set right into his living-room.

'If you want to know what I think,' he said as if confiding a secret, 'I don't think the rock came off by itself.'

'Of course not,' Amália told him, 'it was all the rain we've had recently.'

'No, it wasn't the rain,' he said in a dramatic whisper, 'that rock was pushed down the mountain and it was aimed at someone. Just you wait till the police identify the bodies in the car that crashed into the valley.'

'Oh, come on,' I said, 'there are easier ways of committing murder.'

'Then what were the two men doing on the mountain?'

'Which two men?' Amália asked.

'The ones the police arrested,' he said.

'Perhaps they were mountain climbers,' I explained to Amália when we drove away. 'It has to be a coincidence. You know that mountain-side, it's almost dead vertical, no murderer would be mad enough to want to go up it in blinding fog. Besides, no assassin is going to risk his life unless he's reasonably sure of his victim. Think of it, is that the way you'd choose to kill someone? It's absurd. Country people like to make a drama out of ordinary, natural events, that's all.'

A few miles out of Areal, just past an electricity generating station, we drove along a river on our left with beautiful land beyond it, hills covered with mango-trees and topped with eucalyptus-trees and with grassy slopes where cattle grazed. We had to slow down, going round a bend, for there was a blue jeep in front of us going at twenty miles an hour. A broad-shouldered, white-haired man wearing a maroon beret was swinging from side to side as he drove and a flaxen-haired boy of four or five stood on the seat next to him, holding on to a handle on the dashboard. The road straightened and we overtook the jeep. The white-haired man, whose ruddy face and merry blue eyes we saw as we passed, was singing away in a jolly fashion and the kid beside him appeared to be shouting out the words of the song at the top of his voice.

Past Três Rios the road straightened out on the undulating land which rippled in green masses to a deep, ever-receding horizon. We stopped for an hour at a *charruscarria* outside Juiz de Fora, eating too much meat and drinking a bottle too many of beer. Amália drove for the next two hours while I dozed uncomfortably on the back seat and then I drove while she had a nap. It would have been monotonous and boring had the land not continually held one's astonished attention with its variety and beauty; even when I had tried to doze I had several times raised my head to look across a gentle valley or at the trees bordering a river. Although there were three or four more hours of daylight and plenty of time in which to reach Belo Horizonte before nightfall, I decided to turn off at Congonhas and to spend the night there in the old hotel on the top of the hill beside the church where Aleijadinho's prophets stand in the forecourt, stubbornly independent under the fierce sun as if that were the only quality their maker intended them to preserve to eternity, there in the heart of Brazil, the land shimmering in its undulating gradations on all sides, and a night sky bright with stars.

Amália was still asleep on the back seat and woke up when I ran the car up the narrow, cobbled street which had a rough, uneven surface, making it hazardous to drive fast, and which was so steep that if one did not shift into second gear and press right down on the accelerator of that old Volkswagen one got nowhere, so that it was a matter of going up in a series of bouncing leaps which had the effect of making the occupants of a car feel hilarious or miserable, depending on their mood.

'Where are we, what are you doing?' Amália cried, being thrown roughly in the back, while I held on to the steering-wheel as if to the reins of a bucking horse and yelled in the manner of cowboys in films and, with one final 'Whoopee!' arrived at the church, braked hard and flung the door open.

'Come and meet my friends, the prophets,' I said, tilting the back-rest of my seat forward and bowing.

'Oh, we're in Congonhas!' Amália exclaimed, and smiled.

We walked up the steps to the forecourt of the church and looked with renewed wonder at the soapstone statues of the prophets. We had come here once before, while touring the old colonial towns, but at least two years had passed since that visit. We stood on the stone wall, beside one of the prophets, and looked out on the view he commanded over the wide, rippling plain, a land that might belong to some absentee landlord of feudal disposition but was owned, in that glorious perspective, only by the sky which stretched out its wide blue-white embrace. And I knew then that if any misfortune ever befell me, if a time came when an enemy held a dagger to my throat, I would only need to close my eyes and see the image of this land again and there would be peace in my soul, as there was now. I hoarded images of Brazil within me – the mountains around my father's land, the ocean at Copacabana, the islands in the Bay of Ilha Grande seen from the road to Angra dos Reis, the waters of the Rio Negro meeting the Amazon, and a hundred other images precisely catalogued in my mind, in Bahia and Rio Grande do Sul, in Mato Grosso and Santa Catarina – which kaleidoscopically shuffled their fragments in my mind and always kept alive within me a glittering, colourful composite image of my country, constantly astonishing me by appearing in new combinations and constantly renewing the energy within my soul.

We slept late the next morning, spending the night at the hotel beside the church, but still had plenty of time to reach the airport at Belo Horizonte before noon. The plane from São Paulo came on time, which gave us an hour and a half to talk with the young student we called Nabuco before he caught a connecting flight to Brasília, the meeting with him being one of the reasons why we had driven to Minas.

He was twenty-two years old and had a complexion of that light tan which is not quite brown, black hair which is not quite curly but yet is more than wavy, and lips and nose which had their ancestry more in Africa than in Europe.

We sat in the lounge, drinking coffee, and Nabuco said, 'This is the most exciting thing that's happened to me, going to Europe.'

'Not so loud,' whispered Amália.

'I've had two years of political theory,' Nabuco said in a lowered voice, 'and believe me it's boring when it's not self-evident. Actually, we had more economics than politics and sometimes I wasn't sure if it was not merely geography that the professors were droning on about. I guess there's not much political theory they can give you when the only system you're supposed to value is a military dictatorship.'

He grinned arrogantly, having cumbrously made his way to that punch-line. I looked around the room. There were only a few businessmen drinking cocktails and talking loudly among themselves. I let Nabuco talk on in his boyish manner, realising that he needed confidence to pursue the difficult task that we had delegated to him. We were sending him to Paris in order that he could then make his way to Cuba, and had devised an indirect route for him, calculated to disguise the truth about his designation, which is why he was in Belo Horizonte when he could have taken a direct flight from São Paulo to Paris. He was going to fly on to Brasília and from there to Caracas and only then to Paris. The poor boy thought himself a sort of avant-garde revolutionary who was on a pioneering journey. It was important for us that he believed – and not only so that the Cubans might trust him – that he was on a historical mission for the socialist revolutionary cause, that, thanks to him, things would come to a head in Brazil.

'Last night I talked with—.' He whispered a name so softly that it was hardly audible, and, although I heard it sufficiently clearly, I'm constrained to suppress it for reasons which will be

137

obvious.

'Did you tell him where you were going?' Amália asked.

'I whispered the word Cuba to him,' Nabuco said. 'You can't imagine what a thrill it was to see astonishment on his face. But I told him, I go to pave the way for you, I'm only an ambassador who goes to prepare the visit of an emperor. Obviously, he didn't like the royalist image, but it was better than saying a soldier preparing the ground for a general, and he was greatly impressed. He even gave me a message to deliver to Havana.'

I was pleased to hear him say all that, for we seemed to have calculated correctly the way the man in São Paulo would respond. Capistrano's formula was infallible: 'If you want a man to act, then touch him where his vanity is flattered or pride wounded.'

'Yes,' I said to Nabuco, 'make sure his name is well received by the Cubans, so that they invite him. Unless you can do that, your mission will not have succeeded.'

'Don't you think I can do anything *he* can?'

'That's not it,' I said. 'You know very well what he stands for in the revolutionary underground in São Paulo. You're a leader, too, depend on it, everyone will know of your part in this, but you know what it will mean to the movement to have *him* officially invited by the Cubans. And when he's there, you can be in charge in São Paulo.'

Poor Nabuco, he was such a naïve child he believed anything provided he saw himself in a leading rôle. Capistrano had judged him correctly when, of all his former disciples in São Paulo, he had chosen Nabuco for the present mission. He had just the right blend of eagerness and a love of engaging in a puerile fantasy of being involved in a dangerous adventure, together with a capacity for completely misunderstanding the society in which he lived – all of which, incidentally, is not far from defining a modern liberal whether he be in Brazil or in France or in the United States. We talked with Nabuco to sustain this illusion he had of himself, and even the fact that we had come apparently furtively to Belo Horizonte to give him his final instructions neatly complied with his idea of how such things were done in the complex adult world of secret missions

138

for some desperate political cause. He was the kind of young man who needs a cause to die for, so that his sense of existence is that much more poignant should he survive. Martyrs and supreme patriots are made of his type; and so are terrorists and assassins; and, indeed, so are idiots.

Do not think that we had become so callous as to play with the life of another human being to further our own cause. On the contrary, we took every precaution to ensure his safety and actually were in a position to contrive matters in such a way that Nabuco could have flown directly from São Paulo to Havana had there been a flight between the two cities; no, the round-about itinerary was not to save his skin but to serve another purpose, to convince two of the revolutionary leaders in São Paulo of the sort of truth which they longed to believe in. The phrase has already been used: to bring matters to a head. Nabuco was only an innocent actor who would come to no harm; my real apprehension was for what would follow when he returned.

He went away cheerfully, repeating to himself the names I had mentioned of people he was to contact in Havana and feeling rather proud that he had such an excellent memory that he did not need to write them down, for, he assured us, he was never going to be caught with any evidence on his person. I would have felt pity for him when he boarded the plane did I not believe that I did not have a lifetime long enough to pity all the benign fools of this world.

We had another reason to be in Minas and drove out to the town of Mariana, stopping, since we had time, at the old gold-mining town of Ouro Preto to see again the magnificent golden baroque of the eighteenth century in churches which, in the afternoon sunlight that poured in through the high windows, seemed to be supported by beams of solid dust which in its concentrated massiveness yet possessed the quality of being loose and without substance, just as successive drops of water make up the diagonal lines of rain with a Euclidean formality without actually being visible as drops and without the delineated lines being more than a geometrical illusion. It was a town which we had loved visiting before, and returned to twice, perhaps because here we had felt on our first visit, without having verbalised the idea, that its old solidity and the crazy angles of its cobbled street somehow represented the love we felt for each other, for it too had endured all the shifting of perspectives that come from the passage of years; it had the quality of being established and yet it continued to surprise with a freshness of possibilities, that here one could make a world for oneself; and each time I held Amália's hand or touched her lips with mine or looked into her eyes it was as if I'd just discovered a new love, knowing at the same time that, like the gold of Ouro Preto, it had been glittering with its lovely effulgence for many years already.

Mariana, too, belonged to the era of gold and, although it was a small town, it was not without its own pretensions to piety and (in common with every town in this area) boasted the almost mandatory cluster of churches, each resplendent with gold. Our business here was not in a church but in a barn a little distance out of the town. Some twenty men had assembled there, having been chosen and brought there by a man whom I'll identify only as the Supervisor, for that is what he did for us in the state of Minas Gerais. The men were all administrators on the estates in the area, and while making the speech to them that I had come to make I could not help remembering the traitor Formigueiro on my father's land and, while talking, uttering the vehement, rhetorical phrases which suit any ideology – 'If we are to succeed. . . .' 'The goals of our society. . .' 'The collective wisdom of our people. . . ,' and a thousand others, I kept remembering the land of my childhood, seeing a variety of images of it, now the view from the mountains, now the mountains from the house and now the bewildering montage of several views – that concentration of imagery which is without focus but which, in a dazzling simultaneity, gives us a clear vision of the whole by rapidly projecting a multiplicity of pictures on one's mind in a succession so swift that the parts and the whole are both clearly and definitively envisioned. There was muted applause from the men, who perhaps wished to express their agreement and at the same time maintain their

140

independence, and when I shook hands with them I was not sure if I had said anything other than the empty statements which any politician could have made. The Supervisor was impressed, however, and talked animatedly about several plans, all involving explosives for which he had the sort of enthusiasm a young boy has for fireworks.

'Don't tell me any details,' I said, 'you know very well you're completely free to choose your own means provided you're convinced you'll help achieve the general ends we're after.'

He looked as pleased as a provincial governor who's been given complete power by the federal government, and said, 'The rural movement has to be inspired by the cities. Belo Horizonte and São Paulo and Rio, everything will happen in that triangle.'

'Don't forget,' Amália said, 'Brasília is outside the triangle and thus has the advantage of being able to see all of it.'

Amália and I returned to Belo Horizonte and, since I had no desire to drive during the night, we took a room at a luxurious hotel, deciding to make a celebratory occasion of what was plain necessity. It was early evening and we took a long walk among the busy downtown streets and I could not help remarking that the crowds of people walking from shop to shop or leaving their offices or merely finding themselves there during an idle stroll, like us, had the same dreamy look of the sidewalk crowds in São Paulo and Rio, as if each one was untouched by those two levels of reality which invisibly impinge upon one's daily existence – the larger political reality of an age or an era and that narrower reality which obliges one to wait for the lights to turn green before one crosses a street. It was for these people, dreaming about their dinners or their mistresses, enjoying reveries of their children winning all the prizes at school, calculating in advance how they would spend their expected rise in salary, thinking absently of a thousand tiny details of no large consequence – the outcome of a football match, the price of coffee, the colour of the new car they hoped to buy – it was for the pursuit of their wholly innocent but necessary dreams that men met in secret enclaves and furtively whispered the portentous words of a revolution. I had the

141

image in my mind, which came from I know not where, of a peasant ploughing the land some distance from Hiroshima seeing a blinding light on the horizon, witnessing a mushroom shape itself in the sky and, looking at the position of the sun, cursing the little time he had in which to finish the ploughing. Life, for those of us who were still blessed or cursed by it, had inevitably to shrug its shoulders at someone else's incursions which insisted that we change our mode of living, for the bread must not be left to burn in the oven and the cattle must be herded from the fields for the milking, and in the end, where the ideological intrusion had been unavoidable, one learned to make the minute adjustments, like discreetly taking up the hemline of an old skirt so as not to appear too absurdly out of fashion among those who ostentatiously only wore new skirts; and should the shrapnel of some bomb, exploded at some distance from us, lodge in our flesh for reasons which neither our political leaders nor our patriotic soldiers can make clear to us, once again we would rather shrug our shoulders, call it bad luck and go about our business as best we can than be convinced that it has somehow been an act of patriotic sacrifice.

'But that is defeatist,' argued Amália when we had returned to the hotel and were sitting in the cocktail bar where, over whisky, I had talked of what had passed through my mind in the streets. 'Life *is* changed when a political system changes.'

I tried to explain: 'If you look at the history of revolutions you'll observe that until the twentieth century the motive behind each was to *diminish* or completely *eliminate* the power of the ruling government. The Restoration in England, and the changes in the nature of the monarchy which followed it, the French Revolution and the Declaration of Independence in the United States all removed the ruling power which had become too intolerably powerful, whereas in the twentieth century, whether it's in Russia or Cuba or here in Brazil, it has not been to replace an oppressive régime with a liberal one, nor has it been to distribute power to the people. Instead it has been to *increase* the power of the new rulers who succeeded in seizing it by force. Of course, what they overthrew was an intolerable tyranny but the revolution has not altered the ambience of oppression; all that happens in these instances is that a different person wears the boot that kicks the people, a person who's usually a bit more brutal than the ruler he's overthrown when it comes to kicking. I'm not here questioning the motives behind these revolutions and, as you know, I'm not without a considerable sympathy for our present dictators who came in with the very honourable intention of saving us from the anarchy of an abominably corrupt democracy. My point is a theoretical one: modern revolution, of whatever persuasion, ends by becoming despotic, and those people who were supposed to be saved by it do not discover a different world but live in the same one of common futility and despair with only their dreams to accompany them as they stroll in the streets. The truth has to be that, as long as we need government, we can never have a good government; and since all twentieth-century revolutions, because of the very forces which bring them about, begin with the necessity of suppressing a group or a class of people, then it inevitably follows that any new form of government which can be established has to be more repressive than the one it replaces.'

Amália sipped her drink quietly and I could see that she was disturbed by what I said and she did not want to say what she had accused me of before – that my ideas contradicted my actions, that while I seemed to believe that all action, especially political action, was futile, I spent much of my time pursuing actions which were calculated to effect the political future of Brazil. So that when she continued to look away from me I said, 'No, there is no contradiction, for this is not a question of practising what one preaches, the simple truth being that I don't preach anything. One merely becomes committed, by the force of circumstances, the death of one's parents or the felling of a tree, almost anything – a *favela* being destroyed by a thunderstorm or an obscure paragraph in a newspaper which has been put there only to fill an inch of space for which the editor has no other use, in which one reads that the fish in some river have been poisoned by some industrial waste – oh, just about anything can make us do something which we hadn't thought of before, and that sets off a chain of events.'

'Well,' Amália said, looking up with a quick, bright glance, 'what do you think our Supervisor friend is going to do?'

I understood that she wasn't interested in listening to speculative talk and said, 'I suppose he'll go and blow up some bridges, but we could prevent him, especially if there's danger to people.'

'Otherwise nothing will happen until Nabuco returns from Cuba?'

'Yes,' I said, 'though, of course, there's nothing to keep people in Minas and elsewhere from their own spontaneous demonstrations.'

'How slow all this is!'

I understood her despair but did not say anything, and asked her instead if she wanted another drink.

'Oh, I suppose so!' she said with considerable irritation in her voice, and added after a pause, 'Since you're obviously going to have two or three more.'

I realised that the source of her irritation was what she considered my defeatist attitude, and I thought to myself that it was a nice irony that I had begun to talk, in general and vague terms about mankind at large, not because I believed I had important thoughts to communicate but because it would be boring to spend the evening with nothing to talk about; but my desire to please had resulted only in annoying her, so that I now suffered either a stiff silence from her, or the odd remark thrown out abruptly and in a tone intended to be either icy or ironical. I cast my mind back on what I had said, resolved that I had said nothing which I did not believe in, and yet understood that it was not what I would have chosen to say had I first rehearsed my thoughts, but now, having committed myself to utterance, I could neither retract my words, for I still believed in them, nor wish I had not uttered them, for that would be hypocritical; and nor could I now attempt to redefine the words in order to reveal my thoughts more precisely because Amália would interpret that as a silly persistence on my part and so be annoyed all the more. And thus, when we attempt most earnestly to be convivial or sociable, we fall afoul of people who're closest and dearest to us, whose very closeness has been

144

the reason why we have thought nothing of saying what had spontaneously come to mind, which, of course, we would not have done had they been strangers. Thinking of all this, I remained silent too, believing that an explanation would be received as a clumsy rationalisation calculated to exonerate my error and not – the way I saw it – as an objective perception into the common misunderstanding between two people who love each other, so that my silence, which I dared not break for fear of appearing too frivolous, had the further consequence of giving the impression that I resented not having her full agreement with what I'd said when, in fact, I harboured no resentment and would have said so did I not believe it hazardous to utter another word.

The waiter brought the drinks and I was beginning to think that it was going to be a terrible evening, for sooner or later we would have to leave the cocktail bar and go and have dinner, and I was pondering the various possibilities – one of which would undoubtedly be that Amália would complain of a headache and ask for a sandwich to be sent to the room (which would both relieve me of a miserable dinner in her silent company and at the same time intensify the sourness of the mood by my having to eat alone) – when an acquaintance of some years before providentially walked into the bar and, being alone and seeing us there, came to us with his arms extended. He was a politician, a social democrat of sorts, whose anonymity I shall preserve by calling him simply Pedro and by not describing his physical characteristics, except to say that he was large, bald and of a buoyant disposition.

'Amália!' he called from six feet away, his arms thrown up, and coming to her he enfolded her in an embrace. 'Gregório!'

We shook hands and clasped each other's shoulders, and I noticed a brightness in Amália's eyes and felt within myself that if we had been on the verge of a crisis that, at least, had passed.

'What brings you two to Belo Horizonte?' he asked in a loud voice which nearly made the question a rhetorical statement.

He took a chair at our table while I signalled to the waiter and said to Pedro, 'Well, what will you drink?'

'We're just sightseeing,' Amália said. 'It's so boring in Rio

145

with all the rain we've had.'

'A whisky, like you, Gregório,' Pedro said and added, turning to Amália, 'You should go to Brasília if you want to do some serious sightseeing. They have a zoo there called the Brazilian Congress and you can see fine old monkeys dance while the military band plays popular American tunes.'

'Is that where you're going?' Amália asked, laughing.

'I'm *coming* from there,' he said. 'You know, you can take just so much laughter, after that your sides ache. The stage's all set for Costa e Silva to be inaugurated as the new president. I don't know why Castelo Branco has to step down, his act was funny enough. I told that joke about him to an American I met in Brasília, you know the one, that Castelo Branco joined the army so he wouldn't ever need to wear a polo-neck sweater, and the American just gawped at me and I had to explain that our president just didn't have a neck. It was no joke by the time I finished the explanation. He's a middle-of-the-road man, is Castelo Branco, he can't look to the left or to the right without turning his whole body, so he just avoids the right and the left by looking straight down the middle. You know what the trouble's going to be with Costa e Silva, he's too *tall*. It's like clowns, you have a short one and then you have a tall one. It's too much for me, I can't take any more laughter and I'm on my way to São Paulo. A spell of seriousness is just what the doctor ordered.'

'But Pedro,' Amália said, 'it'll be terrible if our government becomes serious.'

'Oh, I agree, it will be a catastrophe.'

'But who knows,' I said, 'with seriousness we might even get foreigners to believe that life in Brazil is not just a long carnival.'

'That's what I think, too,' Pedro said. 'My motto is that you have a good government when you have foreigners investing in your country. And that's what I'm going to do in São Paulo, go into pharmaceuticals with an American firm to back me. I'll make more money than I ever did saying 'Yes, sir' to the president when I was a congressman.'

Pedro's feeble and rather trite attempts to make a joke of the political situation (from which he was obviously withdrawing

146

before he could be expelled) was not untypical of the older politicians who had been in power when their personal greed and general inefficiency had been partly responsible for the military coup: they could never understand an idea unless it was first translated into a language of personal gain. It was absurd, I thought, that here was a politician who, at least before 1964, had been instrumental in determining the course of the country and yet he was the very type of self-centred person with whom it was impossible to discuss political ideas, for the simple reason that he was incapable of comprehending them. It was an easy stance for him, and many like him, to take, to make derisory jokes about the military leaders, for that absolved him from the necessity of making an intellectual assessment: being incapable of thinking in terms of the larger historical forces which determined a nation's destiny, he resorted to the simple expedient of vilifying that which he could not understand, just as a casual visitor to a museum, having no experience of art and not knowing of the inevitability which has led a painter to cover a large canvas with only white paint, is convinced that the artist is someone to crack jokes about and that he himself is superior in his knowledge not only of the world but also of art.

Now the odd thing was that, while I had the greatest contempt for Pedro's type of imbecility, I was grateful for his presence, for his worthless chatter gave interest to our evening when my own serious deliberations had seemed to guarantee its ruin. He stayed with us during dinner and somehow we preferred his idiotic jokes to our own ideas, even though, when finally free of him, we would spend an hour discussing what a fool he was.

But at dinner he suddenly said, 'Well, Gregório, when are we going to have the revolution?'

'What revolution?' I asked. 'We had one in sixty-four.'

'*We* didn't have that,' he said, 'that was the military's revolution.'

'I didn't know anyone had a counter-revolution in mind,' I said.

'I thought you intellectuals talked of nothing else.'

'But whatever put such an idea in your head?' Amália asked.

147

'Oh, everyone's talking about it.'

'It's idle talk,' I said. 'First, I'm not sure if I like it when people talk of "you intellectuals" in a tone which implies a contempt for intellectuals. Second, I don't believe the label fits either Amália or me. And third, even if it did, just because there might be intellectuals in São Paulo and Rio with revolutionary ideas, it does not follow that everyone else who's to be placed in the same category also has the same ideas.'

'Ha, you're getting too complicated for me,' Pedro said. 'Too serious as well,'

'Not at all,' Amália said. 'It's simply that some people are just not interested in politics.'

'Do you know what the government is going to do?' he said, ignoring Amália's statement, for it was inconceivable to him that there could be anyone in Brazil who was not interested in politics. 'The government is going to *provoke* the revolutionary zealots. Don't ask me how. There are a thousand ways. There was a bank robbery in Rio two days ago which is supposed to have been the work of urban guerrillas, but no one knows for certain. But it's by provoking them that the government is going to get the intellectuals to come out of their ivory towers and on to the streets and, once there, they've had it!'

'That's clever of the government,' Amália said. 'How do you know all this?'

'Go to Brasília, everyone's talking about it. Some things just happen to be in the air.'

He paused, looked intently first at me and then at Amália, and added, 'Don't ever tell me I didn't warn you!' And he laughed aloud.

We remained quiet for a moment and then I said, 'I told you already, you can't put us into one of your categories. The only thing I desire for Brazil is stability. I am too aware of history. Remember the civil war in England? It was better to have a tyranny than to proceed with the civil war.'

'Even if the tyrant is a Stalin or a Mao?' he asked.

'I hope not,' I said, 'but I'm prepared to take the risk.'

'Oh, come on, Gregório, you're only teasing me! You must know that there are Brazilian officers in the United States right now, being trained at military bases in Maryland and Texas. What do you think they're learning there, how to fly a plane? No, my friend, they're learning the fine techniques of making political prisoners talk. Ha, as if Brazilians will ever refuse to talk!'

'You're pretty well informed', Amália said, 'for someone who's not even in politics any more.'

'As I said, just go to Brasília, it's all in the air there. But for my part, I don't care anything about it all. My only interest now is pharmaceuticals.'

'If I may correct that, Pedro,' Amália said with a sweet smile, 'your only interest is money.'

'True!' he exclaimed. 'You put it beautifully. The rest is only the charade of people who don't know what a lovely thing money is.'

'How fortunate for you,' I said. 'You have less to compete against.'

He laughed and embarked upon a series of inane jokes which would have embarrassed us had they not served as a passable diversion and seen us not unpleasantly to the end of dinner.

One event led to another during the next several months, our actions having set off reactions in various parts of the country, especially in São Paulo and Rio. A few days after Amália and I returned to Rio we received a message from Paris that Nabuco had been well received in Havana, and we scarcely needed to repeat the message before it was known among the revolutionaries in São Paulo. Their leader – for whom Capistrano and I had coined the name Avestruz (meaning the Ostrich) – we heard, was vehement in his abuse which, however, was directed at no one in particular since he had no notion of who was behind Nabuco's presence in Cuba, but, receiving a message from his own contacts abroad that Nabuco was arranging for him to visit Havana, he did a quick turnaround and began to say laudatory things – again, of no one in particular, for with him, as with so many political leaders, language was a matter of exaggerated gestures and was un-related to the precise meaning of words. He was so caught up in his own vanity that it did not even occur to him to ask the obvious question: why and by whose direction had Nabuco gone to Havana? In due course he made a secret visit to Cuba but, possessed of the politician's instinct for self-dramatisation (for strict secrecy would have kept him obscure, and what good is obscurity in furthering a political career?), he broadcast a speech of puerile revolutionary rhetoric from Havana, believing in his own vanity that all of Brazil listened to him and not having the common sense to appreciate that by that time, the late 1960s, if any Brazilian still turned away from his television set to switch on the radio it was only to listen either to carnival music or to a football match and certainly not to the ranting of some politician. The public's attention was caught more by the bank robberies that closely followed the pattern of the one I've described, and those too in the course of a fleeting curiosity, without any expressions of apprehension or outrage.

For the three of us it was a quiet time; a time of waiting to see how one event would inevitably lead to another, for there's a strict causal principle at work, men being either imitators and followers of trends or so envious that they're determined to do on a larger scale what someone else has done, especially when it's something they think they ought to have been the first to do. Such behaviour is precisely what we had anticipated; but what we had not anticipated was that there would be a rebound effect, that after a number of events it would be our turn to respond to some cause and find ourselves trapped by what, several steps earlier, we ourselves had begun, and, what's worse, without realising that we had become our own victims.

Much of the last paragraph is in vague language; alas, I'm much more acutely aware of that than you, my friend! I'm my own worst critic and know where my mind resorts to subterfuge, to graceful generalisations, when the truth is embarrassing to reveal. I say this now to lessen the burden on my conscience, to give myself the satisfaction that I've at least hinted at what I do not as yet want to say and, by giving the hint, to enjoy the illusion that the revelation has been made and that I've not faltered from my original purpose of presenting a strictly truthful narrative. Having said this, I'm acutely aware

150

too that the resolve not to evade a truth has led to a subtler evasion and the expression of a generalisation which does not even have the virtue of being graceful. But bear with me in my anguish: what I've not said, you've already guessed, since I've been at such cumbersome pains to say that I've not said it and which, in any case, I shall confess to fully when my mind is as strong as my convictions.

It was at this time, the months during which Capistrano, Amália and I waited for events to develop, that Rubirosa summoned me again, this time asking me to meet him in the restaurant of the Museum of Modern Art. He was there before me, sitting at a table in the patio, a glass in his hand and a half-empty bottle of beer beside him on the table. It was eleven in the morning, I had no desire for a beer and, since I'd only half an hour earlier finished a late breakfast, I had to decline coffee too, so that Rubirosa paid for his drink, rose and, touching my arm with the tips of his fingers, led me across the patio towards the pond with the water-lilies and the flamingoes at the front of the Museum.

'A rather nice place for a mid-morning stroll, don't you think?' he asked with a slight laugh.

I took a step away from him, for I felt a menace in the finger-tips at my sleeve, and said, 'You enjoy the effect of a mysterious rendezvous, don't you?'

'Not at all,' he said. 'I'm within walking distance from my office, it's more comfortable for you to be in the open air than in my stifling office, and I hope you share my delight in the water-lilies. They are, of course, bigger and more beautiful in their indigenous setting in the Amazon. The Victoria Regina species is famous throughout the world, not least in the country whose late queen's name it bears. Animals and plants, they're such a comfort to one's eyes, don't you think?'

'And the ocean too,' I said since he was going to play this game of irrelevance, casting a look across the space between the diagonal concrete columns on which the Museum stood.

'Yes,' Rubirosa said, 'for some people the ocean's massive blue is more impressive than the subtle variations of colour on a

151

plant. I have nothing against that.'

We walked past the water-lilies towards the fountain and past that, in a circular stroll, towards the water-front. A young couple sat on a bench, locked in an embrace.

'Yes, I know what's on your mind.' Rubirosa said, seeing me glance at the couple. 'The future of Brazil is enfolded in their arms.'

'Not merely that,' I said, trying not to be too bothered by Rubirosa's awful vulgarity. 'The present, too.'

'Indeed.'

'For why should we not demand a perfection from the present?'

'And who denies us that?' he asked.

'We ourselves, in the end,' I said, determined to give him no satisfaction. 'For we have an ingrained belief that the present is a time of sacrifice for some future cause and that pure ecstasy, which we're convinced is potentially there to be grasped but unfortunately can't be experienced now or in the next moment but surely will be in the not too distant future. We're born with a commitment to procrastination and, having a certain faith, continue to believe that all the forces in society, social and political, will conspire to allow us our moment of supreme fulfilment.'

And while I spoke, adding phrase to phrase in a tone both cumbersome and portentous, I thought that if evasive nonsense was what he was after then I'd give him a bellyful.

'Oh, you're very wise,' he said, perhaps intending an irony. 'Political forces, well, what about them? Do they prevent your happiness?'

I had no intention of allowing him to believe that his questioning was inevitably bound to lead to some revelation, and said, 'Not at all. As a matter of fact, since I have the knowledge that I myself am the cause of all the feelings within me, I'm therefore independent of the political context of my time. If I'm a slave, it's because I don't have the capacity to enjoy liberty and not because some external force has put me in fetters.'

We had walked across the garden at the back of the Museum

and reached the water-front, where a dark-skinned man in a torn straw-hat sat on a rock, fishing-rod in hand, staring at the ocean.

'Oh come, Gregório,' Rubirosa said, 'let's not beat about the bush.'

I looked at him with raised eyebrows; a trite gesture, I thought even as I affected it, but appropriate for that situation.

'Let me put it to you plainly,' he said, and I sensed that we were in the open at last. 'We're meeting here under the blue sky not out of any love I might have for games suitable to my profession but for the simple reason that we might say what we believe in without fear of walking into some trap.'

He paused. I said nothing, merely looked at the ocean.

'You know my position,' he said. 'Believe me, it's not pleasant for me to have to bring in a friend for an interrogation.'

If I was not already cautious, now I was doubly so: we had never been friends, acquaintances at best, but really only two people who had once, about a dozen years ago, sat in the same room and, leaving it, exchanged a few frivolous words in an elevator.

'I hope you appreciate my dilemma,' he continued. 'I'm under considerable pressure. There have been robberies. All I need to satisfy my superiors is to arrest people who can be shown to have been involved in a certain type of political debate. Proof is not necessary when circumstantial evidence can be made to possess so sinister a threat to society that it's enought to convict a man. Do you understand what I mean?'

'Sure I do, but how can I help you?'

'Why do you pretend to be so naîve? You know very well what I mean.'

'No, I don't,' I persisted.

'Suppose I were to arrest you, Capistrano and Amália? Do you think it will be too hard for me to make you confess your political philosophy?'

'You don't make any sense to me,' I said. 'I don't have the political philosphy you think I have.'

'The point is that you do have one and that would be enough.'

'You're making a mistake,' I said.

'The easiest way out for both of us', he said and paused, casting a look at the man with the fishing-rod, and then continued, ' – for both of us would be for you to give me some names.'

'As I said, you're making a mistake. You talk of acts of violence, I don't even know which ones. You've jumped to the conclusion that I have something to do with them, which is simply not true. How can I convince you that I know nothing of what has been happening?'

'You're going by the assumption that my seeing you at Capistrano's all those years ago is all the evidence I have. You're mistaken there, Gregório. I know a lot more. I have a record, for example, of the journey you made to Minas with Amália some months ago.'

'Yes, just as you have a record of my days in New York.'

'You can see it that way, if you like, but this is a lot more serious. I have the text of the speech you made in Mariana and I have a description of your meeting with Nabuco who, we all know, was sent on a mission to Cuba. You can't disentangle yourself from these facts.'

'I still say you're making a mistake.'

'That is easily said, but you can't deny any of the facts.'

'Since you're the witness of the charges that you yourself make, it would be impossible to deny anything that you raise to the status of a fact.'

'That may be, but you'd no doubt not need to make such a generalisation if you had witnesses who could deny such charges.'

'I could too, but what would they be worth against your word? Come on now, we're in Brazil! You know very well how these things work.'

'It's no use going round in circles,' he said. 'Believe me, I'm acting as your friend. Otherwise I'd simply have arrested you and won myself a promotion. Let us say that you can give me your answer in three days.'

That was his mistake. Or rather, for in these things so much depends on how one perceives a problem, whatever instinct prompted him to give us three days of grace prevented him from committing himself to an irrevocable mistake. As it was, after I'd returned to my apartment and described the meeting to Capistrano and Amália, Capistrano wasted no time in flying that very day to Brasília. Two days later Rubirosa received an order relieving him from his duties in Rio and transferring him to the sleepy old city of Fortaleza on the northern coast. In an objective way I enjoyed the cruel irony since it exemplified so well the turn events take in one's life: had Rubirosa had no scruples and felt no compunction to be lenient to people he considered his former friends, he would simply have arrested us; and his superiors, at least for the sake of form and not wishing to divulge the nature of our work, of which they themselves were fully aware, would have gone through the motions of promoting him, and had he been transferred it would have been either to Brasília or to São Paulo; instead, Rubirosa did the one thing his superiors were glad he did, for it saved them a great deal of embarrassment, but, not wishing to make him any the wiser and in order not to make either him or anyone else in the bureaucracy cognisant of an apparent contradiction, they were obliged to do what on the surface would appear to be the appropriately ruthless thing, to give the impression that Rubirosa had blundered, and so, in effect, demoted him by sending him to a remote city where he would have nothing to do. Thus everyone was convinced that Rubirosa had somehow failed in his duty and he himself, at first crestfallen by his demotion, began to console himself with the conviction that, in a society in which he was one of the secret police, he had been mistaken in not realising that there was a higher level of police, even more secret, which observed his own most secret actions, so that he ended up by praising the system which appeared to him to be extraordinarily meticulous in its vigilance and accepted his own humiliation because it so perfectly vindicated what he understood of police procedure. If what he understood was so clearly meaningful to him, it was because he saw only the expression of a vocabulary which made perfect sense to him; and since few people understand the world

155

outside the limited vocabulary they've learned with which to describe the objects, desires and apprehensions of their lives, they're rarely outraged by an unexpected experience provided it too is explicable in the same, familiar words. But while Rubirosa philosophically accepted his transfer to Fortaleza, he took with him an awareness of a failure which he associated with Capistrano and me and which he no doubt brooded over continuously, as I was to discover much later.

There was, however, a further irony in this episode. By eliminating Rubirosa's mistaken suspicions, the minister in Brasilia had appeared at first to be expressing his faith in us; but by the same act, almost as if the transference of Rubirosa had left a vacuum and someone else must have the thoughts that he ordinarily had, the minister began to have the same suspicions himself. And this is where I must clearly confess to what I've only vaguely hinted at so far: I was not a liberal, not a revolutionary; I had no sympathy with any labour movement or with any form of socialism; at the same time, neither was I a reactionary conservative, nor one enamoured by a military dictatorship even if, at the time, I believed it was the best interim solution for Brazil.

What, then, was I? I wish I could tell you in a few words, but I can't, for the simple reason that no label fitted me. All I can say is that I despised people who derived a complacent satisfaction from belonging to some exclusive camp or another. I know no more today what I was ten or twenty years ago than I did when I was most deeply involved in political action. My only concern was my country, and I did not care if what I did one day was what a conservative would applaud and what I did the next day won the approbation of a liberal. I have never believed in an exclusive ideology, and it astonishes me to think that there are people in this world who do so at this stage in human history: people who talk of class warfare ought to remember that we're in the last quarter, and not the first, of the twentieth century; and people who hold on to privilege ought to be reminded that the nineteenth century has long been dead. But the history of nations is also the history of lapses in memory, and people everywhere are born with the naïve belief that Hitler and Stalin on the one hand and Gandhi and Martin Luther King on the other are only names one has to memorise to pass a school exam. And, memorising the dates of the dead past, we forget to remember the date of the year in which we're actually living. Not only in our political consciousness but in so many other affairs that touch us; for example, in literature and music and painting, or in the running of a shop or a farm, the tradition is lost to us and what is new is consequently rendered meaningless.

Yes, my friend, I know that I'm again turning to generalisations and appear to be evading the particular facts of what I stood for at the time of Rubirosa's being rendered ineffectual. You have no doubt fixed a label on me: an agent of the government; and are wondering how to reconcile this suspicion with the bank robbery in Copacabana and my visit to Minas. And there you have a statement not about me but about yourself –but this is a matter of philosophical subtlety beyond the grasp of most mortals.

No, I was not an agent of the government and nor was I one of the revolutionaries. I had seen my father's land lost to a brother's treachery and ruined by a primitive form of Communism, headed by a barely literate peasant who had not the knowledge to understand that the most perfect Communism had existed in Brazil centuries before the Portuguese ever arrived there. I had also heard the empty rhetoric of young men and women who presumed themselves to be the intellectuals of the country when all they did was to repeat ideas which had been current some time earlier in Europe and in the United States. I understood early in my life that if there is danger to a society it comes invariably from people who're convinced of the superiority of their ideas or from people, like Formigueiro, who consider an existing order so tyrannical that they cannot rest until they have replaced it with their own tyranny. I suppose there is a third type, equally destructive in the end, to which I belonged, people who see it as their duty to prevent the other two from asserting themselves; I had, I hope, the common sense to believe that not one of the three types was better than the other two, but I did believe that if one had a strong conviction then that had to be the point of view which one was obliged to

157

express and even, if the situation was an extreme one, to fight for. In the end, one expressed a prejudice; all one can hope for is that one's own prejudice will do the least harm.

Capistrano said one day, when we had been listening to some records of Brazilian music, something new by Chico Buarque which had moved us quite profoundly, 'There you have an expression of a culture which is specifically Brazilian. It has no meaning to people outside Brazil. To North America and Europe, where they've made an art of reducing all foreign phenomena to neat, little, encapsulated versions, the common belief being that even Homer can, in the end, be reduced to ten pages in the *Reader's Digest,* this music is reduced to two songs by Carmen Miranda and in the inclusion in ballroom-dancing classes of the cha-cha-cha. They understand nothing of the *form*, do not at all comprehend that this is a music which comes from our soul. Now, consider the opposite of this idea. There are elements in North America and in Europe which are the product of the peculiarity of their own culture, whether they are rock music or their political institutions. And these express themselves in forms which are alien to us, their music does not sing in our souls as the samba does. And yet there are Brazilians who, for some reason, some unfounded conviction that what is foreign is somehow superior, or who merely have the desire to be different and to express that difference in some snobbery, are convinced that their lives are incomplete if they can't play the Beatles on their expensive, imported stereo sets, and if they can't also suffer the political anguish of a Hungary or a Czechoslovakia. Modern societies are the victims of mimicry. If the rapidity of modern communications conveys the news from Washington or Moscow to a small village in South America in a matter of minutes, it also ensures that every news item will be surrounded by an aura of such urgency that it would seem natural that it be conveyed only in the briefest phrase, which brevity ends by creating the reverse effect, reducing everything to triviality. We know of everything that's happening in the world and yet remain in near-total ignorance, but at the same time we are entirely convinced that we possess a complete knowledge. What is the result? It's too easy for too many of us to believe that we could make a better world here, it's too easy to think that we know what we're doing. We forget to listen to the music in our souls, we're so anxious to impress our friends with our collection of the Beatles. At the same time we're obliged to suffer the further humiliation of having foreigners, who see us in terms of crude caricature, find us backward or inadequate or failing in some high principles if our policitcal institutions don't mimic theirs or if our culture rejects their influence; for people only approve of you if you speak their language at their level of competency. But consider this: if people in their own culture have not advanced beyond the music of Ives or Elgar or Ravel or Mahler, and cannot hear the new music of their own country with any comprehension, what can they understand when they see us dancing to Chico Buarque?'

With Rubirosa removed from Rio we ought to have felt at our ease, especially as the minister in Brasília, after Capistrano's conference with him, seemed to give the impression that he valued our work more than he did Rubirosa's. But the very speed with which he acquiesced in Capistrano's analysis of the situation gave us cause for concern: could not the minister have in mind thoughts which were precisely the reverse of those which he appeared to profess, and his removal of Rubirosa be only an act calculated to obscure his own doubts? He knew, of course, that he could not observe us more freely than by giving us the impression that we had him entirely in our confidence. We became uneasily aware of a subtle trickery, for the world, in our minds, had become inverted since we ourselves had played too long at being what we were not. This peculiar psychology now worked in a new direction: knowing that the minister probably had doubts about us, we instinctively began to act in a way which would confirm his doubts. We who had despised revolutionary talk as irrelevant and fraudulent rhetoric, we who had acted to provoke revolutionaries so that they would come out of their academies and cells into the open, we, now that they had begun to take to the streets and to commit themselves to action, began to involve ourselves in the same

159

sort of actions almost as if we too had become convinced that the dictatorship had to be replaced by a people's democracy. And the irony of this twist in our behaviour, to which we had been led by no ideological consideration but only by the sheer force of cause and effect, whose persuasiveness within one's own blood is both insidious and irresistible, was that the minister, receiving information of everything we did, believed that we had not defected but were serving the national cause with the greatest fervour: the more liberal our stance, the more derisive we were of the dictatorship, the more he was convinced that we were only pretending in order to lure the true revolutionaries and thus only doing our duty. But so remarkable is life – with the confusing commitments that it involves one in, never allowing one to remain trapped in some pigeon-hole but always insisting on the experimentation of some novelty, always infusing one with the fruitful spirit of contradiction, for otherwise existence would be abominably boring – the more we adumbrated the work of the revolutionaries and shared their convictions, the more we began to see the futile emptiness of their revolt and the utter irrelevance of their ideas to contemporary Brazil, the closer we were taken, on a nice rebound of irony, back to what the minister believed we truly represented.

Meanwhile, Avestruz had returned from Havana and flamboyantly called for an armed struggle as if Brazil were no larger than an island in the Caribbean and revolution was a trivial matter of smuggling guns into a few hamlets. Avestruz was one of those young men of whom nearly every nation had a good number in the late 1960s, people anxious to prove their intellectual credentials by wearing army fatigues and a beret, having long hair and beards, and if they expressed ideas they were always someone else's, and whether they were from Berkeley, California, or from São Paulo or from Stockholm or from Paris, they all had the same phrases with which to applaud the Viet-Cong and to condemn the United States, and to see in the rest of the world, as in Brazil, examples of what they took those symbols, the Viet-Cong and the United States' government, to stand for, the people's struggle and imperialism, but none of them ever paused to examine the precise issues or to

160

note that the issues varied from country to country even if the same clear-cut confrontation could be seen in any one of them (and, if I may add an irrelevant note which, however, is not inappropriate to the understanding of political actions, the most objectionable people in the world have to be the Swedes who, in recent years, entirely bored by their own wearisome welfare state, have taken to flaunting a superior moral posture: it is easy, I suppose, to profess to have a conscience when all natural instinct has been sucked out of the body by the over-solicitous state).

In short, the people who insist on being recognised as intellectuals with advanced ideas are usually, in every society, imbeciles whose loftiest statement is rarely more than a vigorously passionate declamation – the clenched fist hammering the air and the voice charged with emotion – of ideas which have been plagiarised. Such a one was Avestruz, who longed to be a folk-hero but who did not have wit enough to observe that the people already had one in a soccer player.

In 1969, when our actions were ambiguous and were interpreted by the government as loyal and by Avestruz and his camp as revolutionary, Avestruz came to see us in Rio. Various essays by his people into urban-guerrilla warfare, several of them provoked by our early actions, had led to hundreds of young men and women being arrested and Avestruz, assuming that we must have similar forces and must be suffering from depleted numbers too, came with some idea of joining our faction in order to break into two principal jails in São Paulo and Rio to free our people. It was, of course, a ridiculous proposition and we spent the whole evening trying to persuade him of the certainty of failure. He returned the next day and again began talking of the necessity of liberating his people, as he put it, using some grand phrase like 'owing them the sacrifice of my own life'.

It was then that Capistrano said, 'Avestruz, I've been thinking of your friends who're prisoners. I've also been thinking of the history of old Europe. In the old days, prisoners were worth so much money or so much land. If you wanted your men back, you paid gold or ceded a part of your territory. There was a sound commercial basis to warfare, no one believed in causes.'

'Well, obviously you don't intend that I try to buy out our despicable fascist government,' Avestruz said in jargon typical of him.

'No,' Capistrano said, maintaing his restraint, for he always abhorred an abuse of language, 'but money or land are not the only things for which to exchange prisoners.'

'What else is there?' Avestruz asked eagerly.

'In the old wars,' Capistrano said, 'prisoners were exchanged for prisoners.'

'But . . . .'

'Yes,' said Capistrano, 'you don't have any prisoners. But you could get some, could you not? Instead of trying to storm a prison with twenty men, could you not capture a general or a minister with four or five men?'

Avestruz pondered this idea with the amazement of one who's learned for the first time the incredible fact that the earth is round.

Capistrano went on: 'I should think the life of one general is worth more to the government than a dozen or twenty of your men.'

'On the other hand,' Amália said, 'the government might think a general expendable, for they can always promote someone to take his place. You'll need to make sure you go after a really important one.'

Now this is the kind of conversation in which an idea occurs to one by some invisible thrust simply because that is the direction in which the conversation is inevitably leading, each new suggestion and counter-suggestion gradually generating the one idea which is the perfect embodiment of the communal thought of a group of people. So that, as this dialogue proceeded, I found myself saying, 'If you want a hostage, your best bet would be the American Ambassador. If you kidnapped a Brazilian general or a minister or anyone but the president himself, the government would hush it up, would try to get back its man at the risk of having him murdered, and if he were to be killed it would be passed off as some accident, no one would know, and you wouldn't get away with it. What is more, no one

162

outside Brazil would hear of it or, if they did, they wouldn't care, for they'd think of it as one more example of the Latin temperament which they all assume to be unpredicatable and something of a joke. Whereas if you had the American Ambassador, the news would be broadcast within minutes on all the radio stations of the world, the American President would phone the Brazilian President, the U.S. Secretary of State would be on a plane to Brasília, and *Time* magazine would do a cover story. With all that publicity the Brazilian government would give you anything, for it would rather be applauded for having obtained the release of the American Ambassador than suffer the displeasure of the mighty Americans for the sake of keeping a hundred long-haired youths in prison.'

I was astonished at what I said even as I was saying it, for I had not given it prior thought, the words had simply flowed out, formulating, explaining and giving weight to the idea, all spontaneously as if I had been only a mouthpiece for someone else's prepared speech.

Amália took it up from there and said, 'And consider, too, you'd be a hero for capturing the American Ambassador, the Brazilian government will be a hero for winning his release, the Ambassador will be a hero for having survived his ordeal, and your friends will be heroes for having won their liberty. Everyone will have something to be pleased about.'

Avestruz was impressed and, with his friends, worked on the idea for three months. What occurred is history of which I need record only the barest details. The United States' Ambassador was kidnapped in September 1969. Avestruz got his friends flown out of Brazil but two months later was himself hunted down by the police and shot to death.

It set a pattern for future violence. More ambassadors were kidnapped, more prisoners released, and more of the self-styled leaders were hunted down and killed. By the end of 1970, if there was an armed struggle it was from the government which, compelled by the blind principle of cause and effect, had adopted the same cruel procedures which its opponents had earlier plotted against it, thus proving once again that all action is influenced in increasingly strong measures by what it is

163

reacting against.

A lot else happened by the end of 1970. President Costa e Silva, who had been inaugurated soon after that first bank robbery in Copacabana in 1967, had been disabled by a stroke and replaced by Garrastazú Médici, the third president to be hand-picked by the military from among its generals. The changes which follow in an administration on the coming of a new head of state had the crucial effect on us of removing our contacts in Brasília: while the new officials were aware of our existence in the underground they had no notion of what kind of rôle we were playing there and so lumped us with the common rabble of revolutionaries. During the six years of military dictatorship the economy had become stabilised and Brazil had begun to emerge as a world power; such success, proving to the people that the government was dedicated to their progress, made the dictatorship more determined than ever to eradicate the last revolutionary.

In August 1970 Capistrano was visited in the small apartment he had taken in Ipanema by an officer in the military police, one Mauro Arismendi, whom he had known for several years and who had obliged Capistrano on a few occasions and had, in return, enjoyed receiving the gift of a litre bottle of Scotch every Christmas. It was one of those understandings one arrives at with men of vast authority on a score of petty matters, such as traffic violations, which preserves a goodwill between citizens and officers of the law and keeps one pleasantly immune from the minor legal harassments which are of no consequence to one's larger liberty but which, nevertheless, can make life extremely tedious.

Arismendi arrived unexpectedly, but it was not the first time he had done so, for he would come every three or four months, exchange trivialities and depart after having been served a glass of Scotch. On this afternoon, while sipping his whisky, Arismendi said, 'Capistrano, I have a favour to ask of you.'

He paused a moment so that Capistrano would remember the recent favour Arismendi had done for him, and then continued: 'It is my wife's birthday and I have a great surprise for her. The only problem is how to get the surpise to my house. It's a new Alfa Romeo I bought from the dealer in the *praça* here and I was wondering whether you would do me the favour of driving it out to the house for me. That is, if you're not too busy.'

'An Alfa Romeo?' Capistrano said with some astonishment.

'I know it sounds extravagant,' Arismendi said, 'but in my position, you know how it is. The dealer owed me a favour. Of course, it's absurd to ask you to drive the car out for me, I know you're such a busy man, but I didn't know whom to ask. You see, I want someone reliable to drive a new car like an Alfa. It's not far, it'll only take half an hour.'

Capistrano could never understand later why he thought nothing of it, he who had always been quick to suspect sinister motives, especially when dealing with a police officer. And when he wrote to me in detail, describing the way Arismendi had behaved and talked, it was clear even to me that this was an occasion for caution. But I had the benefit of hindsight whereas Capistrano, agreeing to do Arismendi the trivial favour that he asked, failed to exercise his usual prescience. The two took the elevator to the basement where Arismendi had parked his Volkswagen, drove to the car dealer round the corner and took delivery of a brand-new, black Alfa Romeo with a tan interior.

Capistrano drove out in the new car, enjoying its quiet airconditioning and its smooth drive, following Arismendi along the avenue beside Leblon beach towards the new housing development in the Barra, thinking to himself that a police officer with a mediocre salary was doing all right for himself when he could afford a new house for his family and a new Alfa Romeo as a birthday present for his wife. At the end of Leblon, where the road curved up to Avenida Niemeyer and ran high above the ocean, Arismendi speeded up and Capistrano, pressing on the accelerator too, enjoyed the surge of speed afforded by the quiet power of the car – though he wondered to himself, in passing, whether he should be taking a new engine to such high revs. There was a steady stream of traffic from the opposite direction, but during one slight break in it Capistrano, who had been concentrating on keeping up with Arismendi and not bothering to look into his rear-view mirror, was suddenly overtaken by a small, yellow Puma which shot past him and braked hard behind Arismendi's car and kept hard on his tail, hoping for another opportunity to overtake.

Arismendi, himself overtaking three cars ahead of him, found a stretch of open road where he speeded away, leaving the Puma now stuck behind the three cars and Capistrano, much to his frustration, stuck behind the Puma with the long line of oncoming traffic offering him no early hope of catching up with Arismendi. He imagined Arismendi would slow down, for otherwise Capistrano would not know where to deliver the Alfa Romeo. The road turned right, away from the ocean, towards the Hotel Nacional, which seemed to be the destination of the three cars in front of the Puma, whereupon the Puma, finding a stretch of free road, shot away in a burst of speed and Capistrano attempted to do likewise. At this point the road was wide and had become, for a short distance, a one-way system. Capistrano raced into a bend, catching up with the Puma, and accelerated out, nose to tail, into a short, straight stretch. It was here that a police car suddenly appeared on Capistrano's left and, when he slowed down, another behind him. He was obliged to stop.

Of course, he did not have the car's papers and his explanation that he was driving the car for his friend from the military police was laughed at scornfully as being too ridiculously implausible a story. He realised it was no use trying to convince the four policemen and, thinking that Arismendi would get him out of trouble, asked them to go ahead and fine him for speeding. But they were not interested in so mundane a charge, especially when he seemed so blasé about being caught. The worst that could happen, thought Capistrano, was that they would arrest him on suspicion of stealing the car and Arismendi, wondering in the next fifteen minutes what had happened to his wife's present, would come looking and, being a police officer, would no doubt straighten out this awkward matter very quickly. There was no problem: only the irritation of having become involved in an ugly situation.

But the four policement were searching the car. Capistrano,

expecting Arismendi to return at any moment, talked with a certain bravado, using a few earthy expressions, for he was convinced that the policemen would look foolish as soon as Arismendi turned up. His casual and nearly impolite manner only made the policemen suspect him of putting on a brave front. They continued to search the car.

Five minutes later, when nothing had been discovered, one of the policemen took out a knife, slashed the upholstery of the rear seat into ribbons and called to his colleagues just when Capistrano, horrified at seeing the vinyl being ripped, was shouting abuse at him. But then Capistrano suddenly froze and his mouth, which was in the middle of a vile phrase, remained open with the realisation of a greater horror. There were six automatic revolvers concealed among the springs and the foam-rubber of the rear seat.

I had no way of telling what had become of Capistrano when, several days after his disappearance, Amália and I began to be apprehensive that in the current atmosphere of Brazil there could be only one explanation. And how tragic it was, I thought, that Brazil, which needed so desperately the support of its intelligent and commonsensical people, should be so caught up in the malice generated by years of selfish and thoughtless politics that it had reached a stage where it was eliminating those very people who could contribute most to its future. In order not to be caught in the malice ourselves, we made enquiries after Capistrano in indirect ways, using friends whose innocence in all political matters was impeccable. We came up with nothing and began to live in fear ourselves. I would not let Amália go out alone and if I went out by myself I phoned her every half an hour to tell her where I was. We could have attempted to leave the country or put ourselves in a state of readiness to leave at the shortest notice, but I did not want to do so, partly because I believed that we had done nothing wrong and that by attempting to flee we would be offering proof of some guilt, and partly because I did not wish to abandon Capistrano.

Once again, circumstances not of my choosing pushed me

into a rôle which I had never had any intention of playing. Capistrano stood in my mind as the embodiment of clear-headed, down-to-earth, commonsensical wisdom and everything that he said or did was calculated to apply a principled philosophy to those affairs of the country which touched common existence, and he despised especially that which was bogus or hypocritical in political life. And like many a wise man before him, he who showed mankind how its soul could be free was himself rewarded by having his own body imprisoned. I feared worse, for I saw at this time many visiting professors and journalists from North America and from Europe who, in one manner or another, possessed by the pure idea of Brazil, that country of the mind where the most perfect beauty is within human reach, that dream which had driven so many millions to abandon the Old World and search for the purer springs of existence, the very idea which, so abstract and so seemingly inaccessible, saddened the soul and filled it with anguish, and yet also filled it with the tantalising hope that it was there, only barely out of reach, but accessible, in a vast land called Brazil – these men who came to Rio and São Paulo in 1970 came with sorrow in their hearts, for they had received information which had been denied us in Brazil.

That thousands of students and radicals had been arrested since 1967 was no news to me; but after Capistrano's arrest the new contradiction within me was that, while I had been instrumental, however indirectly, in the arrests of some of the radicals, now I deplored all suspension of human liberty. I had suppressed the indignation I ought to have felt at the mass imprisonments, becoming, like everyone else, a hypocrite to myself, professing certain ideals but complacently suspending them when they concerned people whose ideas I did not approve. But now, hearing from my foreign acquaintances that imprisonments were not all, that the secret police, having acquired enormous power in a barbaric attempt to ingratiate itself with the dictatorship, perpetrated forms of torture and cruelty which, but for Nazi Germany, would probably have been unprecedented in human history – now I began to believe that what I had thought to be clear was confused and that, unknown to me, I had become involved in an evil.

Of course, there's always an element of exaggeration in accusations for which there is no evidence readily available to the naked human eye, and while I had no reason to disbelieve my foreign informers I also had no reason to believe every disgusting detail that they had to narrate. I had not forgotten that first meeting with Rubirosa when he had made me witness the four arrested men being stripped in a bare room and had hinted at forms of torture to make them confess; and I knew the Brazilian character which produced such a unique phenomenon as the notorious death squads in São Paulo where a number of policemen took it upon themselves to eliminate criminals, professing a perverted sense of loyalty when all they were doing was appointing themselves jury, judge and executioner, pretending to be dedicated public servants when they were expressing only a deep-rooted envy of the criminal. I knew all this; perhaps I knew too much, was aware of too much. For I knew also of the other capacity of the Brazilian character, the warmth of his heart, his natural ebullience, his inclination to make a joke of everything, for the sun shines on our land, the flowers grow, and really there's no need for us ever to feel any resentment against another; and perhaps it is significant that whenever troubles have come to our country their root has been in some political or economic thinking which was spawned in the grey climates of Europe, whether it be the socialism of our radicals or the fascist response to them of our rulers: these are modes of behaviour that have been learned from foreign copies. Please don't misunderstand me. I'm not trying to exonerate anyone or blame ayone, for the truth has to be that we're victims of our own time and that the communications which prompt a young man at a college in São Paulo to behave like the young man at the Sorbonne whom he reads about in a magazine also prompt the minister of economics in Brasília to think in terms of the graphs depicting industrial growth which he sees in the *Wall Street Journal* flown to him daily from the United States, and no doubt pictures of our lovely girls in their scanty bikinis on Ipanema beach are the inspiration for girls on beaches on Long Island, etc. My point is that, in the race to excel through

169

imitation, in the obsessiveness to copy those models which have the aura of success, what Brazil and a hundred other countries are doing is to suppress elements of their native character. You can see it in Japan as much as in dear old England and in that country which belongs to the hearts of all aesthetes, France. Conversely, those people who try to suppress incursions into their native character end up by adopting quaint mannerisms and committing themselves to the perpetuation of archaisms: folk dances on the stage in Mexico City are no more going to preserve an aspect of Mexican culture long dead than the suppression by the French government of English expressions is going to restore a former purity to the French language. Nothing any more is simply a matter of a nationality or a culture and we have reached a stage where we can no longer preserve this folk tradition or that dialect, for at best that is only a gesture which wins the applause of a small, polite audience which will never itself think of adopting that tradition or that dialect for fear of being laughed at by the neighbours. No, when I talk of foreign influence as a negative force, I do not mean it in the narrow sense of a shopkeeper who blames his falling business on the high level of imports: what I mean is that each culture has its own symbols and when these symbols become blurred or corrupted by the infusion of signs which belong to an alien order of thought, then that original culture, because it begins to lose its identity, begins to feel anarchist pressures in its political structure: its own tribal sense fails it and, giving itself over to mimicry, its own traditions are lost to it, and its rituals, which had their source in the instincts of the race, are reduced merely to a show enacted to an audience of foreign tourists by a troupe of actors subsidised by the state.

I have meandered into these convoluted ideas because my meetings with the foreign professors and journalists at the time of Capistrano's disappearance engendered many of them, for unable to discover any information about him by using the resources available to me, I attempted to see if pure reasoning could not lead me to the truth. It gave me propositions to ponder, neat generalisations whose formulation so pleased the intellect which craved for balanced phrases that it took the form for substance and equated linguistic beauty with truth, but my reasoning led me to no truth about Capistrano. My conviction grew daily that the police took Capistrano, Amália and me for radicals, that he had been trapped in some way and that our turn would soon come. And thus the actions of the very government which I had tried to help compelled me to become what I had never intended to be, a subversive, just as an honest man finding a bag of money outside his front door takes it to the police station, only to find himself accused of having stolen it, and becomes so embittered by the failure of justice to see a simple truth that he ends by losing his honesty.

Some two months after Capistrano's disappearance, when we still did not know what had happened to him, and, for all we knew, he might have gone out for a swim on Ipanema beach and been dragged out by a current – though, of course, this had to be a ridiculously remote possibility, for it was evident that only one thing could happen to a man of Capistrano's persuasions in the political climate that then prevailed in Brazil – when two months of discreet investigation had proved nothing, Amália said to me one day that she was flying out to a remote part of Mato Grosso, adding, 'I believe I might have located Capistrano.'

'Amália, what have you been doing?' I was horrified to realise that she had been making enquiries by herself and, in the process, risking her own life: one did not, at that time, discover that a friend or a member of one's family had been sent to the distant jail in Mato Grosso without having the police begin to suspect one too.

'Trying to find out', she said, 'what's become of Capistrano.'

'But do you realise the danger you've put yourself in?'

'We're in this together,' she said.

'But not to die.'

'That has to be the ultimate risk.'

'I know, but that doesn't mean we should throw caution to the winds.'

'Capistrano is very probably suffering,' she said softly, a pained look on her face. 'How can you talk of caution?' she

171

added with a sudden flaring of bitterness.

'Because it would not serve Capistrano, or the principles he stood for, if we were to be caught too, and made to suffer in the same way.'

'I don't know whether that's common sense or cowardice.'

'Listen, Amália, I have no intention of dying because some bungling police officer or bureaucrat takes it into his head that I'm a traitor of some sort, because I am not. Everything that you and I and Capistrano have done has been for the good of the country and I don't intend to suffer if some idiot has misunderstood us. That is why this is a period of caution, we simply have to wait until someone in the government realises that we're fighting for the same cause.'

'All right, why don't *you* go to Mato Grasso, then? Why don't you find out for yourself what has become of your great friend?'

'All right, I will,' I said, finding myself committed to an action that I had not desired for myself, but seeing in that moment that my going would at least save Amália from becoming involved in an ugly situation. The very thought of Mato Grosso, out in the western wilderness of Brazil, was enough to fill one with the worst forebodings of what might happen to a beautiful young woman visiting a jail run by brutal men. I suspect too that I was unconsciously jealous of Amália's active initiative while I myself tended to be ruled by the laws of inertia; and now, having a line of investigation to pursue, I probably longed to assume the active rôle myself. It could also have been that there was a different sort of jealousy buried within me.

The next day I flew out to Cuiabá, a long, boring flight of seven hours in an old plane, with three stops on the way, and reached the jail a day later after a series of rides in a taxi, two different buses and a spluttering old motor-cycle driven by a youth who twice lost his way. A letter with an official seal, which Amália had succeeded in procuring from the relevant ministry, obtained me an entry. I was still not certain that I would find Capistrano at the jail and so was obliged to talk ambiguously and vaguely but with the confidence of one who was supposed to be an authorised agent of the government

172

come to interrogate a certain prisoner, and gave the impression that if I knew Capistrano was here it was because I, as a member of the secret police, had been instrumental in sending him here.

He was there. I recognised only his eyes. His body had shrivelled, his face hollowed and wrinkled, his arms were thin as sticks. Whatever had happened to him in the last two months had taken his voice away. But he extended a shaking, bony hand to me and I sat there for twenty minutes, holding his hand and looking into his eyes, learning of all his suffering from the blood that weakly throbbed at his wrist and from the deep sadness in his eyes. I talked to him, spoke what words came to my mind, having to keep up a pretense that I was an officer on official business, for a guard was within earshot. Then, calling to the guard to fetch me a glass of water, I embraced my friend, clasped his fragile body, kissed his hollow cheek and wrinkled forehead, and left.

Two days later I returned to Rio and had another shock Amália had gone. She had left a note in which she briefly mentioned that she had run into a radical friend from the old days and that he had set up a company in São Paulo for exporting leather goods to Europe but that it was only a front to get himself and his friends out of the country without anyone being suspicious. She was sorry this had happened while I was away, but she had begun to fear for her life, especially after what I'd said of not taking the sort of risk which she had taken to discover the whereabouts of Capistrano. But the opportunity, a golden one, had turned up so suddenly. She had waited till the last possible moment. She knew I'd approve of what she'd done. Coming hard on the violent emotions which were still raging within me after seeing Capistrano, I don't know what I thought. I followed her last instruction and tore up the letter.

As a matter of fact, once I'd overcome the shock and recovered my rationality, I believed that Amália's sudden going away to Europe was not really a surprise; and nor did I think that it was the kind of action she'd succumbed to on the spur of the moment during three days of my absence when, and only when, chance provided her with what she called her golden opportunity. I had no evidence, but I was convinced that she had plotted her escape for some time and, because I had not been told a word of it, it was an escape not only from Brazil but also from me. There was something in her character that, much as she loved me and seemed devoted entirely to me, prompted her to go away from me, as she had done that time before I went to study in New York. There was a part of her which acted as a subversive to her own best desires. Agreed that there was some danger to her person if she stayed on in Brazil; but I could not believe that she'd want to abandon me so easily or in such ambiguous circumstances: there could be no doubt that she had been planning an escape, for there was a suppressed wildness within her which could not long be tamed by a love, however strong. Normally quiet and timid, she was given to eruptions.

But where did she leave me? Humiliated and alone, disenchanted and embittered: for she had left me when my soul had already been soured by seeing Capistrano withered to a plant that had tried to grow in the drought-stricken north-east. Sorrow does not allow one to rest comfortably against the pillow, it rages in the blood and, whispering soliloquies of despair in the brain, its insomniac mumblings plot subtle treason against the very elements so that the soul may discover an eloquence to match the rain and the thunder, and the body offer the naked, burning arrogance of its sinews to the hurricane. We allow ourselves to be overtaken by tragedy when the mundane circumstances of our existence have left us denuded of common hopes and allow our anti-self to assert his complacent evil over our actions, for the virtuous choices are snatched away from us and we become what we never wanted to be.

I flew to São Paulo and met the activists of the underground, embracing them as my brothers when three months earlier I considered them misguided idealists who had no conception that their idealism was not so much a chimera as an erroneous attempt to impose an alien ideology on Brazil, like trying to grow mango-trees in Canada. They were not without their own sorrows which generated in them a craving for some brutal

174

action, for, after the kidnapping of the U.S. Ambassador, the government, determined to show its strength and believing that that strength was to be measured by the numbers it could imprison, had become callous and indiscriminate and had arrested dozens of young men and women many of whom had uttered no protest of any kind; but in 1970 the expression of even an innocuous desire to wear one's hair differently was tantamount to political protest. It was a time of over-reaction on both sides, it was a time when humour and common sense were in short supply, it was a time of intense suspicion.

My one obsession now was to try and save Capistrano, who was as innocent as the first Indian to have had a bullet shot through his body by a pioneering Portuguese in the sixteenth century. Fortunately, the revolutionaries in São Paulo knew nothing of my ambiguous past and thought of me only as a radical brother, which painful label I was prepared to suffer provided I could work for my own private cause.

Everyone I talked to had only one thing to say: 'We need more money and more arms.'

'We have a duty', I said, and this was my repetitive theme, 'to our brothers and sisters in jails.'

How I wished that I could have spoken this alien jargon to the government, for the words 'brothers and sisters', which had such a false ring in the mouths of the revolutionaries who, even in their direst anguish (and one had to be inhuman not to sympathise) repeated the ridiculous inanities which they'd picked up from abroad, and which, when spoken in a natural language, were words of truth and beauty which came from a pure heart – how I wished that the president and his ministers could be made to understand that these people were truly their brothers and sisters. It was too late, I felt, having only Capistrano's frail and withered body in my imagination, too late for a reappraisal and an accommodation, too late for tragic processes to be reversed.

I convinced the Paulistas that saving our brothers and sisters from jail had to be our priority but was obliged to concede to their demand for money, and we hit upon the one action which could possibly guarantee both. In a bold stroke of repetition, it was decided to kidnap another ambassador; perhaps it was not a bold stroke at all, only a poverty of imagination, but it did occur to me that it was the one thing that could not be expected to happen again and therefore it was worth trying. Obviously, it could not be the American Ambassador again and the Asian and African ambassadors would not have the same impact as one from Europe. The choice almost inevitably fell on the Swiss Ambassador. Again, the facts are recorded by history: the Swiss Ambassador was kidnapped in December 1970, and later released once seventy prisoners had been put on a plane for a foreign destination. Three weeks later I received a picture-postcard of the cathedral in Mexico City on which some American tourist had apparently been persuaded to write the English words, 'Wish you were here,' and I knew that Capistrano was safe.

I had received no word, however, from Amália, although it was three months since she had left for Europe. It was some time later that I received a detailed letter from Capistrano in which he described how he had been trapped by Arismendi; but when I received that letter I was already myself a fugitive.

After the kidnapping of the Swiss Ambassador one of the important leaders of the urban guerrilla movement was trapped and shot to death by the police, and a number of other revolutionaries were imprisoned. I have no evidence but I presume that some of the latter, under the harsh circumstances of torture, revealed my name as one of their leaders, which, of course, was a false assumption on their part. At the same time some other revolutionaries in São Paulo who had escaped the latest raids had somehow hit upon the idea that I was not one of them and, in the bitterness of seeing their own leader killed by the police, looked for an informer and, ignoring the fact that the informer had to be one of their own group who had been captured and tortured and thus forced to reveal the leader's name, they had concluded that I had been an agent in their midst. Consequently I found myself in the rôle of being wanted as a public enemy by the government and as a personal enemy by the revolutionaries when in fact I was enemy of neither and friend to both. Even in the hour of my extreme trouble I had the objectivity to observe that this doubly negative situation perfectly symbolised my life: I was obliged to play a part that I had not intended and was presumed by others to be what I never was.

It was hot in Rio and I had driven away to Petrópolis and taken a room in a modest hotel where no one was likely to know me, spending four days there, idly walking the streets in the evenings, drifting with the crowd or sitting in a square and watching people come and go as if they were figures in some dream, or hearing a fountain splash in a disciplined aimlessness. In cool shades, among green shadows, in that world in the mountains which so easily dissolves into moist mists, inducing one to believe that one's own spirit has been refined to ether, a thing that shivers for a moment like a drop of mercury, I felt as if all life had been transformed to a liquescent shimmering and what I witnessed was a continuous evaporation. I shivered, sitting on a park bench, my bare arms which had come out in a sweat being touched by a gust of cool breeze. I awoke as from a vision which, in the moment of its dissolving, still held me entranced with its promise of a world without feeling, but then the consciousness of the hard bench and the voices in the square took it away altogether. Who would believe this, I wondered, rising and walking to the hotel, resolving that I must return to Rio, to the reality of events over which I had no control, to the harsh loneliness of my days – who would believe that I, who appeared to belong to a world of action, actually understood reality to be without substance, merely the exhaling of a breath in a void of whirling winds?

I drove down the mountains to Rio the next morning, trying at last to confront the options before me of which I had suppressed all thought during the four days in Petrópolis. I could attempt to go abroad, join the many Brazilian exiles who now lived in Paris or London or Mexico City. There would be difficulties – I would certainly be denied an exit visa if I applied for one in my own name – but it would not be impossible. But there was a part of me that resisted, even abhorred, the idea of a foreign exile, for it would solve nothing, only put my body on ice, suspend my existence until some later date when it could be resumed. A second option was to commit myself entirely to the underground movement, become what I had originally set out to destroy; I reviewed the reasons why I should do so: the treatment of Capistrano, the vicious arrogance of the secret police – they did not, however, strike me as sufficiently compelling reasons now that Capistrano was safe, and I realised that my strongest reason was a desire to put myself in a situation of violent extremity, as if life could only have meaning if one intensified the probability of losing it. There was a third option. I could go to the government and confess or strike some bargain with it.

The more I thought of these options, the more objections I found to each one of them. Perhaps that amounted to no more than the realisation that we cannot choose our future for ourselves, and when we think we have choices we become so involved in a rational speculation of the pros and cons, the ifs and the buts, that we're still lost in deliberation when some unexpected event takes place and mocks our philosophy of self-determination.

I arrived in Rio having decided nothing but feeling a little more relaxed than when I had left it. The porter, an amiable, middle-aged man named Mário who spent much of his time washing cars in the basement car-park, greeted me by the entrance to the building. Inside, waiting for the elevator, I thought that one thing I ought to do soon was to leave my apartment and change to an obscure address if I were to continue to live in Rio. The elevator came down, its door slid smoothly open and out stepped Virgílio Távora, the accountant whom I employed to collect the rent from my other apartment and to pay the taxes on my properties. Before I could express my surprise at seeing him there, he looked at me with perfect astonishment and said, 'I don't believe it, I thought you were in your apartment!'

'What makes you think that?' I asked in a quiet voice, already apprehensive that something was wrong and, remembering how easily Capistrano had walked into a trap, I became more alert than ever.

'Why, I was there just now. I rang the bell and after some time it was opened by a beautiful woman with a dressing-gown loosely wrapped around her and her hair slightly dishevelled. Well, I immediately apologised when she said you weren't home and retreated to the elevator. You see, she said it in such a way I assumed you must have been. . . . well, in bed with her.'

'Didn't you say anything else?'

'No, of course not. I thought I understood the situation, the delicacy of it.'

'Virgílio, where's your car?'

'Out on the sidewalk.'

'All right, listen to me carefully. Go out as if nothing has happened, walk quietly to your car and drive round the corner and stop in front of the pharmacy there. I'll probably get there before you if you have to stop at the traffic-lights but otherwise I won't be more than two minutes.'

He walked out of the building. I took the elevator down to the basement car-park, ran up the ramp the exit of which, being at the corner of the building, allowed me the opportunity to leave the building unobserved, in case someone were watching from my apartment, and to run round to the side-street, where I reached the pharmacy a second earlier than Virgílio and jumped into his yellow Volkswagen when he had scarcely stopped.

'Drive to your apartment,' I said.

He turned right at Avenida N.S. de Copacabana where the traffic was heavy and we proceeded in little spurts, half a block at a time.

'Some woman you didn't want to see, eh?' Virgilio said, looking at me with a knowing smile as if to indicate he understood these complicated affairs. I realised what he was thinking of, that the woman he had assumed to be my mistress was someone I had lost interest in and she, determined to win me back, had somehow broken into my apartment – perhaps she possessed a key from a former, happier time – and, dressing

179

herself in a seductive manner, awaited my return. 'Lucky it was me standing there when she opened the door, eh?' he added, chuckling to himself and no doubt rehearsing an elaborate fantasy in his mind.

'Yes, it was damn lucky,' I said.

'You know what I thought when she stood there gaping at me? Even during that one little second? I've put my foot into it, I thought.'

'Never mind about it,' I said, not wanting to listen to his irrelevant thoughts and having a confusing set of ideas in my own mind. 'Look, there's something I want to find out. Can you turn right and go back on Avenida Atlântica and drive past my apartment?'

'Why, you want to go back to her now?'

'Listen, Virgílio, this is not a joke. I'm sorry to take up your time, but you can charge me for it, include it in your next account. I just want you to drive right past the apartment, go as far as the next junction and then turn round and drive along the beach to town.'

'To *town*?'

'Yeah, to your office. I assume you had some business to do, if you came to see me.'

'But you asked to go to my apartment a moment ago!'

'I'm sorry, I've changed my mind. Please be patient, Virgílio,'

He drove down Avenida Atlântica past the building on the sixth floor of which was my apartment. Looking up, it was impossible to tell if anyone was on the terrace, for the building was too near the road and my apartment too high. A little later, driving in the reverse direction, along the edge of the beach, a gasoline station dividing the dual carriageway so that we were sufficiently far away from the building, I was able to see through the windscreen that a man stood on the terrace, a pair of binoculars hanging from his neck.

'Hey, Gregório, isn't that your apartment up there where that man is standing?'

'Yes,' I said.

Virgílio frowned a moment and then broke out in a wide grin, saying, 'She must be some woman!'

I failed to understand what interpretation Virgílio now put on the situation, but it certainly seemed to amuse him. 'You know,' he said, 'I had a woman once I couldn't get rid of, then I had a wonderful idea. I invited her over and also invited a man I knew at the office without telling either of them of the other and quietly disappeared for the day, getting the porter to let the visitors into my apartment. What do you know, the two of them ended up by getting married and I was their best man! Life is funny!'

I looked out at the ocean and at the crowds lying under parasols on the beach, youths playing soccer and volleyball, the swarms of bathers on the edge of the water. We turned away from the ocean towards the new tunnel, and between leaving Copacabana and driving through Flamengo, again along the beach, while listening to Virgílio's bemused chatter and responding to it in a similar vein, I had worked out what I had to do.

We went to Virgílio's office and I said, having firmly closed the door behind me, 'Virgílio, how much money can you lay your hands on in the next hour?'

'Why, how much do you want?' he asked, looking at his watch.

'Twenty to thirty million.' (One still had the habit of talking in terms of the old currency and that astronomical number represented no more than some five thousand dollars.)

'I could manage twenty,' he said.

'All right, let me have twenty on account. You can pay yourself from the rent you collect for me, it won't take more than three or four months, and you can add two per cent per month interest for your trouble. All right? Good. Now, listen carefully. In a few weeks from now find some agent who knows nothing of me, has never even heard of my name, and get him to find someone to rent my own apartment. He should collect the rent and pay it to you in cash. It is most important that no one should be able to trace the money past the agent. Could that be done?'

'Yes,' he said, 'there's no problem. But what's going on, Gregório? That wasn't an ordinary pair of lovers, then?'

'No lovers are ordinary,' I said.

'But you know what I mean. You're running away from something.'

I did not answer.

'Where are you going?' he asked.

'Truthfully, I do not know.'

'But what's the sudden panic for?'

'Virgílio, I've trusted you for several years with my money and value your professional integrity. I will keep that trust. If I appear to be running away, yes, I'm in some trouble, but I do not know with whom. You've seen the face of my enemy closer than I have and you have ten different ideas of what she might represent. But believe me, I have done nothing wrong. It'll be better, I think, if you know no more than that. I shall write to you to tell you where to send me money when I need it. I shall write to you under the assumed name of...' (I picked up a newspaper lying on a small table beside my chair and made up a name by taking two different names) '...Heitor Bandeira, remember that, Heitor Bandeira.'

I gave him further instructions as they appeared to my mind, such as emptying out the contents of my chests of drawers and filing cabinets at my apartment and storing them somewhere, and a dozen other small but important details, and said a few other general things to reassure him that in protecting me he wasn't going to be harbouring a criminal. We then went to the bank, drew the money and parted. I walked to Colombo's and ate a quiet lunch among the businessmen in their white cotton suits. Then I went into a couple of stores, buying a light-weight suitcase in one and some clothes in another and, putting the latter in the suitcase, took a taxi to Galeão airport. It was nearly three o'clock in the afternoon. I scanned the departure notices of the internal airlines; in the next three hours there were planes leaving for Salvador, Recife, Manaus and Pôrto Alegre. Only the flight to Salvador had a seat available on it, so the choice of a destination was made for me by the random movements of mankind.

Only when the plane took off did I feel a sense of temporary relief, like one who in desperate flight from his pursuers crosses a frontier or reaches some asylum; but of course, the land below me was Brazil and the plane not of a foreign flag: but the confusion that had whirled in my mind all day at last subsided and I could think clearly. A woman at the door of my apartment seen by Virgílio and a man on the terrace; surely, there must have been others inside, but who were they? Virgílio's description of the woman seemed to indicate a young urban-guerrilla type while the man I'd seen with the binoculars had the bearing of a police officer. What would have happened if I had not run into Virgílio? I would have opened the door to my apartment. . . and then? I imagined a dozen different sequels to that prologue and each little drama ended with my death. I smiled to myself, thinking that each of my interpretations could be as mistaken as Virgílio's had been, and just as he, on seeing an attractive woman, had jumped to the clichéd assumption of an illicit romance, I, involved of late in the underworld of political terror, jumped to my own clichéd assumptions. But then, as the stewardess came by offering a cocktail, I thought, accepting a concoction of *cachaça* and coconut, that my assumptions were not so speculative as Virgílio's for the simple reason that they concerned my own life, and I had some grounds for concluding what I did: that the people in my apartment were either the police or urban guerrillas. If the latter, then they had decided among themselves that I had betrayed their late leader, and if the police, then they had become convinced that I was the next guerrilla leader, both theories, of course, being false since I no longer had allegiance to any cause. I put down the drink I had accepted from the stewardess, for it was vile: the two substances, *cachaça* and coconut, each perfectly wonderful in itself, just did not mix; it was like two beautiful people producing a deformed child.

I looked out of the window at the land below and saw it as oddly ambiguous, hard and repellent where the sun caught the yellow-brown of the landscape and soft and comfortingly protective where the shadows fell. How I despised mankind from that height! Everyone played his petty little game, armed with a hideous jargon. After 1968, when there were student riots in America and in Paris, and imitative flurries in Japan, West Germany and South America, governments considered parts of their own population as the enemy and groups of radicals everywhere convinced themselves of the necessity of armed struggle. What foolishness, I thought now, wishing that the plane would fly higher and higher, rise above all that vanity, idiocy, mistaken idealism, imbecility and every type of shit to come out of the mouth of man in the last two hundred years, dirtying every corner of the earth and rendering it un-inhabitable, and yet the fuckers wallowed in it, turned daily to new forms for intensifying the putrefaction. An armed struggle, indeed! Did they not see that the enemy was within themselves, the true subversive was the anti-self within one's own soul, but that he was so subtle an ill spirit that he would sabotage empires before he allowed one the understanding that the throbbing in one's own blood was the laughter of a Faust, that what we desired to emancipate was not 'the people' but our own miserable *self*, that wilted flower which longed only for a drop of water while the anti-self set forest-fires in our limbs? Oh, who paused at that time of easy martial gestures, the arrogant philosophy that one believed in so readily as soon as one acquired a gun, the easy convictions one adopted as soon as one was part of a group – who paused to reflect upon the primeval turbulence within one's own soul?

These words, I know, will be meaningless to politicians and radicals alike, they will be dismissed in the moment it takes to flick ash from a cigarette, and that is precisely why their sort of polarity will continue generation after generation, for a failure to understand the words which attempt to describe existence is the root cause of most of mankind's hatred of man.

There was an army officer sitting two rows ahead of me. In mid-flight he rose from his seat and walked down the aisle to go to the toilet, clutching at the top of each seat at the corner and pulling himself as if he were climbing a steep incline, his large waist and protruding belly filling the aisle. He smiled at people sitting in the aisle seats and looked very much like someone who never intended anyone any harm, a benevolent fool with very little in his head except the formulae inculcated upon his mind by his army training. No, he would never understand words but, given a file with a few facts of what I had done, would be convinced that he knew perfectly who I was and what I stood for.

There was a thunderstorm over Salvador just when we were within a few miles of our descent to the airport. It was a spectacular sight from a distance, for the sky was clear and blue and right in the middle of it was a thick, black column being ripped apart by flashes of lightning. Our pilot, who had set the plane on a gradual descent, straightened it, and a moment later the plane began to be pulled on all sides by turbulence. The stewardesses had taken their seats and there was a deadly quiet in the plane, some staring out at the black column which grew larger in diameter the closer we approached it and some, with eyes closed, seeming to be trying hard to concentrate on some silent prayer. The tone of the engines changed and the plane began to gain height again, turning away from the thunderstorm in a wide curve. For a few minutes I saw only blue sky and then, having come full circle, I saw the electrical flashes in the black mass of cloud down below me. We had gained perhaps a thousand feet but we were now directly above the storm and the plane continued to bump severely. I could see the fringe of the city and a portion of the ocean on the circumference of the dark area, and I realised that what had appeared to be a column in fact covered almost the entire city. The pilot took the plane on another wide circle and then, suddenly, threw it into a dive. The engines began to make a loud-pitched whining sound and we went hurtling through the electrical storm, some of the passengers being unable to restrain their screams. The sensation was terryfying and exhilarating. For several seconds we were diving steeply towards the earth through pitch-black darkness which was being illuminated by ferociously brilliant flashes of lightning, and then suddenly there was a jolt, the plane's metal seemed to be twisted by giant, crushing hands, it stopped diving, straightened out somewhat, seemed to go silent for a second, and then fell as through an air-pocket for a hundred feet; and there, miraculously, we were flying steadily low over buildings whose roofs were touched by

185

the setting sun.

The pilot had probably broken all the rules but I admired him for having done the only thing possible, defeating the elemental violence of the air with a determined violence of his own. Only the most skilful commit themselves to such courage, though, of course, sometimes an idiot will blunder into the same area: but in that case there are never any survivors to tell the tale.

I took a room in an inconspicuous hotel a short walk from the São Francisco church and spent the rest of the evening walking about the streets, some of them narrow and cobbled and sloping steeply, but the humblest of them seemed to boast a magnificent church. There were beggars everywhere – old women, rosary in hand, in the doorways of churches, young women, no more than twenty-five years old, already with wrinkles on their faces, their hair gone so thin it appeared it had not fallen but had been torn away, the despair in their eyes touched with belligerence as they walked the pavements, dragging two young children and carrying a baby at the hip, calling out for help in a voice both pitiable and aggressive. And I, the stranger in the street handing out a few cruzeiros to one, knowing my charity would scarcely feed a mouth, withdrew sharply from her claw-like hand and walked into a pharmacy and devoted all my attention to the trivial business of purchasing toothpaste, razor-blades and a dozen other small things.

I spent six or seven days in Salvador, walking the streets in the morning and in the evening with no purpose but like one cursed to motion, encountering the same beggars who never recognised me from a previous time or, if they did, demanded a renewal of my charity as if it were a tithe that had to be paid each time, feeling sometimes while walking on an uphill street that I was some wretched prisoner, in fetters and nearly naked, driven to a public disgrace with each stretched-out hand of a beggar the lash of a whip on my back or a gob of spit on my face.

Exhausted, I would reach the square named after the poet Castro Alves, with its wrought-iron lamp-posts and lovely bandstand, and sit under the shade of a flamboyant-tree. One day, having come to the square for the third morning in succession, I noticed a man dressed in a white shirt and white cotton trousers, a straw hat tilted over his eyes, sitting on a bench diagonally across from me some dozen paces away. There was something in his manner which told me that it was not chance which had brought him there. I rose and softly walked away, returning to the hotel via some side-streets. In the afternoon I bought a pair of swimming-trunks and took a bus to Itapoã beach.

The next day I did not return to the square but, after a morning of aimless but compulsive walking in the streets, I went to the beach. It must have been a Saturday since it was more crowded than on the previous day, whole families sprawled on the sand and several soccer games in progress from one end of the beach to the other. I stretched out on the sand, rising from there every so often to take a dip in the invigorating ocean. After about two hours I walked across the soft sand to the edge of the road where a coconut seller sat on a wooden folding-chair beside a pyramid of green coconuts. I bought one and he handed it to me, inserting a straw in the small circular opening that he had cut. I took the straw out and tipped the coconut over my mouth, my head tilted back. When I was finishing, my head still tilted back and my hands just commencing the motion of taking the coconut away from my face, I saw across the road, beside an ice-cream stand, the same man in the straw hat and white shirt and trousers. I froze for a second, pretending that I was still drinking from the coconut. The hat's shadow fell across his face, obscuring his features, but he stood with a hand on the ice-cream cart, leaning slightly towards it, talking to the vendor but looking in my direction. I paid for the coconut and quietly backed away to my place on the sand, and after another swim collected my things and walked down the beach, hoping by being lost in the crowds of soccer players to leave the beach where my coming up to the road would not be too conspicuous. I caught the first bus that came; it happened to be going to the small harbour beside the market where the fishermen brought in their catches. I dawdled there for an hour or so, had a lunch of *vatapá* and beer, and took the funicular to

187

the upper city to return to the hotel.

During the next two weeks I spent almost as much time in the air, flying from one city to another, as on the ground. From Salvador there was only one flight available that first day, an old Electra hopping all over the north-east and ending its flight at Fortaleza. It went along the coast, stopping at Maceió, Recife, João Pessoa and Natal and then turned into the interior and made two more stops before heading for Fortaleza on the northern coast. It took all night, flying low over the land which lay in the shadow of the night with a few weak lights scattered helplessly here and there. Soon after taking off from Salvador I had realised that Fortaleza was where my old adversary Rubirosa had been transferred to some years ago, so there was no question of my staying there even though it was likely that Rubirosa must by now have been transferred to somewhere else. But I decided not to leave the plane at some other city and I realised that what I desired most was motion and the comforting enclosure of the vibrating, droning plane as it came down to touch land and rose again, came down to brightly lit airports and rose again into the cool darkness; it was both my prison and the one liberty which I could enjoy without suffering the paranoia which the streets induced in me, for that man in the square in Salvador and beside the beach was probably two different men, neither of them interested in me, and it was only my own mood which interpreted their appearance as a disguise, their presence as a threat. I sought to arrive at newer destinations again and again as if a glorious freedom awaited me there. It was that freedom which promises a new beginning at the end of the journey but a freedom which was bordered in black, for there was the continuous pressure on my mind, that pain of realisation that my hopes had to be false, for there was nowhere I could arrive at and feel the conviction that I could live there at peace with myself.

For I was not only in flight from the people in Rio who had chosen to brand me as enemy. I did not understand it then, but I was overwhelmed by a sense of failure and loss which went deeper than the arbitrary misfortunes which befall one in the course of one's life; the blood had soured within me, imbuing my spirit with a vile odour which so enveloped me that I could smell it myself. Pride, that subtle censor who deletes information not flattering to the self, has restrained me from a free expression of my feelings at Amália's going away, and still compels me to hold my head erect and show to the world a body unbent by any grief. Looking down on the land as I flew from Fortaleza to Belém, and during the next two weeks when I flew on and on in my maddened journey, to Cuiabá, to Pôrto Alegre, to Rio Grande, to São Paulo, to Brasília and finally to Goiânia, looking down at rivers and mountains and vast plains, everywhere on the shifting contours of Brazil was imprinted the face of Amália. *Enough!* I do not have to reduce an eternity of pain to a few tawdry sentences which a curious eye will skip over, proclaiming them too sentimental. But there was the other, profounder pain which came from no explicable cause, a sense of pain which took the imagination plunging down into some watery, choking darkness where one was surrounded by menacing, bulbous eyes of silent, bodiless creatures. Sitting in the sleek jets which, even over the darkest jungle, within which some tribe might still use stones for arrow-heads, proclaimed the twentieth century as a sort of immanent and inexorable spirit, I lost the will to be part of the living world.

The same random principle which took me to Fortaleza saw me land at São Paulo and Brasília – but perhaps I had the unconscious desire to be recognised by some agent, for, standing on the edge of a precipice, the mind enjoys the thrilling fantasy of the body hurtling down into the abyss.

A stout, middle-aged man of a light complexion sat next to me on the plane from Brasília and soon after we took off he said to me, 'How boring these jets are!'

'It's only twenty minutes to Goiânia,' I said.

'It's so much more fun in a small plane,' he said.

'Yes, I agree, at least you're closer to the land. I had a very interesting flight in an Electra not long ago.'

'No, I mean a really small plane, a four-seater with an engine stuck to its nose.'

He'd begun the conversation because he wanted to talk of the small plane which he himself owned, parked at the airport in Goiânia, from where he was going to fly out to his ranch in west Goiás, on the border of Mato Grosso. When we were landing in Goiânia he said, 'If your business here can wait a few days, you're welcome to come out to my ranch. There's nothing but land and, at this time of the year, a lot of water, and about two thousand cattle.'

We had struck up a friendship during the short flight and his invitation was the natural concluding gesture. His name was Francisco Nunes de Carvalho. He had been born in Goiás, had mining interest in Minas Gerais, timber in Santa Catarina, real estate in Rio and a head office to oversee it all in São Paulo where he normally lived with his family in a house in Santo Amaro. He rarely had the time to visit his ranch in Goiás but had kept a small plane at the airport in Goiânia with the idea of spending a long weekend at least once a month at the ranch, but in the last two years he had managed to come only three times, failing on two of those occasions to persuade his family to come with him since his wife and his son preferred to go to the seaside. 'It's too expensive to keep a plane for two visits a year, it would be cheaper to rent one. There's only so much you can write off as a tax deduction. Lately I've had more reasons to travel to Europe and to the States than to my ranch. Ah, it's sad, the thing that one loves the most one is obliged to leave to the end of one's days.'

I accepted his invitation and joined him in his single-engined plane, which he piloted himself. He anticipated my apprehension by saying that the plane was kept serviced and in working order at all times and that he was a member of a flying club in São Paulo and spent at least two hours in the air every weekend.

I had never been in a small plane and was astonished by the ease with which it rose from the runway, without the powerful thrust and wrenching away from the earth one experiences in a jet, and swerved up over the city of Goiânia and settled on a comfortable cruise at some three or four thousand feet, giving a little bump from time to time which seemed more like a joyous, carefree hop than a signal of danger. It roared boisterously though, like a small boy shouting at a surprisingly loud pitch, and it was impossible to talk. Much of the land below was deep in water and shone back brilliantly. One area of marshland was dotted with hundreds of little white birds which were probably flamingoes. Where the land stood above the water the grass was a rich green and sometimes covered with vast herds of cattle. We flew west from Goiânia, over Trinidade and São Luis de Montes Belos – I saw the names on a navigation map, my companion pointing a finger to show me where we were – and headed south-west over a *serra*, and after two hours came down on a landing-strip within walking distance of a square, stucco house, painted white with dark-blue window-frames and shutters, and red tiles, which stood on a slight elevation more or less at the centre of the huge ranch. A man in his late forties, black-haired and tanned by the sun, came running out of the house. He was introduced to me as Lúcio Barreto, the general administrator of the ranch.

I need not describe in detail the circumstances which led me to stay there when, after three days, Senhor Francisco Nunes de Carvalho returned to Goiânia to sell his plane before proceeding to São Paulo; suffice it to say that we got on so well together that on the second night, after an exhausting day riding on horseback to inspect the ranch, while we sat in the veranda drinking *cachaça*, I confided my whole story to him. What compulsion led me to do so I do not know, for, being an industrialist, he had no patience with young radicals, expressed a contempt also for politicians and wanted only that businessmen be left alone. But he listened sympathetically to me, understood perfectly my dilemma of being thought an enemy both by the government and the revolutionaries and said, 'Why don't you stay here? No one will know where you are and, as for me, I always have a thousand things in my head and I shall never remember that I'm harbouring a fugitive on my land.'

We talked some more and I accepted his offer, thinking that all the random flying across the country that I had done during the last two weeks, staying at some city for two days and then finding some reason for leaving it, or arriving at an airport only to depart from it three hours later – somehow all the chance

191

journeys had, with some fixed, predetermined plan, placed me in the sky above Brasilia next to the very man who could offer me a sanctuary, and my haphazard flying, which had seemed the expression of a will so free that it nearly adumbrated anarchy, had in fact pursued a plotted course.

His urbanity, good manners and generosity might well, I thought, be deceptive and perhaps, once I had told him my story, his one thought was to denounce me to the police and he hoped to detain me at his ranch by seeming to be kind. But my instinct prompted me to trust him and, in any case, life held no other hope for me. After he left I thought I would stay on his land for a few weeks, perhaps as long as three months when the dry, winter season set in. I ended by staying there for five years.

Senhor de Carvalho returned thrice during those five years, with an interval of over two years during the second and third visit, but never expressed any surprise at still finding me on his ranch; on the contrary, he was rather delighted to have me as a sort of permanent fixture, for he welcomed having someone to talk to in the evenings. The house was always kept in readiness with the expectation that he and his family might arrive the next day, and consequently I've never seen a cleaner house, for everything was kept in order, the furniture regularly polished, the tile floors waxed, the rooms swept daily, but since nothing was actually used the place looked like a well-maintained museum which is visited on very rare occasions by a solitary and reverential scholar.

The room I found myself using the most was a library at the back of the house which looked out on a courtyard. I was drawn there a few days after Senhor de Carvalho had left that first time. I had been sitting in the front veranda before which the land rolled away for several miles, and suddenly I felt exposed, as if what was before me was not luxuriant grassland on which the cattle roamed but some desert on which I was alone and naked, and I felt like a lizard which is driven by some instinct to seek a crevice in a rock. I rose, startled and feeling a giddiness, and retreated into the house, going as far back as possible down a corridor when I remembered the library my host had shown me a few days earlier, saying how he had diligently collected the works of Brazilian writers and those philosophical works of Europe and the Orient which, he was convinced, would be a great consolation to him when he retired. 'One must spend one's old age with the purest thought,' he said. I remarked that he didn't look like a man who would ever retire, but he insisted that it was the one thing he looked forward to most, a life of inner contemplation, so that I thought to myself that no one is without an improbable dream, that what we see of people masks wholly unpredictable desires. So I retreated to the library and collapsed in a leather chair beside the window, holding my head as if doing so would relieve the giddiness.

Hibiscus and bougainvillaea grew in the courtyard and looking at their blossoms soothed me, inducing a profound sense of serenity; the enclosed world of the courtyard appeased my spirit. And that became my place, the chair beside the window and the manageable perspective of the confined space of the courtyard; if I spent any time in the veranda, it was at night when I sat there talking with Lúcio Barreto and not again in the daytime with the blinding depth of the land to oppress my mind. Within a week it became my habit to sit by the window in the library reading a book. I lived in a world of other people's ideas and my own memories; I suppose my solitary existence, a state of total withdrawal from mankind's preoccupations and sharing a community only of abstract thought, made me especially receptive to visionary ideas: for this was the time when, dwelling on my memories, while pausing in an interesting work of anthropology, that masterpeice of Gilberto Freyre's, I found myself thinking of a past time when I realised with a start that that particular image came not from my thirty-five years in this life but from a past much more remote. I dismissed the thought, it was too bizarre, and then tried to explain it by saying to myself that I'd probably transposed two images, one that belonged to my past in this life and another which I had read in Freyre's account of seventeenth-century Brazil, and that all that had happened had been that sudden confusion in the brain when a sense of immediate reality abandons us and we're momentarily convinced that a crazy montage of images is a

193

vision representing a true reality. I tried to laugh it away, deliberately rose from my chair and walked down the corridor, stepping firmly on the tiles so that my heels made a loud sound, went to the veranda and stared out at the horizon, called out to Lúcio who happened to be walking past, then went to the bathroom and took a cold shower. But that strange feeling of having a memory which came from a life in the seventeenth century and the absurd conviction that it had undoubtedly been I who had had that experience would not leave me. Of course, the explanation which most people would arrive at in such a circumstance, that I was going mad, came to me too, and I even thought to myself that people who think they might be going mad are usually too sane to be in any danger of so doing. I resolved that there was nothing I could do but to continue the life I had chosen and so returned to a composed routine of sitting in the library, reading. More memories came to me and soon I took them for my ordinary thoughts and refused to concern myself with explanations until one day, several months later, when Lúcio, returning from a visit to Goiânia, told me about a discussion with some friends on the subject of reincarnation.

And there it was! All ideas fell into place, this world vanished, a multiplicity of worlds whirled in my mind. I became many people while remaining always Gregório Peixoto da Silva Xavier, many pasts resided in me and, therefore, many futures, other realities belonged to my soul than my present body had known, and how easy it was to conclude that of all existences the present one was the most elaborate dream, for it alone suggested such fantastic pasts and futures!

By now I had long read the works of Gilberto Freyre and had finished a score of other authors, picking up a book at random and reading through it. Lúcio, who had had enough schooling to enable him to do the accounts, write letters to his employer and to read the newspaper, confided to me one day that several years ago he had come into the library to dust the books and, finding by chance a book open on a slightly erotic drawing, picked it up and tried to read the words, surprising himself by the discovery that words in books didn't differ essentially from

194

words in newspapers. The book he'd picked up was a novel but, Lúcio confessed, laughing, it was only the hope of seeing a description of erotic passion that had made him try to read it, and he had to say that his expectation was disappointed; but something in the book undoubtedly touched his imagination, for he soon found himself reading more novels. By the time I was using the library Lúcio had read all of the novels there and had also attempted some of the philosophical works, so that he would often talk of a book he'd read, his eyes lighting up when he remembered the life of some fictive character.

It was during these conversations, especially after the experiences buried within me had suddenly surfaced while I read book after book, that I conceived the idea for writing about my past. I resisted the attempt for several months, for it seemed an absurd undertaking to delve into a past which belonged to the very beginnings of Brazil. But one day I came across the novels of Machado de Assis and for a week found myself entirely immersed in his world; and then, when I had come to the last sentence of his last novel, I put the book down and, without thinking about it, found myself sitting at the small desk in the library and writing about the first world in which I had existed.

Lúcio Barreto came from a mixed ancestry, with Indian and Negro blood in his family, but his own features were predominantly Portuguese. He was short, with a wiry frame, but had a Negro's strength and an Indian's sharp senses so that he could tell from two miles away if a cow had fallen in a ditch or a jeep was coming towards the house, information that he derived neither from a keen eyesight, for his eyes always had a dull look about them like the eyes of one who has had too much to eat at lunch and can think of nothing but an hour's siesta, nor from his sense of hearing, which I was convinced was deficient since I had to become accustomed to repeating things twice before he could hear me although he sat a few feet from me, but from what people call a sixth sense and for which I have no explanation.

He lived in a small out-house at the back of the main house with his wife, daughter and two sons, and to all intents and purposes the great ranch of Senhor de Carvalho belonged to them, for Lúcio's wife, Dona Teresa, ruled over the main house in so far as she had the keys to the cupboards where the silver and the crystal and the superb linen bedsheets, pillow-cases and colourful towels with the texture of a young lamb's back were stored, ruled too over the kitchen where there was a store of oils, spices and a larder full of canned products for an emergency, while her thirteen-year-old daughter, Maria das Graças, changed beds whenever necessary, cleaned and waxed the floors and polished the silver, and the two sons were in charge of the twenty or thirty peasants who looked after the cattle. Lúcio himself, being responsible for the work done by the rest of his family, did nothing, like a master who must appear disinterested to the labours of his subordinates and preserve always a cold and weary demeanour in order to exercise fully his control. He had learned instinctively that the greatest authority is invested in one who does nothing himself but on rare occasions can show himself capable of some extraordinary feat, like inoculating an entire herd of cattle against foot-and-mouth disease, or driving a jeep day and night all the way to Brasilia on muddy, water-logged dirt roads, because that was the nearest city where he could obtain some medicine for the cattle, and drive right back.

Normally, however, he sat in the veranda at the front of the house, reading some book from the library; or cleaning a gun or waxing his boots; but the look on his face, withdrawn and dreamy, belied the quickness with which he could suspend whatever action occupied him and immediately *know* what was happening out of range of his vision, and when, an hour later, one of his sons came to inform him that half a dozen bandits had been seen on the distant edge of the ranch stampeding some of the cattle to where they could round a dozen of them up and put them on a truck and steal them, Lúcio already knew what was happening, and if he still sat in the veranda it was because he had, half an hour before, sent some men to chase off the bandits.

As I observed all this in Lúcio, with increasing admiration for his prescience and the rightness of his actions, his wonderful

196

quality of always remaining unperturbed, and found that he grew to discover in me a valuable companion, we first established a mutual trust and then, when I revealed more and more of myself and he in his own limited way – for he was not given to prolixity – described what his own life had been, we reached that stage of friendship where we would exchange the coarsest jokes and have the greatest respect for each other.

When I had been there two months Lúcio needed to drive to Goiânia for some supplies and I accompanied him in the jeep, which he drove in the meditative manner of one sitting alone in an empty church and staring blankly at the altar, his thoughts all his own. It was a full day's drive on a road which was muddy and, when it sloped, treacherously slippery, and I had the impression of going dangerously fast on the rare occasions when we drove at over forty miles an hour. Where the land was not under water it possessed the beauty of landscapes painted by artists in the nineteenth century, having an overwhelming tranquillity even where flocks of birds seemed suspended in the air, frozen in an icy silence in the moment before they landed on trees; there, in the heart of what people who have never left a temperate climate think of as the 'steaming tropics,' was a softness to the light and a weightless clarity to the air, so that the sky, instead of appearing to be a harsh lid which is about to fall on one's head, seemed to be forever dissolving and withdrawing in a deliquescent gesture of tactful delicacy, and the solitary, tall trees, standing here and there on the distant horizon, were seen in such lucid detail that it was incredible to think that one saw them not through some magnifying lens but with the naked eye. We came to a marsh which I was certain was the same as the one I had seen from the plane, for here were thousands of flamingoes, their white feathers, soft and slightly ruffled by a breeze at the shoulders and stiff at their sides where they flapped, brushed by a light pink so faint and so delicate that there was only a suggestion of redness in that mass of white; a colour that at once retracted itself, as if it took no responsibility for its existence in a world which so insisted on proclaiming its substance, when the birds flew up, flapping the pink away in white arcs over the marsh. It was difficult to believe, accustomed as one had become to hearing pessimistic prognostications of people who lived in São Paulo or Rio where the air was thick with soot and chemicals, that such a pure world could still exist, but then, I thought, the very spot on which my apartment in Rio stood had possessed a similar innocent charm not seventy years ago; that too had been a paradise for humming-birds.

The reason why I had agreed to accompany Lúcio to Goiânia was not that I longed for diversion but that I wanted to send a message to Virgílio, which message I had already written as discreetly as I could, so that, were it to be opened by anyone else, its true meaning would not be understood. It stated in effect that he was to send me, who signed himself Heitor Bandeira, a specified sum of money at a bank in Goiânia on a date which was two months from the date of my writing the message. My expectation at the time was that I would spend another two months at the ranch and then, if I had come up with some plan, I would have the money available for it.

As it happened, since we were obliged to spend three nights in Goiânia – for one of the things which Lúcio wanted was a spare part for a tractor used for cleaning the pastures at the end of the rainy season, and the dealer, being out of the part, insisted that he had a quantity of it coming from São Paulo, for he had had it on order, had already received a despatch advice and was bound to receive it in two days – I broke my resolve to remain secluded in my hotel room and agreed, on the second night, to have dinner with two friends of Lúcio, having first been reassured by him that he had said nothing about me to them (which point, indeed, I had stressed to him before we left the ranch: that he should not reveal that I lived with him and that, if he had to explain at all who I was, he was to call me Heitor Bandeira, a travelling businessman who happened to be in Goiânia and who was leaving for São Paulo in a day or two). It all sounds amateurish and irrelevant now but at the time it seemed the logical and proper precaution.

Lúcio drove to the western outskirts of the city, to a street with three-storey buildings painted a dark blue or a gaudy green or bright pink, the ground floor of each being a bar-café or a shop where one bought rice, beans and a few mouldy and nearly rotten vegetables, or being given over to some aspect of automotive repair with crudely painted signs or symbols (a large, worn-out tyre from a truck, a rusted, old radiator) in front of the shop, with the upper floors of the buildings made into dark and dingy little apartments. It was a street common all over Brazil, appearing always on the outskirts of cities or at the centre of villages, and contained a complete community – ragged children running about between puddles and sleeping dogs among whom one sometimes saw a girl of five or six, dressed in a dirty and soiled frock on which small, blue flowers had faded a long time ago, with hair as straight as an Indian's and sparkling green eyes – a girl potentially so beautiful that it saddened one to think that, even before she turned fiteen, long before that potential could be realised, she would already be crushed by some labour in a nearby factory, for in the same street one would see, coming out of the shop with heaped sacks of flour at its front, a girl of fifteen or sixteen in a thin, dirty frock, stooping at the shoulders, her breasts fallen and her stomach swollen, her hips ungainly and rigid as she laboriously walked across the street in dirty, bare feet, carrying a bulging plastic shopping-bag with a pattern of bright pink flowers on it. It was a street always of movement and noise – a truck grinding past in a low gear, a radio in a café, positioned by the entrance, filling the street with its loud music and commercials.

Lúcio parked the jeep outside a café and, entering the building from the side, we climbed up two flights of steps which were lit by one bulb hanging high above the stairwell on the ceiling of the third floor and which smelt strongly of urine. The dimly lit room which we entered seemed bright by comparison and had a small, square table in it with four chairs around it, a narrow bed along one wall and a small sofa, covered in blue plastic, beside the opposite wall; another wall had a door in the middle which led to another room and on its opposite side a door opened on to a small balcony overlooking the street.

We were welcomed into the room by a young man of twenty-five, introduced to me as Emmanuel Xeria, whose dark eyes had a merry glint, imparting a frankness to his light-brown face. He conducted us to the balcony which had just enough room for four folding, metal chairs, where sat an old man with a lean, hollow-cheeked face, a few strands of white hair on his head and a beard so thin that it came down in four or five hairs on either cheek, the tanned white skin glistening in between the strands, and collected together at the chin to create an effect of loose and speckled cotton-wool and then fell away in shreds, the thin hairs seeming to disappear in the air rather than come to an abrupt ending. A similarly frail moustache curled round the corners of his thin lips, leaving his upper lip exposed as a flat, shining surface over which a small nose added to the effect of a body which had become weak and shrunken. It was only when he looked up and the deep blue of his eyes fixed one with a penetrating stare that one had the intimation that if his body was weak it was not because of age but because it was merely the neglected appendage of a being which looked elsewhere than in the world of physical sensations for its intensity. He was Fernando Cardovil.

Since we sat two floors above the café the loud music from its radio throbbed in the very cement of the balcony, but it was such a constant feature of life in the street that nobody seemed to hear it. We sat there an hour, exchanging small talk and drinking beer. Young Emmanuel Xeria, his eyes darting from one person to another, filled up any pause with some comment on a recent soccer match or a film which he had seen and sometimes, pointing to someone crossing the street below us, narrated some comical or tragic episode from that person's life. In the room behind us there was the shuffling of feet and the sound of plates and cutlery being placed on the table until a woman came to the doorway, her hands wringing a soiled apron which she wore at her large waist, and said that dinner was on the table. It was a simple affair of rice and beans, a heap of manioc flour and a little jar of *malagueta* peppers, together with a malodorous stew made of dried meat.

The old man said little during the meal, to which he seemed to give all his attention, eating with a slow, ruminative absorption and observing a very decorous manner at the table. Young Emmanuel, however, recounting anecdotes of the months he had spent working in a chemicals factory which, he maintained, he had left because he could not stand the smell there, kept us highly amused; he talked of leaving the factory in a manner which implied he had been dismissed for indolence, an impression he was eager to convey because he wanted us to understand that he was an intelligent person, even though his family background had not afforded him an education, and had no desire to become an automaton. There was a bravado, almost an arrogance, to his conversation towards which I was not unsympathetic, for he was obviously clever and could discuss an idea he had picked up on the radio or in the newspapers and criticise it with a remarkably astute independence of thought. When, for instance, Lúcio mentioned the government's development of Amazonas, Emmanuel said, 'Thousands of people from the north-east still go packed like cattle in trucks to the *favelas* of São Paulo every month. Our government is given to grand schemes. First it was Brasília and now the highway across Amazonas. We're led to believe that we're witnessing miracles. With Brasília, we imagined that once the streets were paved they'd be of solid gold, and now with Amazonas we dream that once the highway's completed it'll take us straight to El Dorado. It's all a game of power, with foreign money involved. If we have any place in it, it'll be in the new *favelas* which are bound to spring up even in the jungle as they did right next to Brasília.'

'Now you're talking like a Communist,' Lúcio said.

'No sir, you won't catch me spouting their sort of rubbish,' Emmanuel said with some emphasis. 'I came across them in the chemicals factory, but I saw right through them, all they wanted was not to free me from what they never tired of telling me were capitalist chains but to make me turn my body around so that the chains would tighten round me a little more, only I'd be looking at a different view. The way I see it, there never was anybody who wanted political power for himself who had any interest in other people. In a democracy the politician goes to the people like a man goes to a whore, he pays her money, says a

201

few pretty things to her but, once he's got what he wanted, he never sees her again. In a dictatorship it works in another way, the ruler himself is so impotent he can have no relationship with the people, so he surrounds himself with a bunch of pimps known as his cabinet who then go about the world procuring foreign clients to come and screw his country.'

'Come, come,' I interposed, 'that's all very neatly put, but you must guard against ideas that are no more than a neatness of language.'

Fernando Cardovil put his fork down, stared at me a moment and then looked at Emmanuel and said, 'That is wise, remember that.'

That was the old man's first statement during the meal and I was flattered that he should have spoken in commendation of what I'd said.

'Well, I grant you a certain exaggeration on my part,' Emmanuel conceded gracefully, 'but can you give me an example of a ruler who's entirely disinterested?'

None of us answered for a while and then the old man said in a soft voice, 'You might also remember that, when you're taken to task for being imprecise, it is a cheap way of reasserting yourself by asking a rhetorical question.'

'Oh, you are clever!' Emmanuel said, laughing. 'For you deprive me of my next strategem, to insist that the question be answered. Well, so be it, we're all friends here.'

The conversation turned to other subjects in which Fernando Cardovil did not participate but merely looked with a profound interest at whoever spoke as if he were a student witnessing three experts discussing a subject about which he was eager to be instructed. Then, at the end of the dinner, he said to me, 'You have experience of the world. You have, if I may express a view, the wisdom which is acquired only by those who have submitted themselves to suffering. I wish you would come back, there's so much Emmanuel could learn from you. People struggle for this freedom and that in this life. But I believe you know that freedom from the self is the greatest struggle of all and most of us don't even recognise the tyrant who enslaves us, for we walk, like children carrying colourful balloons on the end of a string, with our inflated vanities suspended above our heads like a cloud which we never see to be dark but, instead as that point in the sky where the rainbow begins. Ah, forgive this tortuous metaphor, you who must have forgiven more than the lapses of language in those whom you loved!'

I did not answer, not knowing how to understand his words, and merely stared thoughtfully at my empty plate, wondering what new human struggle it was my fate to witness.

When we left Goiânia a day later I did not believe I would be seeing Emmanuel and the old man again, even if my own business brought me back to the city. The simple truth was that I did not wish to become involved in the lives of people who believed themselves on the verge of deliverance from some oppression, whether it was political or, as old man Cardovil had suggested, that complicated matter of projecting the anguish of one's self to a world which did not live up to one's purest expectations and so became an object in which were concentrated one's desires and one's hatreds and one's belief in the possibility of that perfection which, if it was elusive, was only so because some other force – a lack in our education, the nature of the country's rulers, or something else, like the heavy rains of one year and the drought of another – put it just beyond one's reach. And yet I'd come away with a growing affection for Emmanuel; his ideas had been so ardent and down-to-earth that he seemed, in a slightly crude fashion, to be echoing Capistrano, and I was gratified that there should be in Brazil, far from the centres of intellectual activity, a young man of no education who could still discover ideas independently in an environment which was hardly encouraging to the cultivation of such a mind. If only our rulers could understand this: that men and women who think, *whatever their ideas,* are a country's best assurance of its future; and that to suppress thinking human beings is like poisoning the rivers which supply our drinking-water; that to come across an Emmanuel in the intellectually barren interior is an occasion for national joy, for his existence is a promise given to us by nature that barrenness too will be made fecund in the near future. Meeting Emmanuel

203

was like seeing in some desert a cactus of cumbersome shape, its thick skin covered with thorns, its green colour burnt into brown patches by the sun, but at the top of each of its despairingly uplifted arms a delicate yellow flower blossoming with translucent petals, the flowers conferring upon the plant qualities of elegance and poise, symmetry and grace, so that the plant which had seemed from a distance to be something of a joke, falling this way and that like a drunkard, is seen to possess an inner strength and sense of purpose and an astonishing beauty which is entirely its own. But I resisted the tremendous attraction of wanting to nurture such a plant and told myself that I must not let my vanity think that, with a little encouragement from me, a young man of Emmanuel's sensibility could be raised from his lowly station and even become some sort of a leader.

Again I'm driven to confess my incomprehension at the way we cannot avoid the peculiar destiny reserved for us which, always rooting us in some environment in which we had never expected to find ourselves and committing us to actions we had assumed to be contrary to our own desires, highlighting those aspects of our characters which we had considered alien to them, makes us serve an ideal which we had thought foreign to our natures. For no sooner do we experience some random circumstances than we begin to convince ourselves that some logic has been at work and that what we're about to commit ourselves to is not the fascination of a new experiment in which to engage our vanity but an inevitable consequence of our previous actions; and thus, like the man who has consulted a fortune-teller and cannot resist a compulsion involuntarily to engineer the fulfilment of the very prophecies he had considered too shocking to believe, we end up by doing what we had not intended simply because a confused rationality convinces us, producing a complacent satisfaction, that that indeed has been our destiny all along. And so, the more I tried not to think of Emmanuel and of Cardovil's cryptic words, the more I became obsessed by the two men. When Lúcio paid another visit to Goiânia a month later, I was anxious when he returned to hear if he had met them again, and when, after some vague hints, he said nothing, I was constrained to ask, 'Did you see our two friends?' and was astonished at my own mind which had come up with the word 'friends'. And what's more, I could not explain the thrill I felt within me when he said yes, he had spent an evening with them and they had said that they were sorry I had not returned to Goiânia.

'But how could they expect me to be in Goiânia again?' I asked. 'I was only supposed to be a businessman who was passing through.'

Lúcio looked at me as if he had not heard me and I was about to repeat the words when he said, 'Gregório, why do you think I took you there that time? If it was only entertainment we wanted, to pass the time while we waited for the tractor part to arrive, we could have gone to the pictures.'

'Well?' I asked when he did not continue.

'Believe me, I said nothing to them about you apart from what you heard me say while you were there that one time, except, of course, that you were well and spent much of your time reading.'

'But those words you used just now,' I said. 'About *taking* me there, as if you had a special secret purpose.'

'I wanted to see what would happen,' Lúcio said. 'They had never heard of you before you entered that room.'

'Lúcio, I still don't understand. You know very well what happened, we ate and drank and had a pleasant conversation.'

'What you are saying, Gregório, is that you still haven't heard from me what you'd like to hear.'

I was surprised at his perception into human psychology, for I could not deny that my pretence of not understanding him was only a stratagem to make him say more and more until he came up with the words which would define the idea in my own mind – which idea I had no complete conception of as yet, except that I was tantalised by its hushed whisperings and its partial glimpses, and I also had that anticipation of what it would import which made me instinctively suppress a formulation of it while at the same time wishing Lúcio would do so, thus relieving myself of the responsibility for its assertion.

And when I did not say anything Lúcio went on: 'They've

205

talked of you many times after our visit. They have many conjectures of who you are, and I was quite impressed when Cardovil, twisting the ends of his beard and gazing blankly at the street below while we sat on the balcony, said that he was quite sure you were no businessman but the embodiment of some spirit condemned to suffer in this world.'

I made as if to laugh but Lúcio continued: 'I have to tell you about old Fernanado Cardovil, for it's easy to laugh at the things he says. Everything that he finds interesting or curious he turns into a spiritual phenomenon. You see, he came from a fairly well-to-do family in Minas and had everything available to him in his youth, a time of his life which he has described to us as having been devoted entirely to the pursuit of women and those habits, like drinking and expensive clothes, which go with such a life. He has never told us what made him give all that up, for he simply abandoned that life and walked away into the interior. People do desperate things in search of themselves. I suppose in Brazil we have no certainty of what we are. We might be living happily in Belo Horizonte, carrying on a small business, while within our veins the blood might suddenly have a memory of Africa or even the more mysteriously compelling memory of the jungle in the Brazil of hundreds of years ago. For most people these things mean nothing, such memories might appear as a disturbing dream and that is the end of them, for a few they alter the normal coursing of the blood and we recognise the self, which we had never questioned before, as being false. It loses its composed poise which had artificially been propped up by vanity, and we either go insane or commit suicide or embark upon a quest without any knowledge of the goal we hope to reach. Believe me, Gregório, these are words I've picked up from Cardovil but I've understood them within my heart. I've relived his story in my dreams, I've seen him wander in the interior, just as he described it, staying in villages for short periods and then walking away.'

He paused and I said, 'So, he became a saint, is that what you're trying to tell me?'

'No, that's not the word I'd use, for 'saint' is a word invented by religious propaganda and has no true bearing on this world.

Cardovil simply took up a life of self-denial. And you know how it is in our villages where people live among superstitions older than Brazil, there's always someone supposed to be possessed by the devil.'

'And Cardovil helped them?'

'Yes,' said Lúcio, 'but you must not put him in the common category of healers, you see them all over this country, for he himself will insist that he is nothing and sometimes, in order to put an end to such a discussion, will say he's a spirit in a human body. But that, as I say, is only so that he does not have to talk about himself, for we do that, don't we? Put an absurd label on ourselves, it makes people think they know the truth.'

'But isn't that precisely what he's doing when he puts a label on me too? For that is a common human practice also. When trying to fathom the mystery of another person we settle the matter by fitting him into a concept that we have for one of our own group, we reduce the world to the language we know.'

'I will only say this, Gregório. You have been here three months and I've not observed you suffer the wants of ordinary humans. You eat the simple food given you as if what goes into your body is of no meaning. You appear to show no interest in women. When you look up from the book you're reading it is not to look at this world but at some image of another which is in your mind. You see, I've lived alone here all my life too, though I have a family. I know the kind of man one has to be to seek such loneliness.'

I was about to object that I had sought no such thing but did not, since it occurred to me in that moment that in order to deny his abstract explanation I would need to provide a physical one and end by describing what I was, a fugitive. So he went on: 'But of course, no one goes in quest of loneliness for its own sake. A man is disappointed in love; or he is betrayed by his family; or he comes to experience some bitter disenchantment with the world; or it can simply be a matter of hiding oneself – from the police.'

He was watching me closely when he spoke, pausing while he added one alternative after another to express his hypothesis, and pausing at length before uttering the last three words. I

207

believe some nerve twitched in my face, or there was some involuntary gesture that betrayed my secret to him, and even as I suffered a new anguish within me I could not help admiring Lúcio's subtlety, for all his talk had seemed to border upon the mystical until he had suddenly sprung upon me the concrete word 'police'.

'Cardovil understood this of you,' Lúcio said when I remained silent, 'even when Emmanuel was only talking about some film he had seen. So you see what they make of you? You were not a chance visitor, you had been *sent* to them.'

'But whatever for?'

'People everywhere, Gregório, are longing for revelations.'

During the several months which followed I spent my days entirely in the library, having begun writing about my past, experiencing a strangely ambiguous feeling within me, as if the total realisation of the past which went beyond the thirty-eight years of this existence liberated me from the tyranny of the present which constricts all mankind but, at the same time, subjected me to a new tyranny, that of an insistent subservience to a past with which my present mortality could have no real commerce. In the evenings, at sunset, when the horizon was bearably near, I sat in the veranda at the front of the house with Lúcio, drinking a glass or two of *cachaca*, but he did not talk again of our friends in Goiânia and of what expectations they had of me. But one evening he said, 'We should leave by six tomorrow morning if we're to get there in time.'

He talked as if he alluded to some journey we had already decided to make together when, in fact, it was the first intimation to me that he planned to go somewhere the next day. The odd thing was that I did not question him at all and behaved as if I was well aware of the journey, for I said, 'Knock on my door at five-thirty, just in case I haven't woken up, though I'm usually up before then.'

At six the next morning I was sitting beside him in the jeep while he drove out of the ranch. We travelled through the country in silence, exchanging no more than an occasional remark about the landscape for the next six hours, when we stopped, around noon, for a light lunch at a village, proceeding after that for another four hours and arriving finally at another village some fifty miles from Goiânia. Lúcio stopped outside what looked like a shed with a tin roof. It was apparently the local cinema, having posters of some war film stuck on its brick wall. In the cracked plaster which covered the upper part of the brick wall, whole areas of which had simply fallen away, was painted in a faded blue the sign *Ciné Goiás* but a letter in each of the two words had been eliminated by the dilapidation; directly above it, however, was a more recent sign made of metal and electric bulbs with the words *Ciné Brasília* on it. Inside, a narrow auditorium was crowded with families of peasants, women and children far outnumbering the men. A man sat on a chair on the stage, the cinema screen a blank rectangle bordered in black behind him. There was a microphone in front of him but it was obviously not working. Two young men were also on the stage, in the far right-hand corner, one of them working on a plug with a screwdriver and the other wrapping black insulating tape around a cable which came from the microphone. I recognised the man sitting in front of the microphone as Fernando Cardovil. He appeared to be talking but his words did not carry across the auditorium, for a good many of the children were making a noise and their mothers, attempting to quieten them, were only adding to the din. Lúcio guided me down the hall to the front row where Emmanuel Xeria sat alone with five empty seats on either side of him. We quickly sat down beside him. He remained seated but put out a hand to greet us and when I sat next to him said to me, 'You're in good time, the old man's doing beautifully.'

Just then, as I looked up at the stage, the microphone came to life and I saw the two men in the corner walk off the stage, and Cardovil's voice came loudly from the speakers, saying, 'And now the time has come for me to leave the stage, for I see that our visitor is here. He needs no introduction from me.'

Cardovil came down, stepping carefully on the three steps at the middle of the stage, and walked up to me. I stood up to greet him and he, clasping me in a frail embrace, said, 'These are your people, my friend. Speak to them.'

I stood there for a moment and turned around to look at the audience while Cardovil went and sat in the chair which I had vacated. There was a comparative silence in the room, though some of the children were still making a noise, and I noticed, a man in the third row, sitting in an aisle seat, was chewing a sugar-cane, taking savage bites from the two-foot piece of cane which he held sideways in front of his mouth like a flute, chewing rapidly and spitting the shredded pulp out in the aisle. I turned towards the stage and walked up the steps to the chair and sat facing the microphone. I had no thoughts in my mind. I did not know where I was or what I was expected to do. Some of the men were asking their wives to hush up and some of the women were scolding the children. One woman suddenly got up and dragged a small boy by the arm down the aisle to take him out of the auditorium and the boy, who had been teasing another child, cried loudly all the way to the exit, which had the effect of silencing for the moment all the other children as they imagined the beating the small boy was about to receive out in the street.

'My name is Gregório,' I said, and paused. I looked just then at Cardovil and noticed that his eyes were bright like one who believes that the vision he's seeing represents a profound truth. 'I was born', I continued, 'on a sugar-cane plantation and I was born on a cattle ranch and I was born in Rio de Janeiro. The air that moves over the land gave me breath, the breezes that blow from the ocean inspired me with their music, the atmosphere that hangs over Brazil pressed down upon my mind with its subtle pressure, so that I appear before you as the pure spirit of the country, a mind which contains the purest essence of Brazil and a body which is its completest physical projection. My friends, do not think that you see me, a mortal named Gregório, but that you see the embodied spirit of the past and the future of Brazil. To you the past is a dream and the future a subtler dream, to you the past is a memory invented by history books and the future the promises of a government, to you the past is the failure of your parents and the future a hope of your children's success. Believe none of these dreams, my friends, none of these desperate illusions. We're creatures of our own minds, we're the architects of temples built for the glory of the self in a world committed to turn to ruin and rubble the most concrete edifice. We're the planters of lawns and orchards in a world ruled by nature which prefers the profusion of weeds. We're the emptiness behind the full bottle of liquor.'

A shout went up from the room, mainly from the women who apparently believed that my speech was an attack upon the alcoholism of their men. I paused for a moment and looked at the audience and noticed that the men were glaring at me, as if all I'd said had been calculated to arouse male guilt, while the women had a beatific intensity in their eyes; but in spite of this clear evidence of being completely misunderstood by my listeners, I went on: 'Have we not been warned against vanity? And yet within our minds we see ourselves as if in a mirror without realising that the image we see there is only the reflection of an image on another mirror, for all we can ever see of the self is a multiplicity of reflections which have as their original source only an illusion. The self sits in a barber's shop or in a beauty salon, staring at itself in a new hairstyle.'

At this point the men broke out into applause, no doubt convinced that my intention was not to abuse their love of alcohol but that what I had really come to discredit was female vanity, and the women, I noticed, looked suddenly uncomfortable, as if thinking to themselves that I could not be trusted, and thus, doubly misunderstood, with no hope of being followed by anyone, I continued: 'The self is a monster threatened by shadows, the self is a musician who finds no comfort in melody, such is the suffering it believes it must experience to atone for its secret belief in its fantastic beauty; the self is a dinner guest at our table who eats sparingly to exhibit his sensitive nature, oh, the self appears in a million transfigurations, it is an entire mythology of being which, however, whatever form it takes, has only one end, to assert its importance. Throw a stone upon the mirror, I say, empty the bottle in the gutter.'

I had hit upon a fortunate sentence, for now there was applause from both the men and the women. Realising finally that whatever I said would be meaningless to my audience, that what it responded to was only an impassioned voice and the

211

occasional phrase which it interpreted in a way in which it could relate it to its own experience, without thinking of what truth it could have in the generality of my argument, I abandoned logic altogether and gave myself up to a rhetorical projection of my voice, letting the abstract phrases flow as pure sound and slowing down only with the concrete images in order to clinch the impression of meaning. Surprisingly, people who would not have understood had I said something like 'We must inoculate the cattle against foot-and-mouth disease,' seemed convinced that they entirely comprehended my rhetorical nonsense, so that I had hardly finished when the entire audience was up on its feet shouting, 'Gregório, Gregório, Gregório!'

I thought to myself that I who had proclaimed to the public that I was Gregório was no longer Gregório, for there was some other who stood in my body; and I walked down from the stage, as if wanting to escape from the other. Cardovil embraced me, speaking into my ear while the crowd continued to applaud: 'You have the people's gratitude, my friend, for you have touched their hearts and set off a beautiful music in their souls.'

Emmanuel Xeria came up and embraced me too, saying, 'Ha, now we shall see what stuff the government is made of! They can imprison students and torture radicals, but a people possessed by a religion. . .!'

The statements of both my friends seemed to me as meaningless as my speech had been, but the same obscure compulsion which had brought me to the auditorium and made me utter unrehearsed words of no precise meaning also insisted that I respond warmly to Emmanuel and Cardovil. 'We're brothers of the same faith,' I said to them, thrilling them by unwittingly uttering the jargon which appealed to both, while the real Gregório watching this usurper-Gregório talk in this fashion, grimaced inwardly: for I believed in no faith and did not care to call any man my brother when of my true blood-brothers one had abandoned me and the other betrayed me.

In spite of these contradictions, which I have never been able to explain in any rational language, that meeting was the first of

212

many which saw me address crowds in villages all over the state of Goiás during the next four years. It was like the daring of some folk-hero, an outlaw who, putting on a thin disguise, east at the table of the very guardians of the law.

Meanwhile, back at the lonely ranch, I continued to re-create my past selves who were aliens to this life. While memory made vivid lives which I could only have possessed by some obscure and inexplicable divine principle – of which the word 'reincarnation' is but a feeble adumbration – unless, in that library, my imagination had taken on a wholly new character, and all conceivable lives which could possibly be invented by a mind immersed in fictions could easily be believed in as memories in my soul; while I lived this rich re-creation of lives which had no connection with my present existence, the events in which I found myself, these appearances before ecstatic crowds, had a smimilar irrelevance to my self. Someone else was doing the living for me, and if I caught sight of this other, in the moment when he paused in his speech or when he disinterestedly cast a look at a young woman, it was only to observe how remote his immediate preoccupations were from those I believed to be mine.

At the end of one meeting, when I had already been in Goiás for three years, Cardovil said to me, 'Gregório, I'm glad to have lived to see the people freed from their selves.'

'Truly,' I said, 'I don't think any such thing has happened, or can ever happen. All that they experience is the poetry of language, a fine feeling of being in touch with deep meanings which they can never know. It's only a mystical breathlessness.'

'The main thing is that the people find a happiness,' Cardovil said.

'They could get that by owning television sets,' I said.

'I am well aware of that, and I know too that gambling and whoring could provide the same service. And sex among the poor can be a desperate distraction from hunger.'

'So what does that make me,' I asked jokingly, 'a card-dealer and a pimp?'

'It makes you nothing, Gregório. Only a human being. The label does not matter, only the action does. But that is not what I meant to say.'

He was about to say more, perhaps to reveal some subtle idea, but Emmanuel joined us then with some excited notion of his own, and I never saw Cardovil again. A month later Lúcio, returning from a visit to Goiânia, reported that the old man had left the apartment he shared with Emmanuel.

'Where has he gone?' I asked.

'I believe he has gone to die,' Lúcio said in his quiet, matter-of-fact way.

'What do you mean?'

'Old Fernando wasn't of this world and for him to die among other humans would have been to leave the terrible burden of his body to others. He was the kind of man who, when he knew his end was approaching, would choose to go into the jungle and lie where the ants would leave nothing of his body.'

We never talked of Cardovil again. It was as if he had only been some invisible force which had drawn me into a world to which I could belong only by allowing an alien spirit to possess my body. Capistrano had plunged me into political activity and Cardovil into the rhetoric of a sort of secular spiritualism, but both were pure ideas in my mind now, neither had ultimately helped, for I was still in exile from what I believed was my real world: the only freedom I had now was when I remained confined for months in the library, re-creating the past, having no responsibility whatsoever to the present, for my memories could concern themselves with truth without being bothered by the realm of fact.

Oh of course, there was a tyranny that oppressed my mind! My Amália, where was she? I had broken my resolve not to mention her name and had succumbed to the temptation of writing to Virgílio, asking him to make discreet enquiries to discover if she had returned from Europe. But my letter was composed with so many admonitory qualifications and so much insistence on cumbersome secrecy that Virgílio could come up with nothing. I suffered from the double humiliation of her having gone and never having written and my inability to maintain the proud resolve not to approach her.

I do not believe now that I lived for five years in Goiás because I was a political fugitive. For the truth is that, at the village meetings in which the other me declaimed the poetry of the spirit, the crowds stood up and chanted, 'Gregório, Gregório, Gregório!' for the whole world to hear. No, I had turned my life in Rio into a fiction and my mind refused to see the reality of it, for the one thought which I returned to again and again although I tried rigorously to suppress it was that *Amália had never left Rio.* And attendant on that thought were a thousand explanations which tormented me that she was unfaithful; that she had betrayed me, perhaps under police compulsion, but still betrayed me – that she had never loved me. I drove away the thought by turning more and more to those lives which I could reconstruct, in which she had no life and so freed me from the possibility of her presence; but no. Every time I looked up and stared out of the window, gazing at the hibiscus flowers in the courtyard, there she stood by the wall, framed by the arch of the climbing bougainvillaea, with a smile which, over the years, assumed a bitter mockery. I turned desperately to the inventions of my mind, substituting a possible reality with imagined realities which were no less possible, but an hour, two hours, later I looked up again, and now she sat on the wrought-iron bench, reading a book, the smile still on her lips, as if amused by what she read, and again I was driven by the thought: *she never left Rio.* But still, perversely, as if this torment was precisely what I desired, I continued my exile, prolonging the sweetness of suffering for what little heroism it guaranteed, believing that there would be nothing heroic if on returning to Rio I were to be the target of an assassin's bullet. Contradiction and paradox which had so constantly attened much that had happened to me had become a habit of thought, and I could not arrive at an idea of my own existence without observing the contradictory and paradoxical aspects in its very nature; and I who stood before crowds of villagers preaching against the tyranny of the self never realised that I was doing so only because I wished to escape from my own self.

215

Chapter 4
INTERLUDE:
SOLILOQUY OF THE ALIEN HEART
IN ITS NATIVE LAND

Here the wind blows across the low-lying marshlands and spirals up in random updrafts, making the hawk, poised in the sky's still blue, suddenly flap its wings to convince itself, when the first gust of wind has passed, that the turbulence at its breast was of its own creation, until a second, more prolonged gust sends it skidding in a curve that matches the bay-like crescent of the horizon, and the land is then all curves, parabolas, convex and concave contours, the undulations of tall grass as the wind flows across it, making it fall and rise like a swelling ocean

and does not the heart then mimic the fall and the rise of oceans, of grasslands, as the blood surges, swelling the veins with spontaneous palpitations that send a throbbing rhythm to the brain, a vibrant memory of the darkness of the jungle, O my Brazil,

what knives are these, the cold surgical steel held by white-coated men, what wires as from a cardiogram machine attached to my bosom, compelling the blood to flow into maddening whirlpools, into muddied eddies, what blinding suns rise before my eyes, flooding the brain with a hot whiteness and as suddenly what darkness infuses its ice into the heat-inflamed cells

while the late summer afternoon across the deep perspectives of Goiás and Mato Grosso stifles the afternoon's breath to a whisper, holding the tall high clouds in a tableau of silken vestments edged by gold, pink and purple, while the evening, softer than a woman's sigh, touches the flamingo's wings with a gesture of a gentle caress, while the air trembles with a lover's hesitations and the land coyly withdraws behind veils of shadows, and the air floats as perfume from lavender bushes

the air which is as still as the pomegranate suspended from its stem

and then the sunset over the land with its bloody hands and the wind kicks up its heels once more, briefly, like a shot horse before it dies, a kick, a twitch of the flanks and a violent spasm and then nothing, the whirling clocks of summer winds come to zero, after the violence, a barbarous beauty collapses in the wrinkles of the land, a darkness duplicates the erasure of memory

and what violet light radiates its menace about the heart then, what electrical impulses interrupt the heart's coursing, draining the lungs of oxygen and filling them with the shriek of a whole people

in that darkness which falls over Brazil?

Chapter 5

THE LIBERATION

That Monday morning in late November a crowd of people milled about in the lobby of the bank where I had come to collect a large sum of money – I believe it was twenty-five thousand cruzeiros – for which I had sent a message a month earlier to Virgílio in Rio, and it took me half an hour to go through the three separate phases of seeing an assistant manager who could authenticate the payment, have a clerk scribble the sum in question on a piece of paper, put a rubber stamp upon it and give me a token which, after waiting in a third queue, I presented to the cashier who gave me the money. I had an empty brief-case with me in which I deposited the money and, making sure that its metal fasteners were secure, I began to walk out of the bank in order to return to the hotel and wait for Lúcio to come back from his own errands, and stepped out casually into the street trying not to give the impression that I suspected that someone was following me.

Earlier, when I had waited to see the assistant manager, standing in a disorderly line of six or seven people, I had, as I always did on these occasions, looked around at the people, both those who worked behind the counters and the customers in the lobby, partly out of the normal human curiosity that makes one remark absently on the manner or the dress of another person and partly because I was obliged always to be on the lookout for anyone who might be observing me with a curiosity that exceeded my own. There were three people ahead of me and the one who was actually at the counter had a sheaf of documents over which his and the assistant manager's heads were bent as if they were absorbed in a game of chess. The latter took the papers away at last, sat down at a desk and put a rubber stamp on each together with his initials. Looking at another line of people at another counter, I saw a young man in a white cotton suit leave the queue when he was within two places of receiving the clerk's attention, as if he had suddenly realised that he had left his cheque-book at home. His clothes were not unusual and, indeed, I would not have noticed him with such particularity had I not seen him at that moment when he withdrew from the queue; and even that would not have elicited my concern had I not then seen him walk back to the wall where there was a counter where one filled in deposit slips or wrote a cheque, place his brief-case on the counter, leaf through some papers there, close the brief-case and return to the same queue and take his place at the end of it, with some eight or nine people ahead of him. The entire action, I realised, was play-acting, for he had not actually looked at anything in the brief-case, only given the impression of doing so, and it was obvious that his real motive in enacting this charade was to waste time; if all that were not enough, when he walked back from the counter to rejoin the queue he cast a quick glance in my direction. After I had seen the assistant manager and walked across the lobby to join another line, I saw that the man of whom I'd begun to be suspicious had quietly withdrawn to the counter by the wall again, and a moment later I caught sight of him walking with the absent-minded air of one who is preoccupied with his own thoughts to join the group of people waiting to see the assistant manager. *Who is he*? I wondered while I walked to join the cashier's line. He could not be an agent of the police, for if the police had had any suspicions they would have gone straight to the manager and got hold of all the papers pertaining to my transaction; on the other hand, he could well be a police detective making a first tentative observation, thinking it premature to be seizing papers. While I counted the money and put it in my brief-case, I thought that he could not be out to rob me; but then, it was not unknown for people to find excuses to hang around a abnk lobby, observe a likely victim and then follow him out to rob him. Finally I walked out, looking very relaxed and unperturbed, though each muscle and nerve within me was tensed.

Outside I immediately crossed the street, which I had not needed to do in order to return to my hotel, but a double instinct within me, that of commencing on a false trail and that of being on the side of the street where the crowd of pedestrians was thicker, prompted me to risk running across the traffic, which was moving in spurts, and gaining the farther sidewalk as quickly as possible. Now I believe that I could, by some stratagem – slipping into a shop, say, or jumping on to a passing bus – have escaped from the young man who was following me, which I confirmed by casting a backward glance when I was in the middle of the street, but no sooner was I one of the stream of people on the sidewalk than I slowed my pace; indeed, it would not be imprecise to say that I actually began to *loiter*. I realised what I was doing: I did not want my pursuer to lose sight of me! And when I stood by a shop-window, staring at the shoes displayed there and looking sideways to see what progress my pursuer was making, I understood the nature of my own reluctance to escape: I had to know who he was and why he pursued me in order to seek a true escape; otherwise, even if I could immediately be spirited away to the ranch, not knowing who had pursued me would keep me enslaved to an anxiety which would interpret the most innocent onlooker standing idly at a street-corner as another representative of the same agency which for some reason dogged my steps wherever I went. And now whenever I paused he stopped too, and I realised that my best plan would be not to run away but to draw him to me, like a hunter his quarry – that it was not I but he who was the real victim of this situation.

I walked on leisurely, almost casually swinging my brief-case in my hand, and came to a restaurant where I stopped, noticing that it was nearly empty since it was long past breakfast-time and too early as yet for lunch. Two men at a table were having coffee together and chatting, and at another table a man was lifting a full glass of beer to his lips with the self-congratulatory look of one who the night before had resolved never to drink again but has now found a reason that he had not thought of before which makes it imperative, if his health is to survive, that he immediately take a glass of beer. I chose a corner which was far at the back and ordered a coffee. Before it was served, the young man in the white cotton suit entered the restaurant and sat two tables away from me. I noticed that his suit was stained at the armpits with sweat, and thought rather triumphantly to myself that he was nervous and, ironically, he was trying to avoid looking at me while I stared at him with cold, penetrating eyes. The waiter brought my coffee and went to his table to take his order, which was also for a coffee. When the waiter had shuffled away, I said quietly but so distinctly that my voice seemed to fill the restaurant, 'Perhaps you'd care to join me while you have your coffee?'

The man looked up at me with a sudden start, not expecting that his presumed victim would be taking the initiative. But he smiled, affecting a bravado, and rose with the confident and casual air of a hunter whose successes are the talk of an African nation, and came and sat opposite me, trying to convey a calculated scorn in the smile that he flashed at me.

I sipped my coffee and, the cup before my lips, said, 'I assume you know my name so perhaps you're the one who should introduce himself.'

'Roberto Moniz,' he said, rising from the chair he had taken and offering me a hand which was small and damp. 'And you are Heitor Bandeira,' he added.

Just then the waiter came and placed a cup of coffee in front of him and went away, sighing to himself.

Moniz eagerly drank from his small cup while I still held mine in front of my lips and looked intently at him. He put his cup down and said, 'Or shall I call you Gregório?'

'Call me Dom Pedro if you like, what do I care?' I said, emboldened to utter cheap sarcasm now that he seemed so nervous. And then, as he picked up his empty cup, held it in front of his face and stared into it and put it down again, I said, 'All right, what's your game?'

'I've been looking for you for almost a year,' he said in a tone which struck me as oddly sad. And when I did not respond he added, 'I was in Mexico City a year ago.'

I finished my coffee and put the cup down and stared silently at him.

'Yes, I met Capistrano there,' he said. 'I was coming back from London to Brazil and decided to come via Mexico City, I'd heard so much about Mexico, you know how a country becomes a fashionable place to visit. As usual, wherever you go nowadays, you run into Brazilians and I ran into a group of them in Mexico City, Capistrano among them.'

I continued to stare at him and indicated neither that I believed what he said nor that I doubted his every word.

'Capistrano asked me to look for you and Amália.'

It was at the mention of her name that I lost my composure and covered up by calling the waiter and ordering two more coffees.

'It took me only two months to track down Amália. I found her finally in a little apartment in Ramos, that miserable district in Rio, but it has taken nearly a year to find you.'

'Why such persistence?' I asked. 'Just because someone you met in Mexico City asked you to look me up?'

'He was not just someone, he was Capistrano. And he wasn't asking me to look up just anybody but you, Gregório. You don't know what your name means, you belong to the mythology of this country.'

I decided not to be taken in by his flattery and said, 'Well and now that you've found me, what do you propose to do?'

The waiter brought the two cups of coffee, placed them on the table, keeping his eyes hooded as if he had no intention of concealing his utter boredom with his existence, and sauntered away.

'I can at least write to Capistrano to say that I've fulfilled my duty,' Moniz said.

'How do you expect me to believe any of this?' I asked.

'Why, what don't you believe?' he replied, and I was struck by his spontaneously innocent manner.

'Amália left Brazil for Europe five or six years ago,' I said. 'She fled like so many of her generation, and I doubt if she has ever come back.'

'But that's not true,' he said. 'I tell you she lives in Ramos. She does some kind of social work among poor children. I met her several times, she told me a great deal of the years when you

222

were together, she never mentioned a word about Europe.'

I felt that I wanted to be convinced that he was lying and yet his frank manner suggested that he was not, so I asked, 'How is she?'

'Sad, like someone whose life stopped a long time ago. She goes through the motions of living. Oh, she's very dedicated to her children, but you can see it's a life of sacrifice.'

I did not believe him and began to suspect that all he knew was of my past relationship with Capistrano and Amália and that he had fabricated a story around those two names in order to serve his own obscure ends. We finished the coffee and I said, 'And what is supposed to happen now?'

'Come to Rio for Amália's sake,' he said. 'That was her wish when I told her that I would search the entire country until I found you.'

I pretended to take the idea seriously but decided to play for time so that I could determine with greater conviction whether or not he was telling the truth.

'Why don't we go to my hotel?' I said. 'We can discuss what to do, perhaps even see if there's a plane to Rio.'

'There is, this afternoon.'

'But I've a few things to do,' I said, 'and first I must go to the hotel, for I can't carry all this money about with me. Unless, of course, you wish to meet me at the airport and spend the time looking around Goiânia. But in that case', I added with a disarming smile, 'you run the risk of not seeing me again.'

He came with me to the hotel. It was in my room that, once I had made him feel at his ease, I suddenly pounced upon him and, clutching his throat with both my hands, said in a restrained but vicious voice, 'Right, you motherfucking son of a bitch, tell me the truth now, who the fuck are you?'

'I told you,' he squeaked helplessly, terror in his eyes.

I slapped him hard across the face, two or three times, saying, 'Come on, I've had enough of your lies!'

'It's the truth,' he cried but, the blood raging within me now, I punched his face with both my fists so that he fell back on to the bed and I flung myself at him and, my left knee on his chest and my hands at his throat, shouted into his face, 'Don't give me that shit! You're from the secret police, aren't you?'

'No, no,' he moaned.

'Then why were you behaving like an amateur spy at the bank?'

'I didn't know what to do, I wasn't sure if it was you.'

'You're lying, you fucker, like you lied about Amália living in Ramos.'

'No, that's true, you'll see her there.'

'You're lying!' I cried. 'She's probably still in Europe.'

'No, she's in Ramos, she's been there ever since she left prison.'

'What prison?'

'Don't you know?' he said in a weak voice. 'Some years ago, maybe five or six years ago, when you think she went to Europe. Maybe she was in Europe for a while and came back, I don't know what happened, but she was in prison. It must have been soon after Capistrano left for Mexico City.'

I released him and stood back. He remained on the bed, a trickle of blood at his mouth, looking like someone who has been brought in from the street following some accident. During the entire scene I'd been so possessed by my own enraged feelings that I never reflected that not once had Moniz attempted to fight back: I thought of it afterwards, however, when his meek acceptance of my brutality suggested an entirely different interpretation of his personality.

'Well go on,' I said, leaving him on the bed, 'what else do you know?'

'Just that she was in prison for a while. She couldn't find you when she came out. She waited for you. In a sense, she's still waiting.'

'Then why did she write to me that she was going to Europe?'

'I don't know, Gregório, she hasn't told me everything. I've told you what I know.'

It occurred to me that she had never written to me *from* Europe; I began to have all sorts of doubts in my mind. I reflected that in the great dramatic tragedies a slow messenger who arrives two minutes too late to deliver a letter is the agent of a fatal misunderstanding; and what entirely trivial detail

224

might not be responsible for the tragedy of my life? On the other hand, I was still not convinced that Roberto Moniz was not lying; so much of what he had said was so implausible, and yet it could be the implausibility of one who did not know how else to act; while at the same time, his blundering implausibility could well be a studied act. There was only one way I could find out: by going to Rio.

Could it be possible, I kept asking myself, that she had been in Rio all this time? Except for that one cold letter which I found when I returned from seeing Capistrano in the jail in Mato Grosso, in which she announced her departure for Europe, she had not communicated again while I was still in Rio; and I, finding my soul turning bitter, had begun to imagine that she was so determined to make a new life for herself that she had decided to forget me completely; but how unlike Amália that would have been, I thought now, for if there was any truth in what Moniz had just revealed, then the image of Amália, stoically bearing her sufferings in silence, devoting herself entirely to some charitable work, was more in keeping with her character. A mixture of violent emotions boiled within me – now it was remorse at having lost five years of our lives to empty ideals, now a despair at the callousness of circumstances which had rarely been of one's own choosing but which, coming as relentlessly as waves, finally drowned one in a world one had not wanted, and now the longing to be with Amália again, so that I was possessed by such a great urgency to go to Rio that even that afternoon's plane seemed not early enough.

Lúcio still had not returned from his errands. I took what money I would need and left the rest of it in the brief-case with the manager of the hotel to give to Lúcio, together with a short letter I'd written in which I told him that I was going away with no real knowledge of where or for how long.

It was a long flight, with a stop at Belo Horizonte. I had a thousand questions to ask Moniz, but he either knew very little or was convincingly feigning ignorance. Looking at him as he sat nervously slumped in the aisle seat, trying to see if something in his expression revealed his true identity, I sudden-

225

ly felt sorry for him, he looked so weak and innocent, and apologised to him for having hit him at the hotel.

'My jaw's still sore,' he said, smiling.

'But tell me, Roberto, what is your own interest in all this? Why should you spend your life looking for two lost people?'

'It's a challenge,' he said. 'Also a promise I made Capistrano.'

I found the answer inadequate rather than implausible, it indicated more a youthful idealism and a desire for adventure than the personality of a police agent.

He fell asleep a little after the plane had taken off from Belo Horizonte and, with still an hour to go of the flight, night fell outside. Sitting in the window seat, I looked out at the darkness and saw only the reflection of my own eyes in the window. They looked as if they were two tiny points hung in space, radiating light. I felt again the isolation I had experienced on my interminable flights five years earlier, a sense of being pitilessly suspended above the world to which I could not belong and yet condemned to look down upon it with envy and despair. I had come down from the sky to it but only to live outside my own self, to be the agent of other people's deliverance and not my own, free only as the warden of a prison in which other bodies are confined.

Moniz woke up some fifteen minutes before the plane was due to land in Rio and rose from his seat to go to the toilet. A few minutes later I leaned across his empty seat and looked down the aisle to the back, debating to myself whether I should go and use the toilet or wait until we had landed, and noticed that there was a queue of four or five people. Seeing them, I decided that I had no real pressing need, but just then I noticed that the last person in the queue was Moniz – for at first I'd only seen people waiting and not individuals. Moniz had his arm resting on the back of the last seat and was talking to a stewardess who apparently seemed very interested in what he was saying. It looked as if he was merely passing the time while he waited, making conversation with the pretty, young stewardess. I sat back in my own seat and looked out into the night, seeing a few scattered lights below. A moment later no lights were visible outside and the plane ran into turbulence. I

226

tightened the seat-belt around my waist. The stewardess walked past hurriedly and disappeared behind the curtain which separated the first-class section. Moniz returned to his seat and fastened his seat-belt, saying, 'It bumped just when I began to piss, threw my aim off completely.'

The pilot announced that we were beginning to make our descent for Galeão and instructed everyone to return to his seat. The stewardess emerged from the first-class section and walked down the aisle, checking to see if everyone had fastened his seat-belt. The plane was going through what has always seemed to me the worst situation of all, fighting the turbulence to keep itself in the air while at the same time deliberately losing height to make its descent, so that there was some terrifying bumping. Just when the stewardess went past us, she looked first at me and then at Moniz. For a moment it struck me as an odd look, as if I were someone she had heard something about and was curious to see what I looked like; while the look she gave Moniz was slightly different, though I could not at that moment tell in what way. But it was sufficient to make me turn to look at him when she had passed; his eyes were closed, his hands tightly clasped the arm-rests and he seemed to be holding his breath, for the struggling and descending plane was obviously creating a sinking feeling within his stomach.

It was raining at the airport when we landed a few minutes later. The plane taxied very slowly towards the terminal, stopping twice when it had got off the runway and was following the various roadside signals to the terminal, going slower each time it resumed. It stopped within a hundred yards of the terminal. Many of the passengers stood up but the pilot's voice came on the air to ask everyone to remain seated. The plane remained there for five minutes and then began to crawl forward again. The pilot's voice came on once more: 'Ladies and gentlemen, we regret the inconvenience. . .er. . .we just heard. . .uh. . .all flights originating from Mato Grosso . . . uh . . . Ministry of Health regulations . . . must be sprayed . . . uh . . . some mosquito . . . please remain seated till . . . '

'What a bore!' Moniz said, and a murmur went up from

227

among the other passengers, who complained to each other of the sudden regulations some ministry or other was always springing on the people. 'It's for our own good,' said one voice, and another: 'I bet you some general's got a pay-off from a chemicals company.' And then a silence fell in the plane as a couple of airport employees entered and began to spray the cabin. Some people sneezed, a few coughed and several wiped their eyes with their handkerchiefs. A police officer walked behind the two workers and smiled at the passengers and said to a woman, 'Better to cry now than to die of encephalitis.' The woman was only dabbing her handkerchief to her eyes but on hearing the police officer's comforting words she burst into tears. When the two men had reached the end of the aisle the police officer walked back and, standing near where Moniz and I sat, said, 'O.K., you can leave now.'

Suddenly released from the oppressive atmosphere, many people immediately rose from their seats to make for the exits, Moniz the first among them. He shot off towards the first-class compartment to gain the exit there, but before I could rise the aisle was jammed, there was a crush of people, and the police officer, collapsing in Moniz's vacated seat, said, 'This is ridiculous, why can't people be more orderly, the plane's not on fire or anything. Well, let them go, there's no rush.' He leaned back, crossed his legs in the tight space, one of his knees touching the back of the seat in front of him, and thus had me trapped in my window seat.

Two or three minutes later the plane was empty. The officer looked at me, smiled and said, 'See? It was such a short wait. It only needed a little patience. Well, the time has come, what do you say, Gregório?'

The police officer conducted me down the steps from the plane and led me to a black car which drove up just when we reached the bottom of the steps. He opened the door to the back seat and I entered and sat down, overcome by a feeling of weariness. The chauffeur drove away from the airport, and when he stopped at a gate where he had to present a paper to a guard it occurred to me that this was a strange way for one to be arrested, being driven out of the airport by a solitary chauffeur who had no police authority. He continued to drive in the dignified manner of a well-trained chauffeur, never looking back at me or trying to strike up a conversation, so that I just sat there, wholly puzzled, and it did not even occur to me that all I needed to do to escape was to alight at one of the many traffic-lights.

He drove down Avenida Brasil towards the city. I lost all sense of danger to myself on seeing Rio as we entered Praça Mauá and then drove along Avenida Rio Branco. The old senate building at the end of Rio Branco looked like a ruin and apparently it was being demolished to make way for the new subway system, and I thought to myself that if I had been away for twenty years and had returned to a completely transformed city I would still have been moved, for it would still be Rio; for there, beyond the old senate building, was Flamengo and the distant Sugarloaf at the end of the crescent of the beach, and there at the top of a hill the Glória church with its sentinels of palm-trees and above that, far to the right and high above the city, Corcovado with the illuminated Christ; but it was not merely these familiar landmarks, which even the tourists who see nothing else know so well, which produced a thrill within me; there was, I believe, a feeling in my soul of complete freedom as if it no longer mattered to me what happened to my body. I had thought, while being driven from the airport, of all that had happened during the day and how Moniz had tricked me. I realised now why Moniz had not fought back when I'd beaten him at the hotel in Goiânia in the morning; it had been part of the game he had to play to convince me of his innocence; and I realised that when he'd stood at the back of the plane talking to the stewardess it had been to tell her to convey a message to the pilot; all the events of the day from his con-spicuously odd behaviour in the bank to the plane being sprayed against some fictitious mosquito had been precisely calculated. But in spite of the fact that everything had conspired towards my capture, I felt as though I had been released from some confining prison. I had thought of Amália obsessively during the flight, wondering what she would look like after all those years, what she would say, while at the same time trying to suppress thoughts of her, for I wished to arrive at that moment when our coming together would be a sudden surprise; but now, realising that it was not to see her that I had been brought to Rio, I suffered only a slight feeling of disappointment. A new, unpredictable inevitability was at work now, I had been relieved of all responsibility to my body, and, holding on to the strap beside the window on my right, I leaned across to the window on the left to look at the lights reflected on the ocean when the car turned into the streets of Botafogo. The usual maddened traffic of Rio exploded on all sides, bursting in little spurts of speed. We began to go up curving, narrow streets in a corkscrew motion, zig-zagging on sharp bends. Soon the bay was far below us, lit up in necklaces of beaches, and Christ on Corcovado with his outstretched arms swung over as the car squealed round the bends. I was going giddy with the twisting motion of the car as much as with the intoxication that a native feels on returning to his city.

A gate was opened and we entered a long, steep drive and came to a stop at the entrance to a large house. I remained seated, looking at the carved door of the house, and then across from the house at the garden, which in the darkness was all bushes and still trees. There was an iron fence at the end of the garden and beyond it one could see some of the lights of the city below. The chauffeur came and opened my door. Just then a short man, who I realised had been strolling in the garden in the manner of one nervously awaiting an expected visitor, came up to the car and stood beside it as I emerged. He was a small, stout figure and, seeing his face in profile while he talked with the chauffer, I was struck by his sharply hooked nose and his high forehead. He turned to me and said, 'Welcome! It's a pleasure to have you here. We've been looking forward to your arrival.'

He conducted me inside. Oriental rugs on a marble floor in the hall were a prelude to the palatial luxury of the house. Tapestries and paintings hung on the walls of the drawing-room which was full of colonial furniture. I was invited to take a seat. 'Perhaps you'd like a drink while your luggage is being brought from the car,' the man with the hooked nose said in a soft voice.

I was too bewildered to make an immediate answer and he said, 'Before we go on to business. I'm sorry it can't wait, you must be tired after your long flight.'

I recovered my composure, thinking it odd that he should employ such ambiguous language, and said, 'I don't have any luggage. I left suddenly, it was totally unexpected.'

'I can understand that,' he said. 'You have run an enormous risk; believe me, there are many who appreciate your dedication.'

'Thank you,' I said, not knowing what he was talking about but not as yet prepared to ask questions or to say more than seemed necessary.

'Well, you can take a drink in the library, if you want to,' he said, leading me towards a shut door. 'We don't want to keep our friends waiting.'

We entered the library where three men, all between fifty and sixty years of age, sat in leather chairs round a low table on which was placed a silver tray with a bottle of whisky and some glasses. One of the men wore an army uniform and, although the decorations made him out to be a general, I recognised that the uniform was somehow not Brazilian.

'Here he is,' the hook-nosed man announced. He seemed to be refraining scrupulously from using my name, which I assumed he knew since, on seeing me, he had given the impression that I was the very person he had been waiting for. I walked up and shook hands with the three men and noticed that one of them looked vaguely familiar, but though I searched my memory for his identity I could not remember where I had seen him.

'I hope you had a good flight,' he said.

'The landing was a bit rough,' I said, 'but otherwise it was quite smooth.'

'I've never crossed the Atlantic without experiencing turbulence,' said the general.

'It must be something to do with the trade winds,' said the third man.

I had no comment to make on their flying experiences and

just smiled vaguely, accepting the drink which the host had poured for me. I was invited to take a seat opposite the three men.

I looked again at the man I thought I recognised and realised simultaneously that he was a politician from Portugal and that the army uniform on the other man was Portuguese.

'Well, to business,' said the host.

'Yes,' said the politician. 'What information do you bring?'

I looked at the three of them and then at the host, entirely confused in my own mind as to what was happening, and finally said, 'I'm sorry, I don't know what you mean.'

'Well, that's understandable,' said the third man. 'You want to make sure first that we're the people to talk to.'

He was about to give his own name when the general interrupted him with, 'No, no, our names are unimportant. If you don't know us, so much the better. The only thing that matters is our country.'

'I do see the newspapers,' I said, bidding for time. A momentary smile, which was instantly suppressed, betrayed the politcian's pleasure in his own fame. And I added, 'I can recognise people from photographs, so introductions are almost irrelevant.'

'Yes,' said the politician, unable to restrain a prompting of his vanity, 'you can be sure you know who you're talking to.'

'Well, then,' said the third man, 'let's get down to business.'

I stared at him blankly and then looked at the others. Then I said, 'Life goes on the same everywhere, people have their problems, but nothing really changes.'

'Friend,' said the general, and I could see that he was holding on tightly to the arm-rests to convey the idea that he was being patient, 'we've been waiting five hours. Had we known the flight was going to be delayed in Luanda we would have postponed this meeting till tomorrow.'

'Luanda?' I said with a dumbfounded look, but in the same moment understood what was going on. 'Where do you think I've come from?' I asked, just to test the idea which had occurred to me.

'Come, come, this is not a quiz game on television,' said the

232

third man.

'The flight I came on', I said, 'originated in Mato Grosso I caught it in Goiânia and there was an hour's stop at Belo Horizonte.'

They looked at each other in disbelief and bewilderment. The host rose and with agitated gestures conducted me out of the library and asked me to wait in the drawing-room.

I worked out the confusion and had it confirmed later by the hook-nosed host who was named Adolfo Lobo. A plane from Lisbon had landed two minutes before the one on which I had come. The three men in the library were Portuguese right-wing leaders in exile (which they believed to be temporary) from the revolutionary upheaval going on in their country and they expected a messenger to bring them some important information on the plane which arrived from Lisbon that evening. The chauffeur, who had been given special papers to by-pass the usual formalities, had driven up to the wrong plane, and since the officer who had arrested me had instructions to put me in a black limousine he had assumed that the black car which drove up was intended for me. As for the Portuguese messenger on the plane from Lisbon, he had, for all I knew, been picked up and was now being interrogated by the secret police who, hearing him deny that he was Gregório, probably assumed that he was lying since they were accustomed to such denials and for them it was only a matter of applying a certain pressure to make a man confess that he was the very person they believed him to be. If the man was lucky, the police might have photographs of me to reveal the mistake; and I assumed too that the Portuguese leaders would probably be able to find him through their connections before the man suffered any real harm. As for me, a bizarre coincidence had saved me without actually freeing me, for it left unanswered the questions as to where I was intended to be taken and what, if anything, was true of all that Moniz had said about Amália, for without reference to her situation he would not have succeeded in luring me to Rio.

Senhor Lobo emerged from the library, followed by the three Portuguese exiles who looked at me disdainfully as they walked past, as if from their aristocratic height I belonged to some

233

contemptible class of peasant. They went out and I was left to contemplate the works of primitive art which decorated the wall in front of me, paintings which possessed neither the honesty of down-to earth representation of nineteenth-century works nor the stark power of modern abstraction; they were a product merely of smart commercialism. Such art, having no roots in contemporary existence but being only the saleable product of third-rate minds, was no more than a sophisticated and, of course, expensive souvenir for tourists. I thought it interesting that while the higher class of Brazilians despised the junk sold in tourist shops they never realised that in buying such things as primitive art they themselves were only imitating the superior sort of tourists and patronising a superior, and therefore more worthless, sort of junk.

These thoughts, which served to give me fresh evidence for the fact that human imbecility knows no class barriers, distracted me for some two or three minutes. Just then a door opened and in walked a blonde-haired woman. At first I saw only the rather plump figure, which I judged to be in its late forties, in a white T-shirt and blue jeans; and then I saw her green eyes and, recognising the woman I'd known twenty years ago, said with astonishment, 'Mônica!'

'Oh,' she said, 'I thought everyone had left. Why, you are. . .'.

'Gregório,' I said.

'Yes, I remember now,' she said after staring at me with a puzzled look. 'What are you doing here?'

'I was abducted,' I said but, seeing that the joke didn't amuse her, explained briefly the circumstances of my being there.

'You must stay here tonight,' she said. 'There can be no question of your going anywhere.'

The lovely figure which had once provoked such lust within me was quite gone, and since it seemed that I had last seen her only the other day I almost wondered why her face, which had acquired wrinkles at the forehead and the cheeks, showed no sadness at the body's having become so altered that it was, compared to the earlier perfection, a deformity. There seemed a deliberate masochism in her which insisted on advertising the large waist, with folds of flesh at the stomach, by wearing jeans

234

and a T-shirt which rode up each time she moved an arm to reveal the flabby flesh. It was the perverse vanity of a middle-aged woman which made her dress like a teenager with a view, no doubt, to making herself look younger and achieving the opposite of the desired effect: a gross accentuation of her age. It would have been pitiful if it had not been so ridiculous. Her vivacity was gone too, for now she looked and spoke solemnly and smiled so rarely that it appeared she had made a resolution not to do so.

Senhor Lobo returned to the room, looked surprised at seeing us sitting together on a sofa, walked straight to a marble-topped table where several bottles of spirits were arrayed and poured himself a Scotch. He turned round and looked at me with a mixture of scorn and hatred as if I were directly responsible for the problems of his life. He remained standing there, short and ugly, the works of primitive art on the wall behind him adding to the effect of a simplistic outline which caricatured a ridiculous pomposity.

'What a confusion!' he said, taking a generous swallow, rolling his eyes and staring first at me and then at Mônica.

'Please, Adolfo,' Mônica said, 'I'm too tired to hear of your Portuguese friends. No politics at this time of the night, please.'

Senhor Lobo gave a short, cynical laugh. 'Besides,' Mônica went on, 'if you want to solve a political problem, here's Gregório with more troubles than Portugal. I'll see you both in the morning. Gregório, I'll have your room made ready, Adolfo will show you to it.'

She poured herself a drink and walked out with it in the heavy manner of one who has had to attend to an unpleasant duty and now must proceed to another equally unpleasant one, her large buttocks wobbling heavily in the blue jeans.

It was news to Senhor Lobo that not only had I retarded the plans of his Portuguese friends but also that I was to spend the night in his house. I described my situation to him in the baldest terms, referring to my former acquaintance with Mônica as a most superficial but warm friendship, so that he would not be jealous that I had known the woman he had married before he had met her and at the same time be convinced that he owed it to my former friendship with his wife to provide me with a temporary refuge in his house. While I talked he kept rising from his chair and re-filling his glass, and an hour later the whisky convinced him that he was entirely in sympathy with me and that he simply had to tell me his story. It was pathetically told, I must say, for he became progressively drunk the more he attempted to confide in me and no doubt believed that each new measure of whisky which he poured himself aided his speech, whereas in truth it merely accelerated a general incoherence. I understood, however, that he had been a politician before the military revolution of '64 when he had enjoyed some power in the Ministry of the Interior but that he had been the first to withdraw from politics – which statement I understood to mean that he had been the first to be sycophantic to the military dictatorship, being an opportunist who possessed no ideals but only a desire for personal power. He had withdrawn completely from politics and made his money from real estate in Amazonas – which meant only one thing, that in his years at the Ministry of the Interior he had transferred to himself land which belonged to Indian tribes. I let him talk, encouraging him with sympathetic phrases, so that by the end, while he had the satisfaction of having confided in a person whom in his drunken state he believed to be a friend, he had at the same time a vague feeling that he ought not to have said anything because he would now be obliged to keep his secret.

Mônica looked no more shapely in an elegantly tailored white dress when we had breakfast together in the garden the next morning after her husband had left for the city. She seemed to believe that our chance encounter of many years ago had been a prolonged and a beautifully romantic affair and my attempts to disabuse her of her delusion were futile.

'Life is such a disappointment,' she sighed. 'I would give so much for simple happiness.'

Just then two boys of about twelve and thirteen came running out of the house, one chasing the other.

'Mário!' she called in a shrill voice. 'Alfredo! Don't go climbing up the mountain, do you hear?'

The boys ran away to the end of the garden where, beyond the lawn and the flowering bushes, there was a wide path bordered by eucalyptus trees and beyond that, to the rear of the trees, an elephant-coloured rock jutted up to form a massive peak. Mônica frowned, watching the boys disappear, and said, 'Just like their father, selfish and stubborn, what I say never counts.'

'They're handsome kids,' I said.

'I want to send them to school in Switzerland, but Adolfo won't hear of it. And I long so to go to Europe, life must be so exciting there!'

A white-uniformed maid discreetly placed a pot of coffee before us and took away the plates from which we had been eating papaya.

'Paris in the winter! It must be lovely to wear a fur coat and walk in the Bois de Boulogne.' She sighed again as if she needed to expel some enormous burden from within her. I remembered that this plump, gross and utterly self-centred woman had talked of revolution twenty years ago, had indeed been one of the first to express ideas of rebellion against the class to which her rich, landed family belonged.

We strolled about the garden when we had finished our coffee. Down below was the city, sections of it obscured by pools of pollution but much of it sparkling in the sun, and the dazzling blue bay on which a tanker was crawling slowly towards Niteroí bridge. Mônica was saying something about skiing in Austria while I thought to myself that I had been a refugee too long in the very world where I was most a native and resolved that, whatever the consequences, I would go down to that city where I belonged and accept what reality was to be mine. Mônica continued to talk, obviously determined to complete a tour of Europe, and while I nodded sympathetically and occasionally expressed some polite banality my thoughts were on my own condition.

Two hours later, when she went to her room to change in order to go down to visit some friend in Copacabana, I called Virgílio on the phone.

'I was just going to lunch,' he said.

237

'I'm sorry, I won't keep you long.'

'No, no,' he said, 'I'm glad to hear from you.'

'Listen, I'm in Rio.'

'You need money?'

'Not immediately, but I will soon,' I said. 'What I need is my apartment back. How soon can you get the tenant out?'

'There's no tenant in your apartment,' he said.

'That's lucky,' I said. 'How long has it been lying empty?'

'It was never rented.'

'What do you mean, it was never rented? I told you to rent it, didn't I?'

'Your wife said not to rent it,' he said.

'What are you talking about, I don't have a wife!'

'Your woman, then. Listen, Gregório, I don't know what your affairs are, it's none of my business. You told me to keep things secret and I kept things secret. You never wanted letters from me, except that one time when you wrote to me and I didn't understand what you were talking about. I always did exactly as you asked.'

'Yes, yes,' I said, trying to remain rationally in control, for the blood had begun to throb at my temples with the sudden realisation of a terrible mistake. 'Yes,' I said coolly, 'you've been terrific, doing everything I asked. And very trustworthy, too.'

'It's my business,' he said.

'But this woman, who is she?'

'The one I saw that morning when I ran into you in the apartment building. When I went back to check the apartment to see what sort of tenants I should get for it, she was there. I didn't tell her anything, only that you were not in Rio and that I was to rent the apartment. She said she was your wife and she was going to stay there. Well, I had a feeling she wasn't really your wife, but I played along with her, for a mistress is a delicate matter. She asked how she could get in touch with you and I said I didn't know, I hadn't seen you for a long while and I was only working for an agent. I made it out to be very mysterious so she wouldn't press me because I was following your orders, see, making sure I lived up to the word I'd given you. Well, I left her and thought I'd let the matter rest for a while and then I forgot

238

about it. Maybe a year later I went back but it was locked. The porter said she had gone away with some men. I didn't know what to do, I mean, what do you do when a woman goes away with some men, so I thought maybe I'd come back, for she was bound to return any day. You understand, Gregório, that I had the problem in my mind all the time but somehow couldn't find a solution to it.'

'Do you have the key I left with you?'

'Yes, of course.'

'Can you get a boy to take it to the building right now and leave it with the porter?'

I accompanied Mônica when she was finally ready to drive down to Copacabana in her steel-grey Alfa Romeo. She had changed to a light-blue dress, had done up her hair and inserted pearly ornaments in it so that it looked like a bejewelled basket resting delicately on her head, and when I complimented her on the heavy silver and dark-blue necklace she smiled and said that it was from a set of Navajo Indian jewellery which Adolfo had brought her from a visit to New York, and held up an arm to show the bracelet and ring which went with the necklace. It was a sweet smile, reminding me of her former face when the cheeks had not been so full and the tanned skin had not appeared to need make-up, and noticed that the wrinkles which I had observed earlier were now buried under a layer of make-up. She drove down the winding road, skirting a *favela* at one point, talking continuously of how her house so high up above the city was like a prison, how bored she was with her husband's association with politicians; if she had to marry again it would be to some artist, someone with imagination; she was, she said, made for an exciting life. I fiddled with the air-conditioning outlet, for the winding road and Mônica's heavy perfume in the closed car were adding to the nausea which I already felt after listening to Virgílio's revelation.

'Now that I know where you live,' Mônica said when I was leaving her car, 'I hope to come and see you. It's such a shame when people let old friendships die.'

I thanked her for her kindness but let her transparent

239

proposal go unanswered and left her with an ambiguous smile and the words, 'Please remember me to your husband and thank him for me.'

My apartment was almost exactly as I had last seen it and after a few minutes I felt as if I had not left it for five years but only for a few days, a long weekend in Petrópolis or Cabo Frio, and had returned with no expectation of anything having changed. There was no evidence of Amália having lived there during my absence until, opening a closet, I found some of her dresses hanging there. A few other items belonging to her, shoes, belts, some books and papers, were all neatly put away, suggesting that she had not had to leave in a hurry but had done so with care and deliberation.

I did not know what to think. The thought that it was she who had been waiting for me when the accident of my meeting Virgílio led me to panic and flee from Rio, a victim of my own assumptions, was too painful to contemplate since it was attended by the alternative of what might have happened if Virgílio had not stepped out of the elevator, suggesting an entirely different existence – as with those idle speculations one has in history, such as what would have happened if Napoleon had not lost at Waterloo. Painful and idle too were the many other questions in my mind: where had she been and what coincidence led her to return at the very time when I had gone to Petrópolis, where was she now, what had Roberto Moniz really known. . .?

I sat on the terrace looking at the ocean, seeing nothing, feeling drained of all knowledge of my own existence, experiencing a diminishing sense of being in a world which was withdrawing its physicality as if my senses were dissolving into a vapour and drifting away in the haze above the ocean, which so grew in intensity that I was immersed in the sensation of being bodiless in a world of blinding light.

I shook myself out of this hallucinatory sensation which, in its colourless brightness, had a terrifying beauty and for a moment aroused in me the impulse to leap from the terrace and be sucked away by it like a drop of moisture in the sun. I needed to be active, to participate in the busy-ness of the world. I went out and had a late lunch at a sidewalk café, spent an hour buying groceries and liquor, and returned to the apartment to resume my life. I wrote a letter to Emmanuel Xeria in Goiânia to tell him that I had returned to Rio and asking him to convey a message to Lúcio to send me the papers I had left behind at the ranch. I needed to work to keep myself so occupied that I did not have time for despair, and the only work which could thus absorb me was what I had begun at the ranch, the long chronicle of all that I had experienced, the astonishing history of my soul. But I will be the last to admit that work is a sufficient distraction from the problems of one's existence, for that very evening, after exhausting myself mentally, I still had excesses of energy in my body and, eating a pizza just before midnight at a sidewalk café, I picked up a whore, a slim young Negress, a savage beauty, and brought her back to my apartment: my derelict body needed an elaborate debauchery and it was not until the next morning when she had gone that I realised that what I had desired was not a sexual partner but another body which would be the instrument of my self-annihilation, for I had wanted that superfluity of pleasure which would end by being a pain.

I saw Virgilio two days later at his office and spent three hours discussing the various business affairs which he handled for me and looking at the accounts. I had no desire to question him further about Amália, for he really knew nothing other than the blunder in my life which he had unwittingly caused, and in any case he was more useful to me as a business manager than as a friend to whom I could unburden my anguish. He advised me on improving my other apartment so that it could earn a higher rent and I gave him authority to attend to whatever changes he thought necessary.

Leaving his office and walking down the street which intersected Avenida Rio Branco, I suddenly remembered that the lawyer who had handled my father's estate had his office near there and I decided to pay him a call, especially as the business of my father's land had never been settled as far as I knew. I had to wait twenty minutes, but he was able to see me. He was a robust, stout little man with grey hair and red cheeks.

'You come about four years too late,' he said, looking at some papers. 'I believe we kept the matter open for a year, hoping you would turn up and claim your land.'

'I'm afraid I don't understand.'

'Well, there was some irregularity, if you remember,' he said 'That was sorted out, the land was brought back to the family, an inventory taken, the whole thing surveyed and valued, after which it was a matter of the division.'

He shuffled the papers before him, looked at one and continued, 'Your sister Iolanda wanted her part sold, for she wanted money, and your brother Vicente wrote to say that his part should be given to you. Well, that wasn't surprising. But you were nowhere to be found even though I put an announcement in the paper. I managed to delay the proceedings somehow, dragged it out for a year, hoping you would turn up. But then I had to accept the judge's decision. Your part, and that includes Vicente's inheritance, went to your heir, your younger brother Anibal who also bought Iolanda's share.'

I stared at him dumbly and he said, 'If you want to make a claim, we can look into what legal approach is open to use, but I can tell you it will be complicated and expensive, especially as every effort was made to trace you at the time.'

'No, don't bother,' I said. 'I have no desire to fight my brother. But tell me, what was that you said about Vicente, why didn't you think it surprising that he should cede his part to me?'

'Don't you correspond with him?' he asked with astonishment.

'I haven't heard from him in years.'

'He married into the Austrian aristocracy. Why, there were some pictures of him and his lovely bride in some magazine, in *Manchette*, I think, in the grounds of some castle or palace, or something, quite a grand place.' He flicked through the papers in front of him and added, 'Here is his last letter, see the crown on the notepaper?'

For three days I drove up and down every street in the district of Ramos, looking for Amália, spending fifteen to twenty minutes in every café in the area, stopping at grocery shops and pharmacies and even enquiring at the nearest school. No one knew the person I described. And then a week later, at my apartment, I heard a key turn in the lock, the door opened and there was Amália. I suffered more from shock than I experienced pleasure or surprise at seeing her. We must have stood there for several minutes, simply looking at each other, speechless and filled with despair rather than joy. And then we both eagerly reached for each other and embraced and kissed and looked at each other and kissed again with tears running down our cheeks.

'I've been looking for you,' I said when we finally sat down next to each other on the sofa.

'I know,' she said, 'I have been looking for you, too.'

'What do you mean, you know?'

'Oh, nothing, just that I knew you'd be looking for me wherever you were, as I always did for you.'

'I've been searching the streets of Ramos for you,' I said.

'I rarely leave the house,' she said.

'So you *do* live there?'

'Why, yes. Roberto told you.'

'Amália, who is Roberto?'

'Roberto Moniz. He's a good man, a friend of Capistrano.'

'I don't understand it,' I said. 'I don't know whom to trust. Moniz brought me to Rio to have me arrested.'

'No, no, Roberto wouldn't do that, he admires you.'

'Believe me, Amália, he had me trapped in the plane with a cop and it was the wildest of accidents that saved me.'

'He told me how he lost you. He rose to leave the plane thinking you'd go out with him but you got caught in the crush.'

'No, Amália, he darted out at the first opportunity and disappeared into the terminal. If he wanted to be with me, why didn't he wait at the exit of the plane or at the foot of the stairs?'

'Because he expected you to come to the terminal, he really didn't expect you to be delayed. As he sees it, it was *you* who disappeared.'

'I'm convinced it was a trap, only the wrong car picked me up.'

'Then why should he come to me?'

'How else can he still find me?' I asked. 'As long as you have only his story, his identity is safe.'

'My poor darling!' she cried, embracing me.

She had grown thin, even her cheeks had hollowed and were of a pale colour. I held her face to my chest, patting her head and seeing that there were several grey strands in her hair. Her eyes, when I looked into them a moment later, were expressive of a suffering that I could not imagine. I began to talk of the years of my absence, telling her how all that time had had no relevance to my real existence, how I had seemed suspended above this world to which I could not be said to have belonged during the time I was away from her. She gently stroked my head while I talked, letting the fingers press softly at the back of my neck, kissed my cheek from time to time to diminish the pain of my words or pressed her head to my breast in a natural gesture of despair at what the events of our lives had done to us.

And then I remembered to ask her: 'Who was the man with the pair of binoculars in his hands, standing on the terrace that day?'

'Oh, that was Augusto, a cousin from Santa Catarina, my mother's nephew, who was visiting Rio at the time. He wanted to look at passing ships, but I think that was only an excuse, he wanted the binoculars to look at the girls on the beach.'

I had a thousand other questions to ask her – where had she been after Capistrano's imprisonment, had she really gone to Europe, how had she happened to come while I was away in Petrópolis. . .? But we had expended too much emotion already and I decided it would be best to have a drink and then go out to dinner before we burdened each other with more confessions.

That the freshness of her youth should have vanished by now was not to be unexpected, or that her face should be marked by incipient wrinkles which showed especially when her face seemed to contract in sadness. And if I thought that she had not lost her essential beauty, it is probable that my mind insisted on seeing her still as beautiful. There was another sort of raggedness about her, however, which was more than the natural diminution of a woman's beauty which comes with the

244

passage of time, but I could not define what it was. And what was it that I felt within myself? An abstraction given the word 'love' to which no direct physical cause could be attributed but which became a greater mystery the more one grew to know the woman who evoked the emotion to which one gave that name, herself an embodiment of the same mystery. As we sat in the restaurant eating fried chicken and rice and beans, remembering what her beauty had been and seeing all the more clearly her present tendency towards plainness, and for a moment imagining her to be even ugly, I had a strong desire to make love to her, as I had done a thousand times before, but all the more urgently now since physical attraction was no longer in question, as if I longed for our two decaying bodies to join together to vindicate the abstraction of love which depended not on the body's roundnesses and moistures but on its own ideal, the indescribable ecstasy of the soul than which there can be no greater irrationality.

Back at the apartment we sat having more drinks and I asked, 'Why have you been living in Ramos?'

It was an attempt to prompt her to tell her story, to fill up the gaps in my knowledge, but she said in a casually dismissive voice, 'Oh, it's a long story...!'

'But briefly...?'

'I live in a two-room apartment in an old house a woman left the Church many years ago and look after the children in the house, some poor children.'

'I thought you worked in a school.'

'Well, we call it a school. It's more of an orphanage. I mustn't drink too much, I have to drive back soon.'

She spoke in a matter-of-fact way as if the subject were of no interest to her or as if she wanted to suggest that she was not interested in talking about it so that I might not ask her more questions.

I drew her to me, stroking her shoulder and pressing my lips to her cheek.

'Gregório?'

'Yes?'

'Nothing.'

245

'What is it, Amália?'

'I don't know how to say it. We must not expect everything to be the same again.'

'What are you trying to tell me, Amália?'

'We can't pretend that many years have not passed.'

'Are you trying to tell me about another man?'

'No,' she said quickly, with a sudden sharpness in her voice. 'We have to know each other again. But slowly, patiently. There's so much to understand.'

'I wish I understood what you're saying.'

'You will, Gregório, you will.'

I slipped my hand down from her shoulder to her bosom but she quickly pushed it away, saying, 'I really must return to my children.'

'Amália, I want you to stay the night with me.'

'I can't, it's impossible! Oh, Gregório, I want to, but I can't, I can't abandon the children.'

'You thought nothing of abandoning me,' I said.

'Now I really *must* go if you're going to pick a quarrel!'

She stood up and I could not tell whether she was pretending to be angry or really was angry and was trying so hard to restrain herself that the suppressed anger seemed only to be a pretence. I caught her hand and pulled her back to the sofa and made to kiss her on the mouth. She held me back and looked at me and I thought there was not anger but sadness in her eyes.

'Please, Gregório, be patient. We are different bodies now. We need to get to know each other slowly, like courting lovers. We can't force some emotions to return, it's too much of a shock for the body.'

I let her go soon after that and suffered first the wretchedness of having my desire to make love to her frustrated and then from a more general sorrow that the return of the woman I loved had not brought any happiness. She seemed stubbornly evasive, as if there were some secret within her, something which was too painful for her to confess or something which she believed would be too painful for me to know.

She began to come every evening so that we always dined together. She found the woman who used to be our maid many years before and who was happy to return to work for us. Amália busied herself playing the housewife whenever she was at the apartment but did not stay as a wife, returning at ten each night to her children whose mother she was not, living thus in a world of nice contradictions.

It would perhaps be revelatory of the nature of human behaviour and make a neat comment on the general human situation if I were to state that, while during the five years of my exile in Goiás I had fastidiously kept away from women when I was certain that the one I loved was not miraculously going to visit my bed, now that she visited my apartment each evening I often went out to the streets five minutes after she left and picked up some whore to spend the night with me; to this revelation let me add the interesting observation that it is precisely when we believe that our love is the most authentic, the purest and the loveliest that we demand that it express itself in the most debauched fashion, and if it does not we think nothing of purchasing that debauchery elsewhere and, when we do so, are convinced that that piece of ostensible degeneracy is nothing more than the extension of the very love we believe to be so pure. I wish women understood this; or, rather, that Amália had understood this: that when one's feeling is intense, it's the expression of that intensity which is more important than any conventional scruple; that love is beautiful only as an idea, like religion, that two people have in common, but when it represents a tension in one's genitals it is altogether a different thing, for then, especially in situations of extreme passion, a whore's cunt has a lovelier smell than the perfumed cheek of the woman one loves. But I expect that in this, as in so many other things, I shall be misinterpreted, that no one will perceive my desire to arrive at a truthful understanding of the workings of human vanity and a loathing of the humbug and hypocrisy which pass for explanations of human behaviour: in the end one is obliged to remain alone in this world.

Amália continued to exhort me to be patient and after a short time I did not even attempt to embrace her; I suspect this was the result of an embittered self-pity, but I would rather not talk

247

of it – there are matters to do with one's pride which seem trivial in retrospect, if not downright silly, and a silence on the subject at least assures an aura of mystery about one's person, making one flatteringly a figure of tragedy. She planned to relinquish her work with the orphans and return to live with me, and I supposed that she wanted our relationship to pursue a natural growth. We simply could not throw ourselves into our former relationship but had to re-train our bodies so that they could discover a fresh present which would be a continuation of our shared past.

And when she finally resumed living with me, some three months after I'd returned to Rio, Amália insisted on sleeping in a separate bedroom. Our love-making was no more than that of two adolescents on the beach in the middle of the day who are surrounded by thousands of people. If I kept my peace, it was out of stubbornness and not patience, for in my pride I was determined to do nothing until she came to me of her own will. Ironically, now that she had returned I found excuses to go away, pretending each time that there was someone I had to see or some facts to check for the writing I was doing, but going away for two or three days at a time to be in Petrópolis or Cabo Frio where the only thing I did was to pick up some woman. It was in this way that, looking for some new reason to escape from the silence of the apartment, I decided to pay a visit to the land which had been my father's. I had no prior desire to go there; indeed, when I had learned of Anibal's having acquired it all I had expressed to myself the wish of never seeing it again. But on this day when Amália said, 'Going to Petrópolis again?' I said, 'No, I have to go and see my old farm,' and realised that there must be some unconscious force driving me to do so.

The barbed-wire fence had gone and where, on my last visit, I had had to wait for a gate to be opened there was now a stone arch with the words CENTRAL PARK across it in large capitals and below them, in smaller letters, 'New World Properties, S.A.' The old dirt road which used to lead to the house in the middle of the farm was now paved and had narrower roads going off it, each one named after an avenue or a street in New

York City – Madison, Park, Lexington, Bleecker. The setting was entirely rustic, however, for at every junction there was a sign made of a rectangular piece of wood nailed to a post pointing the direction to 'The Stables' or 'Golf' or 'Tennis'. And where there had been thick vegetation or pastures bordering the old dirt road, the land had now been cleared and there were groups of houses made of timber and stone in a style which one instantly recognises the world over as modern. I drove slowly, looking with astonishment at this wonderful new world, and was overtaken within five minutes by a Mercedes, an Oldsmobile and an Alfa Romeo. I saw a man wearing a Panama hat, a flowery shirt and light-blue Bermuda shorts drive past in the opposite direction in a golf-cart, and then saw emerge from a side road two middle-aged women on horseback. To my left, a small plane seemed to be diving straight at me but when it came near it was some fifty feet above my car and I realised that it was intending to land on an airstrip far to my right. I reached where I believed our old house used to stand. There was a large, rectangular building there, all glass and concrete, with a sign outside: 'Central Park Inn and Clubhouse'.

I thought I recognised the man in a dark-blue uniform of cotton trousers and a short, tunic-like jacket who was cleaning the plate-glass door at the entrance as one of my father's peasants and greeted him with a cheerful 'Good day!' He lifted his heavy eyelids a moment, stared blankly, and returned to his task, no doubt concluding that I had addressed the man who happened to be coming out of the building at that moment. Inside, I found myself in a lobby where there was a reception desk with two young women in bright pink uniforms behind it, one of whom flashed a wide smile on seeing me. I walked up to her, noticing the maroon carpet, the potted plants, the low, formica-topped tables beside the plastic-covered chairs which made the lobby look like a lounge at an airport.

'Can I help you?' the woman said when I reached the desk.

I stared at her rather stupidly for a couple of moments, not knowing what to say, and she said, 'The cocktail bar is open and the restaurant will begin to serve lunch in another half an hour.'

249

'Yes, thank you,' I muttered and then asked, 'Is it all right for me to look around?'

'Most certainly,' she said, smiling. 'There's an elevator to the roof-garden, the view is spectacular. And you might glance at this.'

She gave me a glossy brochure on the front of which was a composite picture of people riding, playing tennis and golf, swimming, and dining in formal evening clothes. I went and sat in a corner, almost concealed behind the broad leaves of a philodendron. 'The twenty-first century comes to Brazil!' proclaimed the brochure. A couple walked past the lobby towards the cocktail bar. I glanced through the rest of the brochure quickly, catching such phrases as '. . .modern concept of leisure. . .' and '. . .luxury as a way of life. . .'. A short, rather stout man in a business suit accompanied by a young woman in a light-blue, polka-dotted frock with a straw hat on her blonde head entered the lobby, walked to the receptionist, the man and the receptionist exchanged some words, he produced a credit card, and a little later he and his companion, taking a key from the receptionist, walked away down the hall.

I took the elevator to go to the roof-garden. There were buttons for four floors and beside each button a label indicating the facilities available on that floor. I was about to press the button for the roof when I noticed the word 'Management' beside the third floor button, and pressed that instead.

There was an office with three secretaries, and I asked the first one who looked up if I could talk to whoever was in charge.

'That's Senhor da Silva,' she said. 'Can I tell him who wants to see him?'

'No, if you don't mind, I'd like to surprise him. You see, we're old school friends.'

She walked up to a door, looked in, spoke a few words and called to me, 'This way, please.'

I tried to remember how many years it had been since I had seen Anibal – at least ten or twelve, I thought, and then, trying to remember what he looked like, I could only remember a large, loutish adolescent. I felt a sudden rush of blood within me as I entered the office, but it was wasted emotion. The man in the

250

business suit was not Anibal. He was a thin-faced, middle-aged, humourless man who kept looking at his watch during the five minutes I spent with him. He knew nothing of my brother and said, 'New World Properties is a corporation in São Paulo with interests all over South America.'

'That must be very reassuring for your clients,' I said. 'They can be in different countries and yet always be in the same place.'

My irony was completely lost on him, for he said, 'How right you are! I've always said that if business interests prevailed all over the world, then we'd have a true united nations. The very fact that man has to eat and have a roof over his head makes him a consumer, in the end his nationality doesn't matter. That's why I love working for an international corporation.'

'I thought your company was based in São Paulo.'

'New World Properties is only a subsidiary, the parent company is in Florida.'

'I see,' I said, beginning my retreat to the door. 'Well, it's been charming meeting you. I've no doubt your progressive ideas will prevail.'

Leaving him, I went to the roof-garden which, in a country of bougainvillaea, hibiscus and a thousand other flowering vines and bushes, was given over entirely to the cultivation of roses. I looked out on the land. Where there had been a pineapple plantation was now the golf course; the corn field was the airstrip; the vast pastures which had once been the home of as many as two thousand head of cattle had clusters of smart town-houses. There were groups of people everywhere, going about ant-like, some on the golf course, snailing about on golf-carts, some splashing in the swimming-pools beside each set of town-houses. Cars were cruising up and down the main road. And below me, in the rooms of the inn, no doubt a dozen or two middle-aged men were locked in an illicit embrace with some mistress or whore.

When I returned to Rio towards evening and later sat having dinner with Amália which she herself had prepared, the maid having taken the evening off, I thought that somehow Amália was the only real thing in my life, the one constant, physical reality in an environment which was never fixed and which seemed to take a perverse delight in reversing its outward appearance like some beautiful woman whose long, golden tresses turn out to be a wig and whose pearls and silken gown are only the outward accoutrements of a transvestite. What I felt for Amália that evening was first an immense gratitude – she had that gentle, solid quality of a candle during a power failure; and then, after dinner, my feeling turned to an intense love, and I had her sit beside me on the sofa so that I could hold her hand, squeeze her shoulder, kiss her cheek, so that I could continually reassure myself that she still existed and was beside me, unaltered by an ideology or by the will of others. I was not trying to make love to her, simply holding on to her, feeling her physical presence to convince myself that I had not lost everything; and I believe she responded to me more warmly than during previous days, when she had almost scrupulously prevented physical contact, because she now realised instinctively that I was in need of consolation. When I kissed her cheek softly and put my head upon her shoulder she turned to kiss me gently on my lips and then pressed her temple against my head. We remained thus for some time, caught in the fragility of feeling, exchanging the poignant gestures of that delicacy which came from a knowledge of the other's suffering.

But suddenly I desired her with all the accumulated passion of recent days. She sensed it immediately and I could feel that she was readying herself to resist. The anticipation that she was again going to frustrate me had the effect of intensifying my desire and in a moment I was possessed by the strongest lust I had ever experienced.

'Gregório!' she cried, pushing my hand away when I had it at her breast (where, being at home, she wore no bra).

I kissed her with a great pressure, almost violently, feeling her struggle, and I was so enraged that I pinned her down with my knees at her thights, my hands at her shoulders and my lips on hers, allowing her no escape from the violent embrace. With an enormous effort she pushed me back, gasping for breath and managing to say, 'Are you trying to kill me?'

252

But I held her arms down and kissed her hard again and released her only to say, 'You're all I've got, Amália.'

'Gregório, please, you're too heavy, you're killing me.'

The turbulence in my blood was too great now, I was diving towards destruction. She was kicking her legs, managing to hit the small of my back with her heels.

'I want you,' I cried. 'I love you, you're my life!'

'Gregório, don't, please don't!' she nearly screamed, shaking her head from side to side to avoid me.

The more she struggled, the more I was enraged and became engaged in a frantic struggle to hold her down and to unbutton her blouse at the same time.

'*No!*' she screamed.

'Amália, I'm going to *fuck* you!' I shouted back, and in that moment, abandoning the struggle with the buttons on her blouse, tore the front away and put my face down to her exposed breast.

For a fraction of a second I must have felt a sweet relief, an anticipated sense of fulfilment at being about to grasp the object I had so long desired. But even in that moment I realised something else: my maddened eye, which had not seen, saw; my lips, already drinking the juices of my beloved's flesh, stopped before they touched the nipple; my violent heart suddenly went dead. Amália had gone limp, she had given up the struggle when I tore away the front of her blouse. She could not hide any more what she had not wanted me to see, she could not pretend any more that the reason why she had refused to share my bed since our reunion was not that she wanted our relationship to grow anew but that she wanted to spare me the sight of her disfiguration.

Her breasts were scarred with slashes and cigarette burns. The pure, white skin on which I had brushed my lips and run my tongue a million times was pitted with little black circles and cut crazily with two-inch pink lines where the slash-wounds had healed to leave an effect of minute pearls of white dots in tiny pink circles of swollen skin strung together in the two-inch lines which stood out in slight relief, this way and that, in a hundred places. I drew forward the torn blouse to cover the hideous sight. I lifted myself from her and sank to the floor and sat there with my head in my hands. Amália had turned her head to the back of the sofa and was sobbing softly.

'Why didn't you tell me?' I asked in a quiet voice.

She did not answer, and when I turned to look at her I saw that she had curled up on her side with her back to me and was continuing to sob. I rose and sat on the edge of the sofa and touched her head softy, stroking her hair.

'I'm sorry, my darling,' I said. 'I do not know what to say. I'm sorry.'

We remained thus for some time, she turned away and I looking at her, touching her face with my finger-tips. Finally she turned her face, looked at me with tearful eyes, and then lifted herself to embrace me, her cheek firmly against mine.

'Oh Gregório!' she cried softly and burst into a loud sobbing, her body heaving in convulsions against mine.

I held her there, rocking her slowly. 'Who did it?' I asked in a low voice.

'Do I have to tell you?' she asked, releasing herself, so that we now sat side by side, my arm round her shoulder.

'I know. But when? Why?'

'It is meaningless,' she said. 'And senseless. This existence. We belong to a disfigured generation. The imbecility of it. Your own people torturing you.'

'*Who* did it, Amália?' I demanded to know, refusing to accept her evasive generalisation.

She remained silent, looking down at her lap. The thought suddenly struck me that she had suffered more than what I had witnessed upon her body, that for me to demand an accounting of her past was to oblige her to suffer again in memory the very horror which she might have schooled herself to forget.

'Does the past matter?' she asked. 'What trivialities have not people been asked to die for? All for this. . .this Brazil. . .this idea of one's country, this empty pride of nationalism.'

'Amália, I want to know about *you*!'

'I survived.'

'You don't want to talk about it, do you?'

'Not now, Gregório. I feel too weak. And frightened.'

254

'Frightened?'

'For you.'

'They seem to have forgotten me. And you yourself said that Moniz was a friend of Capistrano.'

'I believed so, but what can one really believe? He's never tried to see me after that first night when I returned to find you here.'

'I worry about it, too,' I said. 'There are too many things I don't understand. Did you go to Europe that time I went to see Capistrano in the jail in Mato Grosso?'

She did not answer and I turned to look at her face. There seemed to be pain in her eyes and she whispered, 'No.'

'And the letter you left for me?'

'Can you not imagine?'

'Yes, but I want you to tell me.'

'I was made to write it,' she said.

'But that morning when I ran into Virgílio outside the elevator and he'd seen a woman and you say it was you. . .'.

'I had been released the day before. You were in Petrópolis, you said. It had been a brief detention. I was asked to confess, I said I had nothing to confess. They didn't touch me then. Just put me in a room in which they would create a blinding white light and turn on the heat and alternate that every two or three hours with total darkness and a freezing cold temperature accompanied by shrieking sounds on a loudspeaker system.'

'What did they want you to confess to?'

'Oh, something stupid, that you and a dozen on a list were Communists. I told them the question was ridiculous, they could believe what they wanted and my confirmation or denial was meaningless. I suppose they finally saw the logic of that and let me out. Apart from the horrible suffering of being put in that room, I thought the whole thing was ridiculous. I thought that just because the government had put a lot of money into equipment and manpower to interrogate political prisoners they were now obliged to justify the expenditure by creating sufficient numbers of political prisoners. The statistics must always be impressive in these matters, the suffering of innocent people is irrelevant to a bureaucracy.'

255

She was again resorting to generalisation so as not to speak of herself, and I asked, 'And the next time they took you in?'

'That was much later, about two years ago.'

'As recently as *that*? I was under the impression they didn't bother too much with political dissenters any longer.'

'What makes you think that?' she asked.

'The government has shown the world it can produce an economic miracle and is now anxious to show there's nothing but sweet harmony in the country.'

'The terror of 'seventy 'seventy-one has passed, but no one has a guaranteed right to freedom.'

'What did you do that they took you in two years ago?'

'Gregório, I'm tired, I should like to go to bed.'

'I'm sorry. Is it that painful to talk about?'

She did not answer.

'Amália, why don't you come and sleep beside me? Now that I know why you've kept away, there's no longer any reason for you to do so. I want you beside me, holding me.'

She touched my arm and kissed me softly on the cheek.

'Gregório,' she said, 'one day I shall be well and will come to your bed for more than just lying beside you. You see, I desire you too.'

I looked at her and she added, turning her head away, 'I have nightmares, Gregório.'

A tender accord was established between us now that I knew something of her suffering. We were like two convalescents who can only hope for a slow recovery and must live secluded from the potential harshnesses of existence. Mônica visited us a few times, coming burdened with volumes of gossip, but otherwise we saw no one since we had not been in touch with our former friends. Although we seemed to have found peace we could not rid our minds of a sense of oppression, for the past continued to exist as a violation committed upon us which, instead of compensating us for the injury, reversed the logic of justice and insisted on extracting an ever increasing penalty. We decided one day that what we needed was a change of environment; we would go to Europe, visit Vicente in Austria and Iolanda in

256

France, travel around, and see if there were some place where we could find deliverance from the pain of the past. I also wanted Amália to consult a psychiatrist, for her nightmares had not abated, and it occurred to me that such treatment would perhaps be most effective in a foreign country since I imagined the root of her problem to be associated with Brazil itself.

Nearly six months had passed since I'd returned to Rio and on the surface life seemed entirely untouched by personal or political drama. Twelve years after the military revolution there was no reason to challenge the dictatorship which had achieved political stability and economic growth to such a degree that Brazil was being talked of as a world power, and if there were those who did not accept the established order it could only be out of envy or resentment that the apparent success had been achieved by an opposing ideology, for surely political beliefs have their source in no absolute truth – if that were possible, the perfect political order would long have been established all over the world – but in pursuing a formula of promises calculated to appeal to human greed and selfishness with the single aim of winning power for oneself. Our problems as human beings were within us; only, with Amália and me, these had been compounded by our having been involuntary participants in those events which the accidents of time and place did not permit us to exclude ourselves from, so that we had been thought to be that which we were not and were now obliged to leave the country in order to purge ourselves of the evil in which we had been unwillingly involved.

In the first weeks of my return; believing that Moniz had brought me back from Goiás in order to have me arrested and feeling certain that the secret police must be watching me, I rarely left the apartment, and when I did it was always in the service elevator and via the exit of the basement garage. Gradually I abandoned this precaution, thinking that if the police wanted to arrest me they could have done so before then. I did not know what to make of my situation. If Moniz had taken the trouble to track me down to Goiás and then succeeded in having me accompany him to Rio only to lose me at the

257

last minute, it was unlikely that I would now be left to enjoy my freedom; on the other hand, I could perceive no evidence that I was being observed, and yet the absence of such evidence suggested that my senses were deceiving me, that surely I was under surveillance of a subtly invisible nature: it could be that I was not seeing what I thought must be there because I was looking at it too intently.

For a time I played with the notion of surrendering myself to the police, for part of the oppression in my mind came from the uncertainty of my situation. But after we had decided to go to Europe I began to fear that, once I had committed myself to the idea of an escape, chance, which had left me free when I had had no notion of seeking a liberation, would now block the passage to freedom. We tend to forget that the blade of a knife is lodged in our flesh at birth and, from time to time during the course of our lives, when we least expect it, pushed a little deeper and twisted.

We applied for exit visas, without which a Brazilian cannot leave Brazil. One had to produce papers to prove that one had paid one's taxes and had also to perform various gestures of obeisance to the state, the most ridiculous of which was to furnish proof that one had voted the last time there had been an election. The entire thing was an exercise in bureaucratic constriction of human existence, involving one in a thousand frustrations and leading one to conclude that one of the most important freedoms one could have was the freedom to leave one's country if one so wished. For most Brazilians who wanted to go abroad on business or for a holiday, obtaining an exit visa was simply a matter of paying a sum of money to a middle-man who used part of the money to bribe the officials who had access to the necessary rubber stamps, and over the years the middle-man, known as the *despachante*, had become a semi-official bureaucrat himself, a known agent of bribery who invariably had his office next to the appropriate agency of the bureaucracy. Well, we paid our money to one such *despachante* and left our passports with him with applications for exit visas. When I did not hear from him for ten days I phoned him and he said there was no problem, he was doing all he could. A week

258

later he called and asked if I'd heard of the new law.

'What law?' I asked.

'You have to pay a bond of twelve thousand cruzeiros to leave the country.'

'*Twelve thousand!*'

'That's the law,' he said. 'Remember last summer when everyone had to go and line up at the minstry?'

'Yes,' I said, recalling the news accounts of people standing all day in a line. 'I thought things had improved since then.'

'Well, the problem has been everyone wants to get an exit visa to buy dollars legally and then they don't go. Or there are those who go to Buenos Aires for a weekend to take advantage of the weak peso. The government's put an end to it all, no one goes unless they post a bond.'

'All that means is that the rich can travel and not the poor.'

'Yes, but it's the law,' he said.

There was no point in discussing the matter with him. Amália went to see him that afternoon and posted a bond for the two of us. Another week passed. Now that I had set the procedure in motion for leaving Brazil I longed to be out of the country and felt each day's delay a threat to my security. The *despachante* called a few days later and said, 'There's a problem with your voting papers.'

'How much do you need?' I asked, cynically concluding that all he needed was more money.

'I don't know,' he said, 'I've never had this problem before.'

'Well, what's wrong with my voting papers?' I asked.

'You didn't vote at the last election.'

'That's a joke,' I said. 'What's there to vote for in a dictatorship?'

There was a silence for a moment and then he said, 'I'm sorry, I don't understand.'

I realised he didn't want to compromise himself and so said, 'All right, find out how much you need to get the papers straight.'

I never heard from him again. Two days later he returned our money by a messenger who also conveyed the stunning information that our passports had been confiscated.

And yet our life continued to seem normal. No one came to knock on our door and to take us away and, although within ourselves we felt imprisoned in the apartment, we were free to go out, loiter on the beach, walk the streets and sit in restaurants. But each moment was fraught with the apprehension that in the next second there would be a knock upon the door or a hand would stop us in the street; we felt that we were the victims of another's will, that someone knew of our past and was slowly and deliberately drawing a net around us. In order to escape from this continuing sense of uncertainty and the frightening suspense which it created in our lives, we decided to go away from Rio for some days and to see if some friends in São Paulo could help us leave the country.

Amália's sister Odila, who had grown stout and matronly, put us up in the small house where she lived with her husband Basílio, who was a professor at the university, and their three children. It was a mistake, we should have stayed at a hotel, but – as in so many of the details of one's existence in which one is obliged to choose the more trivial alternative for the sake of one's family or some other absurdity – it was difficult to escape the conclusion that destiny, which pushed one into a world of boring triviality, did so with some obscure logic which, when it made its final meaning clear, had but one end: to reveal some appalling drama in one's existence. So during this visit to São Paulo, when we had no intention of staying with Odila, the simple act of phoning her from the airport while we waited for our luggage, just to tell her that we were going to be in the city for a few days and hoped to see her, produced her insistent invitation that we stay with her. Amália had some reservations when we drove out to Odila's house in a taxi but I thought that perhaps being with her sister and nephew and two nieces might be an interesting change from her secluded existence with me. As often happens in such circumstances, everyone was involved in making a sacrifice: Odila had enough on her hands with her children to be entertaining two guests but did so out of what she felt was her duty to her younger sister; I had no desire to listen to Odila's gossip and her husband Basílio's high opinion of himself, to say nothing of the noisy children, but did not object

260

because I thought Amália would prefer to be with her sister than be alone in a hotel with me; and Amália, feeling she had a duty to her family and believing that the society of people who belonged to the world, as opposed to we who had withdrawn from it, would be good for me, suppressed her own misgivings. The only person who seemed delighted by our visit was Basílio, for it afforded him an occasion to talk about himself to a new audience.

He was a professor of comparative literature, the aims of which discipline escaped me completely, for in my ignorance I had believed that literature was literature wherever in the world it was written and if there were symbols common to two writers of alien cultures this was so for the very simple reason that all writers were born as human beings and, that being the case, could not help arriving at intellectual structures common to all mankind. Basílio, however, laughed at my naîveté, and if I said a great deal else on the subject it was, I must confess, mainly to keep up the pretence of my total ignorance, knowing that the attitude greatly flattered my host, and since we had to endure his pretentiousness it was one way of amusing ourselves and also, I tend to talk aggressively and with a great show of conviction when my only aim is to prevent my having to listen to the tedious talk of another. And actually, given the choice of having to listen to Odila's nonsense about her children, or having to hear the children themselves, and keeping up a mock-intellectual argument with her husband, I much preferred the latter. So I amused him enormously by asking why there was not a study of comparative bridges, for bridges were such vital things in any nation's life, adding, 'No, I don't mean to be funny, Basílio, for since you yourself have told me that the relationship between our own Machado de Assis and an English writer called Sterne is a fertile ground for comparative study, why should not the old iron bridges one sees in the country be studied in a similar way by comparing them to the iron bridges of England?'

He laughed uproariously, but I could see that it was the laughter of one who's convinced that he possesses an exclusive truth and that anyone who expresses a commonsensical doubt

261

about it has to be tolerated as one tolerates someone who has had the misfortune to be born an idiot. Since what I said was mainly nonsense and uttered primarily as a defence against Basílio's pretentiousness, I must add that this is not the place to argue against his kind of intellectual humbug which passes for a serious profession – people are impressed by the appearance of complexity, all those cross-references and footnotes, for whether the man who produces it has a mind or not is never in question provided he can show himself capable of copying down other people's phrases. Well, all this led, on the third evening, to Basílio talking of dreams as symbols in the work of Dostoevsky and some modern Argentinian writer, and I said, quickly making up a fresh piece of nonsense so as to keep him quiet for a minute or two, 'Dreams, ah yes! I'm reminded of a wise old man I knew in Goiás, Fernando Cardovil was his name, and we were talking once about the psychology of dreams and he said, more or less something like this: "I have one remark to make on the subject of vivid dreams. I don't think they have any meaning whatsoever and certainly not the ponderously symbolic meanings assigned them by psychologists. I think all we do when we have vivid dreams – whether they are erotic or horrifying or absurd – is to tell stories to ourselves to pass the time of night. We create fictions to amuse ourselves whether we're awake or asleep – we go to the theatre: because more than any other semiological structure which the mind can invent, fiction is a precise mirror of reality – and what can be more appropriate than that our dreams be the purest fiction? Nightmares with a most complicated plot and a grippingly fascinating imagery are a luxury enjoyed by those with the money to eat and drink well, those who actively fill their leisure with imaginative diversions. But how gratifying it is to our vanity to be told by a learned man that these amusing images have a special *meaning* which explains something extraordinary about our characters!" '

Basílio laughed, though for a moment, when I used his own favourite phrase 'semiological structure', he had nearly taken me seriously but realised by the time I finished that I was entirely ignorant of the subject. Odila, however, who had been looking at me with the excited expression of one who has had an association in her mind and had obviously not listened to what I said, for she was merely waiting for an opportunity to talk herself, said, 'That reminds me of the dream I had two nights ago, just the day after you arrived, of seeing Capistrano and Amália—'

And then she suddenly stopped, either feeling embarrassed or realising her error in raising the subject, and the expression on her face could not suppress the idea that she was searching desperately to complete her statement with some untruth, for she finally came out with, 'Oh, it was a silly dream, really, just the three of us in a field full of cows.'

When she had hesitated I had glanced at Amália and noticed something odd in her expression too; as though she had been taken off guard or as though her sister had been unwittingly on the verge of revealing a secret; and, as my eyes quickly darted from one to the other of the two sisters, I felt that finally, when Odila ended by talking about the cows, there was a sense of relief on Amália's face. So all that irrelevant and inconsequential prattle about bridges and dreams had not been without direction: in its aimless way, intellectual silliness had led to *this*, a sudden plunging into past reality.

That night Amália was anxious to go to bed early (she had a small bedroom while I slept on a couch in the living-room) and, on the pretext of getting a book from my suitcase which was lying in the bedroom, I accompanied her. Basílio too, having to be up early for work, went to bed while Odila was busy putting the children to sleep. Amália went to the bathroom and stayed there for fifteen minutes and raised her eyebrows on seeing me still in her room.

'Didn't you find the book?' she asked.

'I wanted to say goodnight to you,' I said. 'And to wish you happy dreams.'

'That's so sweet of you,' she said, preferring not to see any subtle meaning in my words.

She sat down on the edge of the bed to remove her shoes. I stood in front of her and, touching her chin softly with my hand, raised her face so that she looked up at me, and I said, 'Is

263

there anything you should tell me?'

'I'm tired, Gregório,' was all she said and turned her attention to her shoes.

'Amália, look at me!' I said, my voice a little too loud for that small room.

'Gregório,' she said in a harsh whisper, 'there are children trying to sleep in the next room.'

'All right.' I spoke softly. 'Are your nightmares about something other than what the police did to you?'

'You don't know what you're talking about, and please, Gregório, this is not the place for any drama.'

'Shall I tell you what I think? Shall I call Odila to come and tell you of the dream she really had?'

She stood up and put her hands on my shoulders, saying, 'Gregório, we've been killed once already, the past is dead in us and this reincarnation is not worth murdering. Please go now, I want to sleep.'

I left her then, feeling a bitterness within me, and returned to the living-room where I poured myself a whisky. I sat brooding, thinking of the past, trying to puzzle out the shape of the idea which was floating as a whirling abstraction in my mind. The only thing I could be certain of was that the woman I had been closest to was the one who remained mysteriously distant. Some experiences, the explanations of which appear implausible, seem to suggest that the apparent implausibility is our own fault, that we have been inattentive to some crucial detail, and so we rehearse the images of the past again and again in our minds, become involved in complex exegesis, but finally are left with images which do not relate to one another and the mind reverts to its commonest state, that of perceiving the essential incoherence of things.

'That's exactly what I need, a drink!' Odila exclaimed brightly, entering the living-room. 'You don't know how boring this life is, Gregório,' she added, pouring out a whisky for herself, 'and I must say it's been cheering to have you here, at least the conversation has been lively. But look at this household, it's not ten o'clock and everyone's gone to bed.'

She sat down opposite me and went on, 'We ought to have

264

music, we ought to dance, we're still young! But poor Basílio has to be up at six and the children have to be taken to school and the maid is bound to have a headache. Oh, what a mess we make of our lives!'

'Why don't we go out and enjoy ourselves?' I asked, making a frivolous suggestion merely to have something to say.

She looked at me with rounded eyes and then laughed. 'Why not?'

'Where shall we go, to a film?'

'One doesn't dance at the movies,' she said in the tone of voice one uses to indicate that the person being addressed is stupid.

'A night club, then?'

'Seriously?' she asked with a bright glance.

'Yes, why not?'

'Why not!' she exclaimed, swallowing the rest of her drink and putting the glass down with a thump.

Twenty minutes later she had changed into a pink frock, done her hair and put a generous quantity of make-up on her face, I'd put on a jacket and a tie, and we were driving in her car. She had turned the radio on high, apparently convinced that she was already enjoying herself.

At the night club we sat at a corner table, drinking cocktails. A band was playing at the other end of the room, two or three couples were dancing rather languourously. It was still early, just eleven o'clock, and people were slowly drifting in from a late dinner.

'You know, Basílio used to love going out,' Odila said. 'Now he works so hard he doesn't even have time to have a mistress.'

'Do you want him to?'

'Oh, I don't know what I want! But I certainly don't want to be bored to death by one day being like another. All Basílio ever wants to do is to stick himself in his study and write his book.'

'What's he writing about?'

'God knows! It's all to do with symbols and myths but how can you expect me to understand anything which is not real?'

I did not say anything, and after a pause Odila said, 'You know, he used to be a Marxist critic once.'

'Really?' I said, prompting her to reveal more and glad that in

265

her desire to keep the conversation going she had begun to utter a confidence.

'That was when I first met him, oh, back in the early sixties. Then he changed overnight, burned some books he had. It was the best thing he did. He found himself, discovered what he really believed in while some of the people he knew went to jail. Now he's quite famous, you know, two years ago he was even invited to give a paper in the United States. A pity I couldn't go too, I'd have loved to have stopped off in Florida.'

We had another drink and, so that she might get the impression that I was confiding something personal to her, I told her how my father's land had been developed by some corporation. The band livened up and, on looking around, I realised the place had imperceptibly filled up. 'Let's dance,' I said, and Odila rose eagerly from the table.

Surprisingly, I enjoyed dancing with her. She was so convinced she was having a great time that she gave herself to the samba rhythm with intense abandon and I could not help being infected by her enthusiasm, so that to her it appeared that it was I who was giving the lead, dancing with such vigour, which she took to be a compliment, with the result that she felt an excessive warmth for me and on the occasions when our bodies came together she pressed herself close to me, putting her head on my shoulder or throwing it back with shut eyes and experiencing God knows what reverie.

We sat down, exhausted but exhilarated, and she said, mimicking an Americanism she had no doubt heard in some film, 'Wow, that was terrific! It's been such a long time since I danced like that.'

'I loved every minute of it,' I said and, seeing that I now had her in a mood to reveal more confidences, added, 'You know, I felt a great passion for you when I first saw you all those years ago in Rio.'

She leaned forward, her elbows on the table, her eyes dissolving in mists of remembrance, her mind eager for a theoretical, retrospective romance.

'Actually, Odila, if I can say so now, I used to long for you at that time. Seeing you at Capistrano's, I'd go away and dream of

266

you, lying alone in my bed.'

Her eyes were bright and moist and she was smiling. 'Can I tell you something?' I asked. 'It's difficult but it's true and I'll say it if you promise not to be offended with me.'

She was all burning eagerness to know.

'You're sure you won't be mad with me?' I asked, torturing her with suspense.

'Positive.'

'You're still awfully desirable,' I said, staring at her in a gesture which passes for 'looking deep' into a woman's eyes. 'There! I've said it, please forgive me for my presumption. But that time – twelve, thirteen years ago was it? – seeing you at Capistrano's I went quite mad desiring you.'

'Shall I tell you a secret, Gregório? I liked you at that time. I thought you were not just handsome, you were beautiful. If you'd come to me...but then, you never even looked at me.'

'I pretended not to,' I said, 'for you were Capistrano's girl, but I saw you out of the corner of my eye all the time.'

'You're wrong there,' she said. 'No one was Capistrano's girl. Or, if you like, everyone was, sooner or later. I thought for a time I was someone special to him, but I was wrong. My vanity got the better of me, I began to show off. You see, all the girls fell in love with him, he had a funny power over women. I forgave him all his former affairs, believing I was the one he'd really fall in love with. So he used me like he used everyone else and for a while I had the illusion that I'd succeeded in making him fall in love with me. I began to show off. I had even to show off to my sixteen-year-old sister.'

'Yes,' I prompted, 'that's what I understood from Amália.'

'Well, you know the rest.'

I did not want to press her to tell me her version for fear that she might realise that I really knew nothing, and so I remained solemnly silent for a moment or two and then, shaking my head sympathetically, said, 'I believe it was very sad for you.' A woman like Odila, I calculated, must enjoy casting herself in a tragic rôle.

'I made an elementary mistake. I assumed that Amália being only sixteen, would be impressed by her elder sister's grand affair. I should have known the truth about people. She was jealous. She didn't want to know that I'd succeeded in making Capistrano love me, she wanted to prove that I was wrong. It became a matter of her own vanity. She could not live with herself until she'd succeeded in making Capistrano sleep with her. Oh, that wasn't too difficult with Capistrano, the younger they were the more willing he was.'

'I suppose that must have been when he had left Rio for São Paulo,' I said coolly, suppressing my own emotion.

'Yes, we had quite a scene. That's when I married Basílio. It was too much for me, the look of victory on Amália's face and that terrible look on Capistrano's which suggested that he couldn't care less if I jumped out of the window. He was totally callous about women, he never loved anyone.'

'But Amália left him soon after that,' I said.

'Well, by that time she must already have been eighteen or nineteen. You see, she was at college in Rio and had come to São Paulo to have her showdown with Capistrano. What I mean is, he already had a new young girl at the time, and took Amália only because he wanted to get rid of me. Actually, he soon threw Amália out too.'

'Is that why she disappeared for three years? To go and repent? Or to feel sorry for herself?'

'She went to have his child.'

'Oh, of course,' I said, forcing a smile, 'but that doesn't take three years.'

'She's a strange one, Amália. No, she never told me what she did during those years.'

We rose to dance again, for I wanted to keep up the pretence that nothing of what Odila had said was news to me, that it had only been conversation made to pass the time pleasantly. I danced clumsily, but I don't think Odila noticed, for she saw action only as the fulfilment of her own preconceived notion of what people did.

It was two in the morning when we returned to the house. Wanting to prolong the sensation of enjoying herself, Odila joined me in a final drink in the living-room, saying, 'I'm going to be terribly sick tomorrow, but what's the point of life if one can't enjoy oneself?'

'Yes,' I said, 'better to kill yourself with drink than with boredom.'

She laughed aloud and then suppressed the laughter, remembering that people were asleep in the house. We talked for some ten minutes of trivial matters and finally, finishing her drink, she stood up to go. I stood up too, thinking that I'd pour myself another drink when she left and hope for oblivion to overtake me. She walked up to me and hugged me with genuine affection, saying, 'Thank you for a wonderful evening.'

'Thank *you*, Odila,' I said, kissing her cheek. 'you've been just terrific, and beautiful too.'

She was greatly touched and, overcome by some impulse, kissed me on the mouth, and then said, 'There! See what you missed many years ago?'

She drew back and had begun to walk towards the door when she stopped suddenly, for Amália was standing in the shadow of the doorway.

'Well, hello there, sister!' Odila called brightly. 'We've been talking of you all night. Well, good night, you two old-fashioned lovers. I suppose this is your secret, to surprise each other in the middle of the night. Much more romantic than getting married and spending the rest of your life in the same old bed!'

Amália stood there watching me gloomily as if she expected me to make some announcement. I had no intention of saying anything and merely turned away to fill my glass. When I looked again she was gone. I don't know how many more drinks I had that night, but it must have been four in the morning before I passed out, having gone through the various stages of self-pity, self-loathing and a desire for self-annihilation again and again, a dozen times.

It was past noon when Amália woke me the next day. At first I could neither see nor hear and had only a dim consciousness of her presence; a terrible pain in the head was my only certainty. She gave me some pills to swallow and brought me a large mug of black coffee; when, an hour later, the world was resolving itself into a misty blur, she took me into the bathroom and left me under a cold shower. I saw things clearly when I emerged from the shower but still felt as if my feet didn't touch the ground when I walked, my progress through the rooms in a sort of motorised levitation making me feel ridiculously pleased with myself. I had no appetite, but Amália made me eat a plate full of rice and beans and some roast beef and gave me a bottle of iced beer to drink. Completing the meal, I felt a thrilling sensation of total clarity in my mind.

'Where's everybody?' I asked, my refreshed senses finally giving me a knowledge of mundane reality.

'Basílio's at work, the children at school and Odila's gone shopping,' Amália said, coldy reciting the facts.

'Oh, of course,' I said. 'What are we going to do? We'd better try calling some of the people we came to see.'

We walked across the hall to the living-room where Amália had tidied up the couch where I'd slept.

'That is,' I added, sitting down, 'if you want me to.'

She stood beside a table, her fingers in a vase of flowers, taking out the stalks on which the flowers had died.

'I suppose you're pleased with yourself,' she said.

'Absolutely delighted,' I said, leaning back on the sofa, thrusting my legs out and crossing my feet.

'How could you be so cruel!' she cried, choking a sob.

'*I* cruel! Oh, come on, Amália, you have kept secrets from me for fifteen years, you have deceived me all the time that I've known you, and you accuse *me* of being cruel!'

'You don't know,' she mumbled, 'you don't know.'

'What don't I know? That you ran away from what I thought was our perfect love in order to go and get laid by Capistrano? That you went away to have his child? But why did you take three years doing it? What kind of a monster were you breeding that it took so long?'

She had sat down, leaving the stalks of dead flowers on the table but having restored fresh life to the arrangement in the vase, and was weeping quietly.

'And why did you come back to me? It wasn't a revival of that perfect love, was it? Oh no, it was the only way you could be near Capistrano again. You lived with me because he as good as lived with me. I understand now why you never wanted to marry me. You really loved him, didn't you? You had no interest in his ideas, there was only one idea in your head, that you were in love with a hero. And you went about with me, got yourself involved in all our political shit, hoping that you'd have the chance of doing something heroic which would so impress Capistrano that you'd finally have him for yourself. Come on, tell me, isn't this true? And a lot else I figured out last night. You didn't get picked up by the police, you *made* it possible for them to pick you up, because you *desired* to suffer pain, you wanted to feel what you knew Capistrano had felt, you put yourself into exile because he was in exile. What use are these tears, Amália, why don't you shout back, why don't you tell me none of this is true?'

She wiped her eyes and looked at me. Her mouth was quivering and she said in a weak voice, 'It is not true and it is not untrue. So much has happened without my understanding it that I don't know what I am.'

'Don't give me any more evasive generalisations, Amália, just be honest.'

'Nothing is that simple.'

'Oh, to hell with human anguish and to hell with human conceit, there's no greater deception than to suggest that one's life has been so complicated it's impossible to talk about. Life is composed of facts and facts are simple. Either you got fucked by Capistrano or you did not. Either you chose to throw yourself at him or you did not.'

'But who knows why one is compelled to do anything.'

'I'm not talking about psychology, I'm talking about *what you did.*'

She remained silent, her face turned towards her lap where she held her hands clasped together.

'You don't know what your love means to me,' she said at last, not looking up.

'Why don't you tell me what it means?' I said bitterly.

'You are the only fixed thing in my life, the only true person.'

'I'm greatly touched,' I said with excessive sarcasm. 'I'm overwhelmed by your kind consideration.'

271

'No, please, Gregório! Believe me, a part of me has always loved you.'

'A part? That's wonderful!'

'Oh don't be so cruel! Don't misinterpret everything I say. I've loved only you all these years but how can I say what went through me when I was sixteen or eighteen. I'm *twice* that age now, Gregório, and I've loved you for nearly half my life. There! Does that not make me less guilty for the mixed emotions of my youth?'

Now I was lost for an answer, and she said, 'If we are to have any future, we must break from this terrible past. We have to find a new life for ourselves. If our present is going to be only one of tearing at each other because of the past, then it's not worth going on.'

Odila arrived from her shopping and said cheerily, 'Wow, did I have a terrific hangover this morning! It was beautiful, just gorgeous. Listen, I've had an idea, why don't we *all* go out tonight?'

Amália and I flew back to Rio the following afternoon in an old Electra, which I much preferred to a jet on this short flight because it landed in the downtown Santos Dumont airport, making a spectacular swoop over Botafogo and Flamengo to avoid the Sugarloaf. I stared out at the sky and the sea during the entire flight while Amália devoted her attention to a magazine. We had not looked up any of the people we had intended to see in São Paulo, for after Odila's revelations the feeling that dominated us was one of estrangement, and it seemed almost as if the force which had compelled us to make the pilgrimage to São Paulo had done so to enable us to discover a new knowledge of ourselves.

A small, single-engined plane landed immediately behind the Electra and taxied up to the terminal even as we were alighting. Two businessmen emerged from it and I recognised the elder as my former saviour from Goiás who had brought me down from the skies to give me refuge on his ranch, Senhor Francisco Nunes de Carvalho. I felt first a thrill of recognition and then a vague sense of excitement that, after all the chance occurrences of my life, this coincidence might well be not without some relevance. Taking Amália's hand, I hastened to meet him. He recognised me at once, expressed a great pleasure at seeing me, spoke some elegant phrases to Amália on being introduced to her, and then said, 'Meet my son Francisco who, I blush to say, was named after me at my own insistence.'

A plane preparing for take-off was making a loud whining sound and it was impossible to hear anyone speak. We walked into the terminal building after young Francisco had shouted some instructions to a man in overalls who had come to attend to their plane. Father and son made a smart pair in their business suits, in which they managed to look quite cool in spite of the heat.

'I see that you've kept your plane,' I said when we were inside the terminal.

'No, this is a rented one,' Senhor de Carvalho said. 'I sold the one in Goiânia. And no sooner had I sold it, I discovered I needed one to visit various properties. Francisco finds these small planes boring, he prefers to fly a jet.'

'Can you fly a jet all by yourself?' Amália asked with a look of amazement.

'Well, there're always two of us,' Francisco said. 'The company keeps a small jet in São Paulo, a Lear with—'

'Come, you don't have to give us all the specifications,' Senhor de Carvalho said, smiling. 'You know,' he went on, looking at me, 'I finally found time to pay a visit to the ranch again a few months ago. Nothing had changed. It seemed you'd never lived there.'

'Did Lúcio tell you I ended up by living there for five years?'

'Yes, I couldn't believe it! By the way, I heard the police didn't like what you were doing in the villages.'

'That's news to me,' I said.

'Father hears everything,' Francisco said.

'You see, in a country like ours only soccer players and film stars can afford to be popular. The state is threatened if the people show their adulation of anyone else. The trouble with you was that the police couldn't work out what to do because their agents who heard you at your meetings could never understand what you were talking about!'

Francisco and Amália laughed, believing it to be a joke, but he added, 'Good thing you left. The police mind hates incomprehension and would rather twist your words to make them fit what it can understand than continue to remain baffled. Well, can we give you a lift somewhere?'

We declined since they were only going a short distance away to their office. He gave me his card, which I put in a pocket, and said that, since he was in Rio at least once a fortnight, I ought to phone his secretary so that we could arrange to have an evening together.

Amália and I took a taxi to Copacabana and, although I'd told her of my first meeting with Senhor de Carvalho, I narrated the story again so that we could talk about something and not return to our earlier silence. She listened with some interest and even asked a few questions; but I was uncomfortably aware that if we had succeeded in ridding ourselves of the silence we had endured since leaving Odila's house, a silence in which one knew that the other was thinking of the errors of the past, it was only to begin a dialogue which excluded reference to the subject matter which estranged us and thus, in spite of the continuing verbal noise, we in fact maintained a silence, for that which we did not talk about remained constantly in the air about us, louder than the words we spoke.

The building porter brought up some mail which had arrived during our absence from the apartment. There were two or three bills and a larger, thicker envelope which looked as if it might contain some advertising rubbish. I put it all on a small table in the hall and went and had a shower. It was only late in the evening, after we had finished dinner, that I thought to open the mail. The larger envelope contained Amália's passport. On looking inside, I saw that the Departamento de Polícia Federal had stamped a page with her exit visa. Nothing else was enclosed in the envelope: there was no indication as to who had mailed the passport or who had been responsible for obtaining the visa and the oddest thing of all was that the envelope was addressed to *me*. I would have liked to have believed that some delay in the post had held up my passport, that I could expect to

274

receive my visa shortly, but the anonymous manner in which Amália's passport had been sent to me suggested that I was being told something: perhaps that I could not expect to escape from my situation or perhaps that this was a subtle hint that I was being observed.

At least Amália's receiving the exit visa was a release from our present torment. If I suffered more from bitterness than I felt the warmth of her love, I still did not desire a separation; if her visa had not come, I would certainly not have asked her to leave me, and nor would she have gone of her own choosing; and yet, had she continued to live with me, my suffering would have intensified, for the knowledge that she had kept the truth about herself from me for so many years generated a throbbing sort of suppressed violence within me. Having her visa at least allowed us to maintain the pretence that we were not separating but only carrying out the former plan of going to Europe, and that I would join her in London as soon as my visa had arrived. It gave us an excuse not to talk about the past.

Our last few days together were taken up by mundane reality, and although I began to miss her the day after she left and thought that the hours we had wasted finding worthless details to preoccupy us should have been spent embracing each other, yet when she was there I was grateful that there were the details to distract us – looking for old diaries and address-books to see if we could find the names of people who had left Brazil and whom she might be able to locate in London, or going to the city to buy foreign currency and travellers' cheques, or working out some code phrases with which she could cable me. The distance that we had maintained when we were together I wished to annihilate when she had gone.

And it was difficult, at the airport on the night of her departure, to say anything or even to have a farewell embrace, for there we assumed a new fiction to preserve the distance between us, that I would very soon be joining her in London, and as soon as her flight was called the first time she picked up her hand-luggage, quickly offered her cheek for me to make a gesture of kissing it, and went away hurriedly like one who has waited for the final possible moment and must reluctantly tear herself away for fear of missing the plane. I went upstairs to the bar from where I could watch the plane. It was nearly an hour later that the passengers boarded it, coming out of the terminal in groups and straggling across the ill-lit apron, casting long spokes of shadows from the lights which seemed to serve the function only of creating the shadows, so that all I could see were clusters of bodies moving in the darkness without there being any individual definition to the people. A few minutes later the doors of the plane were closed and I could only assume that one of the flickerings I had observed among the moving shadows had been Amália. I waited a little longer. The plane taxied away into the darkness, its long row of windows lit up, and looked as it stood at the end of the runway like the habitation of some mysterious people. Soon, it rushed down the runway, lifted itself from the ground and, turning its nose up at a steep angle, as if disdainfully dismissing the earth, made for the sky which offered only an obliterating blackness.

A few days later I felt again that I was living in a vacuum: the world around me would not exist did I not consciously create it anew for myself each morning. I heard from no one. I walked out of my apartment building and loitered about Copacabana, but no one followed me. I sat in sidewalk cafés but there was never anyone sitting across the café or standing just outside it with a hat tilted over his forehead, watching me from behind a newspaper. I lay on the beach for hours on end, but even the vendors left me alone. If my mind had not possessed a knowledge of my history, it would surely have exulted in this seeming liberty.

I realised that what I needed most was someone to talk to, I needed to destroy the freedom I was enjoying because I knew that it was not really freedom. I remembered Senhor de Carvalho and decided to phone his office. I looked in several places for the card he had given me but could not find it until I remembered that I'd slipped it into the hip pocket of the trousers I'd been wearing when he gave it to me and never taken it out since. I found it at last and walked with it to the phone and it was only when I'd picked up the receiver and had a finger pointed to commence dialling that I looked at the card for the first time. Beneath the name of Francisco Nunes de Carvaho were the words 'President, New World Properties, S.A.' I put the receiver down and went out to the terrace and sat staring at the ocean. No, I tried to convince myself, I could not blame him for transforming my father's paradise into a modern hell, for I could no more blame the waves for changing the coastline of continents. It was simply a piece of property he had bought on the open market, it was merely the changing face of the world.

I phoned his office only to be told that he had left that morning for Florida, but, the secretary added, stunning me with the idea that a man could go that far for a day's business, he was going to be back in two days. I asked her to let him know I'd called and to arrange for me to see him, having explained my friendly relationship with him. It occurred to me that a man who enjoyed such power that he could fly to another country at a moment's notice simply to attend to a few hours of business could probably help me to leave the country.

A week passed and I received no phone call. I rang up the office again and talked to the secretary who said that Senhor de Carvalho had flown straight back to São Paulo from Miami but two days later had had to fly to Frankfurt. She did not expect him to be in Rio for another fortnight.

The only other communication I had with the outside world at this time was to receive a cable from Amália with the words 'Smooth landing ran into few clouds hope you rise in world', which meant that she'd arrived safely in London and had already met a few Brazilian exiles and that she hoped that I would be able to leave Brazil. A letter followed a few days later in which she said nothing that an ordinary tourist would not say, but it served the essential purpose of giving me her address. I wrote her ten letters, long chronicles of my soul, and tore them up.

My anxiety to leave Brazil had become intense and I longed to be with Amália; I hated my own pride which had so easily seized upon the chance to send her away, and now that she was not with me I made speeches to her, forgiving her her miserable affair with Capistrano; I wrote her page after page and then, as

277

if I deliberately sought estrangement, tore up the pages into tiny bits.

In the confusion of my mind I decided to call the *despachante* to ask him where I could locate my confiscated passport. He gave evasive answers but finally agreed to ring me back as soon as he could find out. I expected never to hear from him and was surprised when the phone rang two hours later and I heard him say, 'Gregório, do you really need to travel?'

'Yes, why do you ask?'

'It's not my business, of course.'

He seemed about to say more but did not. After a moment's silence, I asked, 'Have you been able to locate my passport?'

'I have it here.'

'What?'

'Your passport. I have it here. But there's no visa.'

'Where did you get it?'

'Your passport without an exit visa is useless, you know that?'

'Yes, but I must have it nevertheless,' I said, feeling within me a tremendous compulsion to have it in my hands again as if I could touch the essence of freedom by doing so.

'Do you want to come and pick it up?'

'Yes, I'll come in half an hour.'

At his office the *despachante* greeted me amiably and I asked him, clutching my passport, if he knew why I'd been denied an exit visa.

'You didn't do your military service,' he said.

'But I was in the United States at the time, I was pursuing my higher education.'

'That is irrelevant. You have no papers exempting you.'

'Is that the only problem?'

'I guess so. Though there are the voting papers which are not in order but that could have been fixed.'

'You're sure there's nothing you can do about my military papers?'

He smiled, shrugging his shoulders, probably suggesting that the military papers were only a technicality and that there

278

would always be one to prevent my leaving. He offered me a cup of coffee, which meant that he had nothing more to say. I declined and left his office. I walked down the corridor to the elevator. A man in an ordinary business suit appeared from nowhere and entered the elevator with me. We had to go down eight floors. There was no one else in the elevator. Between the fifth and fourth floors he suddenly said, 'Would you like to surrender your passport to me now or at the station?'

I gave him a look of incomprehension but realised at once that the slight hesitation in the *despachante*'s statements, a touch of ambiguity to some of his answers, had been due to the fact that he was under police pressure, that when he had asked if I really needed to travel he had been attempting to warn me. I had been so desperately determined to take back my passport, and my recent loneliness had been so intense, that I had not stopped in my blind rush to the *despachante* to consider with any measure of prudence what I was doing.

'Well?' the man in the elevator said.

I noticed that we had just gone past the third floor.

'First of all, I do not know who you are,' I said, speaking slowly. 'Secondly, you have no right to touch me or my property.' The elevator went past the second floor. 'Thirdly, if you have any authority to take me to what you call "the station", and I assume it's not a railway station or a bus station and that you're too ashamed of your barbaric profession to call it a police station, then I insist upon seeing my lawyer before we go anywhere.'

We had arrived at the ground floor, and he said, 'We shall see.' Two policemen stood outside the elevator door and a police car was parked just outside the building.

I was obliged to sit between the two policemen in the back seat. A blindfold was placed around my eyes just when the car moved away. The man in the business suit sat at the front next to the driver, but no one spoke during the journey which followed. We must have spent some fifteen minutes negotiating the heavy traffic of the downtown area. Then the car began to cruise at a sustained speed and I guessed we must be driving along the beach at Flamengo. From there it was obvious that we were heading for Copacabana along the beach road, for I knew the rhythm of that journey from having done it a million times. At the end of Copacabana the car turned into a side-street and then began to move in spurts, a few blocks at a time, in what must have been thick traffic. The noise of the buses confirmed to me that we were now heading back towards the city, and that the entire journey was an amateur attempt to confuse me so that I would not know where I was being taken. Finally we arrived at our destination and the car seemed to go down into what I imagined must have been an underground garage. I was conducted down a passage and taken to a room. My eyes still blindfolded, I was made to sit down. No one spoke a word and there was no sound of footsteps but I sensed that there were two or three people in the room. One of them pushed up the sleeve on my left arm. I had the sudden sensation of a wasp stinging my arm. A moment later I heard a door click shut. Believing that I must be alone, I put a hand up to the back of my head and pulled off the blindfold. But I saw nothing. The room was absolutely dark. I touched the object on which I was sitting. It seemed to be a narrow bed. I moved back on to it and was about to turn sideways in order to lie down when I suddenly passed out.

Brightness flooded into my consciousness and I opened my eyes to see that the room was dazzlingly white. It hurt to look up at the ceiling from where the intense light was pouring down in scorching waves. It was like being in a desert at noon. The light was so strong it mocked its own laws and revealed nothing. It had also grown hot and I decided to remove my shirt, and doing so I found that by holding the shirt just above my eyes as a shade I could see, for three small, rectangular, glassed-in windows high on one wall caught my attention. Presumably someone observed me from there. I noticed too a small tray which had been placed beside my bed. It contained a slice of soft bread and a glass of water.

I remembered the room which Amália had described to me where she had suffered alternating light and dark, heat and

280

cold, and thought that this was possibly the same room. I suppressed what other thoughts came to me, a mixture of sentimentality and bitterness. I had no desire to let my mind wallow in its memories, that absurd accretion of images which had been my life, for in this blinding desert of light I longed only for the state of absolute nothingness which alone could guarantee a survival of sorts.

Suddenly the lights were switched off and I had the sensation of plunging down into a deep well. I lay back in the bed but could not sleep, imagining things in the darkness. I thought of Amália in this room or another like it and insistently a host of memories came rushing to my mind. I began to invent situations in which I had not been, with people I had never met, in order to drive away the memories, and played fantasy games, now as a pilot bringing a plane down through a storm, now as a soccer player scoring the winning goal in the last minute of the final of the World Cup, now as a film celebrity being inter- viewed on television – a dozen such adolescent daydreams which served to keep the mind engaged in utter irrelevance.

How many hours, days passed in that confinement I could not tell. Now it was light, now it was dark; sometimes for hours on end, sometimes only for minutes. Always some food was left on a tray beside the bed, sometimes only bread and water, sometimes rice and beans, sometimes a banana. I kept myself awake in the darkness for long periods to see who brought the food, listening for a footfall, for the clicking of the door, but always the food was brought in when I was unconscious.

What I was looking at was the inside of my own brain. The light and the darkness, the heat and the cold, what were they if not the alternating worlds of a brain possessed by its own chimeras? What I saw was what my mind had already constructed in its formulations of conceivable perceptions; it was but a confirma- tion of beliefs that had hitherto been speculative, proving merely that what was capable of having a shape in the imagina- tion was capable too of real substance, that the very abstract nature of my mind had reached a stage where it saw only the purest abstraction, the white and the black, the light and the darkness, the heat and the cold. I thought I no longer needed a self, a being, for that state required that the mind feed upon the vainer dreams and not relinquish its substance to the worms. There was no hunger in my brain, only a desperate desire to witness its own drama, its self-made world which, in that closed room, would have created the breezes of the ocean had it not obsessively stared at the images which represented the language of its own invention.

Muffled and distant, a voice entered the room and I strained to listen, wondering if it was an echo within my own brain. But no, it was there, outside my self, a voice whispering hoarsely words which I could not comprehend. And then it became louder and clearer and then so loud that it had to be a voice on some concealed amplifying system, the very volume of which robbed the voice of its identity. Where I had strained to listen when it was muted, I wanted to shut my ears when it became loud and inescapable; and where, straining to its earlier whisperings, I might have caught a word, now it was too loud to be heard, as if all meaning had gone out of language and it had been reduced to a ringing sound only, the consonants knocking within my brain and the sibilants hissing through my blood. I heard no words but was shouted at by a language, a violent rhetorical flow of speech thundered incoherently at my ears as if a thousand tyrants were each simultaneously speaking into batteries of microphones and I, encircled by giant loudspeakers, were the entire audience. I stood in the middle of the room, my fists on my hips and thrusting my bare chest out, letting the words fall on me like hail, letting their meaningless clatter bounce off me, and then shouted back against the continuing loud voice:

'I am Gregório, born anew to this existence. I was there in the merchant ships which plied the Mediterranean three thousand years ago, and who takes my blood away cannot touch my soul, for I was there a thousand years ago, a dealer in goatskins in Cyprus, and who pricks my flesh with a knife cannot touch my being, for I was there five hundred years ago, fishing the waters off Portugal, and who puts electrical wires to my brain cannot take my mind away, for I was there in the heart of Europe when its soul dreamed of a country which was to be called Brazil. That world of pestilences and wars needed an alternative and it dreamed of Brazil; that barbarous old Europe, butchering its own peoples on a scale unprecedented in human history, needed an alternative world and dreamed of Brazil. This is a land of renewal, not of vengeance, for here come the pilgrims who love not a nation but a country, who, fleeing from the oppression of the state, seek the liberation of the land, for whom Brazil is the free improvisation of a dance to the throbbing, primeval music of an earthly paradise.'

Louder and faster I shouted, yelling against the intense volume of the other voice, not stopping to think what words came from my brain, spilling it all out in a high-pitched scream, until suddenly I realised there was no other voice in the room but my own. My speech slowed itself, the rapid flow of language became sputtered phrases as if I had had a violent coughing fit and found that something still choked my breath and must spit it out. '. . .who came here. . .', my voice threw out weakly, and I found myself sinking to my knees. My body was sweating, I noticed, putting my hands out to check my collapsing against the floor and finding myself fallen on my hands and knees, my voice coughing out '. . .to this Brazil.'

The voice returned, clear and at a low volume but still distorted by the amplification. 'Is that what you wanted, Gregório? Just to yell against blank walls?'

'Who are you?' I asked. 'Why was I brought here?'

'You brought yourself. We tried to ignore you as much as we could.'

'That's not true, you had me under observation even in Goiás.'

'That's another matter,' he said. 'It's our job to watch over the country. What you were doing there was not political, just downright silly so far as I can judge from the reports.'

'Is that why you sent Roberto Moniz to bring me to Rio?'

'Oh, Moniz! No one asked him to bring you, he was simply

283

expressing the enthusiasm of a young recruit. He did it in his own time, he was out to prove how smart he was. Wanted a quick promotion, like everyone else nowadays. The truth is, we never bothered with you after Moniz lost you at Galeão. If we'd really wanted you, we'd have picked you up easily enough. But I realised the best way to get you was to leave you alone, for, left alone, your life was completely meaningless and you're the kind of person who'd rather suffer than have no meaning in your life.'

Silence and darkness, and the echo only of my own voice when I called out 'You lie! You wanted me and would have taken me in just as you trapped Capistrano, you'd have done it just for the sport of hunting down someone you believed was to be identified as an enemy. How stupidly wrong was your assumption! You didn't pause to consider how inhumane was your sport, you didn't care to determine who was guilty and who innocent, in fact you enjoyed your sport all the more if the victim was innocent, for that intensified your sense of power. What did you care if the balls you attached electrodes to belonged to an innocent man or the breasts you slashed were those of a woman who'd done no wrong? All you wanted was the enjoyment of power, what did you care for the ceremony of justice?'

No answer, only darkness for several hours. I must have fallen asleep but at one stage I heard the voice say, 'We didn't want you, what use could we have had for one whose worst guerrilla activities were directed only at himself? You needed us to prove to yourself that you've not wasted your life following a false god and an even more false woman. If we hadn't picked you up, you'd have spent the rest of your life feeling sorry for yourself.'

But I couldn't be sure afterwards if these words had not come from my own brain.

When the voice returned and was unmistakably not invented by my brain, I heard it say: 'We might as well entertain you now that you're here. You should eat that plate of rice and beans, you'll need the strength.'

The light dimmed but did not go out completely. A beam flashed out from one of the rectangular windows and began to project a film on the opposite wall. It looked like a travelogue with shots of Rio and other parts of the country. I put on my shirt, for I was beginning to feel cold, and lay on the bed. I paid no attention to the film and only glanced at it occasionally. There were shots of workers assembling Volkswagens in a factory, coffee being loaded on ships. I put my arm across my eyes and tried to sleep.

'Find your country's progress too boring, Gregório?' the voice asked. I looked up to see the image of a plane landing at an airport followed by a shot of the skyline of Brasília. Just then the projection was switched off, and the voice said, 'It's typical of liberals that if a right-wing government achieves the objectives that they cherish they will immediately complain that the methods have been immoral or invent some other lie. If a factory has been set up to create two thousand jobs and bring some prosperity to people who would otherwise have nothing, the liberals will scream out that the factory was established by American capital and that the goods it produces sell exclusively in American markets; but if it's pointed out to them that the factory in fact is financed solely by Brazilian capital, they will then complain that the government is hand-in-glove with big business and is out to rob the middle class by producing consumer goods expensively and not allowing foreign competition, etcetera, etcetera. But I can see you're pretending to be entirely bored, so let's find something more absorbing for you, something really entertaining. You know what's the big thing in movies in the States and in Europe? Pornography. Anything passes for art when civilisations begin to decay. Well, you judge for yourself, we have a couple of native examples.'

A rectangle of light flickered on the wall and was followed by a very fast succession of images, each a monstrously enlarged close-up of some organ, now male and now female, until the lens stopped on a pink nipple and retracted slightly to show the entire breast and moved along the body past the navel to the patch of hairs. The image cut to a dark, hairy hand holding a thigh, the fingers making indentations in the flesh. The next

285

perspective was shot from over the woman's breasts and showed her thighs held apart by two hands. It cut to the image of a dark-brown penis entering the vagina. The camera was held there until the rapid pumping ceased and the slightly less swollen penis withdrew. The camera stayed there and another penis entered. I lost count of how many times this action was repeated. I turned my face to the wall beside me, deciding not to see any more, but though my face was averted my eyes continued to see. It was all very crude and would have been laughably amateurish had I not been aware of the cruelly sinister motive behind the projection.

The bright light came on and the voice said, 'You didn't find that interesting? Perhaps it lacked variety a little. We could show you more but you seem to be in a bad mood. You should have eaten the beans.'

'Barbarian!' I shouted, rising from the bed. 'Is that all you can do, take your revenge on people who have ideas by mutilating their bodies? Is obscenity your answer to the beauty of the mind? Is youth such a threat that you must rape it?'

'Come, Gregório, what are you talking about? You're unduly disturbed, perhaps you need to rest.'

'Goddamned barbarian!' I yelled. 'You would rape your own daughter in your demented lust for power!'

'Get one thing straight, my friend,' he said. 'The lady in question wanted what she received.'

'Liar!'

'No, believe me, we had nothing against her. She put herself in a position where we had to pick her up. She was just like you in that. We ignored her at first just as we ignored you. You see, like you, she wanted to suffer, and we merely obliged her.'

I fell back on the bed, exhausted, clenching my teeth and suppressing within me the name of the woman I loved. The film had been entirely in close-ups, all of them so enlarged on the wall that the common shapes of the human body appeared at first unfamiliar, but I had no doubt that what was being conveyed to me was that if the woman in the film was not Amália then her experience was precisely what Amália had gone through too. I had felt a terror within me while looking at

286

the film that the camera would suddenly turn to reveal her face, a terror which was intensified by the feeling that, were the face *not* Amália's, I would suffer no less than if it were, for not having the certainty that this was in fact what she had experienced made me imagine she had suffered a worse fate. My oppressor knew that it was a greater torment for me to live without certain knowledge, for he had realised before I had that no physical pain could torture me as much as the one in my mind.

I must have passed out in my exhaustion, for when I awoke there was soft music and a dim light in the room, a distant samba rhythm, and I could not tell for a few minutes where I was until I focused my eyes on the blank wall to make sure that the image I thought I saw there, of a burning cigarette held against human flesh, was only a projection of my own imagination. The light brightened and I looked beside the bed at the tray of food. The plate of rice and beans which had been there earlier had been taken away. The glass of water was still there and placed beside it was a flat object which it took a few moments for me to recognise as my passport. I picked it up and flicked through its pages. It contained an exit visa, and I stared at it for a while, as if I looked at some foreign language, trying to guess at a meaning.

The voice came on: 'The door is open, Gregório, you are free to go if you have the strength. It's too expensive for us to amuse people like you, you never seem to know what you want, though I must add that it has been my personal pleasure to be your host and to taste a little of the sweetness of revenge. But for me, you would still be waiting in the emptiness of your meaningless world. Where will you go now? To Mexico City perhaps? Well, goodbye and good luck. Remember me to old Socrates.'

I had been mistaken, when I had been brought to this place blindfolded, to think that it had been an amateur attempt to confuse my sense of direction: in fact, in my presumption that I was not at all confused, I had actually been so, for what had

287

seemed to me the rhythm of the drive on the beach road had been Avenida Brasil and what I had assumed was a return to the city had been an arrival in a seedy surburban area. I'd been taken in precisely the opposite direction to the one I'd imagined.

I drove back to Copacabana in a taxi, going through some dilapidated suburbs, the windows broken on the shells of burnt-out tenement houses which an earlier government had put up for the people; a little later the taxi skirted a *favela* and there seemed to be a relative tidiness to the shacks, outside some of which women were hanging clothes to dry. Copacabana was sparkling under the sun and, returning to my apartment, thinking I should take a shower before I did anything else, I had the strong impulse to bathe in the ocean.

The water was invigoratingly cold under the hot sun and pleasantly numbed my senses. I swam about or floated or merely stood submerged up to my neck, soothed by the immensity of blue around me which seemed to be the very essence of beauty after the harsh white and black from which I had been released. I was free, I told myself, free to go and join Amália in London, and the more I thought of my freedom the more I enjoyed floating there, at one with the ocean.

Later that afternoon I spoke to Virgílio on the phone to check my financial situation, and then walked down Copacabana to a travel agency. I had to wait some twenty minutes before a clerk was free to see me. Passport in hand, my index finger on the page on which the exit visa was stamped, I sat across the desk from the clerk and said, 'I want a flight to Mexico City.'

He began to look at a fat book of airline schedules and I had a sudden thumping within my chest. What had I said, Mexico City? I was astonished at what had unconsciously slipped out, and wondered at what was going on in my mind, when the clerk said, 'There's a Varig flight on Friday morning at ten, with a stop at Manaus.'

The thumping within my chest subsided and I said, 'No, I'm sorry. I made a mistake. I meant to ask for a flight to London.'

He looked at me with amazement and then laughed, saying,

'There's quite a difference. Mexico City and London are poles apart.'

He began to turn the pages of his book again. I felt another sensation within me, a giddiness and a slight nausea. He was about to speak when I said, 'Listen, I need to think about this, I'm sorry to have wasted your time.'

I rose and left, leaving him staring after me as if he looked at a madman. I walked down the street and stopped at a fruit-juice stand and asked for a *suco de cajú*. I stood sipping the juice, watching the crowds of pedestrians and the thick traffic. The juice seemed to fill my body with a new vitality; the nausea left me.

A few days later, Senhor de Carvalho's son, Francisco, phoned and said he wanted to see me. I was glad to have company and invited him to the apartment. He was a slim, dark-featured man of twenty-seven and wore blue jeans and a light-blue cotton shirt.

'I called all last week,' he said when I'd offered him a drink, 'but there was no answer.'

'I was away,' I said.

He looked at me with apparent admiration which I could not understand, and then he said, 'Yes, I found out. They'd taken you in for interrogation.'

'No, that's not true,' I said. 'No one wanted to interrogate me.'

'That's all right, Gregório – can I call you that? You don't have to hide it from me. As I was saying, I called you all last week without getting an answer. And then father flew into Rio and I was in his office when his secretary said that you'd left a message and wanted to get in touch with father. So I told him I'd been trying without success. Well, father said to his secretary, since he won't ever stand for any mystery, why don't you phone our police friend and find out in case anything's wrong? That's father genius, I guess, he gets right to the heart of any problem at once. And sure enough, he found out you'd been taken in. Don't ask me what he did next, but believe me, if you're not still there it's because father spoke to the right people.'

'I'm very grateful to him and I'm sorry he can't be with us too.'

'He flew to Johannesburg yesterday,' Francisco said. 'There's no knowing where he'll be tomorrow.'

'He has saved my life more than once.'

'Gregório,' Francisco said, ignoring my tribute to his father, 'I didn't tell you what a great thrill it was for me to meet you that day at Santos Dumont. Father had never spoken about you and I had no idea you'd spent five years hiding out on our ranch. Father's like that, he makes decisions and then forgets about them because in business he's got used to people carrying them out and he usually doesn't need to think about them again unless something goes wrong, and then, as quickly as he'd made the first decision, he spots what's not gone right and will immediately make another decision. That's the secret of his success, I suppose, to have the strength to commit himself quickly and finally. Most people let an opportunity pass because they can't make up their minds.'

'Yes,' I said, 'he's a remarkable man.'

'But what I was going to say was that, of course, I'd known of you. I heard of you some years back when I was still at college in Rio before I went to the States. You and Capistrano were quite a team in the underground movement. There are some people I know who still argue about you, whether you master-minded the kidnapping of the American Ambassador or whether you were really out to trap the guerrillas in São Paulo.'

'Oh, that's old history now,' I said, not wanting to reveal the part I'd played.

'I imagined you wouldn't want to talk about it, but you don't have to. We can all see for ourselves what you've had to go through.'

'To tell you the truth, I don't know what I've gone through.'

He took that to be an assertion of modesty and looked at me with renewed admiration.

'Anyway,' he said, 'I'm lucky to have found you in time. What I wanted to know is, do you feel like coming on a plane ride tomorrow? I have the jet in Rio and if you're not doing anything

290

I'd like to invite you to come and meet some friends.'

'In the plane?'

'No,' he said, 'in Paraguay. It's only three hours away.'

We flew out of Rio at seven the next morning, Francisco and a co-pilot at the controls and a young woman of about twenty-two with reddish-brown hair cut short like a boy's and I in the cabin, which had six seats and a cocktail bar. The young woman was named Márcia, and when I first saw her in her blue jeans and matching denim safari jacket over a white cotton T-shirt she struck me as possessing the coldly aggressive manner of one out to prove the unimportance of one's sex in the world of action. It was too studied an attempt to be asexual, and while her attitude insisted that one take no notice at all of the fact that she was a woman, it obliged one to note nevertheless that she was a feminist. That was my first impression of Márcia; events were to prove the impression a superficial one.

'Do you know our destination?' I asked after the small jet had settled at its cruising height.

'TWIN,' she said.

I thought it was some trendy new expression meant to tell one to mind one's own business and I looked puzzled.

'Third World Insurrection,' she explained.

'I see,' I said, feeling a little lost, for I was hearing a new language and thought that already a new generation had inherited my youth and was projecting an idea of the world which I would never understand. 'And what exactly is that?' I asked.

'You'll see,' she said.

To make conversation, I asked if she had known Francisco for long.

'I live with him when I'm in São Paulo, he lives with me when he's in Rio. They tell me that you never married either.'

I didn't want to take credit for having unknowingly conformed with modern liberalism and didn't answer.

'We don't have to explain anything to society,' she said. 'It understands nothing and the originality it mocks today it soon adopts as a rule. But you know this. You were a pioneer.'

291

I realised that her clipped, humourless way of talking was a mannerism, that beneath her affected superciliousness was a warm regard for me.

'I didn't realise Francisco was into politics,' I said, anticipating having to answer questions about myself.

'It's not politics, it's revolution.'

'I've been out of this world,' I said, 'I don't know what's going on. But I was under the impression there were no more revolutionaries in Brazil.'

'Why do you think we're flying to Paraguay?'

'I see,' I said, and let the conversation drop. Márcia began to read a French quarterly in which the pages were printed in double columns of small type. I looked at the *Journal do Brasil* which I'd picked up at the news-stand on leaving Copacabana, but I could not concentrate on the news-story of the U.S. Secretary of State flying back and forth in the Middle East. Francisco involved in revolutionary games? It occurred to me that, once mankind possessed an idea, be it some such abstraction as *justice* or *revolution*, then each new generation demanded a finer refinement of it and no number of reforms by a government could satisfy the people, for the idea, gathering about it the sophisticated vocabulary of idealism, constantly changed and remained ahead of what was practical; and even in a country with stable institutions, like England, where, from a foreign viewpoint, any notion of revolution seemed ludicrously redundant, there would be young people arguing out its terms and plotting a strategy for its execution. I ought not to have been surprised, and yet was, to know that Francisco, the son of one of the richest men in the country, should secretly be set on a course to destroy his father. I learned from a few things that Márcia said and from Francisco himself that he'd been educated at one of the best universities in the United States and that, while in the presence of his father he appeared to be a young technocrat devoted entirely to the profits of the corporation, in his private life he gave himself entirely to fighting American imperialism. I did not even try to point out the contradiction of his existence, for he seemed to think nothing of the power that his position in his father's American-backed company gave him to cross borders, to have arrangements with both the Brazilian police and the controls at foreign airports, which he used to the end of destroying precisely that power: he took the company jet, flew on what apparently was company business, but his mission not infrequently was to annihilate the company.

We landed at a small airport and were soon driven away in a dented old car to a plantation house. A dozen or so young men and women, most of them wearing blue jeans and cotton shirts, a few dressed in surplus army clothes and two in Arab garb, sat or stood about the veranda. They all turned to look at us as we alighted from the car. Francisco and Márcia gave a fist salute in the direction of the veranda and walked up the few steps with a military urgency. I came up just behind them.

'Everyone here?' Francisco asked, and added, 'We have two hours.'

A black American with an unshaven face and a blue beret on his head said, 'Who's the spirit from the past, brother?'

'This is a friend,' Francisco said, waving a hand at me. 'He's seen action. He's seen the inside too. We'll need his advice. You'll know his name later.'

Francisco seemed very much in control. He could have been talking to the employees of a subsidiary company to which his father had appointed him the chairman.

'Right honoured to meet you, brother,' the black American said and offered to clench my hand, adding, 'The name's Wilson.'

He reminded me of the black radicals I'd met in New York back in the early sixties and struck me as pitiably anachronistic both in his dress and the manner of his speech, which together betokened a mind capable only of mimicry.

'I read in the paper that Eldridge Cleaver's returned to the States,' I said to test my opinion of Wilson.

'The man's washed out, man,' was all that Wilson had to say, and obviously he had not even bothered to read his soul-brother's moving statement that he preferred the justice of America, which might imprison him, to the hypocrisy of countries which gave him refuge but oppressed their own people. Wilson's kind of young man was never willing to see the truth witnessed by another person.

We went into a large room with a high ceiling and sat around a long refectory table, Francisco at the head with Márcia to his right and me to his left, and Wilson at the opposite end. There were two other young women in the group; a blonde whom I imagined to be an American but later found to be South African sat next to Wilson. The third was a beautiful dark-haired girl who had looked Brazilian, but seeing her sit between the two Arabs made me realise she was a Palestinian. The rest of the group was made up of young men from Argentina, Chile, Ghana, Kenya, India and Malaysia, and there was one older man, not much younger than me, who looked oddly out of place and who called himself Polo, which obviously was not his real name. I felt as though I knew him but could not think where I might have seen him.

Francisco called the meeting to order and again pointed out that they had only two hours. 'We've talked enough of the three proposals, discussed every angle, and now I think we should come to a quick decision as to which one to pursue and work out the details of the action.'

'Right on,' Wilson said.

'First, I call on Omo to make his final argument for the African proposal,' Francisco said firmly, having no doubt learned the manner at board meetings of New World Properties.

The delegate from Ghana made a colourful speech, giving a sensational account of the African struggle, but his proposal was nothing less than the assassination of the Rhodesian Prime Minister. Francisco next called on the Asian delegation, and the Indian made a flowery speech in which he talked of India as the blushing rose of democracy which had been visited by the canker of tyranny and ended by saying that the tyrant must be nipped in the bud. His proposal was the assassination of the Indian Prime Minister. The Latin American delegation had its own list of people to assassinate but could come to no agreement and so aligned itself with the African proposal.

I found the entire proceeding ridiculous and would have

laughed at the childish idiocy of it had I not seen, when the group was assembling in the room, one of the Arabs and the man called Polo carrying machine-guns which they had placed beside them when they had sat down. These people were deadly serious; the urban guerrillas of the last decade had had to rob banks for money in order to acquire weapons but these people had foreign governments behind them. And all this was not for any idealism, not for the emancipation of a people, but mainly because they had inherited a language: the imagery of a tribal sub-group had fired their imagination and they longed to enact its rituals without realising that the language was far subtler than their minds comprehended. It almost seemed to me that the human race was born with the desire to destroy itself.

Francisco turned to me and said, 'What do you think of the three proposals? Which one would you vote for?'

'None of them,' I said.

'Oh, come on!' Wilson said. I looked in his direction and in doing so caught the eye of Polo, who was staring at me curiously.

'Your reasons,' Francisco demanded in his businesslike manner.

'I don't think assassination will achieve anything,' I said. 'It causes a sensation, that's all. But it's an event which takes place and is complete in itself. You cause a slight confusion but there's nothing you can bargain with. If you want revolution, your main weapon is the threat of killing, not killing itself; an atmosphere of terror will give you results.'

I paused but no one said anything. Just to make my point, I said, 'Did you read the paper this morning?'

Everyone looked at me silently.

'The U.S. Secretary of State will be in Latin America next week,' I said.

There were murmurs, Wilson used some worn-out, trendy expression, and Francisco tapped on the table and asked, 'What do you propose, another kidnapping?'

'I propose nothing,' I said, 'for I would not want to presume upon the rights of your distinguished delegates. I merely state a fact. You can proceed as you think best.'

The assembly obviously enjoyed being treated with such respect. A vote was taken and they agreed to defer the earlier three proposals and to work on a new plan of action involving the visiting U.S. Secretary of State. In giving the idea to them – which had suggested itself without any prior deliberation – I expected that I'd given them something which would be impossible to do, especially as there was so little time in which they could come up with any feasible plan. But I was to be surprised by the ingenuity of this group.

Francisco nominated a sub-committee, composed of Wilson, the Palestinian woman, Polo and two other South Americans, and charged it to report to him in two days with a detailed plan of action. Before adjourning the meeting he made a brief speech thanking me and then, looking across the table, announced my name. There was a gasp from the Chilean man and everyone broke out into applause and stood up. I rose too, to acknowledge the applause, and noticed that Márcia, standing opposite me, was beaming with delight. I was astonished at the spontaneous response of the group, for all that Franciso had said was, 'Gregório.'

We adjourned to the veranda, where a couple of servants brought us drinks. People stood in groups and chatted and came to me in ones and twos to shake my hand and to say a few polite things. Only one person did not come: Polo. He stood at the end of the veranda, leaning against a column, tapping his machine-gun which he had slung over his shoulder. His head was lowered but he was looking at me with a sideways glance, his mouth open in a sneer. I recognised him then: my brother Anibal. I decided not to reveal that I'd recognised him and was glad when, a few minutes later, Francisco said that we had to fly back to Rio.

Why, I wondered, had Francisco brought me to this meeting? Why should he have assumed that I could be trusted? His motives were probably far more complicated than I'll ever discover, but I thought that he was engaged in an act of flagrant exhibitionism. In me he had discovered someone he believed to be a revolutionary of the previous generation, possibly the last survivor of a group of people who had either been killed or were in exile, and so had placed me in the position of a retired teacher who is invited to visit the academy to see how well his work is being continued by younger people. He wanted my admiration: whatever he did would destroy his father and he saw in me a surrogate father who was bound to approve of his behaviour.

In the car back to the airport I asked Francisco what he knew of Polo, and since Francisco had been excited by the sensation he had created by presenting me to the meeting he was in the right mood to tell me anything I asked.

'One of the properties developed by the company originally belonged to Polo's family. Father raised two million dollars in the United States to buy it. No one met Polo at the time, it was all done by agents and lawyers, but Polo turned up some years later. He's an incredible guy. Do you know what he did? He went to New York and played the stock market with his two million dollars. I don't know when exactly that was, but it was just at the beginning of the famous recession. In three months Polo's fortune had dwindled to half a million. He flew to Las Vegas and gambled away the half million in just one month. So you can understand how bitter he is about American imperialism. He went back to New York and fell in with some Puerto Ricans and became involved in the armed struggle. He's one of the best men in the movement. He's been around. Some of the things you've read about happening in Europe and the Middle East, Polo's master-minded them.'

We flew back to Rio. Márcia was a little less surly and seemed eager to make an impression on me. She was clearly flattered by the privilege of flying alone in a plane sitting next to the man her companions considered some sort of a hero, At one point she suddenly clutched my arm in both her hands and pressed her bosom to it, saying, 'Flying scares me.' The flight was perfectly smooth and was no different from the outward journey when she had sat coolly reading her journal. I did not want to encourage her and at the same time did not wish to appear rude, and so patted her gently on the head which she had placed on my shoulder when pressing her bosom to my arm. 'There's nothing to fear,' I said and added, pointing out of the window, 'Look, what an interesting cloud formation.' She leaned towards the window to look and I pulled myself up on the seat so that she would find it difficult to resume her earlier intimate position. She talked of her life in Rio and how boring it was, there were so few interesting people to meet.

'I live a secluded life,' I said, playing with an idea in my mind. 'Why don't you and Francisco look me up?'

'Francisco is often away.'

'Then come by yourself.'

We exchanged addresses and phone numbers.

I wondered what I should do when I returned to my apartment. I had no idea what plan Francisco's sub-committee would come up with; having saved the leaders of several countries from possible assassination, I'd unwittingly placed the U.S. Secretary of State in danger. Surely there was too little time in which they could discover enough information to devise a serious plan; and surely the Secretary of State was in no fear for his life, at least not in South American capitals where he was probably safer than in Washington. But we were dealing with people like my brother and that Palestinian woman, some of whose past actions had stunned the world.

I had to warn someone but could not think who. I did not want to phone Francisco's father in case Francisco, as an obvious precaution, had bribed the secretary to tell him if I tried to get in touch with his father. It was no use my contacting the U.S. consul in Rio: he would consider it a hoax, or, if he knew my name and connected it with my ambiguous past, he would believe something else altogether. The worst aspect of it all was that I had nothing specific to relate, only a general threat which might not materialise after all, which would only lead the people I contacted to believe that I'd gone mad with fantasies of insurrection. There was only one hope: Márcia. If nothing happened in three days, I'd call her.

On the third day she called before I did, and came over to my apartment in the evening, having, for the occasion, abandoned her denim outfit and wearing an off-white cotton pants-suit with an open-necked shirt of white silk and a string of white pearls. Her short, reddish-brown hair added to the

298

sophisticated effect, but it was precisely the boyishness of her hairstyle together with the pants that made her breathtakingly beautiful as a woman: it was femininity which, seeking its strength by denying its own form, expressed itself with aggressive provocation, so that its very strength was a lovely fragility.

'Francisco's gone away to Manaus,' she announced as soon as she arrived. 'And tomorrow he'll fly to somewhere in Pernambuco and then on to São Paulo to report to his father. Luckily the old man is off to Europe again next week. You've no idea how that man works. Francisco is just like him in that, always on the go, and they're both out to conquer the world.'

I made some drinks and we sat for some time on the terrace. It was near sunset, the ocean was calm. She talked of her college days, which could not have been too long ago. 'You know,' she said, 'there was a picture of you in some underground student newspapers, and we always heard a lot of rumours, how you and Capistrano were living with the same woman. No one really knew you but everyone had a story to tell. And I used to think how wonderful it must be to know you. Isn't life funny? Here I am with you all to myself.'

We went to a restaurant and had dinner. I have to confess that I enjoyed her company and was flattered to be seen with a woman about half my age who drew glances from everyone present. I talked of some of the episodes of my past and she listened with eager excitement. We strolled down the avenue towards my apartment building after dinner and I offered to drive her home – unless, I added, she wished to come up for a drink.

'Oh, the night is young!' she cried, flinging out her arms.

I poured out the drinks and we sat on the sofa in my drawing-room. 'I told you earlier', she said, sitting on the edge of the sofa and turned towards me, her knees touching my thigh, 'that I used to think how wonderful it must be to know you. I didn't have the courage to tell you then that I also used to have fantasies of being with you.'

'What sort of fantasies?' I asked.

'Oh, you know, like one has with film stars.'

'And what are they?'

'I wanted to fuck you,' she said, speaking in English, and then continued in Portuguese: 'Isn't English a wonderful language? It's direct and to the point.' And she used the word again, laughing slightly and seeming to derive a pleasure both from its sound and the effect it might have on me of shocking me: 'Fuck.' And she held her mouth open at the sound, savagery in her glinting teeth.

I looked at her with quiet deliberation and then said, 'We shall come to that soon, but I have to tell you first that I respect Francisco as a friend.'

'And I love him,' she said, 'but this is our night.'

'How can you love one person and sleep with another?'

'Haven't you ever done that?'

It was then she reached forward and kissed me on the mouth, repeating in a whisper, 'Haven't you?'

'Yes,' I said, kissing her too, 'Yes, Yes, Yes.'

We remained on the sofa, sipping from our drinks and engaged in exploratory caresses, and continued to talk. I realised that she did not merely desire to sleep with me but to have the experience in a context of believing me a revolutionary hero, so that some of my reminiscences were as stimulating to her as the most intimate fore-play, some of which, of course, I indulged in too, so that there was an intertwining of physical sensation and verbal images, inducing in her the rarest of ecstasies. By the time we went to the bedroom I too had begun to enjoy the dual stimulus, and when we lay naked in bed there was no violent crushing of body against body at first, only the continuation of the caresses and of the soft talk about the armed struggle, and it was in that drugged state that a murmured question from me about the plan for next week made her disclose all she knew while she slowly ran her tongue around my chest. Strangely, I'd never felt such a strong sexual excitement as when learning of the fate in store for the U.S. Secretary of State.

'This is like sleeping with history,' she said when our bodies were finally conjoined.

'No, my dearest, this is the liberation of Brazil.'

I had no idea what my phrase meant but she pressed her heels down harder at the back of my thighs.

I wished the next morning that Márcia had not disclosed the plan to me, for now my responsibility was greater than ever: if I did not somehow succeed in preventing it, the consequences were potentially so dangerous they could conceivably upset the earth's fragile peace. But observe again the workings of chance and contradiction: Márcia had come to me in the form of a romantic cliché and revealed the plan to me with the conviction that she was doing no more than sustaining the intensity of her aggressive seduction of a man she believed a revolutionary hero, who in truth had never been one, thus putting me, who desired precisely this knowledge of her and yet would have been happier to have been denied it, in a situation which demanded heroic action, but one of which the heroism would not be that of a revolutionary but that of his opposite. And since her behaviour had taken the form of drama in which the expression of ardour was artificial, a pure acting out of a fantasy – for her vanity was engaged in the ritual possession of a hero's body – it was not unnatural that my vanity should respond with a like fraudulence of emotion and engage me in a melodrama. I had desired, since the meeting in Paraguay, to make some invisible gesture of intervention, to frustrate at least one piece of madness in this world, but before Márcia came I had not expected to become physically involved; and yet the moment when I began to think that only through her could I receive knowledge of what the revolutionaries planned was already the moment when I had unconsciously begun a personal involvement, and her coming and the subsequent revelation were almost like a fulfilment of my own fantasy; it was as if I myself were bringing about the events which I wished to be my final vindication.

If the plan, which Márcia revealed to me, appeared unbelievably daring and downright impossible to execute, I soon reminded myself that when, a dozen or so years earlier, in that famous conversation with Avestruz, Capistrano and Amália, I had come up with the idea of kiddnapping the U.S. ambassador, it too had seemed a near impossibility. And now that was a banal, almost a forgotten, footnote in the history of international terrorism.

The plan which Francisco's sub-committee had come up with amounted nearly to an act of war against the United States. Francisco was going to pilot the company jet to Brasília on the day when the U.S. Secretary of State was to land there in his Boeing. Wilson, Polo, the Palestinian woman and the two other South Americans would be inside the jet armed with machine-guns, hand-grenades and explosives. Francisco intended to land a few minutes ahead of the American plane, to stop as soon as he could on the main runway and begin to crawl along it and then to move to a feeder road which fire-trucks used in emergencies, telling the control tower that he had an engine malfunction and was stalled. He and his plane were known to the tower and he did not anticipate that anyone would become suspicious. He calculated on being parked in this manner just off the main runway within a few seconds of the American plane landing. And then Francisco would take his jet down the runway behind the American Boeing and, just when the latter was slowly turning at the end of the runway to taxi to the terminal, he would manoeuvre ahead of it and block the passage of the Boeing. From there, Francisco would judge the situation and choose one of several alternatives his team had worked out. I did not know all of them but one was to immobilise the Boeing by shooting its tyres and for the two Latin Americans to wire its undercarriage with explosives, so that if troops began to move to the area Francisco could hold them back by threatening to blow up the American plane. He also calculated that since there would be a ceremonial gathering of government V.I.P.'s, a guard of honour and a band waiting to receive the Secretary of State, his arresting the American plane at the end of the runway would cause first disbelief, then consternation and finally a stunning impact, and he expected that in the general confusion it would be at least five minutes before anyone thought to order troops to the runway, and since they would need to come in jeeps it would take them three or four more minutes to arrive at the scene. He had time to capture

302

the American plane.

And what did he and his companions hope to achieve? Simply, a blow at what they believed was U.S. imperialism by making some outrageous demands. It sounded naïve and unbelievable, but so had so many terrorist acts of the past. The conditions which Francisco's sub-committee had drawn up reflected its composition. It was obvious that Wilson had authored the demand that a cheque for $1,000 be sent to every Negro in America, the money to be raised by a special tax on corporations – 'as a token payment', so ran the rhetoric, 'for a century of free labour'. And no doubt it was the Palestinian woman who had inserted the demand that the U.S. stop arms supplies to Israel. But the most extraordinary demand came from the Latin American delegates: they wanted the U.S. president to fly to Havana, appear in a public rally with Castro and announce U.S. recognition of Cuba.

I had no time to reflect upon the stupidity of my fellow-creatures and upon the evolution of the self-destructive principle which informed the behaviour of youth in its desire to be free of its parents: a primitive instinct for rebellion against the father had become a weapon of international terrorism, threatening the entire human family.

I needed to act to prevent the impending tragedy and I spent the entire morning sitting on the terrace, staring dazedly at the ocean, wondering what to do. About noon, I rose and phoned the office of the Federal Police and asked to speak to Rubirosa.

'How do you expect me to believe you?' Rubirosa asked, taking his stance to drive the ball, for we had met on the Gávea golf course. 'You most of all,' he added, his nearly black face turned down to the ball while he shuffled his feet to be at the correct distance from it and swung the club to rehearse his shot. A caddy stood a dozen paces away from us.

'Look at the facts,' I said. 'The Secretary of State comes in three days. You've heard of TWIN, you said you had a file on my brother, and you know very well what sort of mad people belong to TWIN.'

'You know, Gregório, I hate this game. I see no point at all in hitting a ball and then walking after it. It has acquired an exaggerated importance because of the vast purses put up by sponsors all over the world.'

I looked away at the mountains in the distance, finding Rubirosa's essays into contrived irrelevance tiresome.

'That is why I play it,' he went on. 'Because I have a complete contempt for the game.'

He finally took his shot, driving the ball away into the sky. The caddy came up and took the club. We began to walk in the direction where the ball had gone, the caddy keeping his discreet distance behind us.

'Yes, I know about the people in TWIN,' Rubirosa said. 'But what you tell me are two separate facts. TWIN met in Paraguay and the Secretary of State is coming to Brasília. Why should I presume a connection between them?'

'Why should I come to you and tell you about it?'

'That, Gregório, is precisely *my* question!' He looked at me with an ironical smile and added, 'Unfortunately, because of circumstances beyond my control, our friendship has not been the happiest one in this world.'

'I know,' I said. 'You have every reason to be suspicious of what I say. Will you believe me if I say I have no bitterness in my heart, no desire for vengeance?'

'Belief is something I hope will make my peace with my maker in the after-life. In this life I can deal only with facts.'

'The very fact of my coming voluntarily to you, which makes you have the greatest doubt, is precisely the one which ought to convince you of my disinterested honesty. After all that's happened, you'd be the last person I'd wish to see again. I live now in such isolation that the world hardly exists for me, and it would scarcely concern me if instead of an act of terrorism the world were to be blown to bits in three days. What compulsion has led me to want to prevent one more act of madness I do not know. Perhaps it's only vanity, the desire to be seen as one who has tried to preserve the order of society, a small gesture against the disintegration that threatens us.'

The ball had fallen among some bushes. Rubirosa, looking at me with a smirk as if daring me to accuse him of breaking the rules, calmly picked it up and placed it on a grassy bank and prepared to take his next shot.

'Here's your guarantee,' I said, ignoring his game. 'You can hold me, put me under house-arrest or even in custody. If in three days you discover all this has been a trick to trap you in some way, then you'll have me to proceed against in whatever way you think fit. I offer you myself as a hostage but you must believe what I have said and do something to stop Francisco.'

'Why are you doing this?' he asked, commencing to swing at the ball.

'I don't want my country to be humiliated,' I said.

He hit the grass, making a dent in the turf. The ball plopped a few feet away.

'To hell with this game!' he said. 'Come, let's go to my office.'

A chauffeur saluted Rubirosa when opening the door of the black limousine.

'To the office,' Rubirosa said, settling back in the seat and crossing his legs in the car's ample space.

'This is a change from having to wait for a taxi outside the zoo,' I said.

'You should spend a year in Fortaleza sometime,' he said. 'Nothing like leading an empty life to fill your mind with dreams of conquering the world.'

'Or', it came to my mind to say but I refrained from doing so, 'of taking revenge against people you mistakenly think your enemies.' I was not interested in hearing his story of a triumphant return to Rio to a higher position than the one from which he had been expelled, for I did not want to have to look at his gloating face: not because I resented what he believed was his triumph but because whatever he believed was based on incomprehension of the truth about Capistrano, Amália and me. Fearing that he might well embark upon his story since we had a half-hour's drive ahead of us, I began to talk of the new hotel developments which we were passing, and then about whatever immediate irrelevance occurred to me. Then, when we were briefly caught in a traffic jam just before entering the new tunnel, I asked, 'Why did we have to meet in Gávea?'

'Oh, nothing mysterious about it,' he said. 'There was a

convention of visiting officers in a nearby hotel and I had to be there in the morning.'

At his office I waited for nearly two hours in an anteroom while he shut himself in a conference with two of his colleagues who came loaded with files. An attractive young woman brought me a cup of coffee, smiled and left me alone. Periodicals and newspapers were scattered on a table and one wall had shelves of books from floor to ceiling. Putting the cup down on the table after finishing the coffee, I observed that many of the periodicals were from abroad and that the newspapers included *Le Monde*, *The Times* and *The Washington Post*. I walked across to look at the titles of books and found that they were a collection of contemporary revolutionary thought. I must have spent an hour picking out a volume at random and glancing at a few of its pages and then examining another one. Much of the language was incomprehensible to me although certain jargon phrases – 'armed struggle', 'workers' co-operatives' – indicated the drift of the argument. The world seethed with discontent, it seemed, and I had no doubt that everyone had a sound reason for rebellion, for no one can bear his existence if he cannot possess the illusion of an alternative existence. I sat down, suddenly overcome by despair, like one condemned to perform so enormous a labour that he is crushed by the very thought of it. It was perhaps the realisation that all over the world people were arguing the terms of change and that they would succeed sooner or later in creating a world so different that I would not recognise myself as a member of the race which populated it. Millions of words seemed to be springing out of the wall as I stared at the books and reproaching me for my indifference. But who perceived the paradox that the keener one possessed the will to change the less one could understand that no change, that *nothing*, could ever be of any help? Visionaries and prophets among us were given to verbal enthusiasms, that is all; mankind rallied to slogans. But who saw that only the nature of the sustenance changes, the hunger remains?

The door opened, the two men walked out and Rubirosa, seeing me staring at the books, said, 'Yes, we keep up with what the revolutionary world is up to.'

'In order to know your enemy?' I asked.

'Not necessarily,' he said. 'We are not closed to new ideas.'

'If you really believed that, these books wouldn't be banned and you wouldn't censor newspapers.'

'Come, come, there's no time for a debate. Let me simply say that if a man has a cold one doesn't prescribe chemo-therapy. Most of these ideas are an extreme form of cure for an illness that's unknown in Brazil. But tell the people the drug exists and they'll soon begin to believe they've developed that illness.'

'And what gives you the right to decide what the people can and cannot know?'

'Power. Raw power. No one has a right to anything. But come, we have work to do. We could talk all day about these political niceties, but no fire was ever put out by words.'

We went into his office.. It was like an operations room in a war, with a large map of South America on a wall, different coloured dots next to the names of cities and arrows and crosses suggesting some coded intelligence. There were other charts on the wall with diagrams and statistics. Rubirosa offered me a chair but remained standing, leaning against the desk.

'We've collected the basic information,' he said. 'The U.S. Ambassador in Brasilia has been requested to keep us informed of the Secretary of State's movements and especially of any last minute changes in his schedule. If what you say about the plans of the Third World maniacs is true, then we need concern ourselves only with the Secretary of State's arrival in Brasilia. The security people will look after the rest.'

'Surely they could also look after Francisco and his friends?'

'No, this is a tricky matter,' Rubirosa said, walking pensively away to the end of the room and coming back to lean against the desk. 'For one thing, there's no certainty that Francisco will commit himself to this madness. And then, for a number of reasons, if Francisco did attempt what you say he's planned, it would be best to eliminate the threat without anyone else knowing. But the problem is, we don't know where Francisco is. We're checking with all the airports in the country to locate his plane. We have, what, forty-eight. . .' – he looked at his

307

watch – '. . . say the arrival schedule is for ten am., forty-two, say forty hours in which to find Francisco and his plane.'

'But that's the day after tomorrow!'

'Yes, there's been a change, he's coming a day earlier. With luck, Francisco won't hear of the change, but then it gives us twenty-four hours less to find him. If we don't, then I'll put an emergency plan into action which we devised in the last hour. I shall need you for it.'

'What is the plan?'

'We might never need it, but you'll know if we do. Now, I want you to go to your apartment and stay there until I call. I don't have to tell you that it'll be no use trying anything.'

I returned to my apartment, puzzled by what I had become involved in. Rubirosa obviously did not trust me and yet he did not wish to take a chance in case there was a real threat to the U.S. Secretary of State and, therefore, he wished to proceed secretly and cautiously. My first impulse to prevent a piece of insane terrorism had become complicated in my mind with feelings for Francisco's father, whose dream of a world business empire would be shattered should Francisco's playing with revolutionary ideas lead to a bloody reality. I sat on the terrace, looking at my watch and seeing the hours pass, and feeling a nauseous emptiness within me: glancing at the blue ocean, which had so often relieved me from oppressive thoughts, did not help.

The doorbell at my apartment rang early on the morning of the day of the U.S. Secretary of State's scheduled arrival in Brasilia. Rubirosa was downstairs in the car, the uniformed chauffeur told me. I was to join him within five minutes.

Rubirosa was sitting in the rear corner of the limousine, his eyes closed, when I joined him. He opened them with a start when he heard me enter and bang the door behind me. The chauffeur drove along Avenida Atlântica down town.

'We haven't been able to locate Francisco or his plane,' Rubirosa said.

'When does the Secretary of State arrive?' I asked.

Rubirosa looked at his watch and said, 'In three hours and

seventeen minutes.'

'Francisco has got to be somewhere in this country,' I said.

'We've checked with every little airstrip, even the private ones on the big ranches.'

'He could be in Paraguay.'

'How much fuel does his Lear jet carry? Enough to bring him to Brasília and take him back?'

'I don't know. I don't know where that place in Paraguay is, assuming he *is* there. So what are we going to do?'

'Fly to Brasília.'

'Do we have the time?' I asked.

'I've commandeered an air force jet,' Rubirosa said. 'We'll get there in ninety minutes after take-off. And, by the way, the air force doesn't know what we're up to. No one does.'

'Why is that?'

'If Francisco doesn't turn up and the American plane lands safely, we won't even need to descend, we'll come right back.'

'Believe me, it's not a hoax,' I said, thinking that I was being taken to Brasília as a sort of hostage. 'If he doesn't turn up, it'll be for some good reason.'

'Such as?'

'No, I have said nothing. In fact, I've spoken to no one since I saw you.'

He looked at me with his ironical smile and I added, 'No doubt you know that as a certainty, having my phone tapped and everything else.'

We drove up the overpass opposite Santos Dumont and made for Avenida Brasil, heading for Galeão.

'And if Francisco does come?' I asked.

'I shall know what to do.'

'I'm sorry for his father,' I said after a while. But Rubirosa did not respond, only looked out at the early morning activity at the docks as we drove past them.

The engines of the air force jet were revving at a loud pitch when we arrived beside it. Rubirosa and I hastily walked up the steps to the cockpit where I took one of the two seats behind the pilot. Rubirosa and the pilot exchanged a few words and then the co-pilot, after being told something by the pilot, left his seat and disembarked from the plane. Rubirosa and the pilot talked for two or three more minutes, but I could not hear a single word since they had their heads close to each other and the noise of the engines coming through the open door was too loud. Then Rubirosa left the plane too. Nothing happened for ten minutes. The engine noise diminished somewhat, but the pilot remained in his seat, occasionally speaking words into the microphone at his chin and listening absently to the words and the static that came on the air from time to time. Outside, as I watched the scene through my window and also through the windscreen ahead of the pilot, mechanics were going and coming in their usual lackadaisical manner, presenting a fine human contrast to the urgencies of jet flight. Suddenly, there were Rubirosa and the co-pilot running in the direction of the plane and rushing up the steps. They came in breathless and took their seats, the co-pilot pulling back and locking the door. A moment later we had taxied to the runway and, without pausing there for the customary warm-up that I'd always experienced on a commercial flight, were speeding down it for take-off.

Five minutes later, after the steepest take-off I've known, we had settled at our cruising height, and Rubirosa leaned over towards me to say, 'We just got word. Francisco's plane has the code name Third Wing. He was spotted somewhere over Mato Grosso. He must have been hiding out on some airstrip there, probably bribed some fool to say nothing.'

'Couldn't the plane have been intercepted?' I asked.

'No way,' Rubirosa said. 'There just isn't the time. Besides, get the air force in on this and you'll have an international drama. It's unfortunate, but the military mind goes in for spectacular effects and has no sense of logic.'

'It's interesting to hear you say that,' I said, smiling.

'Yes, I know,' he said in a slightly impatient voice. 'We do live in a military dictatorship, but not everyone in the government is a soldier. The military would have liked nothing better than to be told of Francisco's plan. They love opportunities for a public display of looking after the country's interests. And what would the generals have done? They'd have lined the runway in

310

Brasília with troops and staged a dangerous drama for the world's television crews. But it wouldn't occur to them that a visible presence of more than the usual quantity of troops might invite a desperate act from people like Francisco. The troops would also create the wrong impression on the Secretary of State, for Brazil is anxious to promote the image of a country which enjoys internal stability. And then there are so many aspects of the unpredictability of human behaviour which are beyond the comprehension of the military mind.'

'How are you going to stop Francisco?'

At that moment the pilot looked back and made a sign to Rubirosa, who put on a set of head-phones and adjusted a plug by his seat, and then shifted a lever on his head-phones so that the little coffee-bean of a microphone was in front of his mouth. He and the pilot talked to each other for a while. From time to time Rubirosa leaned forward to say a word to the co-pilot, who would nod and then touch some knobs on the instrument panel in front of him, after which Rubirosa would concentrate on listening to his head-phones.

Our air force jet entered the sky over Brasília some fifteen minutes before the American plane was scheduled to land.

Rubirosa said to the co-pilot: 'O.K., you can switch on the tape and the audio. I want everything heard by the three of you in case we ever need witnesses to confirm what gets recorded.'

Millions of people saw on television the American Boeing land, the Secretary of State step out with a cherubic smile and be ceremoniously greeted by a Brazilian general. No one saw the drama which was taking place in the sky right above the airport.

Rubirosa was in touch with the control tower, which diverted all commercial traffic out of the area; if Francisco's plane, whose code name Third Wing and registration were known to the tower, came in to land, the tower was to behave normally, but to let us know its position.

Rubirosa ordered the pilot to circle over Brasília at twenty thousand feet. We had made two wide circles over the city when we saw a small plane seven thousand feet below us circling the

311

city, and the tower came on at the same time to say the plane had been identified as Third Wing but as yet there had been no request from it to land.

A black mass of clouds with vast thunderheads which seemed to be swirling up to forty thousand feet was building up far to the north.

The tower came on again, confirming that the small jet was Third Wing.

'Isn't it normal for you to ask it what the hell it's doing there?' Rubirosa said.

Two minutes later the tower said that Third Wing reported a jammed undercarriage.

'He's stalling for time,' Rubirosa said, looking at me, and then shouted at the tower. 'Where's the American plane?',

'Eight minutes away from final approach,' the tower said.

'What's the weather doing?' Rubirosa asked. 'There's that black shit in the north, which way is it going?'

'Severe thunderstorm activity twelve miles north of the city proceeding south at approximately twenty miles an hour, winds north-north-west, twelve to fifteen miles an hour, gusting to thirty in vicinity of storm. Must interrupt with urgent message. General B— wants to speak to you.'

'Who the hell told *him?*' Rubirosa said.

'Now listen here, the air force should be handling this,' the general said angrily. 'What is that plane doing there? Why didn't you report to us? Who gave you authority to. . . ?'

'There wasn't the time, sir.'

'You had time to commandeer one of my planes!'

'I had to act fast, sir.'

'I've put four jets on alert.'

'Please, general, don't send them up. We're not dealing with an enemy's air force, we're dealing with a crazy kid. Any more planes in the air and he'll suspect something's wrong.'

'I'm responsible to the president, this is a national security matter.'

'Yes, sir, I know. But don't you see, if you scare the kid he might do something wild?'

'Like what?'

312

'Like crashing into the American plane.'

'I order you to leave this to the air force,' the general said. 'I order you to land at once.'

'But general. . .!'

'I order the commander of your plane to be courtmartialled.'

'General, we're trying to save Brazil from a catastrophe!'

'And I order you to be arrested and tried for violating national security,' the general said and went off the air.

'Shit!' Rubirosa shouted in the plane.

I was scanning the sky with a pair of binoculars and keeping an eye on my watch. We were far to the north of the airport, feeling the turbulence at the edge of the advancing thunderstorm, and Third Wing was below us to the south, circling in a direction opposite to ours.

'What's the position of the American plane?' Rubirosa shouted desperately to the tower.

'Your orders are to come down. Repeat, land at once,' came from the tower.

'If it's five minutes late, we'll all be in that mother-fucker of a thunderstorm,' Rubirosa said bitterly to himself. '*What* are you doing?' he suddenly shouted to the pilot who had swung south and was losing height.

'Obeying orders,' the pilot shouted back.

'Will you quit that and do as *I* say? Remember what I promised if this mission succeeds?'

The pilot seemed to be hesitating between his instinct of obeying his commander-in-chief and whatever agreement Rubirosa had privately made with him. Just then I saw, far to the west, a little black speck, and said at the top of my voice, 'There's the American plane!'

Francisco must have seen it five seconds later, for he began to make a landing approach. At that very moment I saw four air force jets take off from the airport. Our pilot, probably concluding that he was already irretrievably committed either to dishonour or to some glory, seemed to abandon his intention to land immediately and said to Rubirosa, 'O.K., what is it to be?'

'Operation Ski Slope,' said Rubirosa, pulling at his seat-belt.

We went hurtling down at a steep angle, while the four other air force jets went roaring up, and then we banked in a tight curve to be in the same direction as Third Wing. We were immediately behind and above to its right with the runway below and ahead of us. Francisco had reduced speed to make a landing and we came up along his right just when he was fifty feet from touching down. We overtook him and swung across his path, banking to the left and then straightened and went into a steep ascent, just missing a building. This sudden manoeuvre worked, for it threw Francisco into a reflex action which prompted him to pull up his plane and to overshoot the runway: he must have also seen the other four air force jets and it is conceivable that he made a quick decision to gain altitude, not wishing to be a sitting duck for the air force planes above him, for he must have had an operation in mind in the event of his being attacked. As our plane was roaring up in a curving ascent, I had for a moment a complete picture of the airport and its environs in my sight. Third Wing had overshot the runway but had gone out of control. A second later I saw the explosion as it crashed out of the airport into a *favela*, and as our plane swung over the airport I saw the American Boeing coming in to land, followed by the four air force jets. The people waiting to receive the U.S. Secretary of State had probably seen the drama as an air display specially put on for the occasion, the four jets looking like a well-rehearsed escort for the visiting dignitary.

Suddenly, all went black and our plane began to bump severely. We had shot right into the thunderstorm.

'Fly back to Rio,' Rubirosa called to the pilot, his voice nervous and exhausted.

'If we don't get hit by lightning,' the pilot said, no doubt as a joke, for we were soon out of the clouds and cruising smoothly towards Rio.

I learned later that there had been no survivors from Third Wing and that seven women and five children who lived in the *favela* had also been killed.

Chapter 6

CODA: THE UNDISCOVERED COUNTRY

See it from the ocean when, after the voyage across the Atlantic, you sight the land and first believe it to be another provocation of illusion, or on the ferry after a weekend at one of the fashionable islands, when you are unprepared for the dimensions of a continent; and seeing the lush, green mountains just behind the shoreline consider how irrelevant is the uncertainty in your own heart;

come into the interior, you who disembark in cities, come where the green depths – flocks of parrots descending upon the high tree-tops – unfold the spaces of innocence

where, in Congonhas, the prophets sculpted in soapstone, arrayed in the forecourt of a church, cast their bright, vigilant eyes which are both blind and glitteringly visionary at the horizon that throws its halo in a gleaming circle over the dark, forested land or twinkle at the sky's blue merriment (for there is among prophets, as among gods, a comical indulgence of Time) or at the throbbing stars whose enduring luminosity holds the perpetuity of the present in transient pulsations

– the spaces of innocence, the kindled darknesses of the interior –

where tribal ceremonies initiate a youth into the customs of the community, burning animal-fat for the dance of flames, the male and the female consorting together, the blood renewed by being spilled, drawn by the knife honed on the tribe's memories

where
the air whispers inspirations and the serene palms, scarcely
indulging the air's tumult, become the focus of your tormented
perception which aches for comprehension

(when there is only
the direction of the wind in the dry season, the clouds high over
Amazonia while the wind whirls towards the equator)

where in the larger temporal constancy, the jungles older than
the New World, the urgency of your anguish can hang for a
hundred years as moss from a tree and not be touched by light;

but see it from the ocean, see it from the air: O
voyager to Brazil (and coming from the ruins of Warsaw or
from the parched fields of Portugal): see how the blue air
excites your expectation of freedom, see how the waters
dissipate along the shore, and the land, absorbing projections of
your sentimentality, seems to promise a riot of liberality,
though as yet the country is still undiscovered and is only a
secret dream in your soul:

come, O voyager, the voice
of the tribe calls the exile home, it is not the lamentation of the
dead or the frozen shriek of the dying that stifles the air, it is
only the dust rising when the floors have been swept, the dried
blood washed.